volume four **POISON**

written by **GREG RUCKA**

pencils by **MICHAEL LARK**

inks by **MICHAEL LARK** and **TYLER BOSS**

colors by **SANTI ARCAS**

letters by **JODI WYNNE**

"Artifact" pages by **OWEN FREEMAN & ERIC TRAUTMANN**

cover by **OWEN FREEMAN**

publication design
and additional content by **ERIC TRAUTMANN**

edited by **DAVID BROTHERS**

Special thanks to **JONATHAN GITLIN** and **MICHAEL BROUND**.

OWEN FREEMAN

INTERLUDE
MERCY

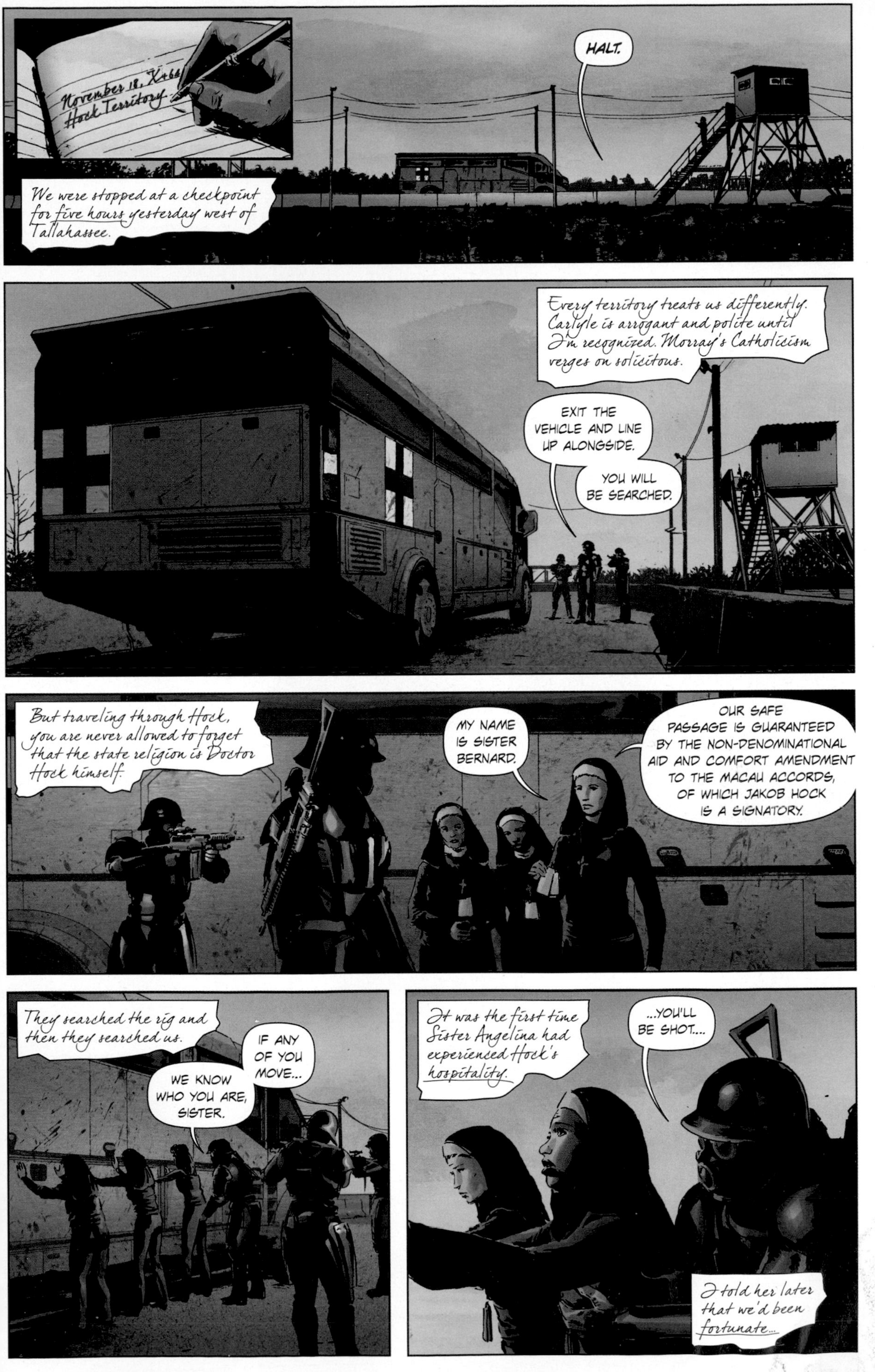
November 18, X+64
Hock Territory
We were stopped at a checkpoint for five hours yesterday west of Tallahassee.
HALT.
Every territory treats us differently. Carlyle is arrogant and polite until I'm recognized. Morray's Catholicism verges on solicitous.
EXIT THE VEHICLE AND LINE UP ALONGSIDE.
YOU WILL BE SEARCHED.
But traveling through Hock, you are never allowed to forget that the state religion is Doctor Hock himself.
MY NAME IS SISTER BERNARD.
OUR SAFE PASSAGE IS GUARANTEED BY THE NON-DENOMINATIONAL AID AND COMFORT AMENDMENT TO THE MACAU ACCORDS, OF WHICH JAKOB HOCK IS A SIGNATORY.
They searched the rig and then they searched us.
IF ANY OF YOU MOVE...
WE KNOW WHO YOU ARE, SISTER.
It was the first time Sister Angelina had experienced Hock's hospitality.
...YOU'LL BE SHOT....
I told her later that we'd been fortunate...

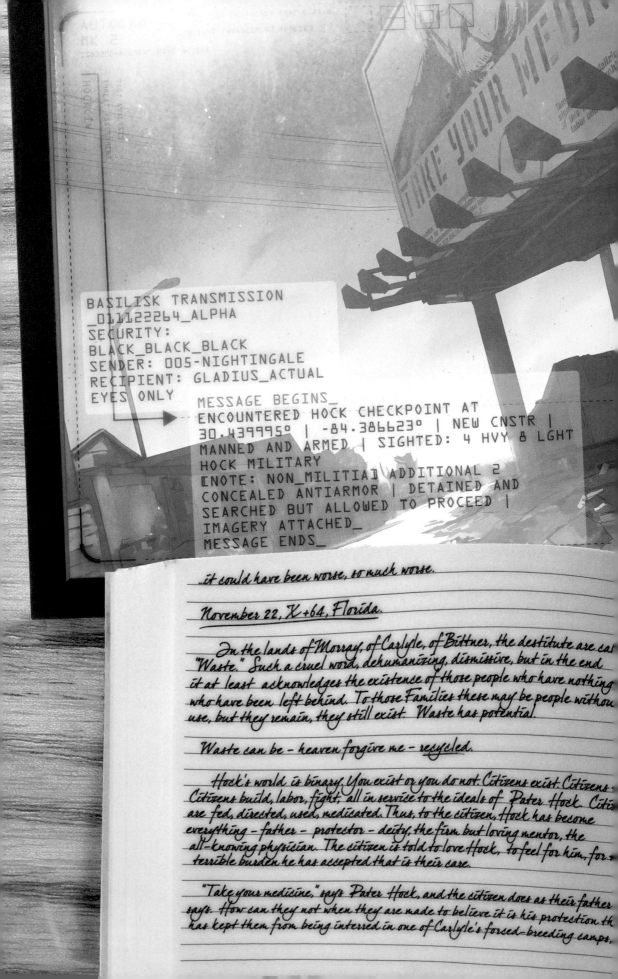

BASILISK TRANSMISSION
_011122264_ALPHA
SECURITY:
BLACK_BLACK_BLACK
SENDER: 005-NIGHTINGALE
RECIPIENT: GLADIUS_ACTUAL
EYES ONLY

MESSAGE BEGINS_
ENCOUNTERED HOCK CHECKPOINT AT
30.439995° | -84.386623° | NEW CNSTR |
MANNED AND ARMED | SIGHTED: 4 HVY 8 LGHT
HOCK MILITARY
[NOTE: NON_MILITIA] ADDITIONAL 2
CONCEALED ANTIARMOR | DETAINED AND
SEARCHED BUT ALLOWED TO PROCEED |
IMAGERY ATTACHED_
MESSAGE ENDS_

...it could have been worse, so much worse.

November 22, X+64, Florida.

In the lands of Morray, of Carlyle, of Bittner, the destitute are cal "Waste." Such a cruel word, dehumanizing, dismissive, but in the end it at least acknowledges the existence of those people who have nothing who have been left behind. To those Families these may be people withou use, but they remain, they still exist. Waste has potential.

Waste can be - heaven forgive me - recycled.

Hock's world is binary. You exist or you do not. Citizens exist. Citizens Citizens build, labor, fight, all in service to the ideals of Pater Hock. Citi are fed, directed, used, medicated. Thus, to the citizen, Hock has become everything - father - protector - deity, the firm but loving mentor, the all-knowing physician. The citizen is told to love Hock, to feel for him, for terrible burden he has accepted that is their care.

"Take your medicine," says Pater Hock, and the citizen does as their father says. How can they not when they are made to believe it is his protection th has kept them from being interred in one of Carlyle's forced-breeding camps.

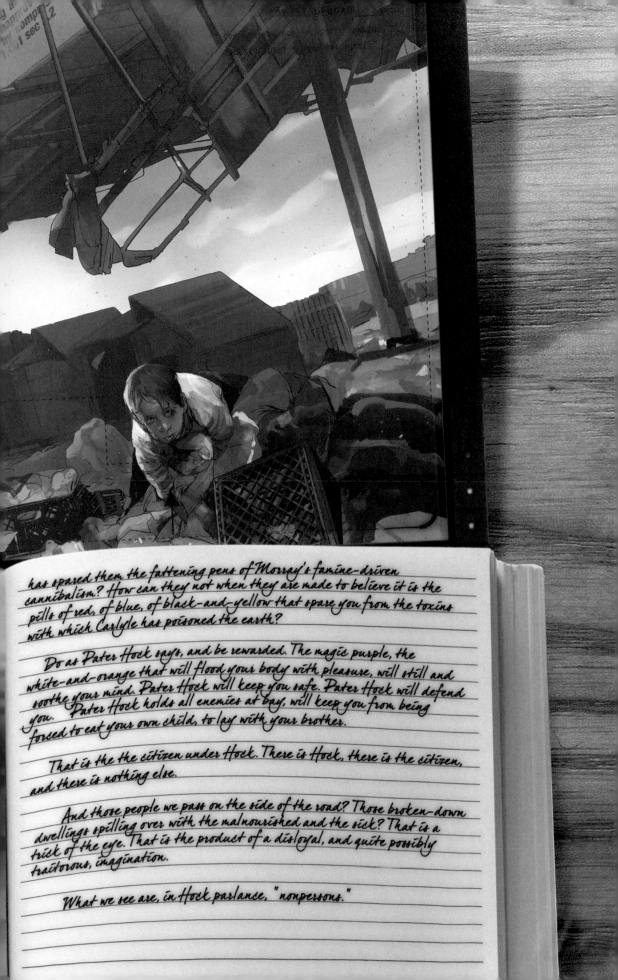

has spared them the fattening pens of Morray's famine-driven cannibalism? How can they not when they are made to believe it is the pills of red, of blue, of black-and-yellow that spare you from the toxins with which Carlyle has poisoned the earth?

Do as Pater Hock says, and be rewarded. The magic purple, the white-and-orange that will flood your body with pleasure, will still and soothe your mind. Pater Hock will keep you safe. Pater Hock will defend you. Pater Hock holds all enemies at bay, will keep you from being forced to eat your own child, to lay with your brother.

That is the the citizen under Hock. There is Hock, there is the citizen, and there is nothing else.

And those people we pass on the side of the road? Those broken-down dwellings spilling over with the malnourished and the sick? That is a trick of the eye. That is the product of a disloyal, and quite possibly traitorous, imagination.

What we see are, in Hock parlance, "nonpersons."

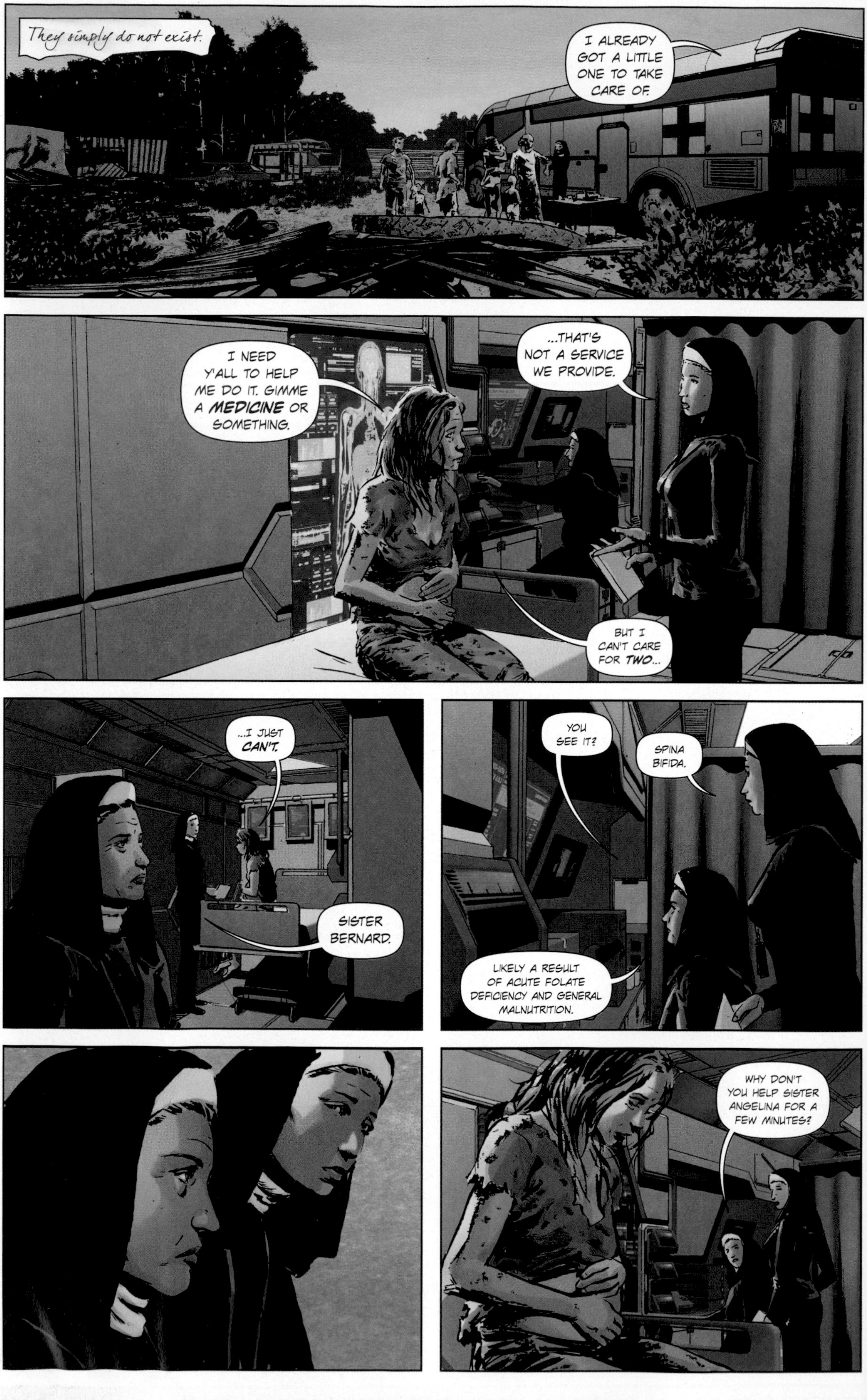
They simply do not exist.
I ALREADY GOT A LITTLE ONE TO TAKE CARE OF.
I NEED Y'ALL TO HELP ME DO IT. GIMME A MEDICINE OR SOMETHING.
...THAT'S NOT A SERVICE WE PROVIDE.
BUT I CAN'T CARE FOR TWO...
...I JUST CAN'T.
SISTER BERNARD.
YOU SEE IT?
SPINA BIFIDA.
LIKELY A RESULT OF ACUTE FOLATE DEFICIENCY AND GENERAL MALNUTRITION.
WHY DON'T YOU HELP SISTER ANGELINA FOR A FEW MINUTES?

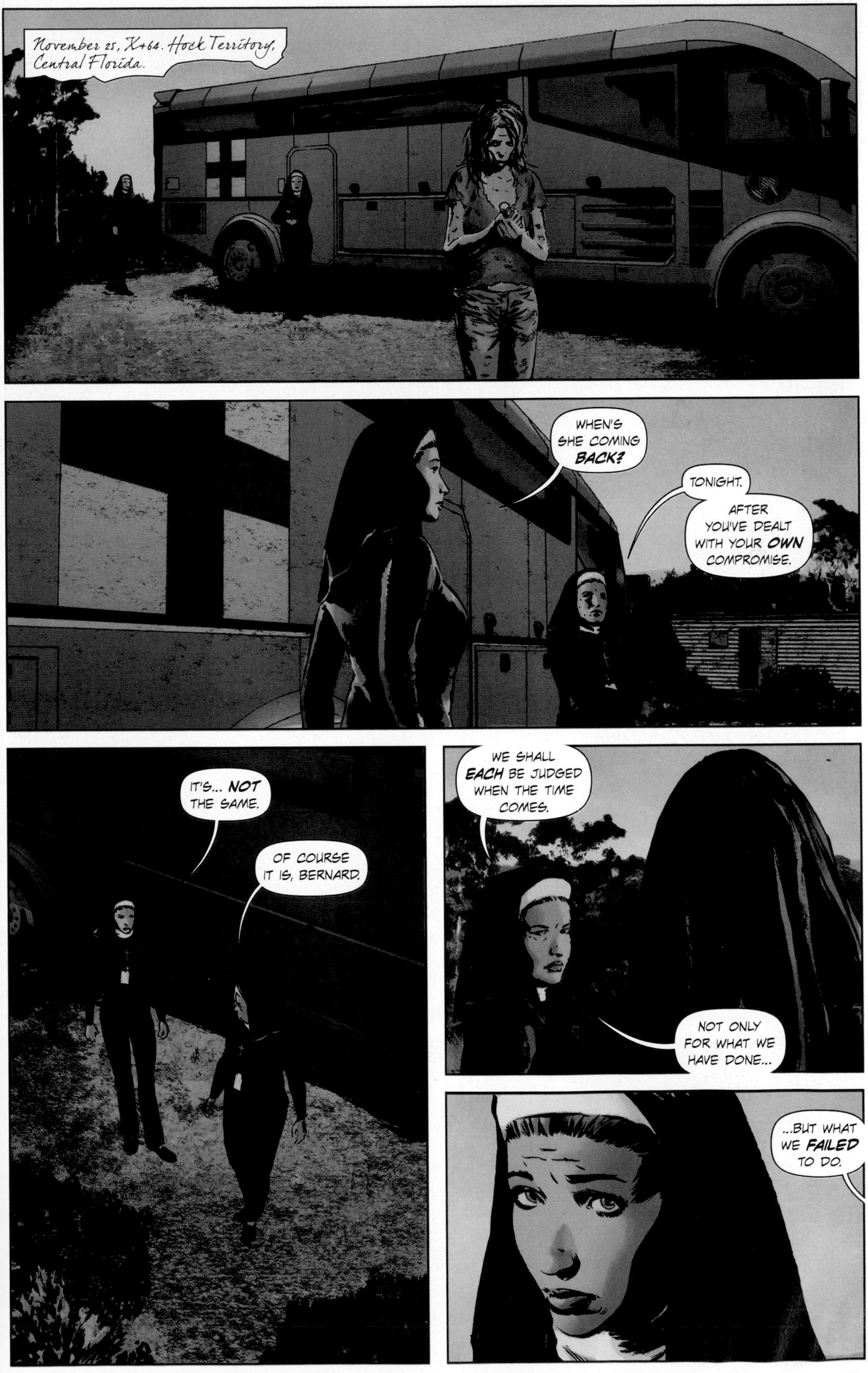
November 25, X+64. Hock Territory, Central Florida.
WHEN'S SHE COMING BACK?
TONIGHT.
AFTER YOU'VE DEALT WITH YOUR OWN COMPROMISE.
IT'S... NOT THE SAME.
OF COURSE IT IS, BERNARD.
WE SHALL EACH BE JUDGED WHEN THE TIME COMES.
NOT ONLY FOR WHAT WE HAVE DONE...
...BUT WHAT WE FAILED TO DO.

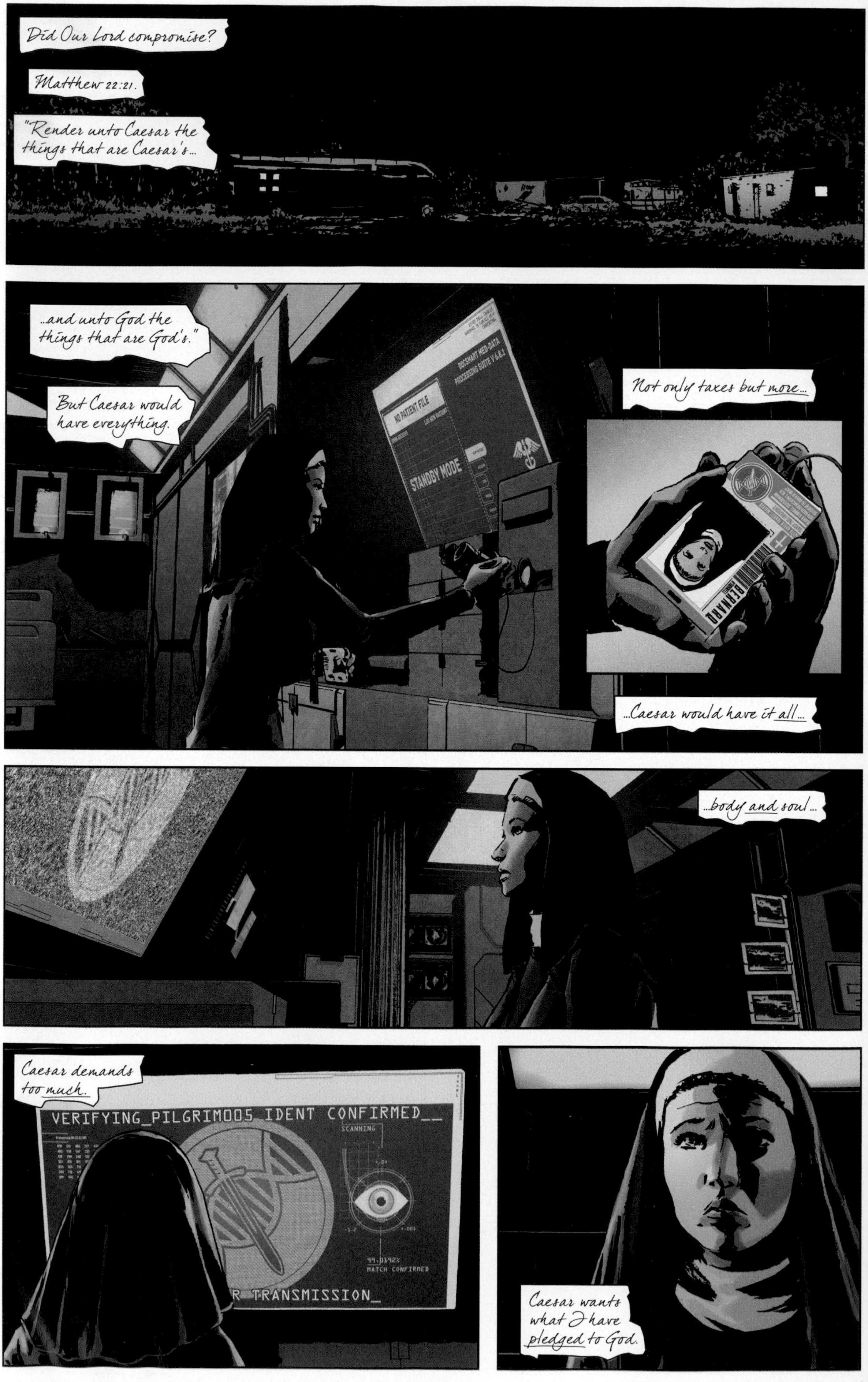
Did Our Lord compromise?
Matthew 22:21.
"Render unto Caesar the things that are Caesar's...
...and unto God the things that are God's."
But Caesar would have everything.
NO PATIENT FILE
STANDBY MODE
Not only taxes but more...
BERNARD
...Caesar would have it all...
...body and soul...
Caesar demands too much.
VERIFYING_PILGRIM005 IDENT CONFIRMED__
SCANNING
99.0192%
MATCH CONFIRMED
R TRANSMISSION_
Caesar wants what I have pledged to God.

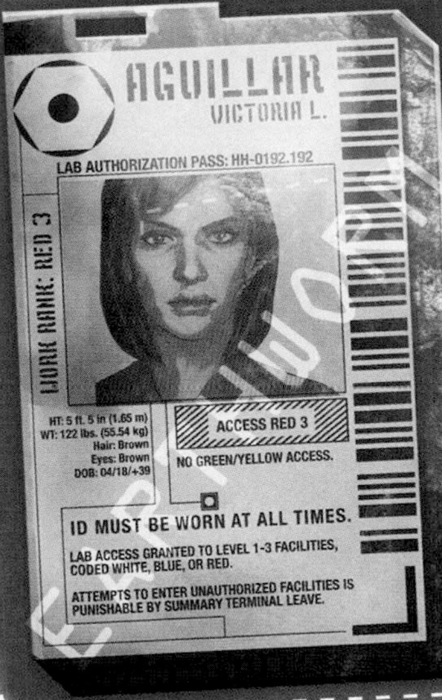
AGUILLAR
VICTORIA L.
LAB AUTHORIZATION PASS: HH-0192.192
WORK RANK: RED 3
HT: 5 ft. 5 in (1.65 m)
WT: 122 lbs. (55.54 kg)
Hair: Brown
Eyes: Brown
DOB: 04/18/+39
ACCESS RED 3
NO GREEN/YELLOW ACCESS.
ID MUST BE WORN AT ALL TIMES.
LAB ACCESS GRANTED TO LEVEL 1-3 FACILITIES, CODED WHITE, BLUE, OR RED.
ATTEMPTS TO ENTER UNAUTHORIZED FACILITIES IS PUNISHABLE BY SUMMARY TERMINAL LEAVE.
EARTHWORM

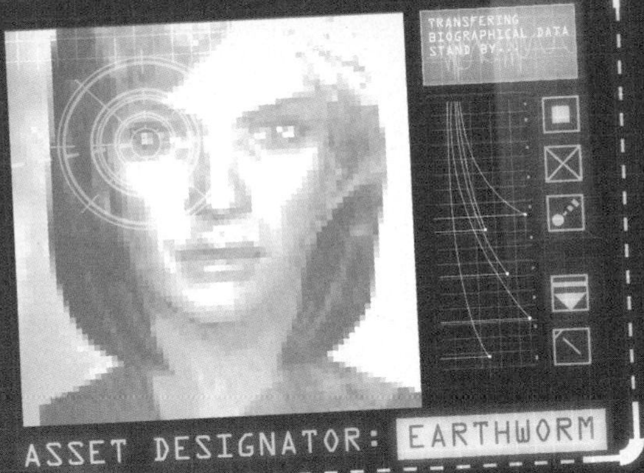
TRANSFERING BIOGRAPHICAL DATA STAND BY...
ASSET DESIGNATOR: EARTHWORM

BASILISK
TRANSMISSION_011125564_ALPHA
SECURITY: BLACK_BLACK_BLACK
SENDER: GLADIUS_ACTUAL
RECIPIENT: PILGRIM005
|| PRIORITY TRANSMISSION ||
MESSAGE BEGINS_WAR DECLARED BETWEEN CARLYLE ALLIED FORCES AND HOCK COALITION AS OF 1948 HOURS GMT THIS DATE_||

_|_BRIEFING TO FOLLOW_|||_STAND BY___|||__STAND BY__|||__BRIEFING BEGINS:_

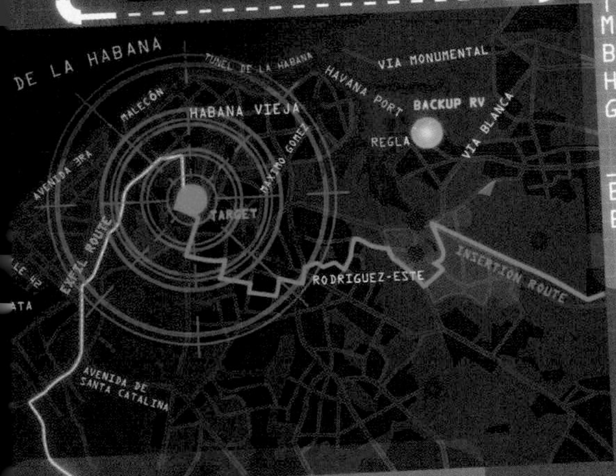
DE LA HABANA
TUNEL DE LA HABANA
VIA MONUMENTAL
HAVANA PORT
BACKUP RV
MALECÓN
HABANA VIEJA
REGLA
VIA BLANCA
AVENIDA 3RA
MAXIMO GOMEZ
TARGET
EXFIL ROUTE
RODRIGUEZ-ESTE
INSERTION ROUTE
AVENIDA DE SANTA CATALINA

TRANSFERRING SITE INTEL

SCIENCE STAFF SHIFT SCHEDULE
SHIFT 1: 2400-1000
SHIFT 2: 0630-1630
SHIFT 3: 1400-2400

SHIFT CREW
3 R&D
10 FABRICAT...

|_PILGRIM005
ACTIVATED_OPERATION:
RAVENVECTOR_OBJECTIVE:

| CONFIRM HOCKLABS DEVELOPING NEW VARIANT STRAIN H7N11_M | PILGRIM005 ORDERED TO RZ POINT TRACER, HAVANA | MISSION: PILGRIM005 ORDERED TO LOCATE AND RECOVER EARTHWORM [982290_HY_27_ATTACHED] AND H7N11_M VARIANT STRAIN SAMPLE | PILGRIM005 DIRECTED UPON ACQUISITION TO RZ PIERCE FOR EXTRACTION |

| RECOVERY OF SAMPLE IS HIGHEST PRIORITY |

_MESSAGE ENDS

They've declared war.

May the Lord protect us all.

May the Lord...

... and I fail, Jesus, help me, I am failing.

I read the words Gladius sends me (my Roman master and I his Christian slave, my service pledged in exchange that I may practice my faith, that I may give comfort, give aid, give help, that I might do as Our Lord did...) and at first I feel nothing, nothing at all.

Then I read the briefing, and I feel terror beyond any I have known before.

And the questions come. Why me, why are they sending me? I am not trained for this, I am not adept at this. I am the wrong person for this, the wrong agent, I am no agent, no spy, I am a nun, and I fear a poor one, at that.

But there is no answer, there never is an answer for that kind of why. Gladius compels me to serve and my choices are simple – do as I am ordered, or do not; do, and risk peril, capture, torture, death; do not, and give the Family yet one more reason to suspend our ministry, to take from us the right to offer our aid, to spread our word, feeble though that may be.

And is not our mission to help? And if what they tell me is true – and there is no reason to believe that it is, I know, but if it is – then is this not a mission of mercy?

I was born the year of Hock's Flu. My mother died of Hock's Flu.

Hundreds of millions died of Hock's Flu.

Is this not, then, an errand of mercy?

SECRET

CLASSIFIED BRIEFING MATERIAL
DIGITIZED ARCHIVE
CODE REF 923742.2387423.298347
cc: ARCHITECT
cc: BLENDER

ARCHIVE
SUBREF: VIROLOGY
SUBREF: HISTORICAL
SUBREF: HOCK FLU

BRIEFING_||_SUBJECT: H7N11_M INFLUENZA VARIANT – COLLOQUIAL: "HOCK'S FLU"
THIS REPORT IS GRADED: SECRET|||

The H7N11_M Influenza A Virus is a manmade modification of the H7N9 and H7N7 Influenza A viral strains. This resulted in a variant of exceptional virulence as well as zoonotic capacity that allowed airborne transmission from multiple infected sources including horses, pigs, domestic and wild birds, and other farmed carnivores.

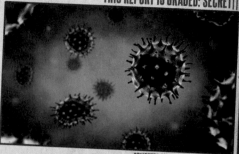

COMPUTER ENHANCED SCAN OF H7N11_A

Beginning in X+25, the H7N11_M virus pandemic lasted until X+29, infecting approximately 30% of the global population at the time, or roughly two billion people. Global fatality estimates run between two hundred million and four hundred million, though an exact accounting has never been verified. Like the 1918 Spanish Flu (H1N1), the virus predominantly killed previously healthy young adults as opposed to more traditional influenza outbreaks which trend towards fatalities amongst juveniles and the elderly.

Coming as it did less than ten years after the cessation of hostilities in the North American Dissolution War (X+13 - X+17), and following on the heels of similar conflicts around the globe, the H7N11_M pandemic damaged the already fragile recovery. In many Domains around the globe this lead in turn to a "cascade failure" due not solely to raw manpower loss, but also the loss of individuals with advanced training and specialized knowledge. Widespread slaughter of all animals feared to be carriers, famine, civil dissolution, rioting, and other effects were commonly felt around the globe, including, it should be noted, in Hock Territory, where the virus was late to strike, but no less virulent when it did.

SURVEILLANCE ASSET: H89382.927: HOCK FLU VICTIM

CENTER Intelligence concluded in X+25 that the H7N11_M virus was developed at HOCK R&D 018, outside of Paducah, Kentucky, and further concluded that the introduction of the strain was likely deliberate. Intelligence gathered from the period out of Hock Territory reported distribution of innoculations to Territory "Citizens" as part of their health regimen, and the late spread of the illness into the region further supports this. By X+26, however, this was insufficient to deter the progress of the virus. Comparisons of the virus from X+25 with strains from X+27 indicate natural mutation, or drift, though evidence also exists to suggest Hock had taken initial steps to prevent just such an evolution from occurring.

SURVEILLANCE ASSET: H881928927: HOCK FLU VICTIM

SURVEILLANCE ASSET: H8734923.183472: HOCK R&D 018 SITE

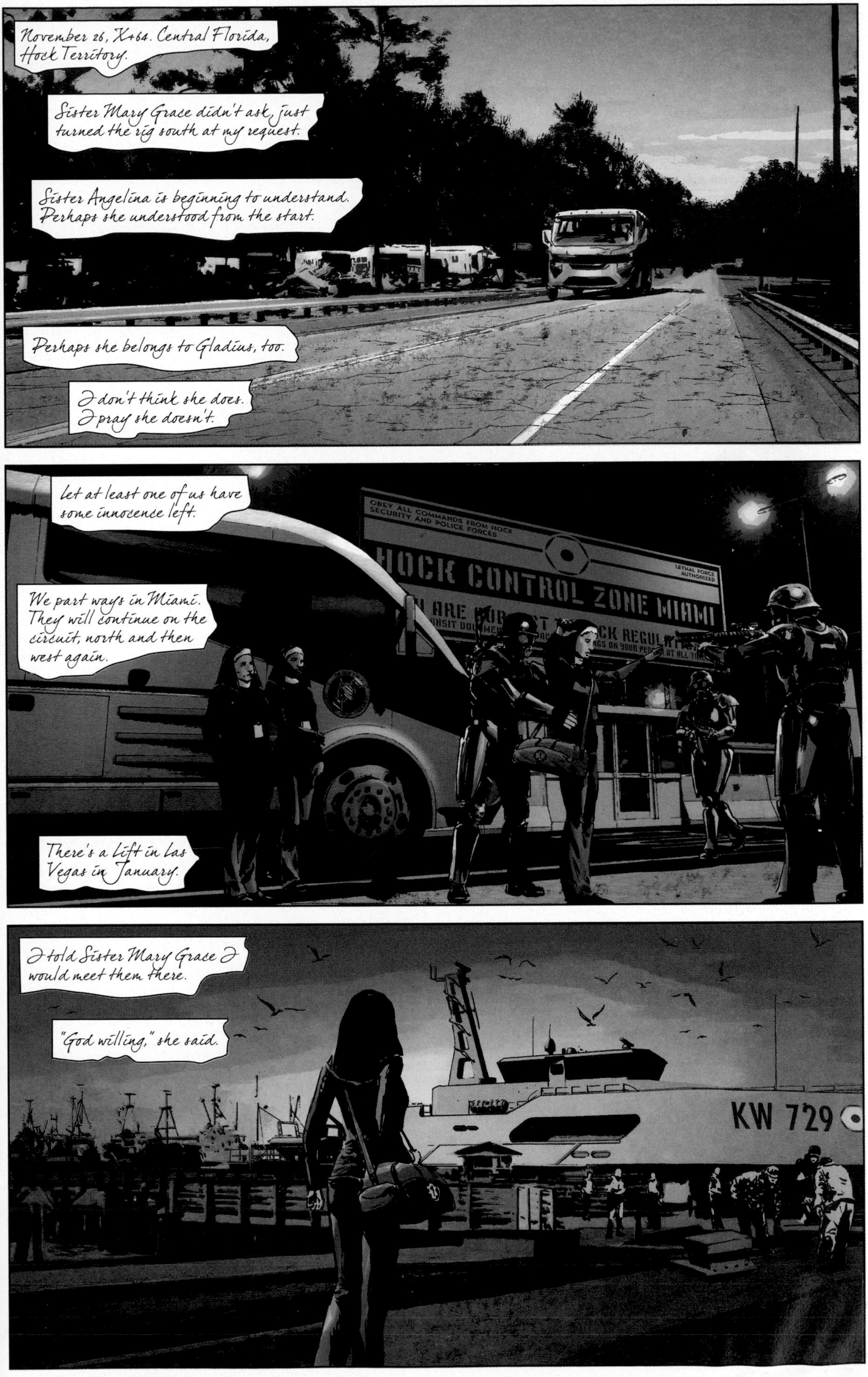
November 26, X+64. Central Florida, Hock Territory.
Sister Mary Grace didn't ask, just turned the rig south at my request.
Sister Angelina is beginning to understand. Perhaps she understood from the start.
Perhaps she belongs to Gladius, too.
I don't think she does. I pray she doesn't.
Let at least one of us have some innocence left.
OBEY ALL COMMANDS FROM HOCK SECURITY AND POLICE FORCES
HOCK CONTROL ZONE MIAMI
LETHAL FORCE AUTHORIZED
We part ways in Miami. They will continue on the circuit, north and then west again.
There's a Lift in Las Vegas in January.
I told Sister Mary Grace I would meet them there.
"God willing," she said.
KW 729

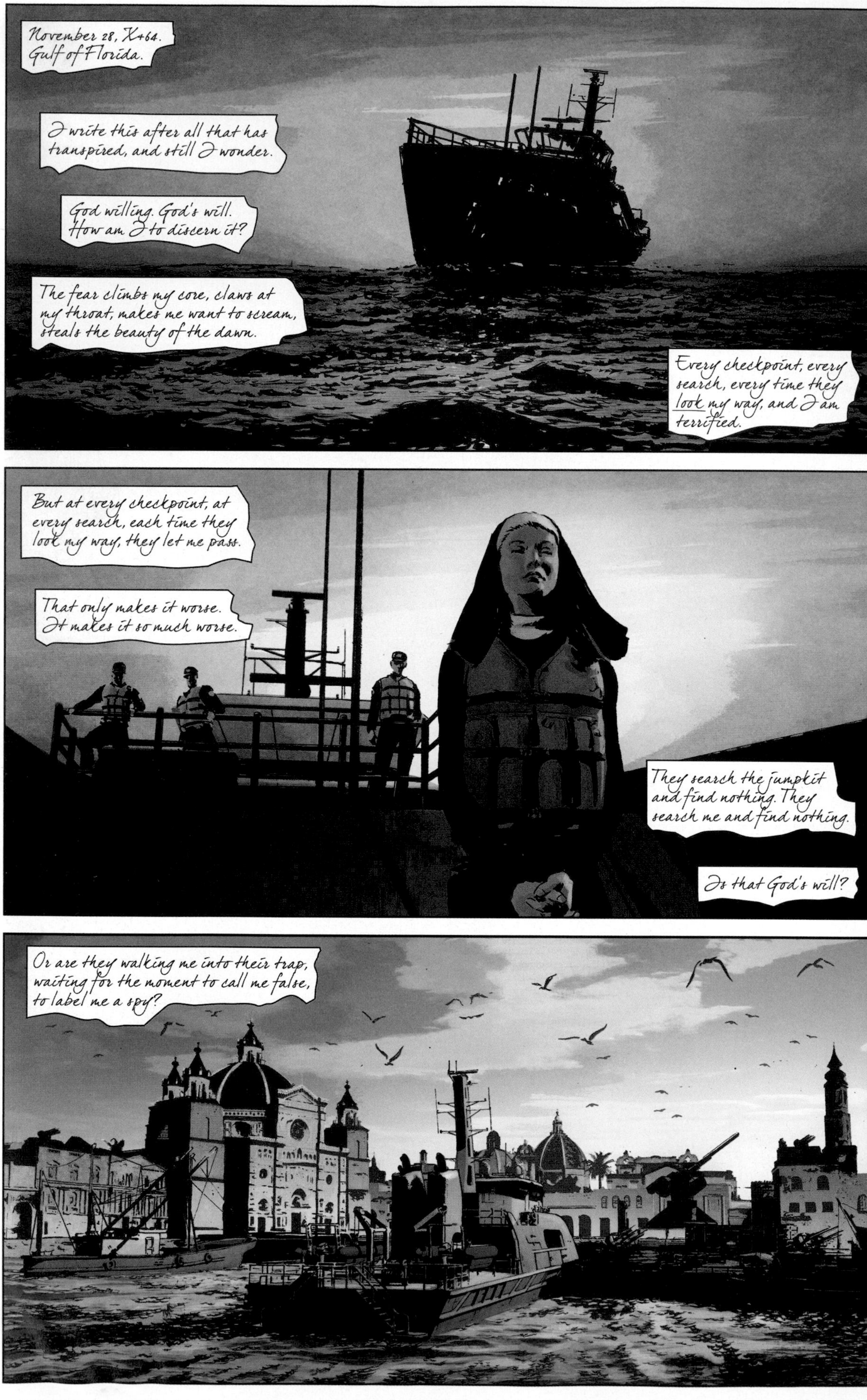
November 28, X+64.
Gulf of Florida.
I write this after all that has transpired, and still I wonder.
God willing. God's will. How am I to discern it?
The fear climbs my core, claws at my throat, makes me want to scream, steals the beauty of the dawn.
Every checkpoint, every search, every time they look my way, and I am terrified.
But at every checkpoint, at every search, each time they look my way, they let me pass.
That only makes it worse. It makes it so much worse.
They search the jumpkit and find nothing. They search me and find nothing.
Is that God's will?
Or are they walking me into their trap, waiting for the moment to call me false, to label me a spy?

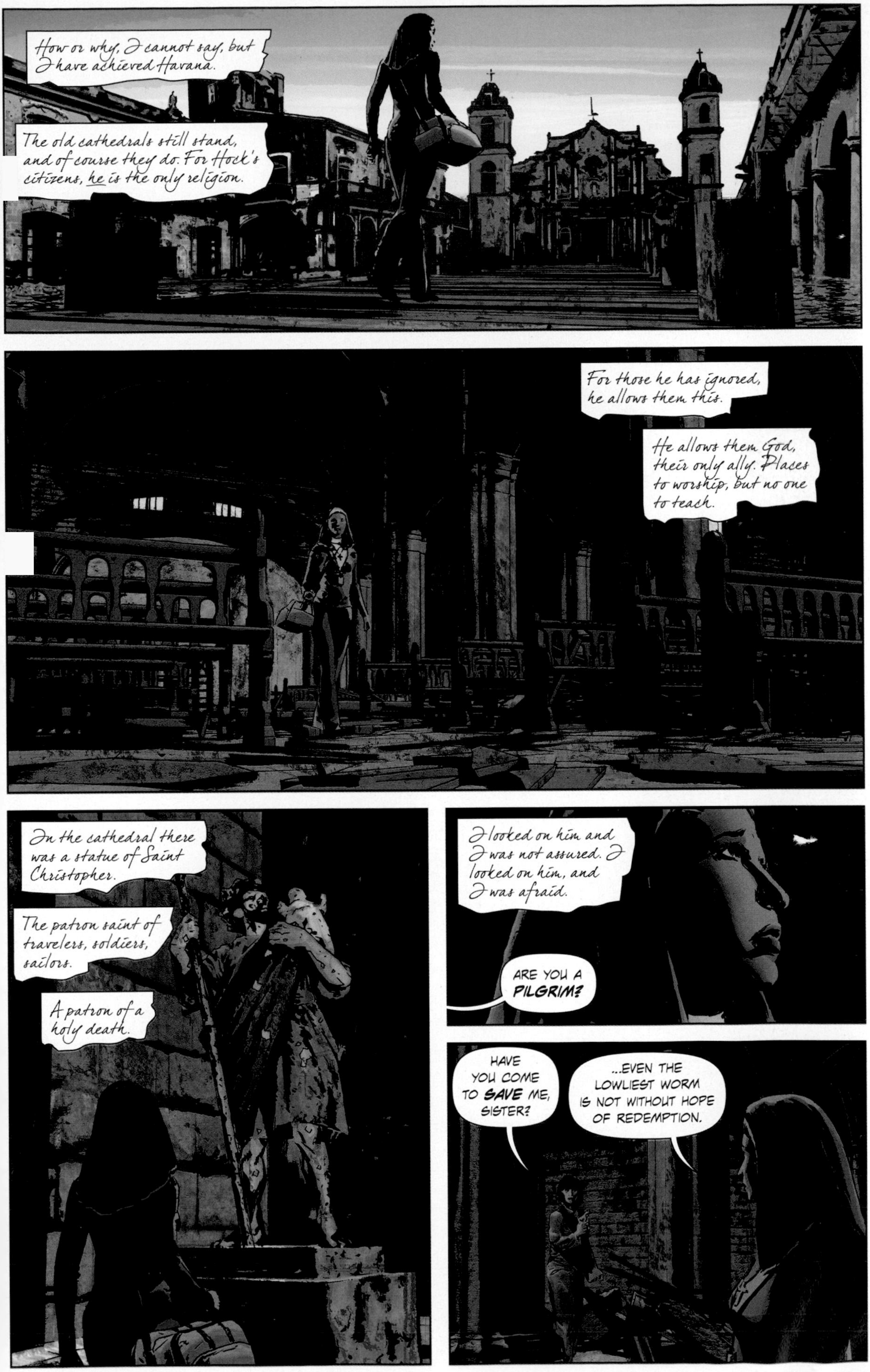
How or why, I cannot say, but I have achieved Havana.
The old cathedrals still stand, and of course they do. For Hock's citizens, he is the only religion.
For those he has ignored, he allows them this.
He allows them God, their only ally. Places to worship, but no one to teach.
In the cathedral there was a statue of Saint Christopher.
The patron saint of travelers, soldiers, sailors.
A patron of a holy death.
I looked on him and I was not assured. I looked on him, and I was afraid.
ARE YOU A PILGRIM?
HAVE YOU COME TO SAVE ME, SISTER?
...EVEN THE LOWLIEST WORM IS NOT WITHOUT HOPE OF REDEMPTION.

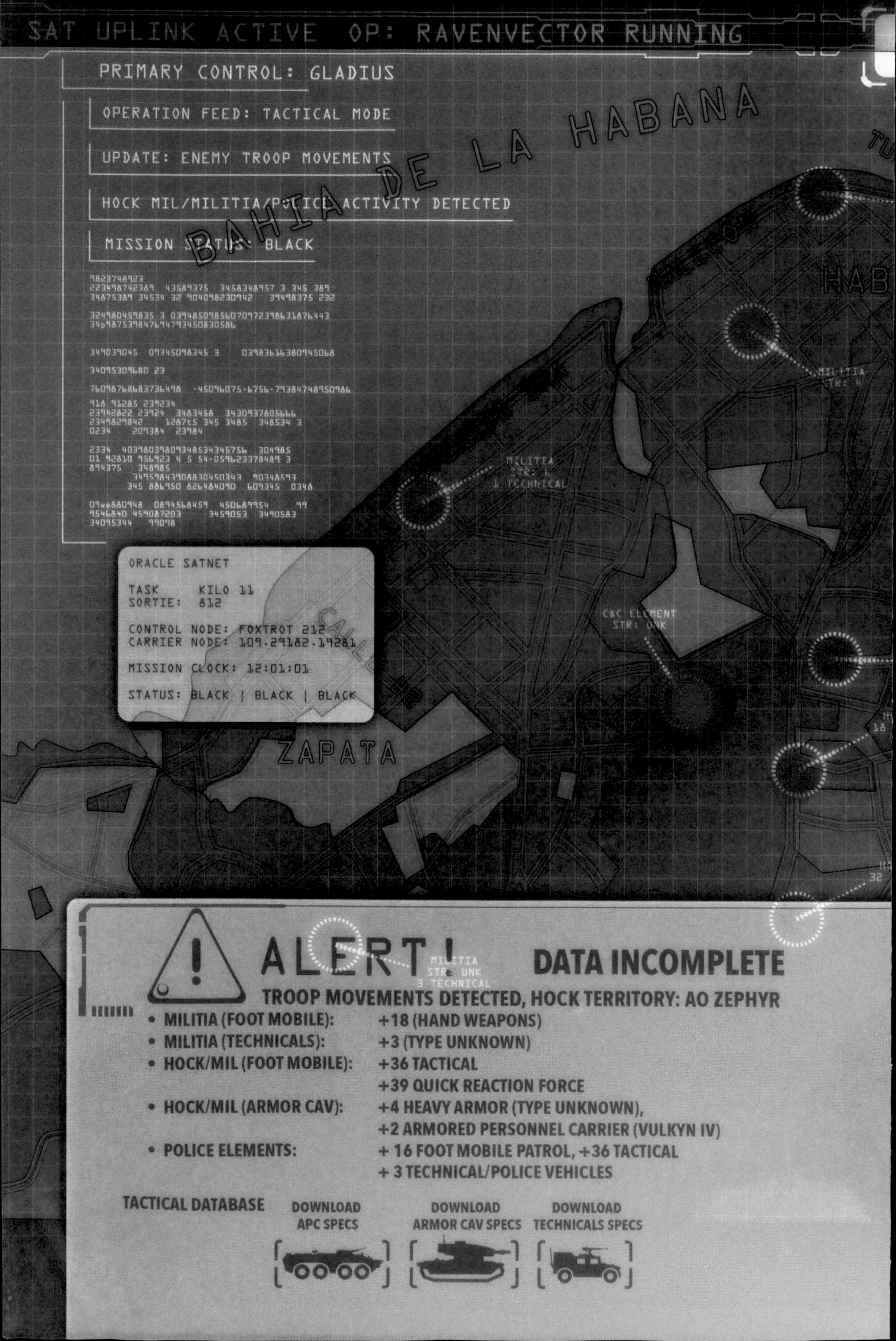
SAT UPLINK ACTIVE OP: RAVENVECTOR RUNNING
PRIMARY CONTROL: GLADIUS
OPERATION FEED: TACTICAL MODE
UPDATE: ENEMY TROOP MOVEMENTS
HOCK MIL/MILITIA/POLICE ACTIVITY DETECTED
MISSION STATUS: BLACK
BAHIA DE LA HABANA
MILITIA
STR: 6
1 TECHNICAL
C&C ELEMENT
STR: UNK
ORACLE SATNET
TASK KILO 11
SORTIE: 812
CONTROL NODE: FOXTROT 212
CARRIER NODE: 109.29182.19281
MISSION CLOCK: 12:01:01
STATUS: BLACK | BLACK | BLACK
ZAPATA
ALERT!
MILITIA
STR: UNK
3 TECHNICAL
DATA INCOMPLETE
TROOP MOVEMENTS DETECTED, HOCK TERRITORY: AO ZEPHYR
• MILITIA (FOOT MOBILE): +18 (HAND WEAPONS)
• MILITIA (TECHNICALS): +3 (TYPE UNKNOWN)
• HOCK/MIL (FOOT MOBILE): +36 TACTICAL
+39 QUICK REACTION FORCE
• HOCK/MIL (ARMOR CAV): +4 HEAVY ARMOR (TYPE UNKNOWN),
+2 ARMORED PERSONNEL CARRIER (VULKYN IV)
• POLICE ELEMENTS: + 16 FOOT MOBILE PATROL, +36 TACTICAL
+ 3 TECHNICAL/POLICE VEHICLES
TACTICAL DATABASE
DOWNLOAD APC SPECS
DOWNLOAD ARMOR CAV SPECS
DOWNLOAD TECHNICALS SPECS

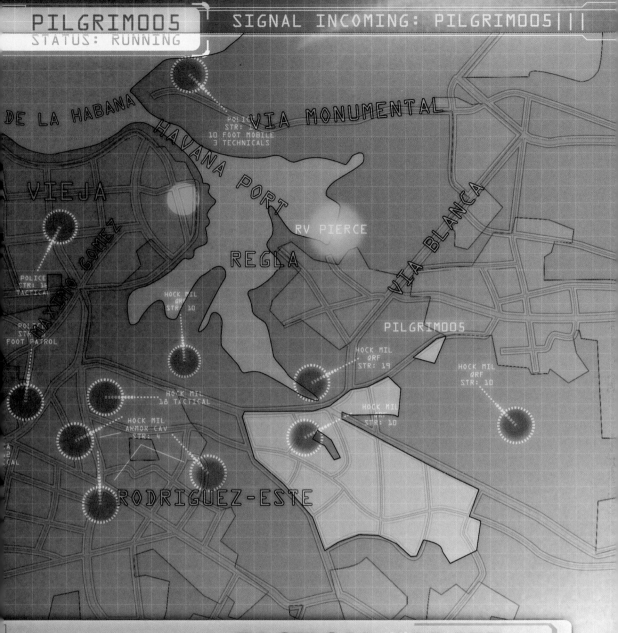

DE LA HABANA

VIA MONUMENTAL

POLI
STR:
10 FOOT MOBILE
3 TECHNICALS

HAVANA PORT

VIEJA

MAXIMO GOMEZ

RV PIERCE

VIA BLANCA

REGLA

POLICE
STR: 16
TACTICAL

HOCK MIL
QRF
STR: 10

PILGRIM005

POLICE
STR:
FOOT PATROL

HOCK MIL
QRF
STR: 19

HOCK MIL
QRF
STR: 10

HOCK MIL
18 TACTICAL

HOCK MIL
STR: 10

A
2
CAL

HOCK MIL
ARMOR CAV
STR: 4

RODRIGUEZ-ESTE

OPS/TAC/CONTROL: GLADIUS

TACTICAL UPDATE
ORACLE OVERFLIGHT

ACTIVITY ANALYSIS:
COMBAT PATROL ACTIVITY DETECTED.

SIGINT INDICATES ENHANCED STATE OF ALERT. PRESENCE OF MAINLINE HOCKMIL
UNITS AND A C&C ELEMENT OF UNKNOWN SIZE/STRENGTH/COMPOSITION IN ZONE 2
INDICATES ESCALATION OF HOCK THREAT LEVEL.

SIGNAL PROCESSING UPDATE: AUDIO BURST TRANSMISSION DETECTED
PRELIMINARY ID: PILGRIM005 AUTORECORD

SIGNAL DECRYPTION INCOMING...

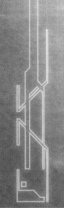

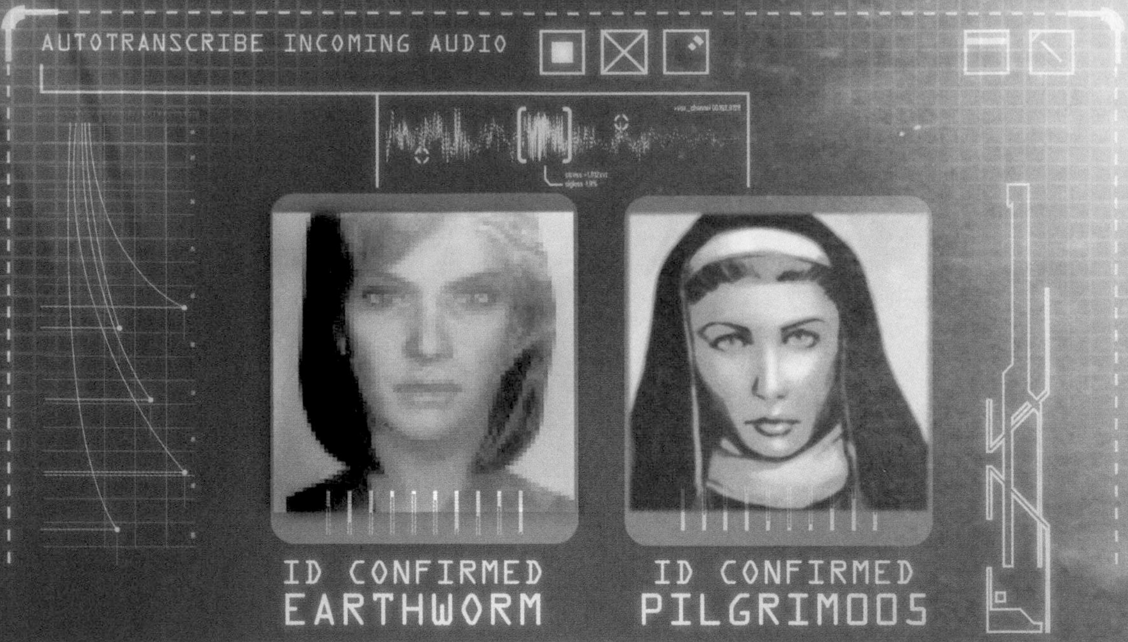

ID CONFIRMED
EARTHWORM

ID CONFIRMED
PILGRIM005

__RECORDING 26_11_64_17:03.17 EARTHWORM||PILGRIM005_CONT'D__

EARTHWORM:	I've been waiting two days. I thought they would send more. Don't they realize how important this is?
PILGRIM005:	Do you have it?
EARTHWORM:	I have it, yes, I have it. This one is different. It's not the old one, not H7N11.
PILGRIM005:	What do you mean?
EARTHWORM:	This one, it's… re-engineered. We went into the RNA, he- he had instructions for us, specific, everything.
PILGRIM005P:	He?
EARTHWORM:	Him. Doctor Hock. Rewrote it from the RNA up. Everything.
PILGRIM005:	If you have the sample--
EARTHWORM:	[laughs] I am the sample.
PILGRIM005:	What do you mean?
EARTHWORM:	You have to get me out. It's in me. I'm the sample.
PILGRIM005:	God in Heaven--
EARTHWORM:	No, no, it's okay, Sister. It's asleep. It'll stay asleep for another… seventy hours or so. Then I become patient zero.
PILGRIM005:	You're… you're not contagious?
EARTHWORM:	Seventy hours, give or take. How's that for motivation to extract me?
PILGRIM005:	You have… you have data? Treatment? A cure?
EARTHWORM:	Everything on a micro-drive, what we were developing, all of it.
PILGRIM005:	Give it to me.
EARTHWORM:	Not on your life, not until I'm safe, not until–

[[UNINTELLIGIBLE / AMBIENT NOISE]]

[[UNIDENTIFIED/VOICE]]|
[NO FILEMATCH]: What's going on here?

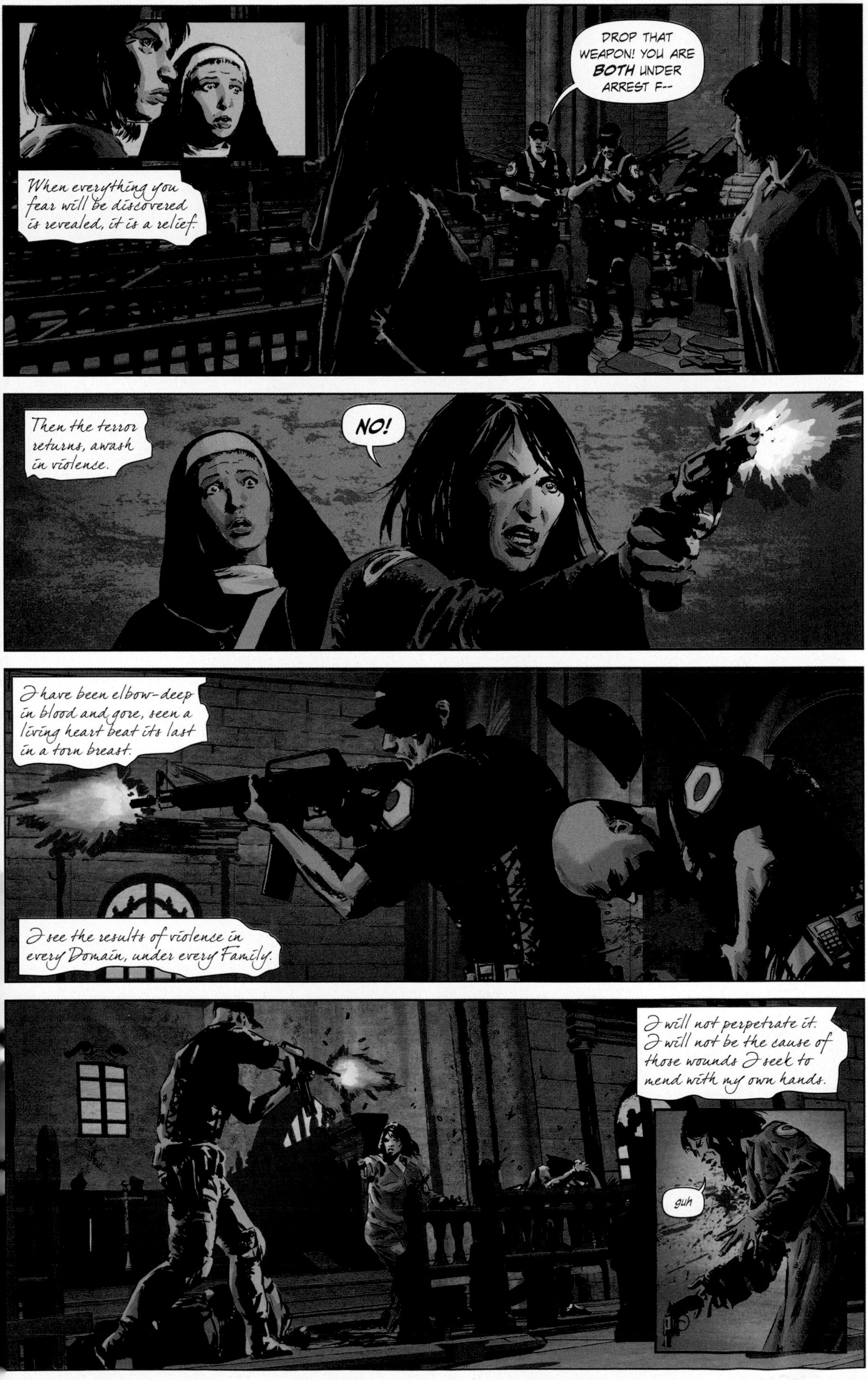

DROP THAT WEAPON! YOU ARE **BOTH** UNDER ARREST F--
When everything you fear will be discovered is revealed, it is a relief.
Then the terror returns, awash in violence.
NO!
I have been elbow-deep in blood and gore, seen a living heart beat its last in a torn breast.
I see the results of violence in every Domain, under every Family.
I will not perpetrate it. I will not be the cause of those wounds I seek to mend with my own hands.
guh

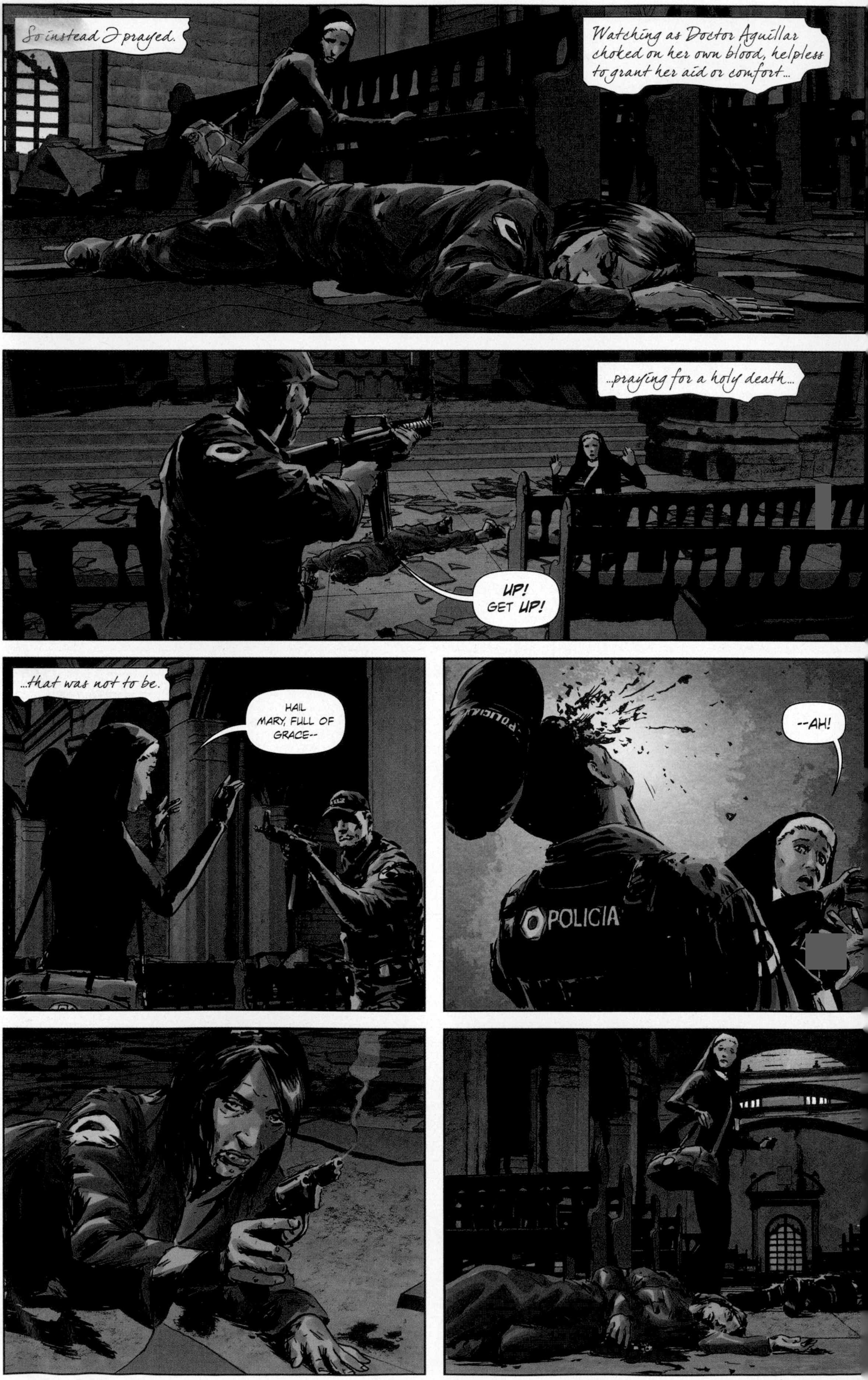
So instead I prayed.
Watching as Doctor Aguillar choked on her own blood, helpless to grant her aid or comfort...
...praying for a holy death...
UP! GET UP!
...that was not to be.
HAIL MARY, FULL OF GRACE--
POLICIA
--AH!

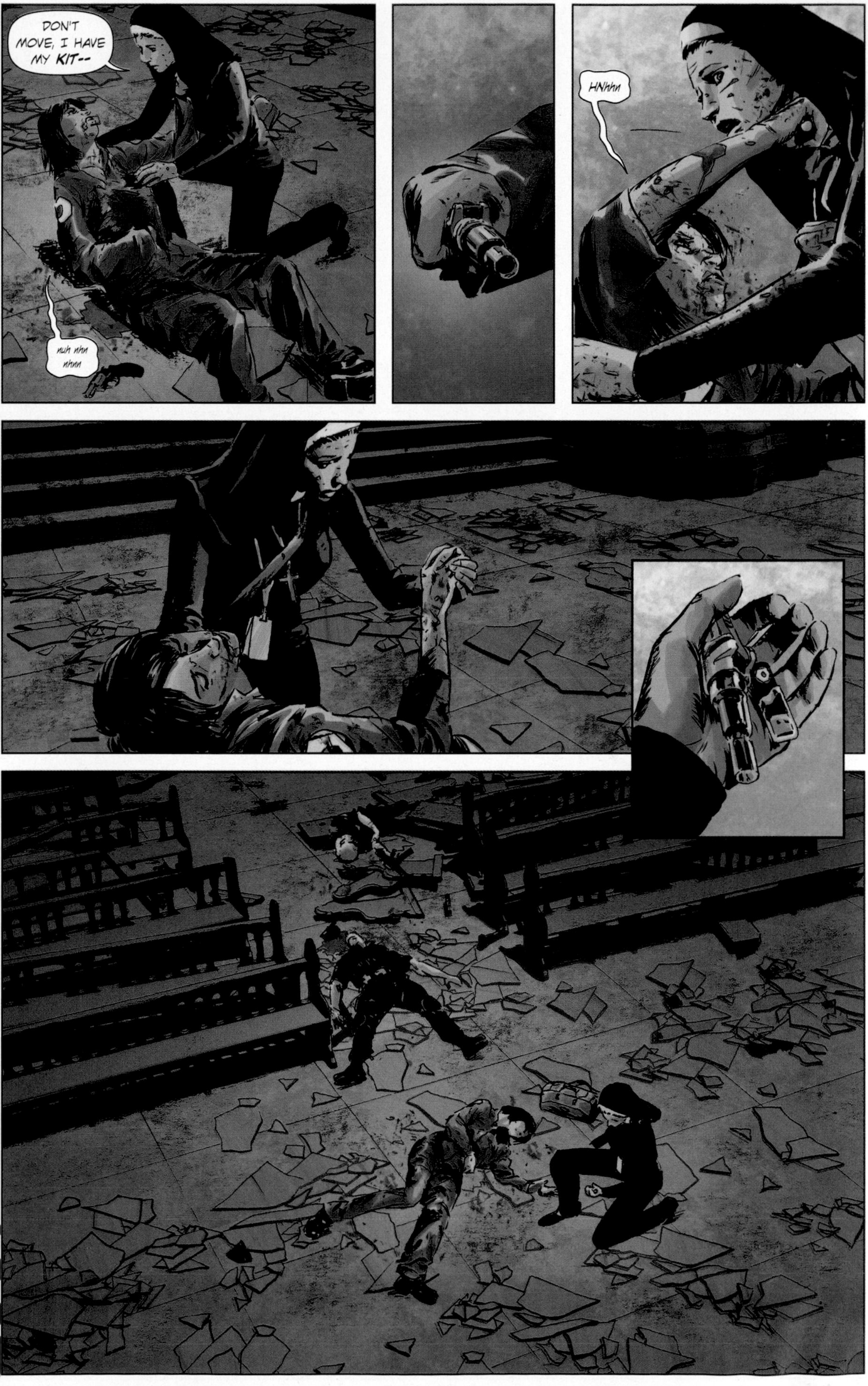
DON'T MOVE, I HAVE MY KIT--
nuh nhn nhnn
HNhhn

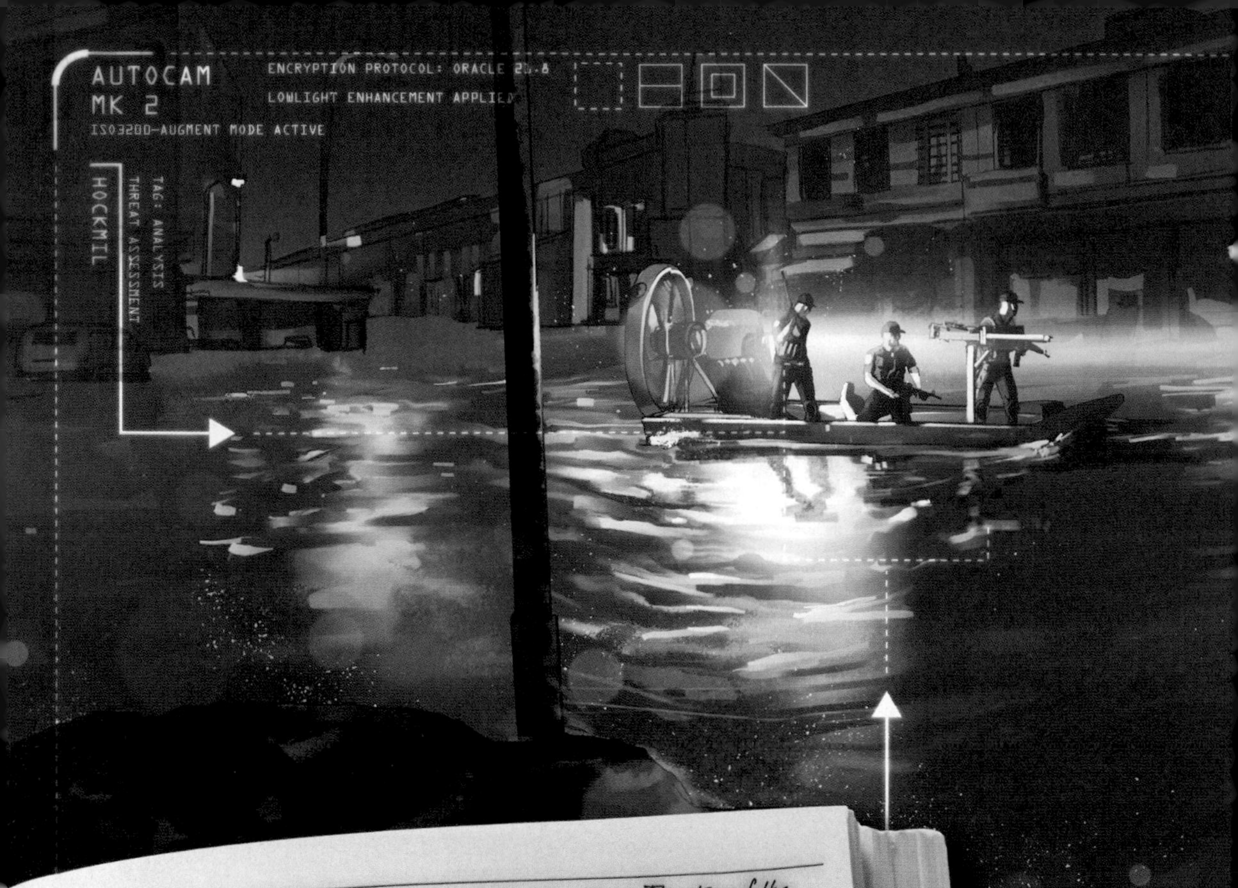
AUTOCAM
MK 2
ENCRYPTION PROTOCOL: ORACLE
LOWLIGHT ENHANCEMENT APPLIE
ISO3200-AUGMENT MODE ACTIVE
HOCKMIL
TAG: ANALYSIS
THREAT ASSESSMENT

In my imagination, I could feel what she had done to me. The sting of the injection lingering, festering, spreading. In my mind, I imagined the virus within me, replicating, growing. It did not matter what she had said, how could it? When one is afraid, one loses reason.

When one is truly afraid, all one has left is faith.

We had been set upon in a church, and I left her body there, and I ran.

She had been as frightened as I.

I ran, and I hid, and my fear changed and became anger. Anger at Aguillar, who had turned me into the very thing I had been sent to prevent. Seventy hours? More? less? And when it was over...

Anger at Aguillar. Anger at Carlyle. Anger at God, and my faith dying even as I was certain I was.

They had given me a beacon, hidden in the jumpkit, precisely for emergencies like this. Activate it and reach the location I had been ordered to, and perhaps I could be recovered, I could be rescued, saved. And perhaps what Aguillar had given me would be enough, would allow for minds better than mine to deliver a cure.

And that would be fine, that would make it right, but for one thing: the same beacon that could bring my rescue would certainly bring my end. The signal would call to friend and foe alike. It would be a matter of which reached me first.

What choice did I have?

What choice did I have but to summon the last of my faith and try?

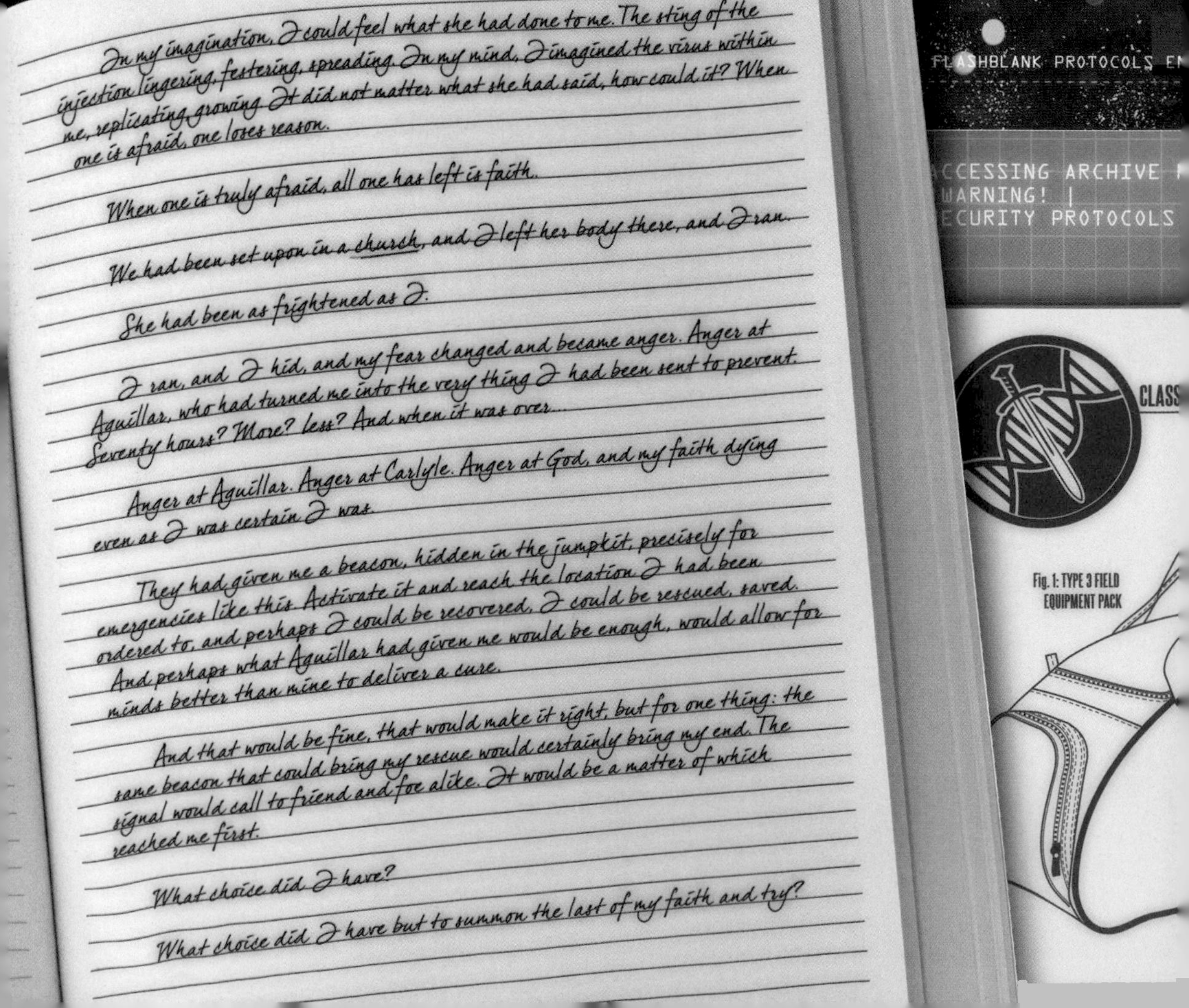
FLASHBLANK PROTOCOLS EN
ACCESSING ARCHIVE
WARNING! |
ECURITY PROTOCOLS
CLASS
Fig. 1: TYPE 3 FIELD EQUIPMENT PACK

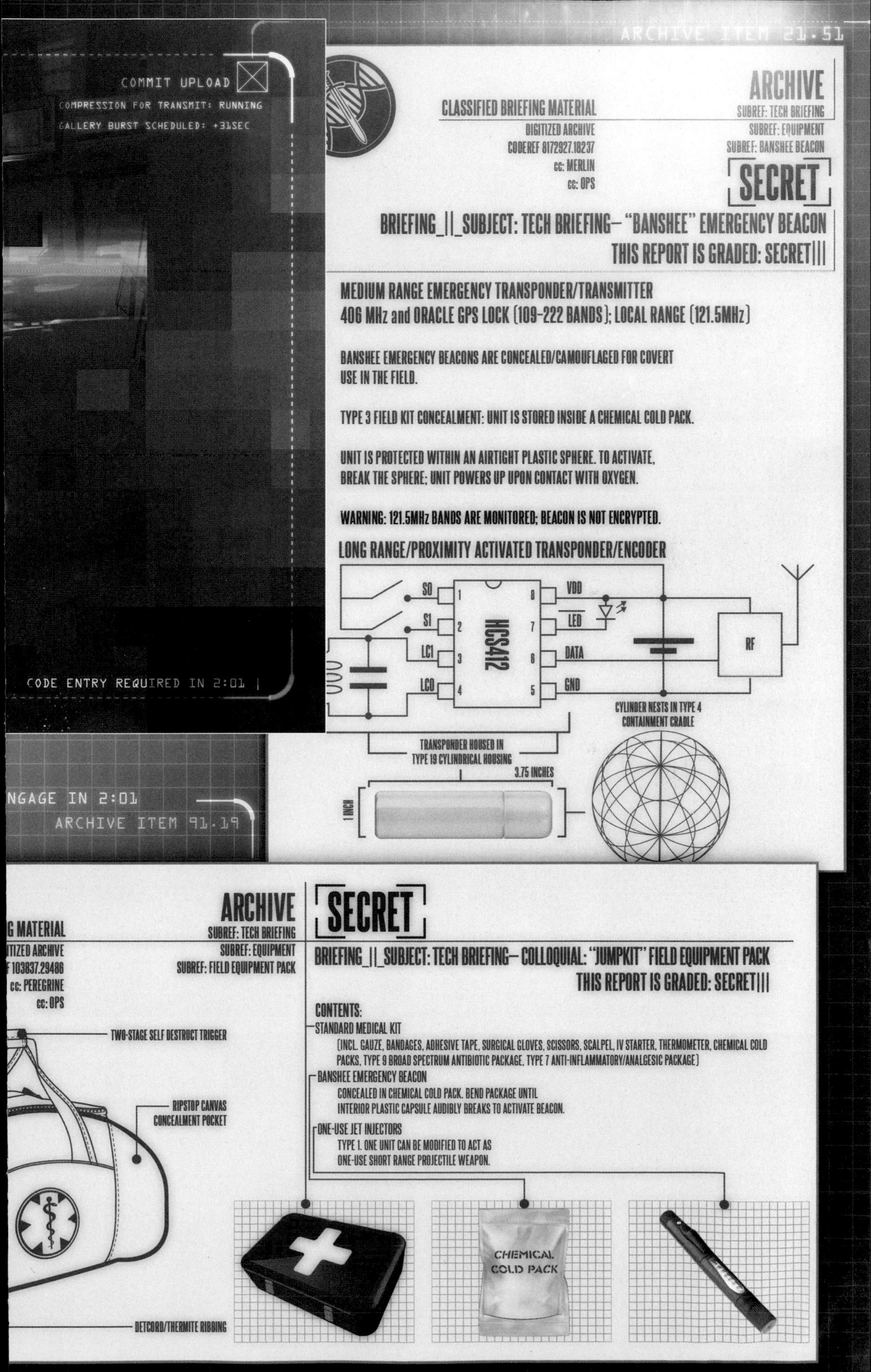

ARCHIVE ITEM 21.51
COMMIT UPLOAD
COMPRESSION FOR TRANSMIT: RUNNING
GALLERY BURST SCHEDULED: +31SEC
CODE ENTRY REQUIRED IN 2:01
NGAGE IN 2:01
ARCHIVE ITEM 91.19
CLASSIFIED BRIEFING MATERIAL
DIGITIZED ARCHIVE
CODEREF 8172927.18237
cc: MERLIN
cc: OPS
ARCHIVE
SUBREF: TECH BRIEFING
SUBREF: EQUIPMENT
SUBREF: BANSHEE BEACON
SECRET
BRIEFING_||_SUBJECT: TECH BRIEFING– "BANSHEE" EMERGENCY BEACON
THIS REPORT IS GRADED: SECRET|||
MEDIUM RANGE EMERGENCY TRANSPONDER/TRANSMITTER
406 MHz and ORACLE GPS LOCK (109-222 BANDS); LOCAL RANGE (121.5MHz)
BANSHEE EMERGENCY BEACONS ARE CONCEALED/CAMOUFLAGED FOR COVERT USE IN THE FIELD.
TYPE 3 FIELD KIT CONCEALMENT: UNIT IS STORED INSIDE A CHEMICAL COLD PACK.
UNIT IS PROTECTED WITHIN AN AIRTIGHT PLASTIC SPHERE. TO ACTIVATE, BREAK THE SPHERE; UNIT POWERS UP UPON CONTACT WITH OXYGEN.
WARNING: 121.5MHz BANDS ARE MONITORED; BEACON IS NOT ENCRYPTED.
LONG RANGE/PROXIMITY ACTIVATED TRANSPONDER/ENCODER
S0
S1
LC1
LC0
HCS412
VDD
LED
DATA
GND
RF
CYLINDER NESTS IN TYPE 4 CONTAINMENT CRADLE
TRANSPONDER HOUSED IN TYPE 19 CYLINDRICAL HOUSING
3.75 INCHES
1 INCH
G MATERIAL
ITIZED ARCHIVE
F 103837.29486
cc: PEREGRINE
cc: OPS
ARCHIVE
SUBREF: TECH BRIEFING
SUBREF: EQUIPMENT
SUBREF: FIELD EQUIPMENT PACK
SECRET
BRIEFING_||_SUBJECT: TECH BRIEFING– COLLOQUIAL: "JUMPKIT" FIELD EQUIPMENT PACK
THIS REPORT IS GRADED: SECRET|||
CONTENTS:
STANDARD MEDICAL KIT
(INCL. GAUZE, BANDAGES, ADHESIVE TAPE, SURGICAL GLOVES, SCISSORS, SCALPEL, IV STARTER, THERMOMETER, CHEMICAL COLD PACKS, TYPE 9 BROAD SPECTRUM ANTIBIOTIC PACKAGE, TYPE 7 ANTI-INFLAMMATORY/ANALGESIC PACKAGE)
BANSHEE EMERGENCY BEACON
CONCEALED IN CHEMICAL COLD PACK. BEND PACKAGE UNTIL INTERIOR PLASTIC CAPSULE AUDIBLY BREAKS TO ACTIVATE BEACON.
ONE-USE JET INJECTORS
TYPE 1. ONE UNIT CAN BE MODIFIED TO ACT AS ONE-USE SHORT RANGE PROJECTILE WEAPON.
TWO-STAGE SELF DESTRUCT TRIGGER
RIPSTOP CANVAS CONCEALMENT POCKET
DETCORD/THERMITE RIBBING
CHEMICAL COLD PACK

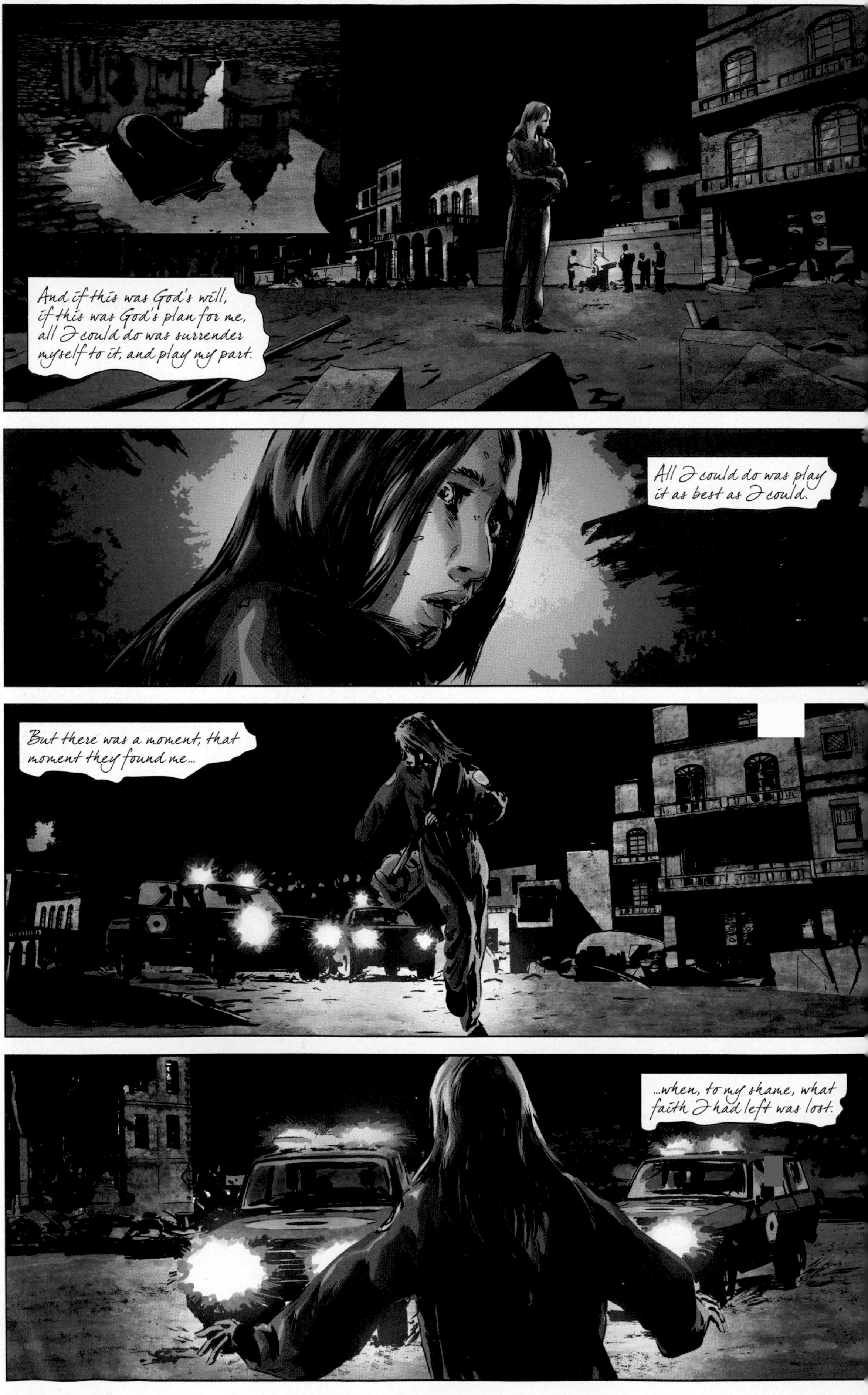
And if this was God's will, if this was God's plan for me, all I could do was surrender myself to it, and play my part.
All I could do was play it as best as I could.
But there was a moment, that moment they found me...
...when, to my shame, what faith I had left was lost.

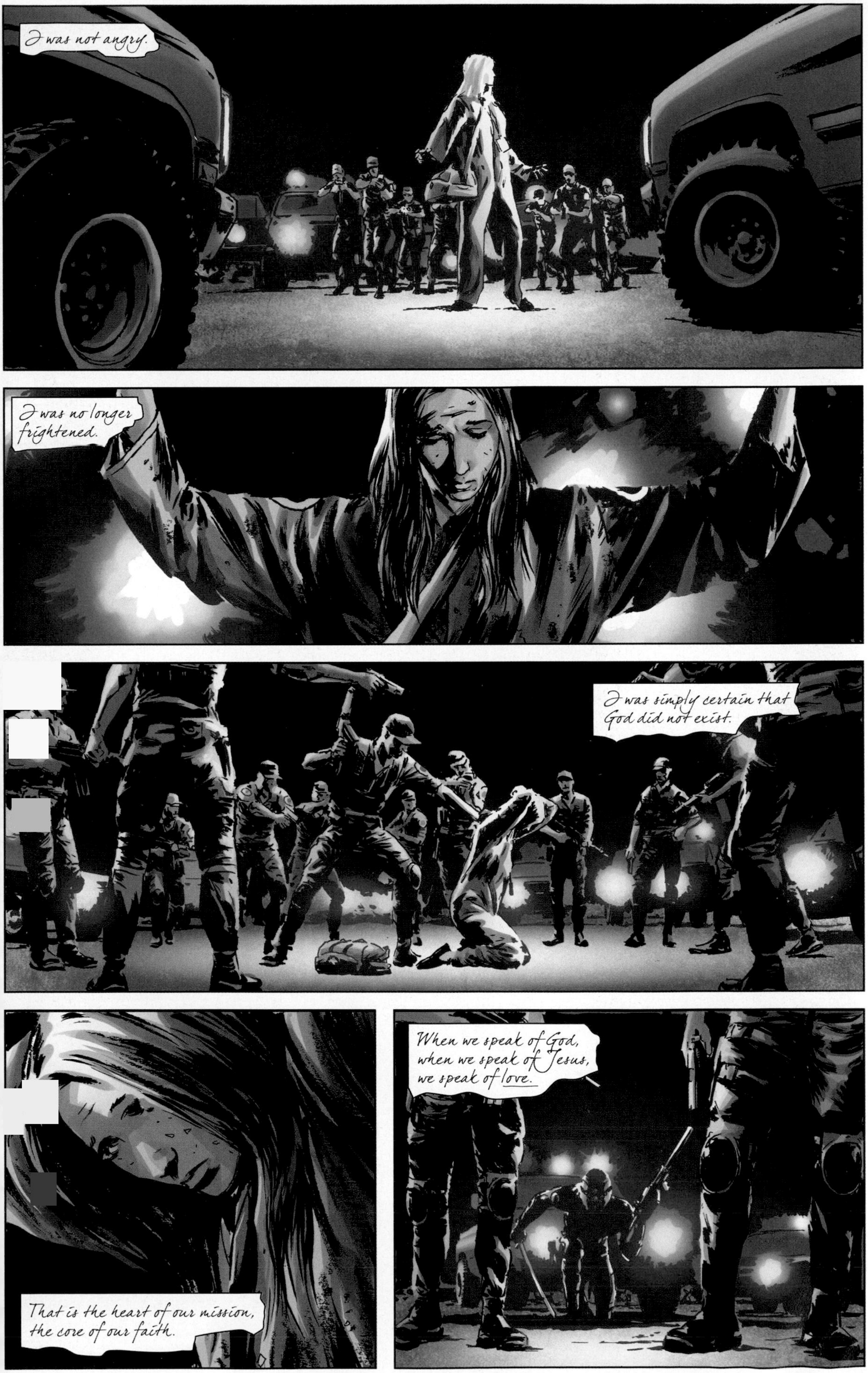
I was not angry.
I was no longer frightened.
I was simply certain that God did not exist.
That is the heart of our mission, the core of our faith.
When we speak of God, when we speak of Jesus, we speak of love.

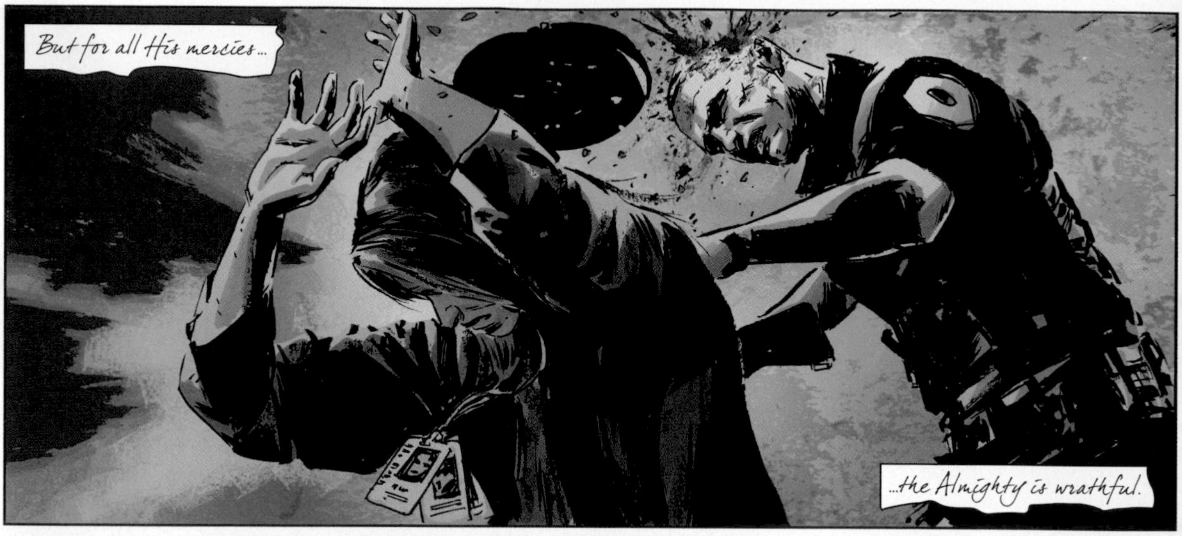
But for all His mercies...
...the Almighty is wrathful.

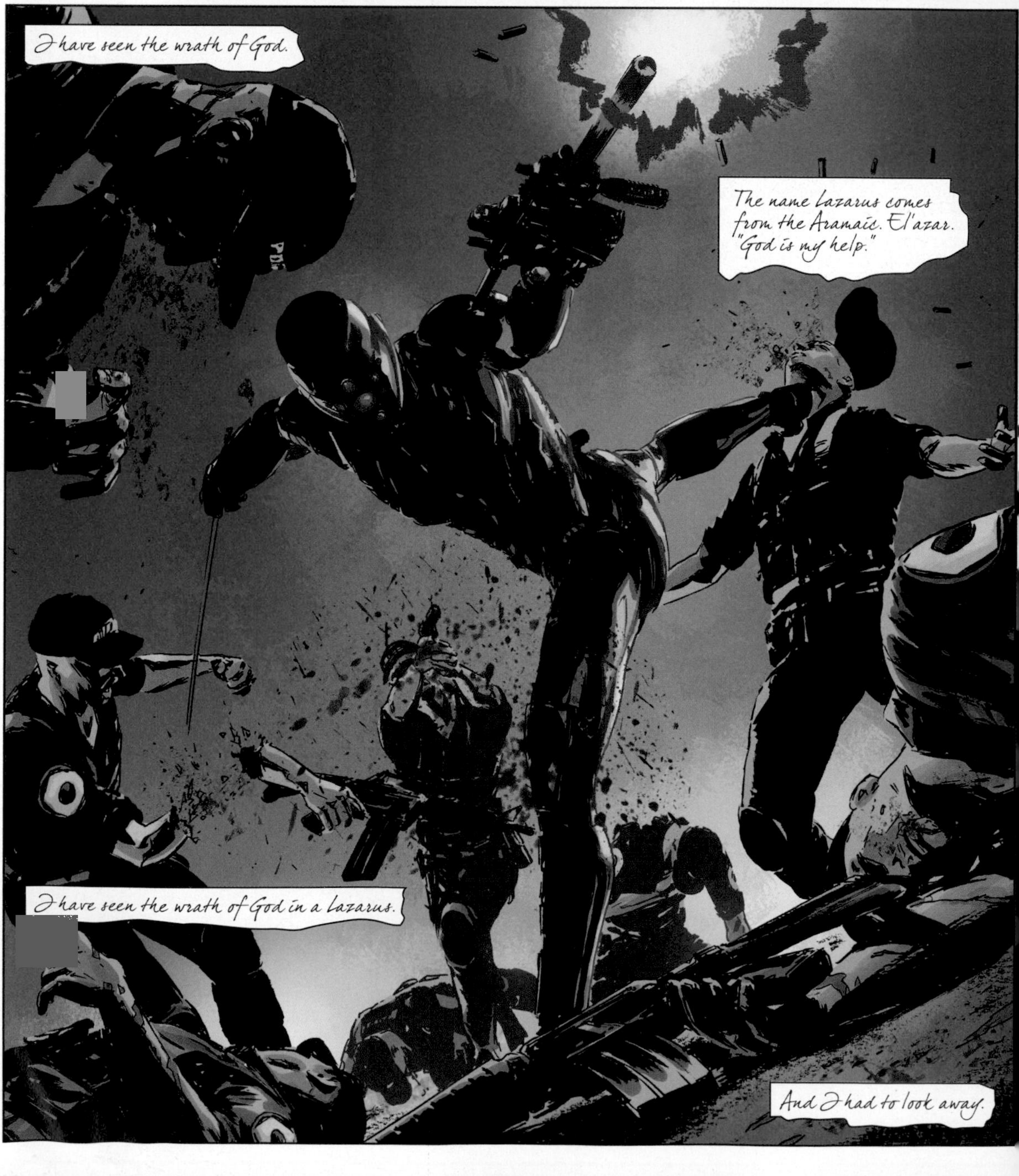
I have seen the wrath of God.
The name Lazarus comes from the Aramaic. El'azar. "God is my help."
I have seen the wrath of God in a Lazarus.
And I had to look away.

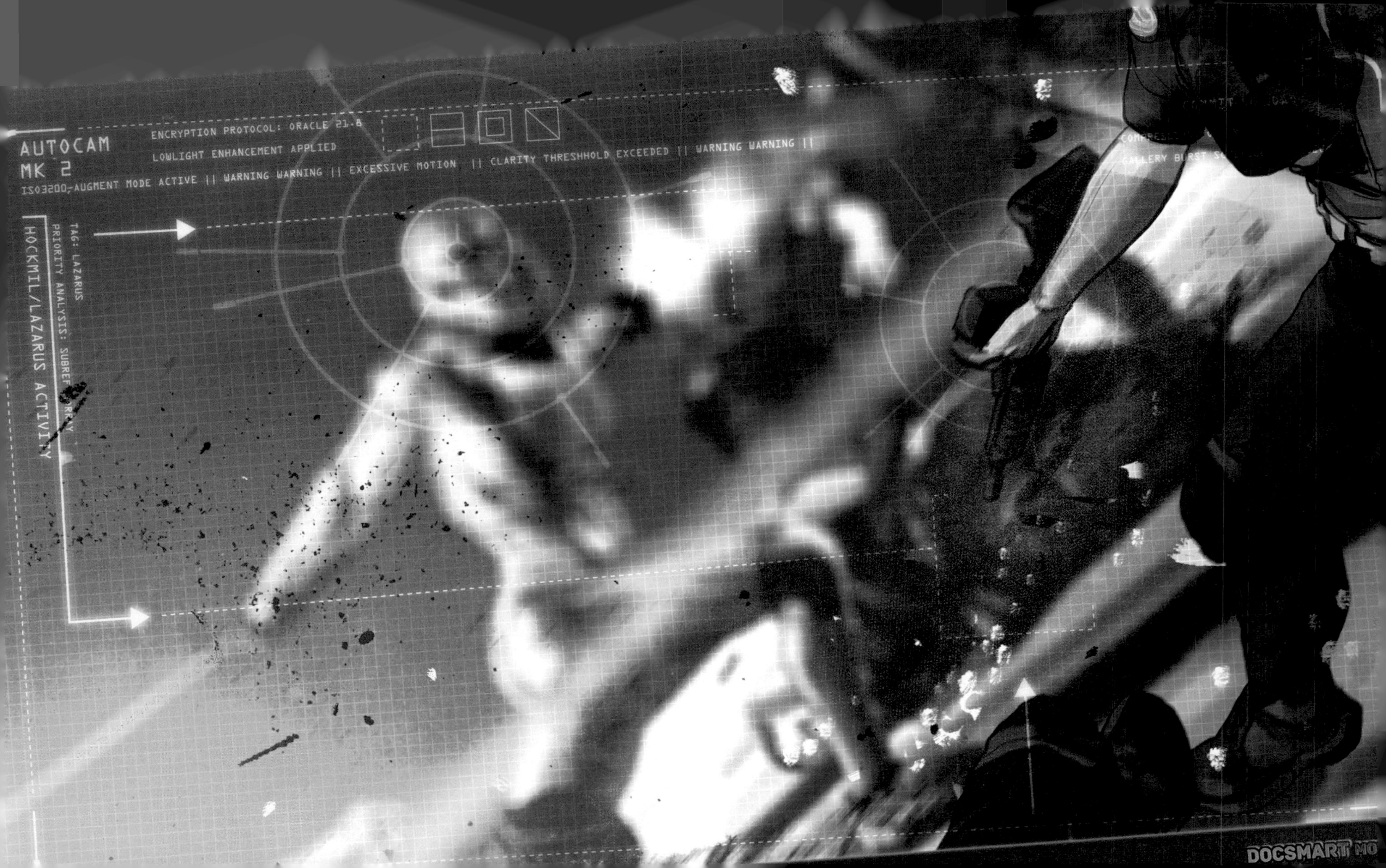
AUTOCAM
MK 2
ENCRYPTION PROTOCOL: ORACLE 21.8
LOWLIGHT ENHANCEMENT APPLIED
ISO3200-AUGMENT MODE ACTIVE || WARNING WARNING || EXCESSIVE MOTION || CLARITY THRESHHOLD EXCEEDED || WARNING WARNING ||
TAG: LAZARUS
PRIORITY ANALYSIS: SUBREF ARRAY
HOCKMIL/LAZARUS ACTIVITY

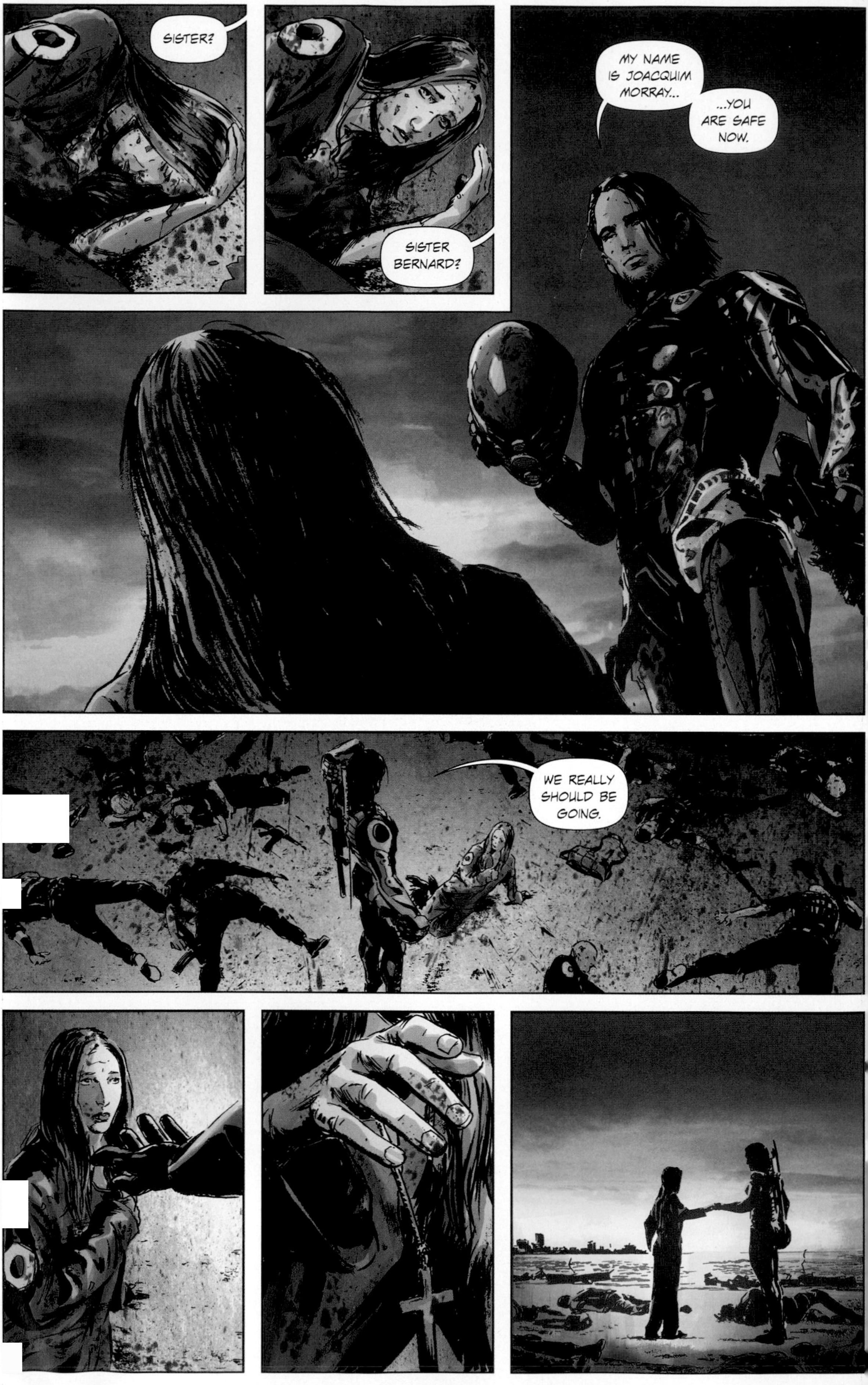
SISTER?
SISTER BERNARD?
MY NAME IS JOACQUIM MORRAY...
...YOU ARE SAFE NOW.
WE REALLY SHOULD BE GOING.

CARLYLE

ODERINT DUM METUANT

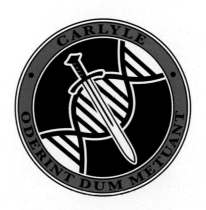

OWEN FREEMAN

POISON
CHAPTER ONE

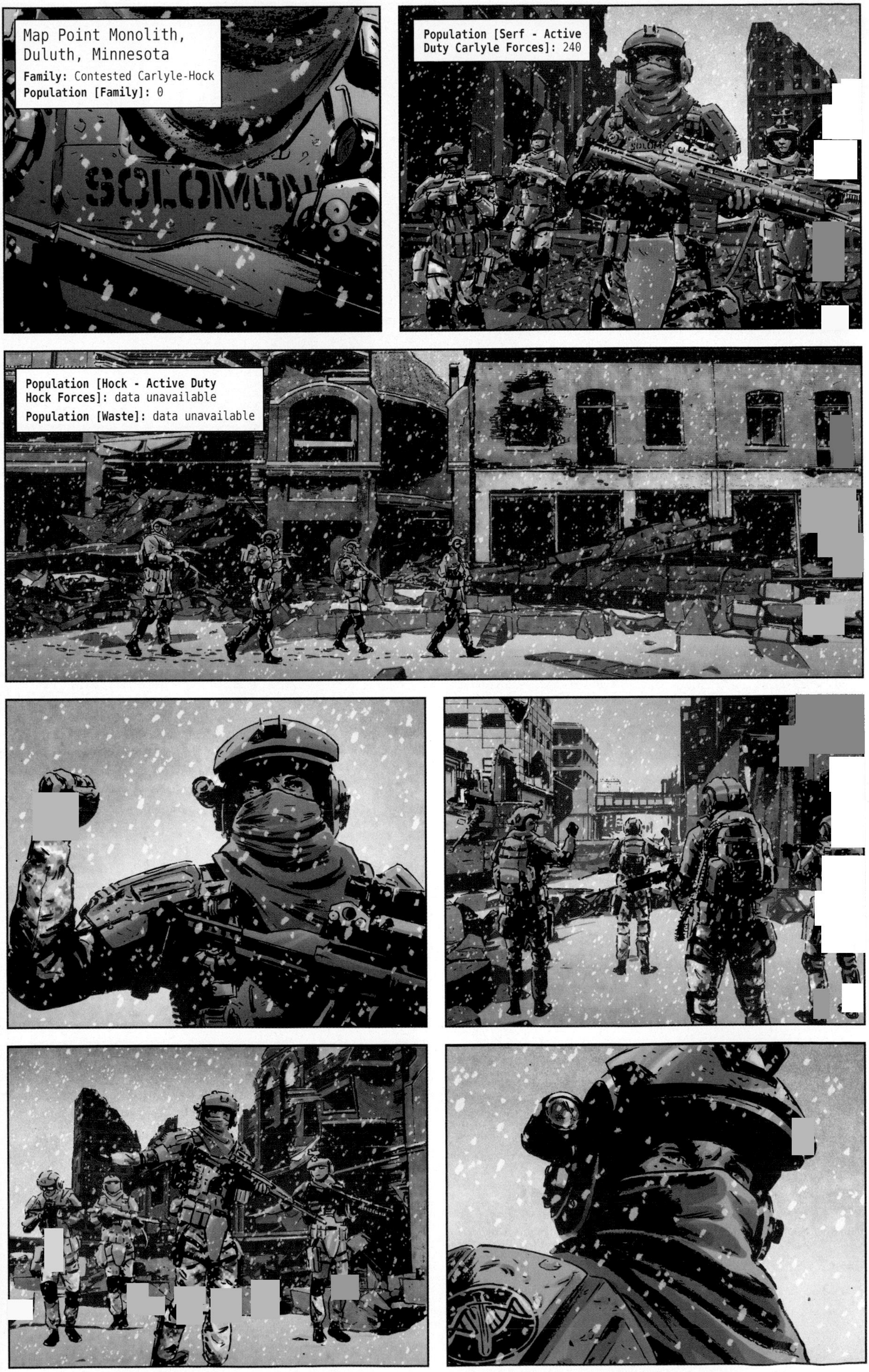
Map Point Monolith, Duluth, Minnesota
Family: Contested Carlyle-Hock
Population [Family]: 0
Population [Serf - Active Duty Carlyle Forces]: 240
Population [Hock - Active Duty Hock Forces]: data unavailable
Population [Waste]: data unavailable
SOLOMON

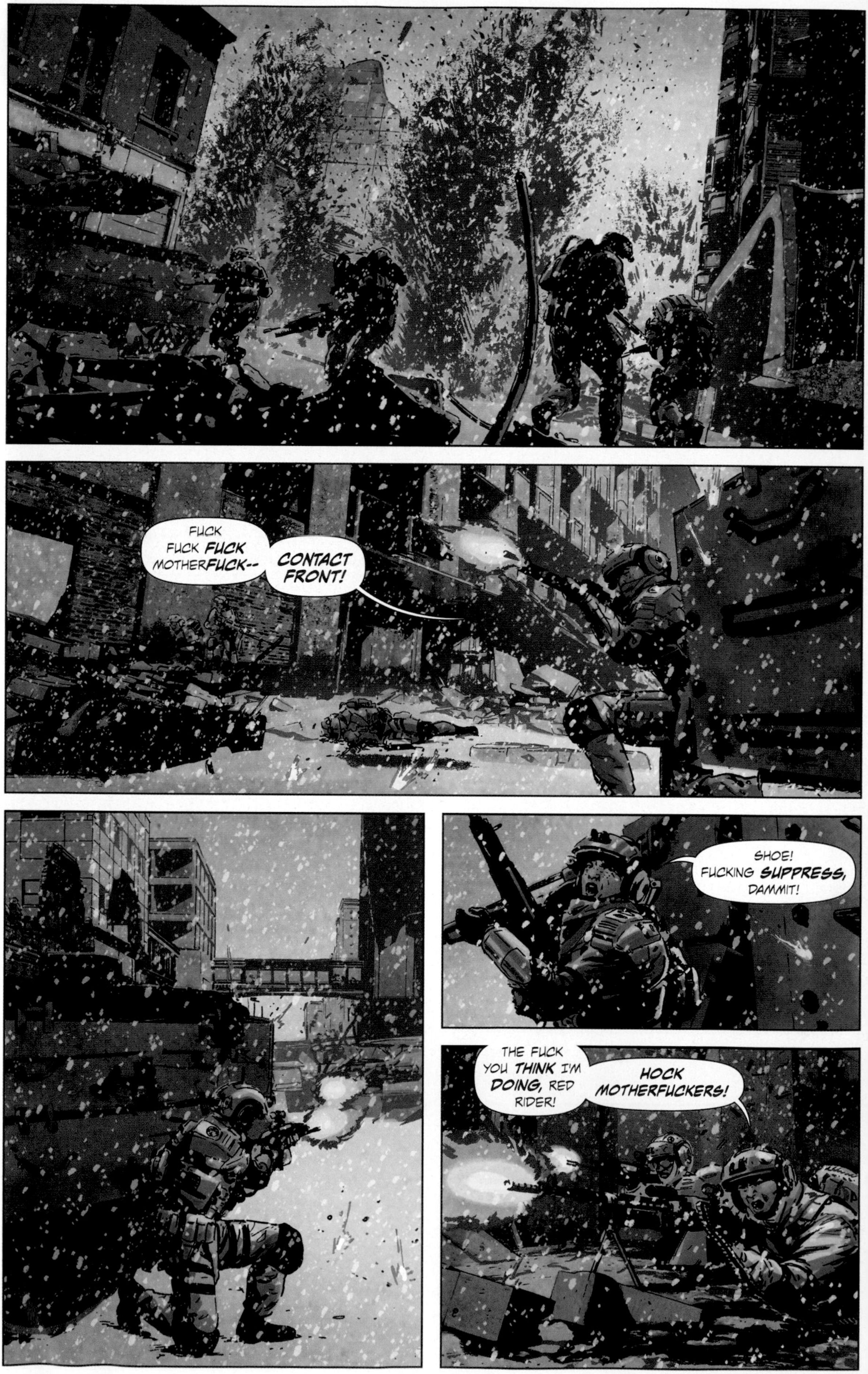
FUCK
FUCK FUCK
MOTHERFUCK--
CONTACT FRONT!
SHOE! FUCKING SUPPRESS, DAMMIT!
THE FUCK YOU THINK I'M DOING, RED RIDER!
HOCK MOTHERFUCKERS!

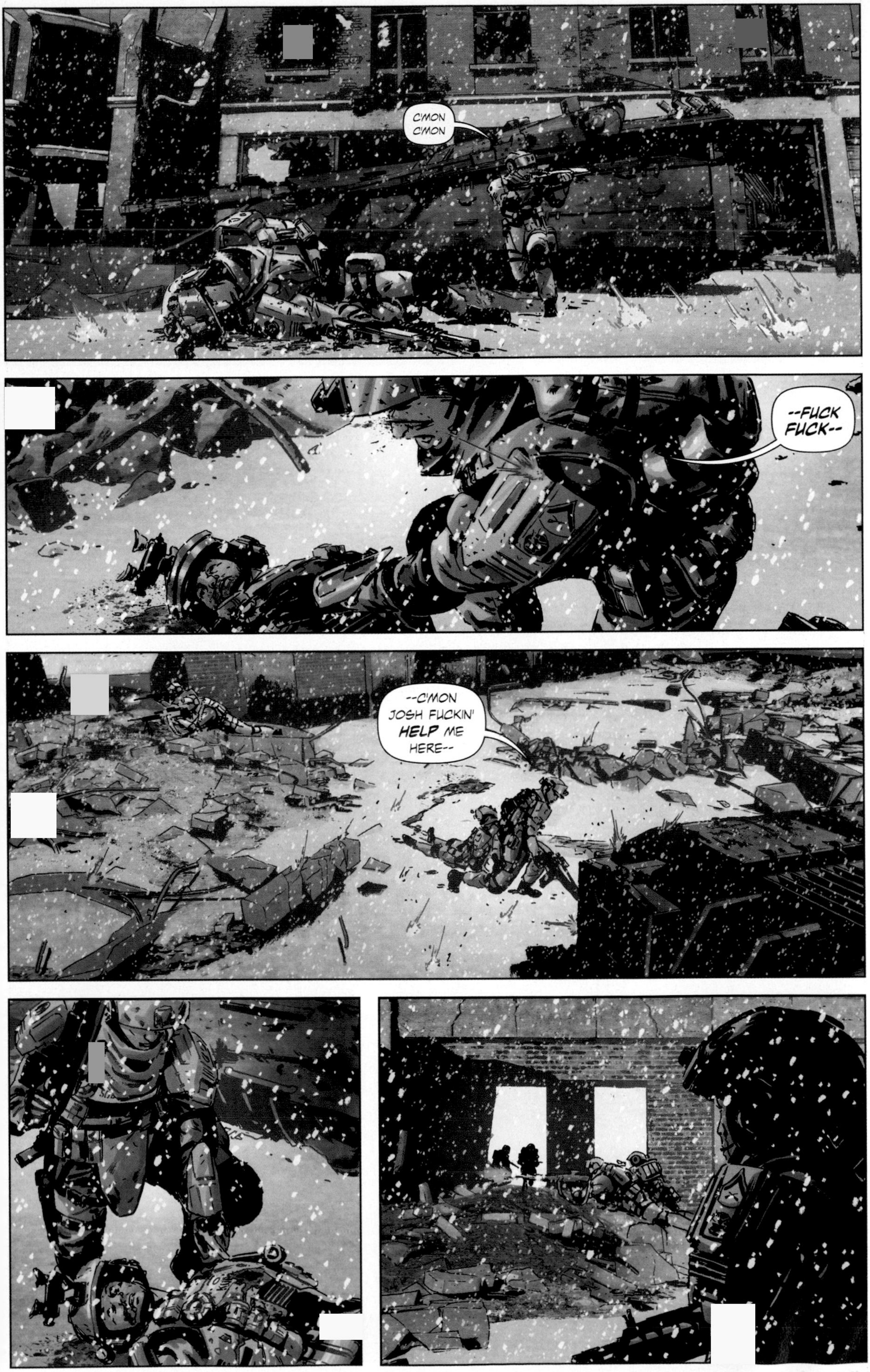
C'MON C'MON
--FUCK FUCK--
--C'MON JOSH FUCKIN' HELP ME HERE--

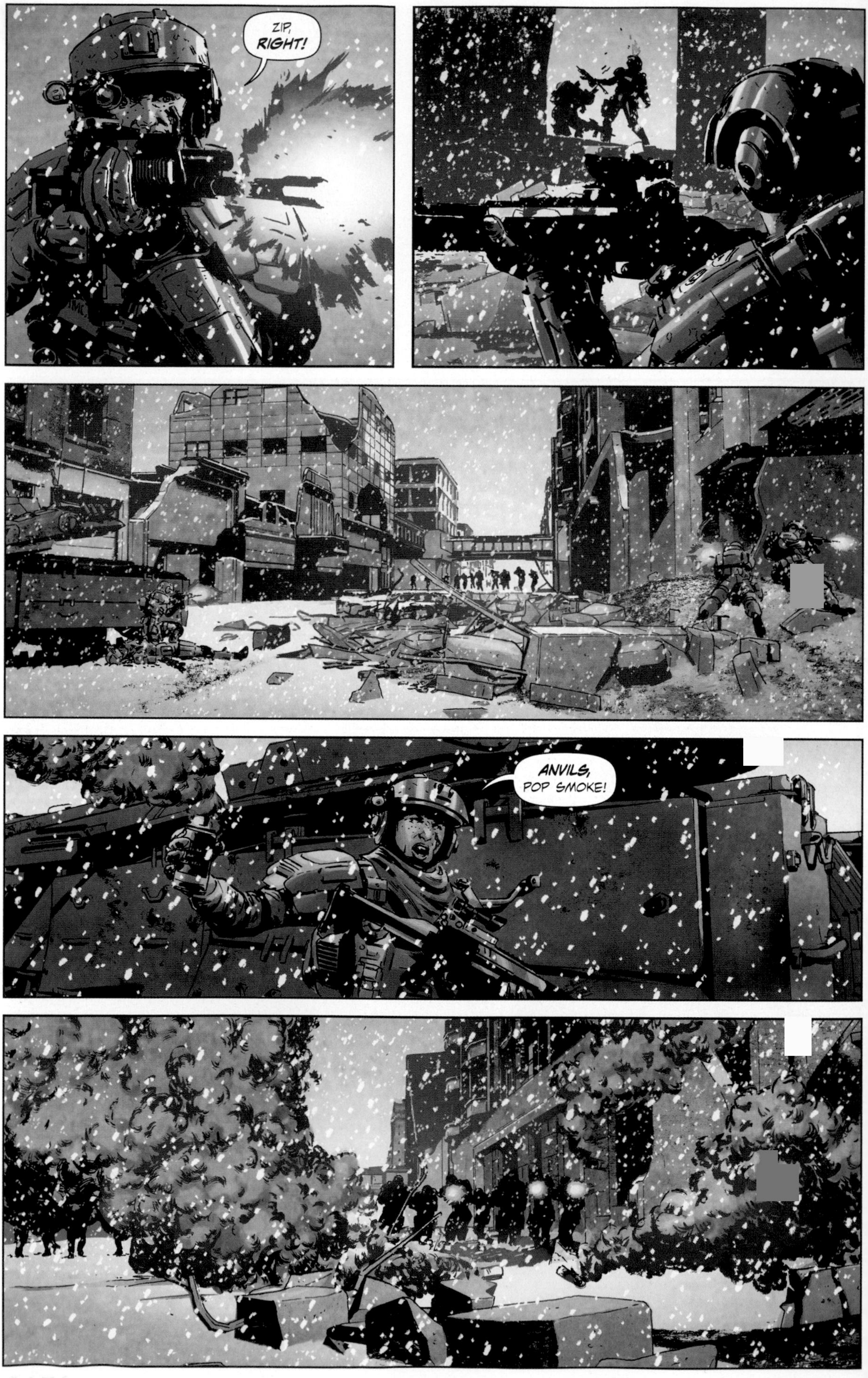

ZIP, RIGHT!
ANVILS, POP SMOKE!

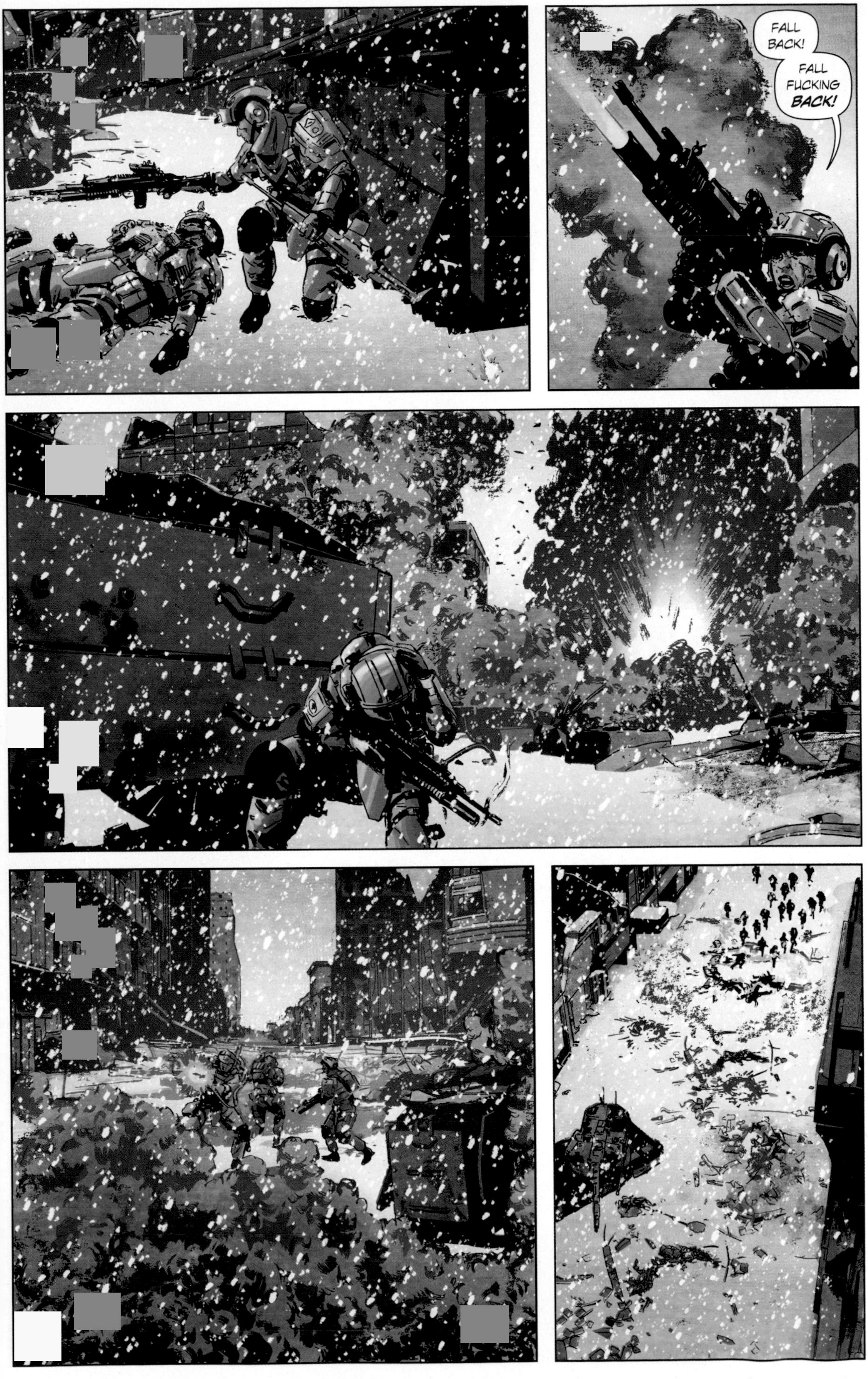
FALL BACK!
FALL FUCKING BACK!

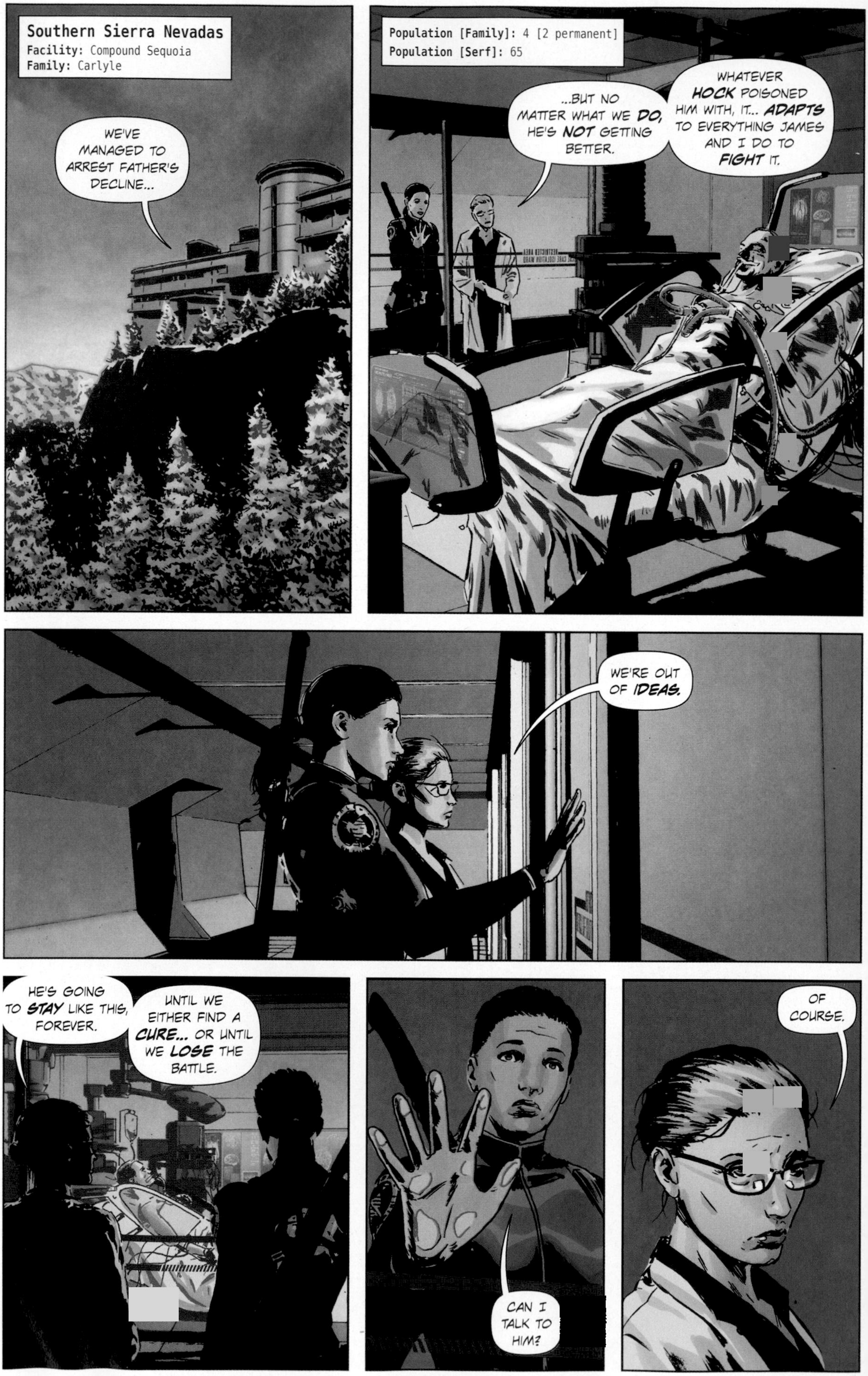
Southern Sierra Nevadas
Facility: Compound Sequoia
Family: Carlyle
WE'VE MANAGED TO ARREST FATHER'S DECLINE...
Population [Family]: 4 [2 permanent]
Population [Serf]: 65
...BUT NO MATTER WHAT WE DO, HE'S NOT GETTING BETTER.
WHATEVER HOCK POISONED HIM WITH, IT... ADAPTS TO EVERYTHING JAMES AND I DO TO FIGHT IT.
WE'RE OUT OF IDEAS.
HE'S GOING TO STAY LIKE THIS, FOREVER.
UNTIL WE EITHER FIND A CURE... OR UNTIL WE LOSE THE BATTLE.
CAN I TALK TO HIM?
OF COURSE.

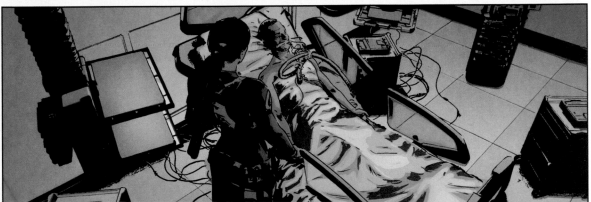

DADDY? DADDY, I DON'T KNOW WHAT TO *DO.*

THE WAR... IT ISN'T GOING *WELL...*

...YOU *PLANNED* FOR THIS, I KNOW YOU DID... YOU HAD A *PLAN...*

...WHAT DO I *DO,* DADDY...

...TELL ME WHAT I SHOULD *DO....*

hhrrk

ZONE BETA

<Oh my God-->

--hNNHHHHH

WE STARTED MISS BITTNER ON HER **REPLACEMENT THERAPY** THIS MORNING...

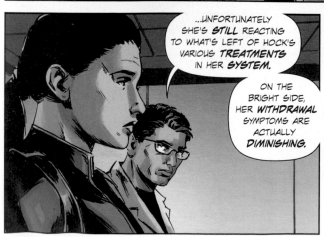

...UNFORTUNATELY SHE'S **STILL** REACTING TO WHAT'S LEFT OF HOCK'S VARIOUS **TREATMENTS** IN HER **SYSTEM**.

ON THE BRIGHT SIDE, HER **WITHDRAWAL** SYMPTOMS ARE ACTUALLY **DIMINISHING**.

NOT THAT YOU WOULD BE ABLE TO **TELL**.

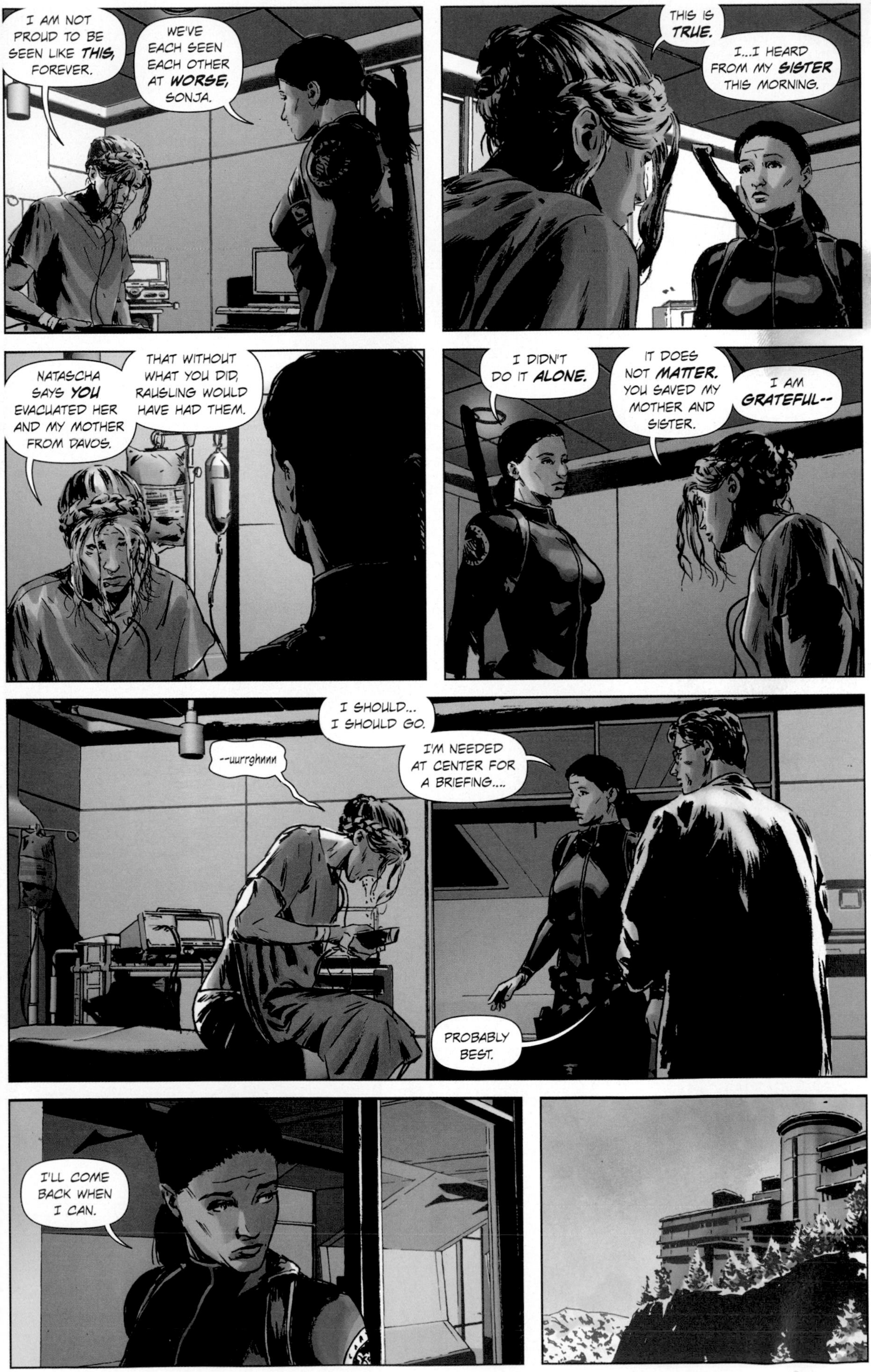
I AM NOT PROUD TO BE SEEN LIKE THIS, FOREVER.
WE'VE EACH SEEN EACH OTHER AT WORSE, SONJA.
THIS IS TRUE.
I...I HEARD FROM MY SISTER THIS MORNING.
NATASCHA SAYS YOU EVACUATED HER AND MY MOTHER FROM DAVOS.
THAT WITHOUT WHAT YOU DID, RAUSLING WOULD HAVE HAD THEM.
I DIDN'T DO IT ALONE.
IT DOES NOT MATTER. YOU SAVED MY MOTHER AND SISTER.
I AM GRATEFUL--
I SHOULD... I SHOULD GO.
--uurrghnnn
I'M NEEDED AT CENTER FOR A BRIEFING....
PROBABLY BEST.
I'LL COME BACK WHEN I CAN.

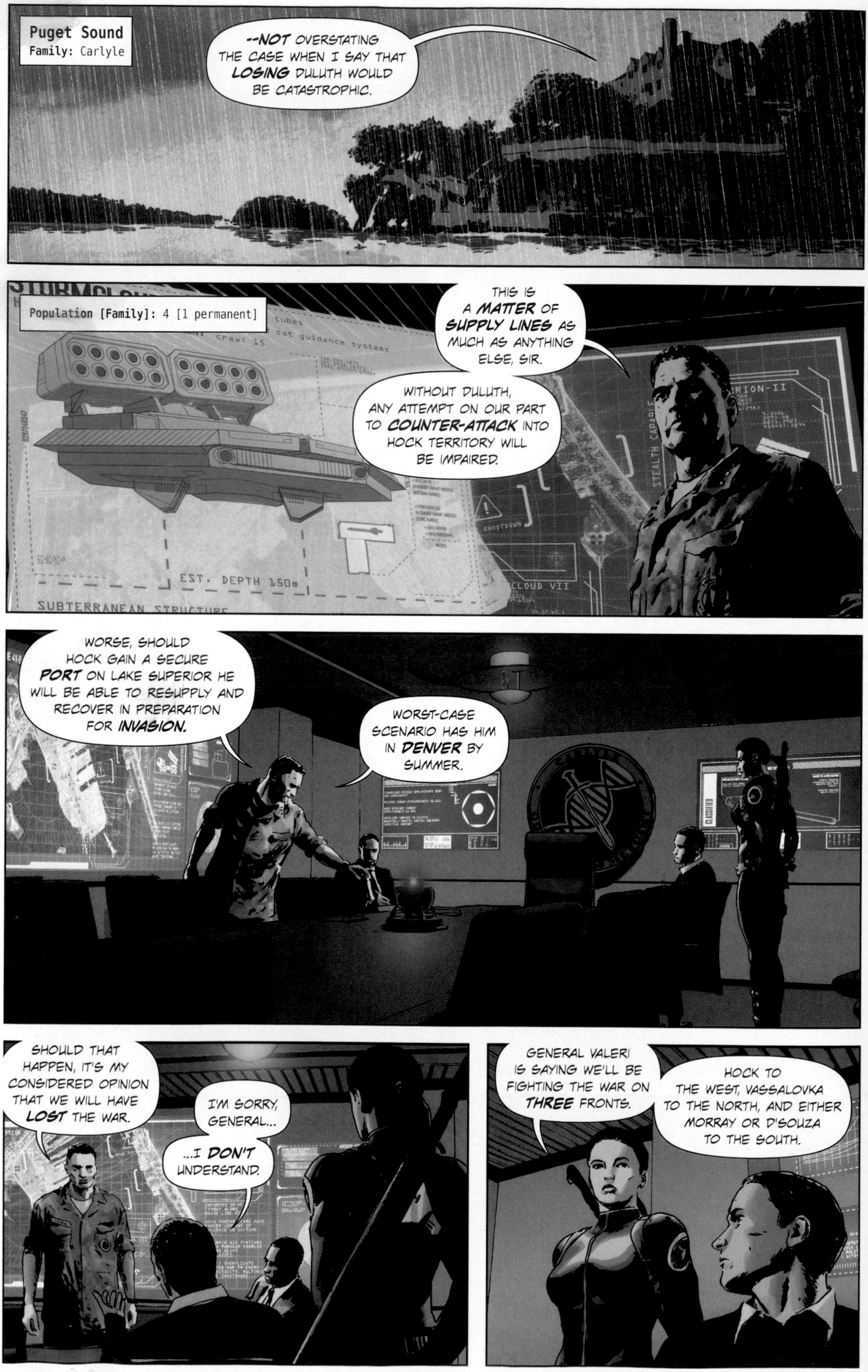
Puget Sound
Family: Carlyle
--NOT OVERSTATING THE CASE WHEN I SAY THAT LOSING DULUTH WOULD BE CATASTROPHIC.
Population [Family]: 4 [1 permanent]
tubes
crew: 15
sat guidance systems
EST. DEPTH 150m
SUBTERRANEAN STRUCTURE
STEALTH CAPABLE
THIS IS A MATTER OF SUPPLY LINES AS MUCH AS ANYTHING ELSE, SIR.
WITHOUT DULUTH, ANY ATTEMPT ON OUR PART TO COUNTER-ATTACK INTO HOCK TERRITORY WILL BE IMPAIRED.
WORSE, SHOULD HOCK GAIN A SECURE PORT ON LAKE SUPERIOR HE WILL BE ABLE TO RESUPPLY AND RECOVER IN PREPARATION FOR INVASION.
WORST-CASE SCENARIO HAS HIM IN DENVER BY SUMMER.
CLASSIFIED
SHOULD THAT HAPPEN, IT'S MY CONSIDERED OPINION THAT WE WILL HAVE LOST THE WAR.
I'M SORRY, GENERAL...
...I DON'T UNDERSTAND.
GENERAL VALERI IS SAYING WE'LL BE FIGHTING THE WAR ON THREE FRONTS.
HOCK TO THE WEST, VASSALOVKA TO THE NORTH, AND EITHER MORRAY OR D'SOUZA TO THE SOUTH.

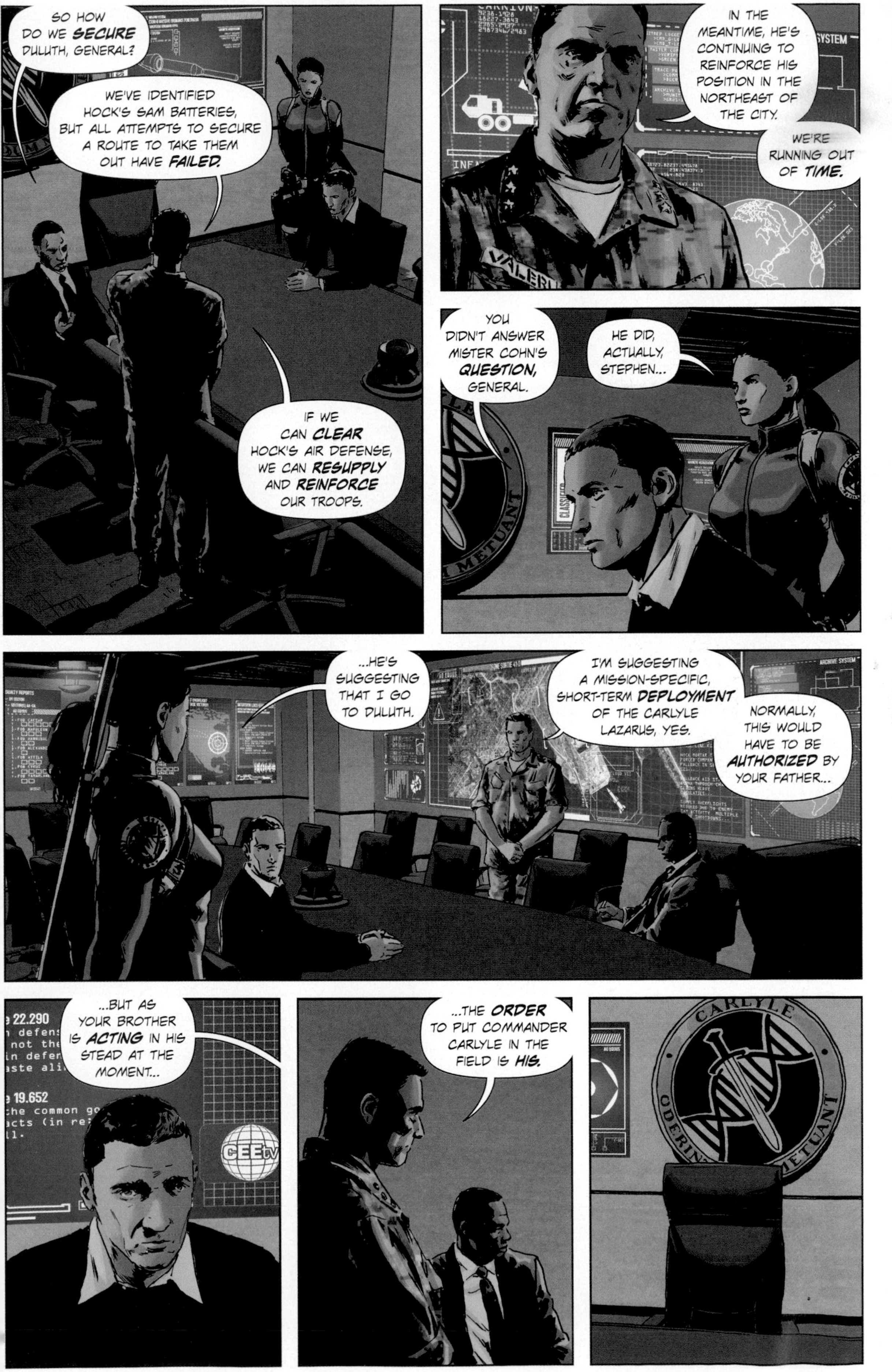
SO HOW DO WE SECURE DULUTH, GENERAL?
WE'VE IDENTIFIED HOCK'S SAM BATTERIES, BUT ALL ATTEMPTS TO SECURE A ROUTE TO TAKE THEM OUT HAVE FAILED.
IF WE CAN CLEAR HOCK'S AIR DEFENSE, WE CAN RESUPPLY AND REINFORCE OUR TROOPS.
IN THE MEANTIME, HE'S CONTINUING TO REINFORCE HIS POSITION IN THE NORTHEAST OF THE CITY.
WE'RE RUNNING OUT OF TIME.
YOU DIDN'T ANSWER MISTER COHN'S QUESTION, GENERAL.
HE DID, ACTUALLY, STEPHEN...
...HE'S SUGGESTING THAT I GO TO DULUTH.
I'M SUGGESTING A MISSION-SPECIFIC, SHORT-TERM DEPLOYMENT OF THE CARLYLE LAZARUS, YES.
NORMALLY, THIS WOULD HAVE TO BE AUTHORIZED BY YOUR FATHER...
...BUT AS YOUR BROTHER IS ACTING IN HIS STEAD AT THE MOMENT...
...THE ORDER TO PUT COMMANDER CARLYLE IN THE FIELD IS HIS.
CARLYLE
ODERINT DUM METUANT

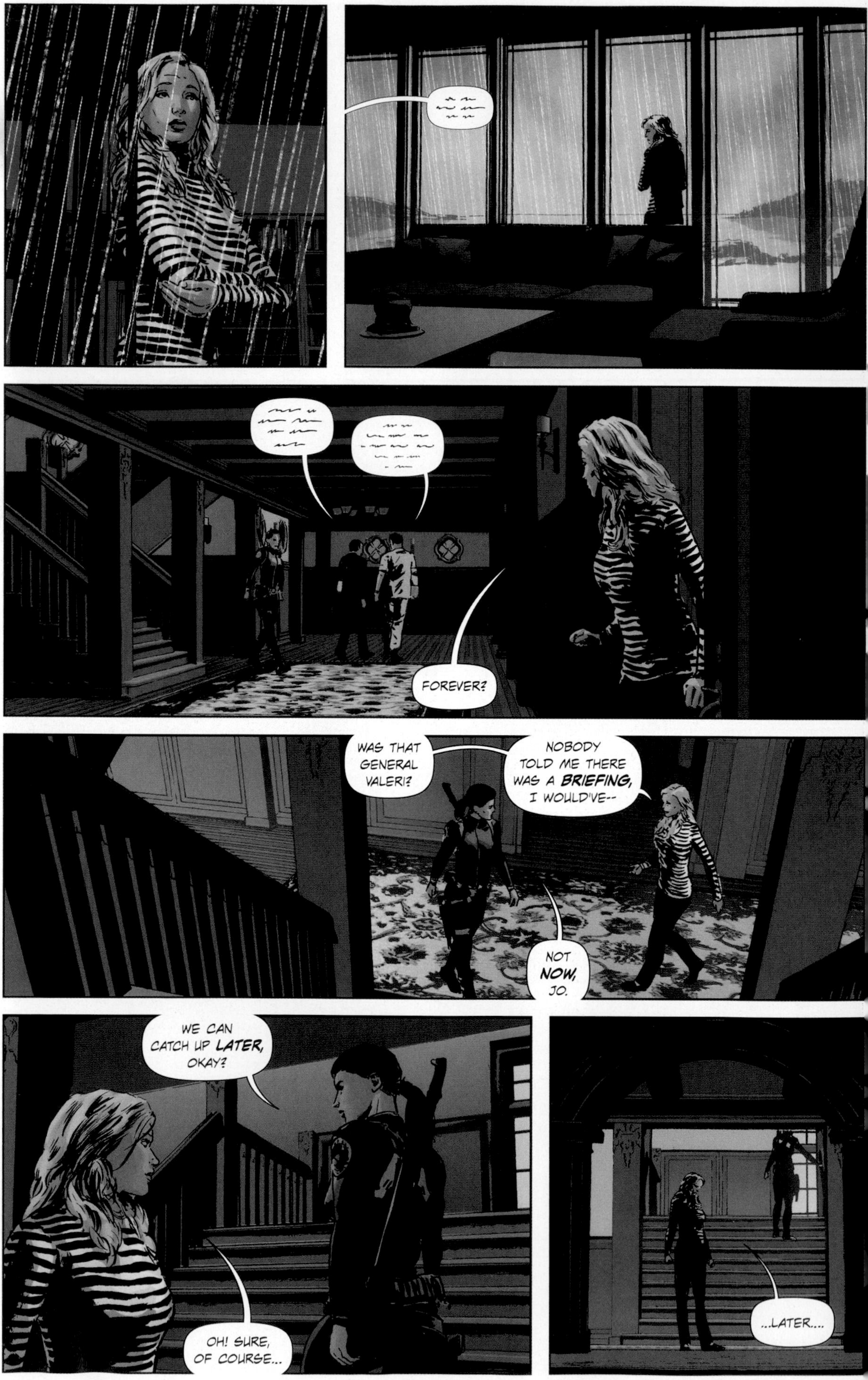
FOREVER?
WAS THAT GENERAL VALERI?
NOBODY TOLD ME THERE WAS A BRIEFING, I WOULD'VE--
NOT NOW, JO.
WE CAN CATCH UP LATER, OKAY?
OH! SURE, OF COURSE...
...LATER...

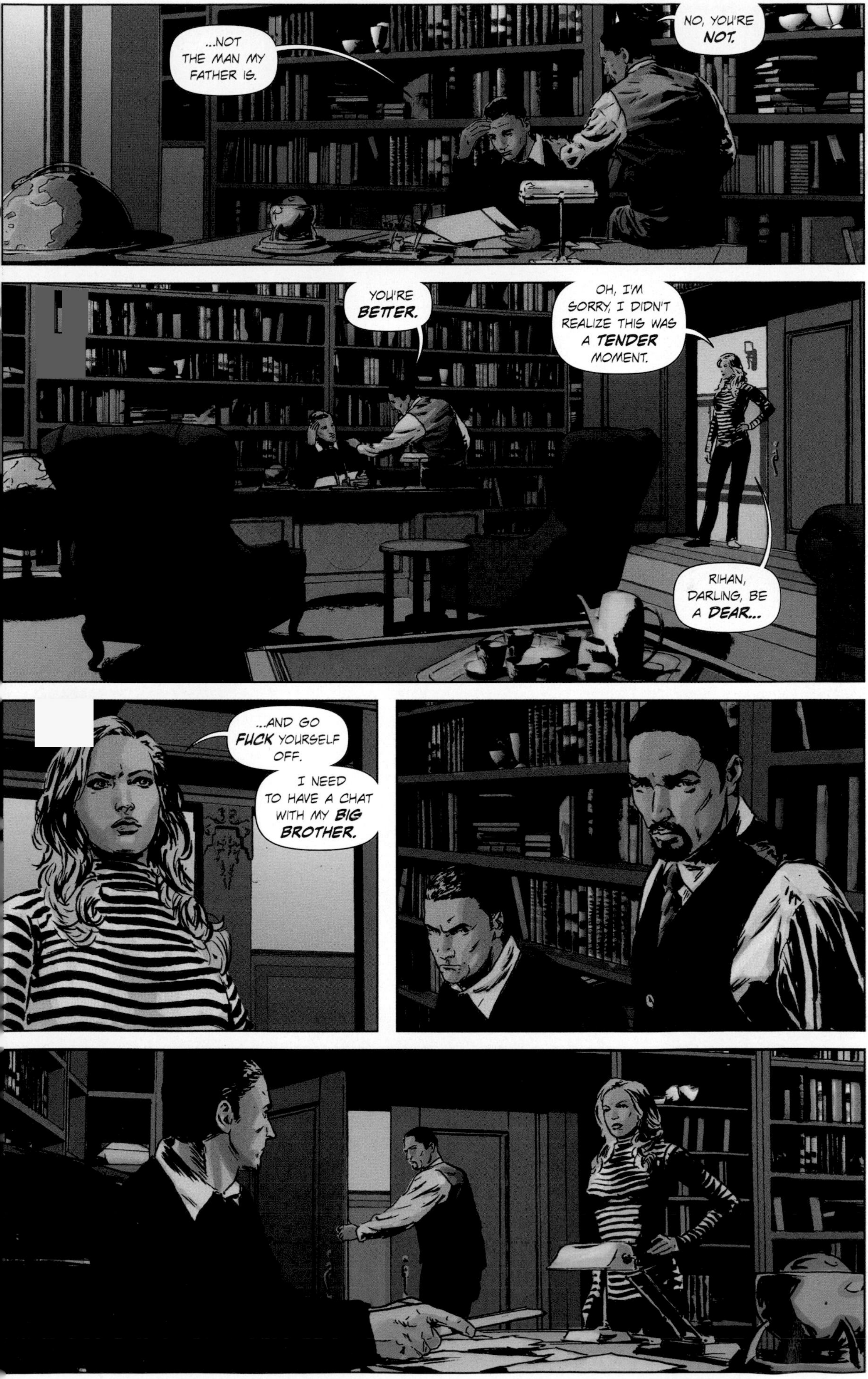

...NOT THE MAN MY FATHER IS.
NO, YOU'RE NOT.
YOU'RE BETTER.
OH, I'M SORRY, I DIDN'T REALIZE THIS WAS A TENDER MOMENT.
RIHAN, DARLING, BE A DEAR...
...AND GO FUCK YOURSELF OFF.
I NEED TO HAVE A CHAT WITH MY BIG BROTHER.

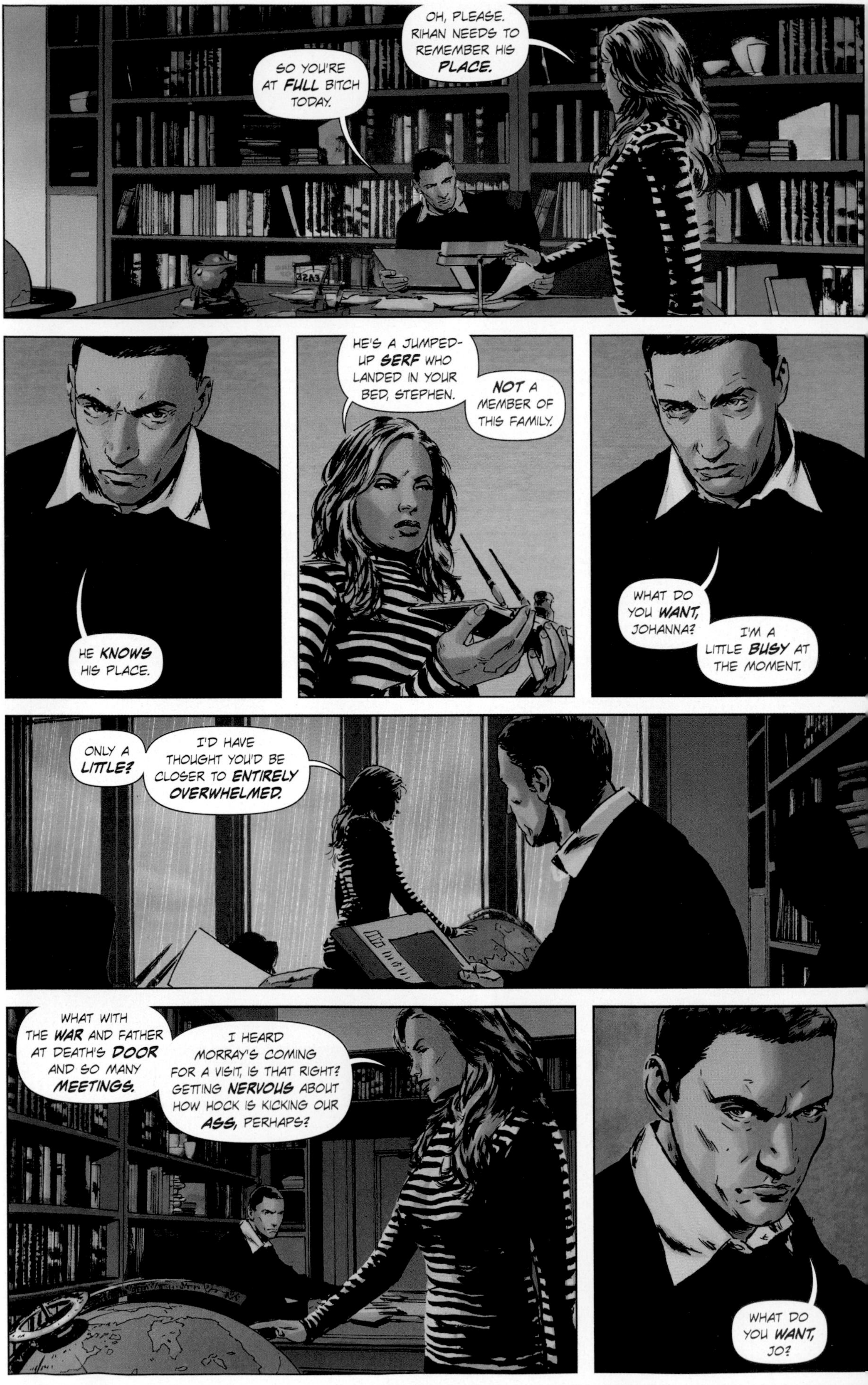
SO YOU'RE AT FULL BITCH TODAY.
OH, PLEASE. RIHAN NEEDS TO REMEMBER HIS PLACE.
HE KNOWS HIS PLACE.
HE'S A JUMPED-UP SERF WHO LANDED IN YOUR BED, STEPHEN.
NOT A MEMBER OF THIS FAMILY.
WHAT DO YOU WANT, JOHANNA?
I'M A LITTLE BUSY AT THE MOMENT.
ONLY A LITTLE?
I'D HAVE THOUGHT YOU'D BE CLOSER TO ENTIRELY OVERWHELMED.
WHAT WITH THE WAR AND FATHER AT DEATH'S DOOR AND SO MANY MEETINGS.
I HEARD MORRAY'S COMING FOR A VISIT, IS THAT RIGHT? GETTING NERVOUS ABOUT HOW HOCK IS KICKING OUR ASS, PERHAPS?
WHAT DO YOU WANT, JO?

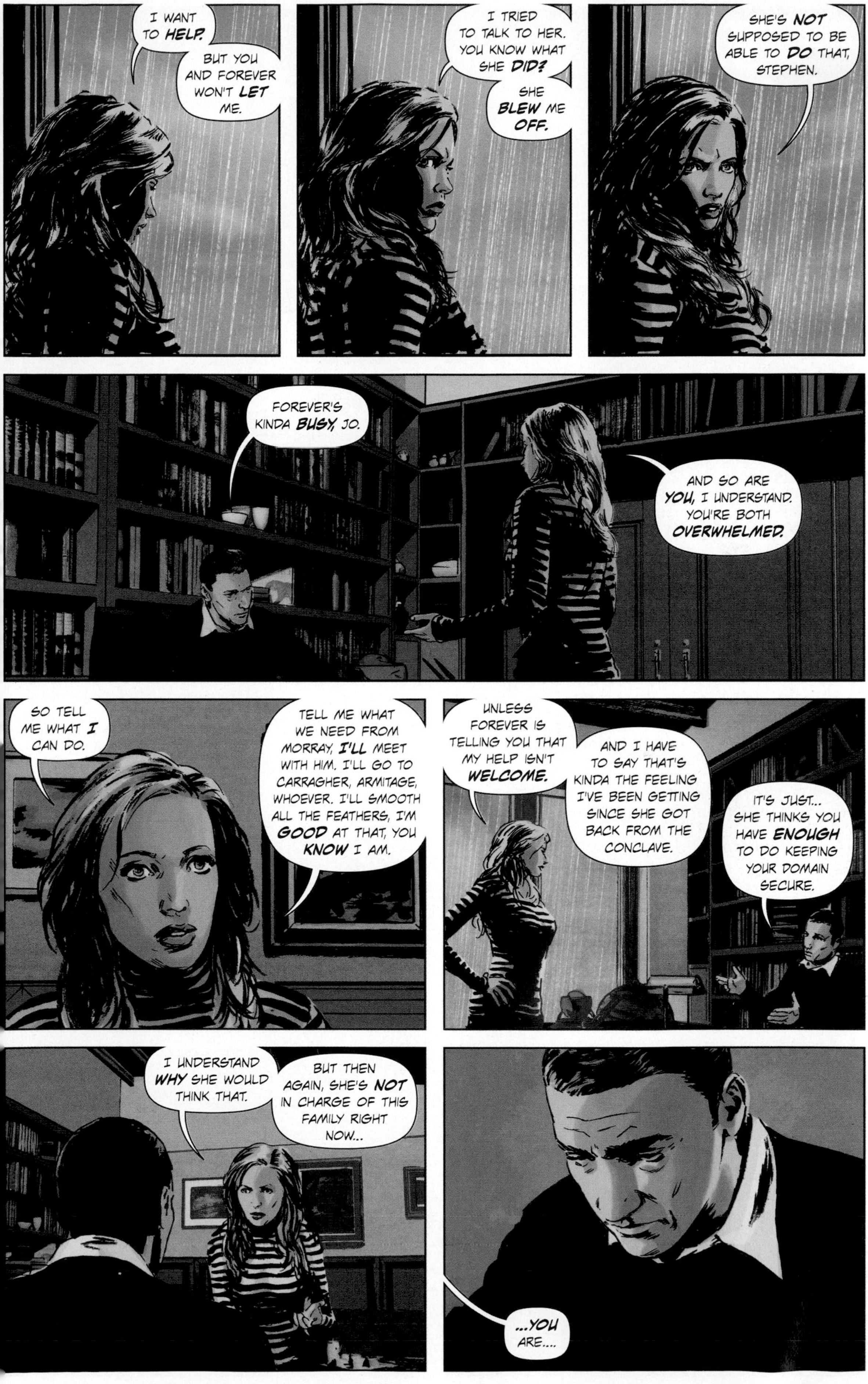
I WANT TO HELP.
BUT YOU AND FOREVER WON'T LET ME.
I TRIED TO TALK TO HER. YOU KNOW WHAT SHE DID?
SHE BLEW ME OFF.
SHE'S NOT SUPPOSED TO BE ABLE TO DO THAT, STEPHEN.
FOREVER'S KINDA BUSY, JO.
AND SO ARE YOU, I UNDERSTAND. YOU'RE BOTH OVERWHELMED.
SO TELL ME WHAT I CAN DO.
TELL ME WHAT WE NEED FROM MORRAY, I'LL MEET WITH HIM. I'LL GO TO CARRAGHER, ARMITAGE, WHOEVER. I'LL SMOOTH ALL THE FEATHERS, I'M GOOD AT THAT, YOU KNOW I AM.
UNLESS FOREVER IS TELLING YOU THAT MY HELP ISN'T WELCOME.
AND I HAVE TO SAY THAT'S KINDA THE FEELING I'VE BEEN GETTING SINCE SHE GOT BACK FROM THE CONCLAVE.
IT'S JUST... SHE THINKS YOU HAVE ENOUGH TO DO KEEPING YOUR DOMAIN SECURE.
I UNDERSTAND WHY SHE WOULD THINK THAT.
BUT THEN AGAIN, SHE'S NOT IN CHARGE OF THIS FAMILY RIGHT NOW...
...YOU ARE....

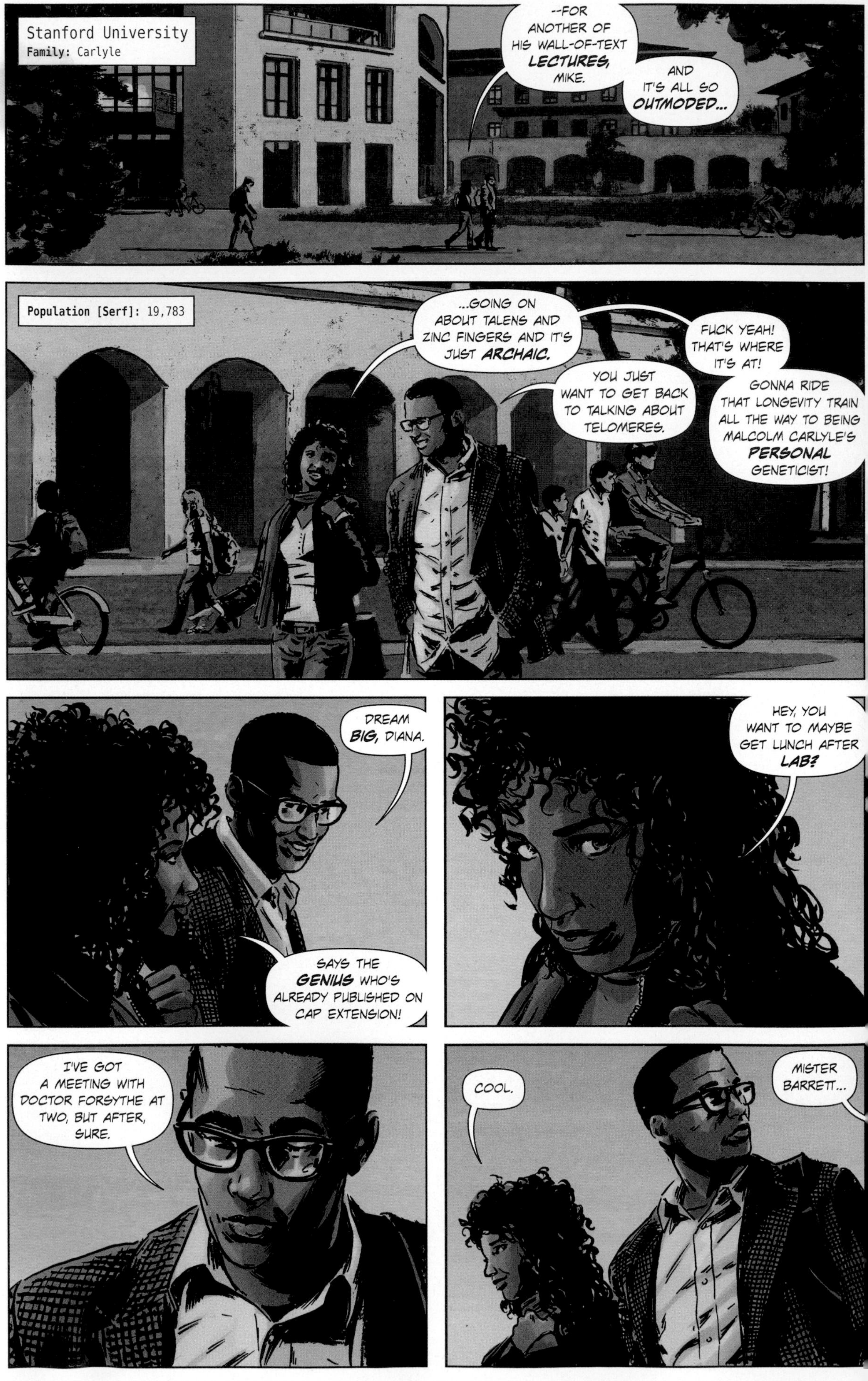
Stanford University
Family: Carlyle
--FOR ANOTHER OF HIS WALL-OF-TEXT LECTURES, MIKE.
AND IT'S ALL SO OUTMODED...
Population [Serf]: 19,783
...GOING ON ABOUT TALENS AND ZINC FINGERS AND IT'S JUST ARCHAIC.
YOU JUST WANT TO GET BACK TO TALKING ABOUT TELOMERES.
FUCK YEAH! THAT'S WHERE IT'S AT!
GONNA RIDE THAT LONGEVITY TRAIN ALL THE WAY TO BEING MALCOLM CARLYLE'S PERSONAL GENETICIST!
DREAM BIG, DIANA.
SAYS THE GENIUS WHO'S ALREADY PUBLISHED ON CAP EXTENSION!
HEY, YOU WANT TO MAYBE GET LUNCH AFTER LAB?
I'VE GOT A MEETING WITH DOCTOR FORSYTHE AT TWO, BUT AFTER, SURE.
COOL.
MISTER BARRETT...

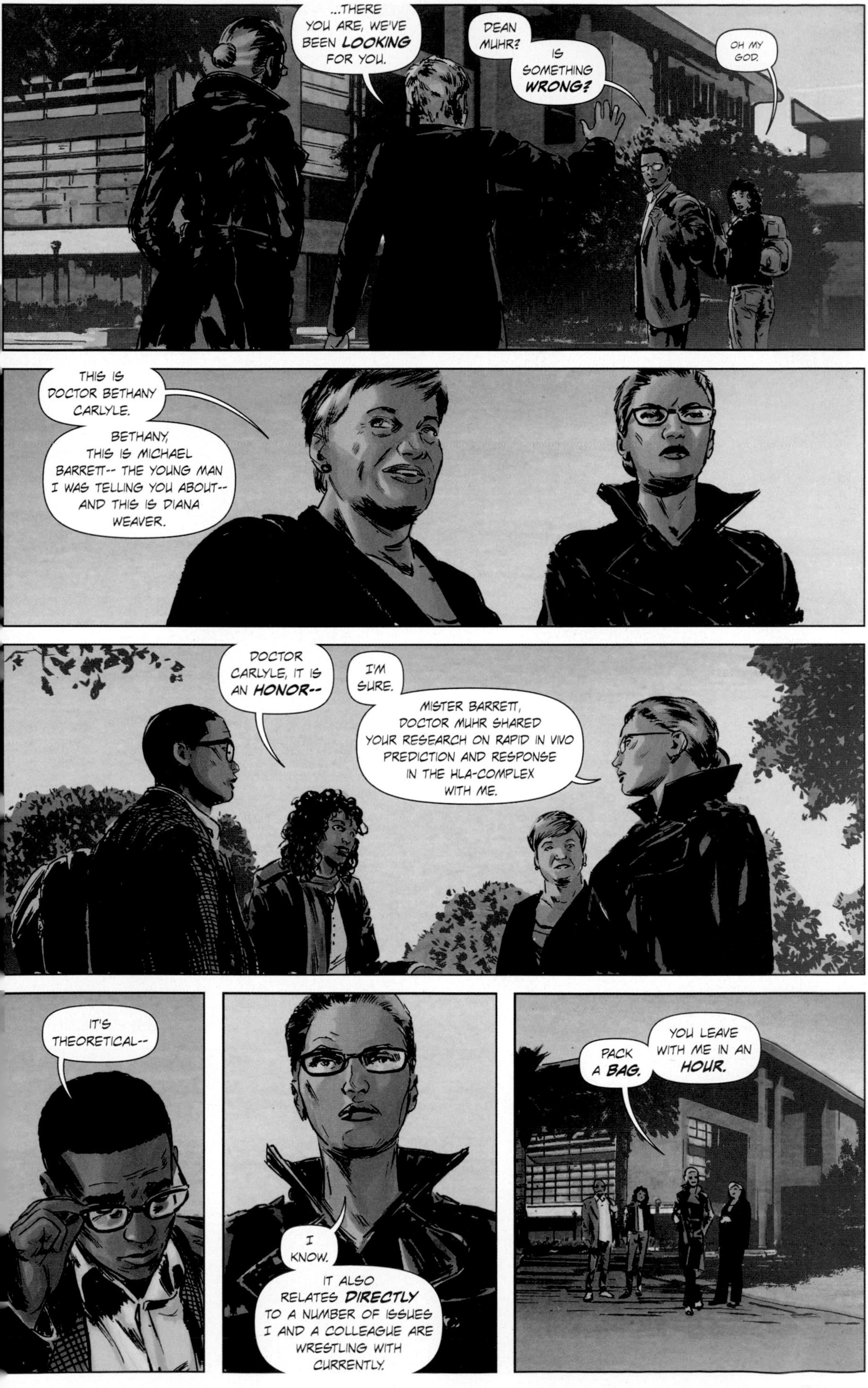
...THERE YOU ARE, WE'VE BEEN **LOOKING** FOR YOU.
DEAN MUHR?
IS SOMETHING **WRONG?**
OH MY GOD.
THIS IS DOCTOR BETHANY CARLYLE.
BETHANY, THIS IS MICHAEL BARRETT-- THE YOUNG MAN I WAS TELLING YOU ABOUT-- AND THIS IS DIANA WEAVER.
DOCTOR CARLYLE, IT IS AN **HONOR--**
I'M SURE.
MISTER BARRETT, DOCTOR MUHR SHARED YOUR RESEARCH ON RAPID IN VIVO PREDICTION AND RESPONSE IN THE HLA-COMPLEX WITH ME.
IT'S THEORETICAL--
I KNOW.
IT ALSO RELATES **DIRECTLY** TO A NUMBER OF ISSUES I AND A COLLEAGUE ARE WRESTLING WITH CURRENTLY.
PACK A **BAG.**
YOU LEAVE WITH ME IN AN **HOUR.**

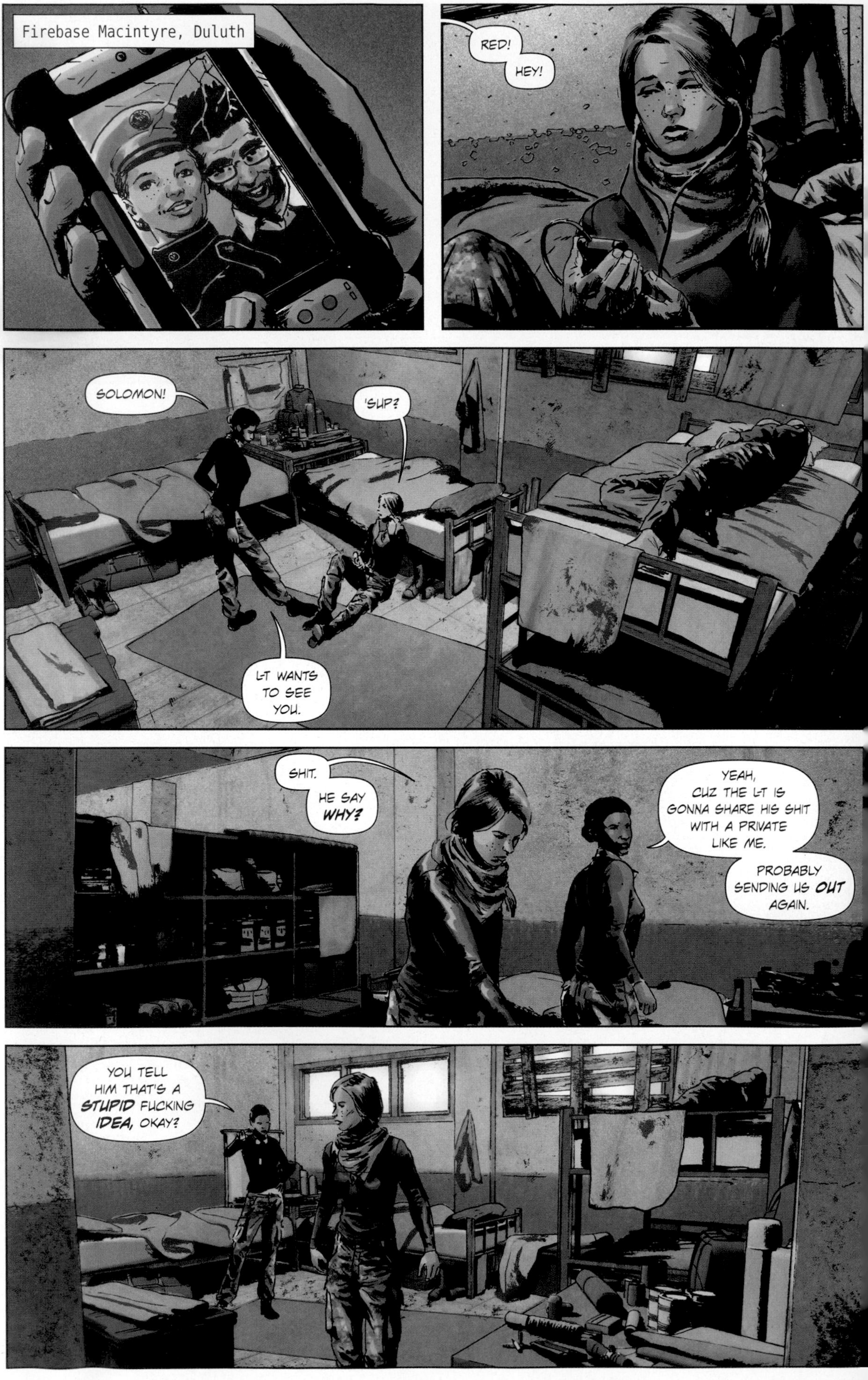
Firebase Macintyre, Duluth
RED!
HEY!
SOLOMON!
'SUP?
L-T WANTS TO SEE YOU.
SHIT.
HE SAY WHY?
YEAH, CUZ THE L-T IS GONNA SHARE HIS SHIT WITH A PRIVATE LIKE ME.
PROBABLY SENDING US OUT AGAIN.
YOU TELL HIM THAT'S A STUPID FUCKING IDEA, OKAY?

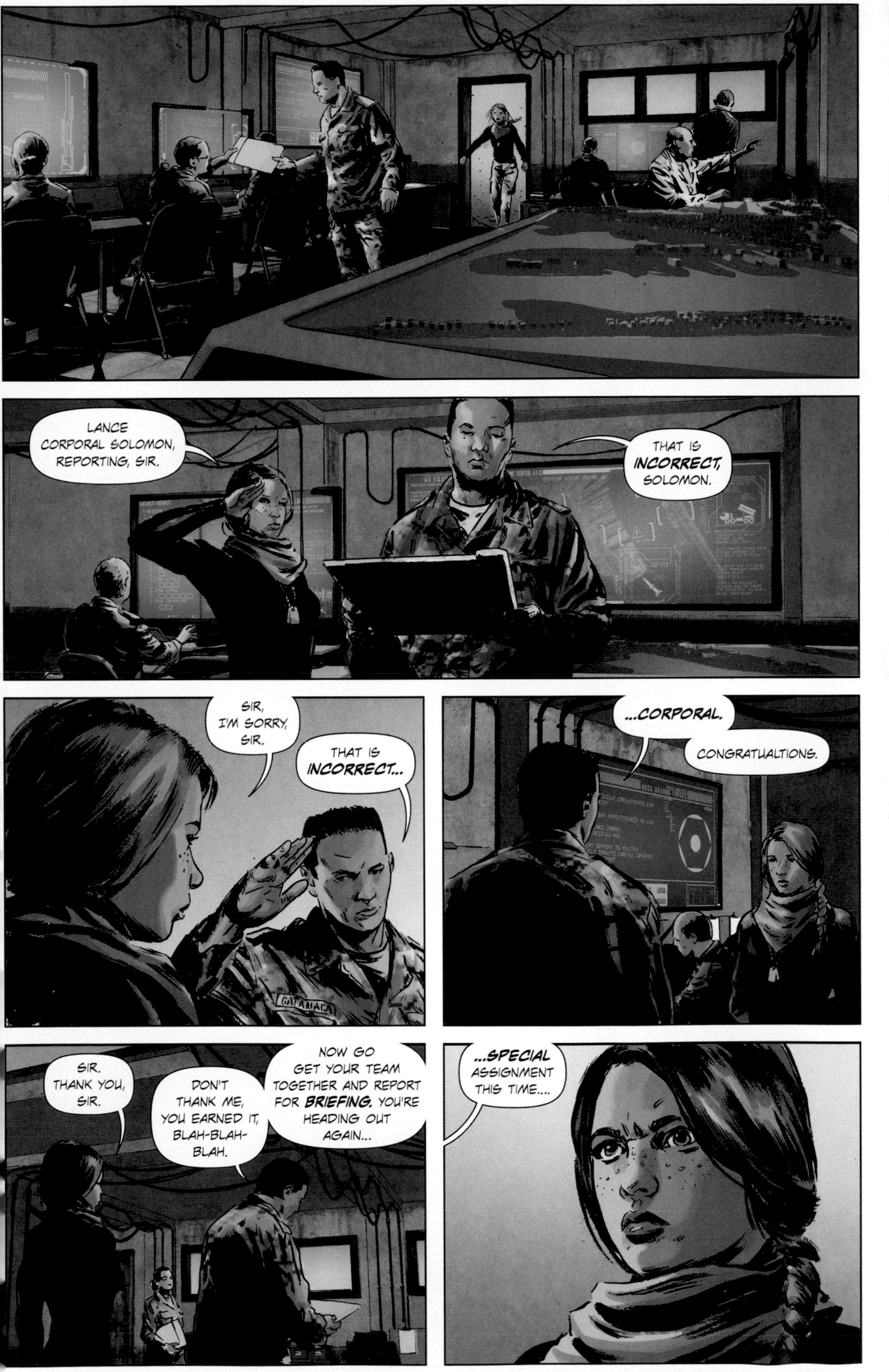
LANCE CORPORAL SOLOMON, REPORTING, SIR.
THAT IS INCORRECT, SOLOMON.
SIR, I'M SORRY, SIR.
THAT IS INCORRECT...
...CORPORAL.
CONGRATUALTIONS.
SIR. THANK YOU, SIR.
DON'T THANK ME, YOU EARNED IT, BLAH-BLAH-BLAH.
NOW GO GET YOUR TEAM TOGETHER AND REPORT FOR BRIEFING. YOU'RE HEADING OUT AGAIN...
...SPECIAL ASSIGNMENT THIS TIME....

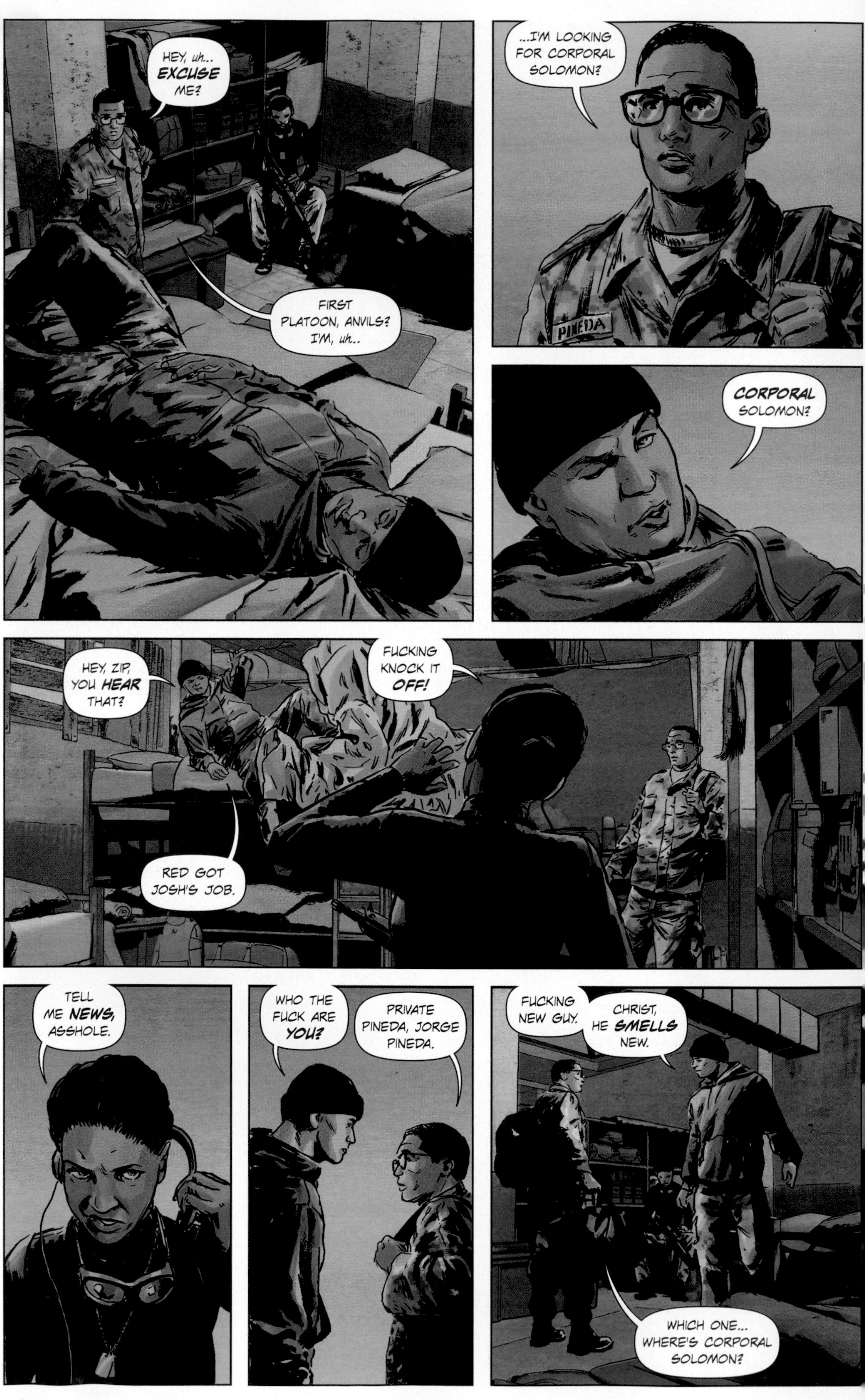
HEY, uh... EXCUSE ME?
FIRST PLATOON, ANVILS? I'M, uh...
...I'M LOOKING FOR CORPORAL SOLOMON?
PINEDA
CORPORAL SOLOMON?
HEY, ZIP, YOU HEAR THAT?
FUCKING KNOCK IT OFF!
RED GOT JOSH'S JOB.
TELL ME NEWS, ASSHOLE.
WHO THE FUCK ARE YOU?
PRIVATE PINEDA, JORGE PINEDA.
FUCKING NEW GUY.
CHRIST, HE SMELLS NEW.
WHICH ONE... WHERE'S CORPORAL SOLOMON?

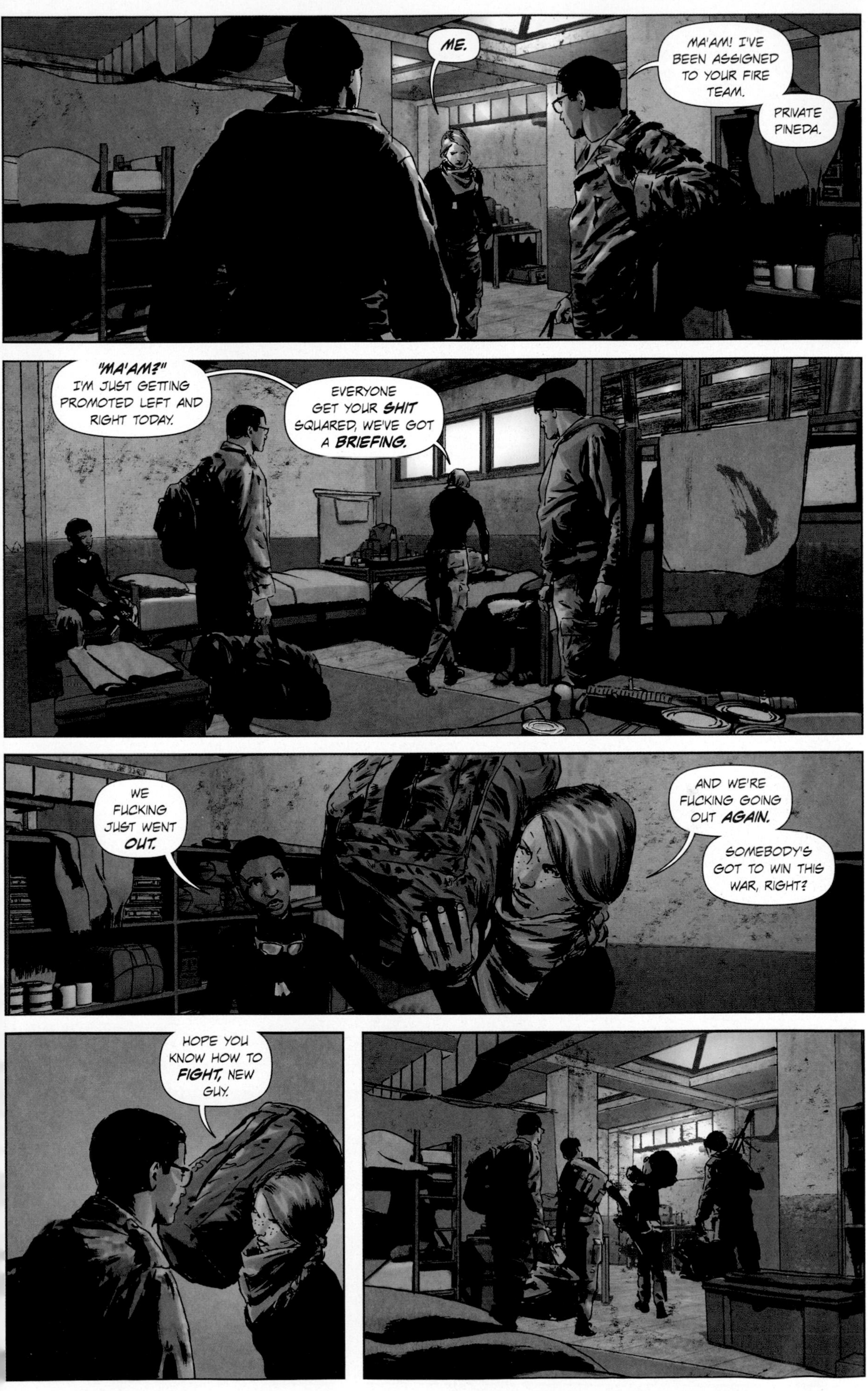
ME.
MA'AM! I'VE BEEN ASSIGNED TO YOUR FIRE TEAM.
PRIVATE PINEDA.
"MA'AM?" I'M JUST GETTING PROMOTED LEFT AND RIGHT TODAY.
EVERYONE GET YOUR SHIT SQUARED, WE'VE GOT A BRIEFING.
WE FUCKING JUST WENT OUT.
AND WE'RE FUCKING GOING OUT AGAIN.
SOMEBODY'S GOT TO WIN THIS WAR, RIGHT?
HOPE YOU KNOW HOW TO FIGHT, NEW GUY.

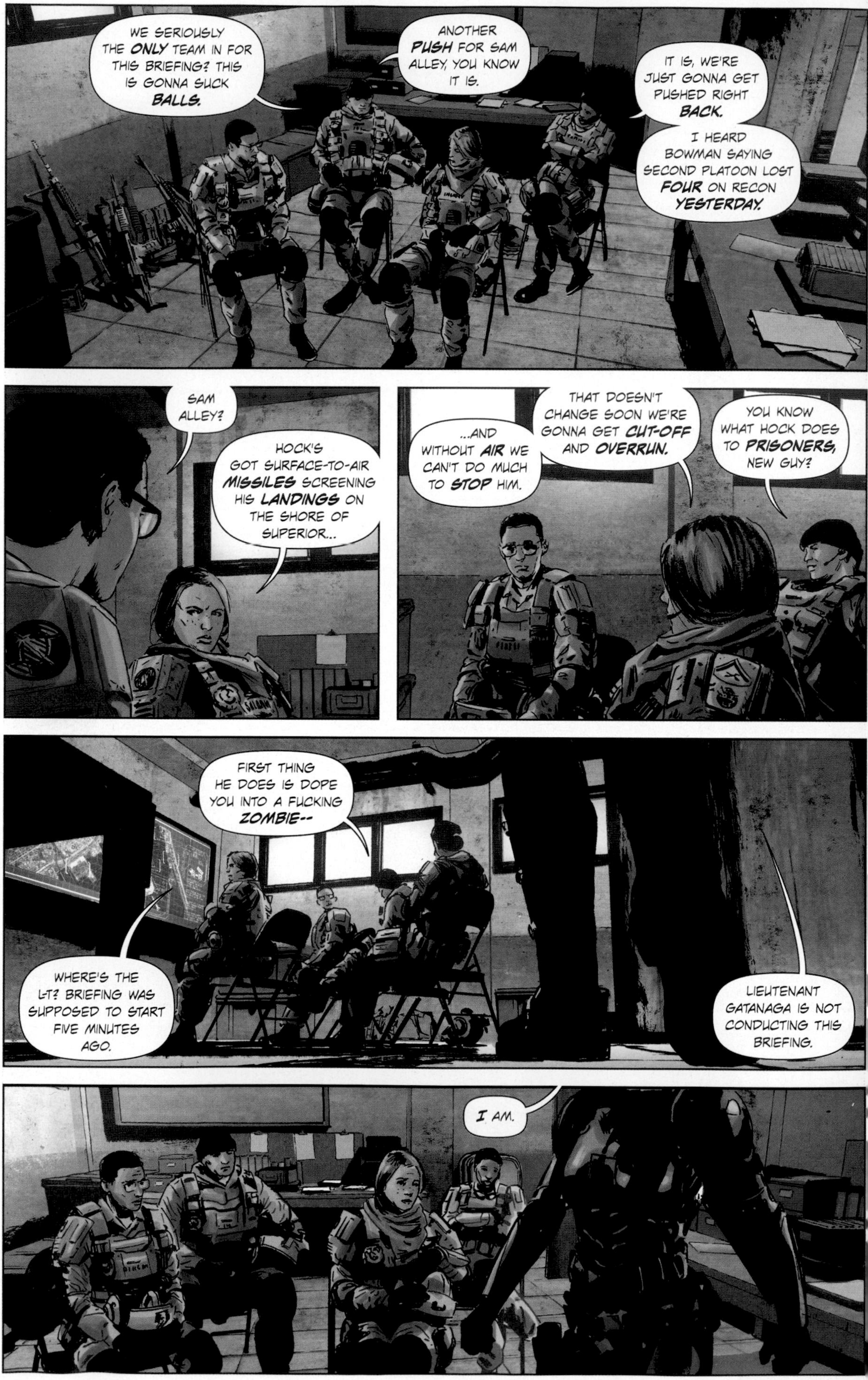
WE SERIOUSLY THE ONLY TEAM IN FOR THIS BRIEFING? THIS IS GONNA SUCK BALLS.
ANOTHER PUSH FOR SAM ALLEY, YOU KNOW IT IS.
IT IS, WE'RE JUST GONNA GET PUSHED RIGHT BACK.
I HEARD BOWMAN SAYING SECOND PLATOON LOST FOUR ON RECON YESTERDAY.
SAM ALLEY?
HOCK'S GOT SURFACE-TO-AIR MISSILES SCREENING HIS LANDINGS ON THE SHORE OF SUPERIOR...
...AND WITHOUT AIR WE CAN'T DO MUCH TO STOP HIM.
THAT DOESN'T CHANGE SOON WE'RE GONNA GET CUT-OFF AND OVERRUN.
YOU KNOW WHAT HOCK DOES TO PRISONERS, NEW GUY?
FIRST THING HE DOES IS DOPE YOU INTO A FUCKING ZOMBIE--
WHERE'S THE L-T? BRIEFING WAS SUPPOSED TO START FIVE MINUTES AGO.
LIEUTENANT GATANAGA IS NOT CONDUCTING THIS BRIEFING.
I AM.

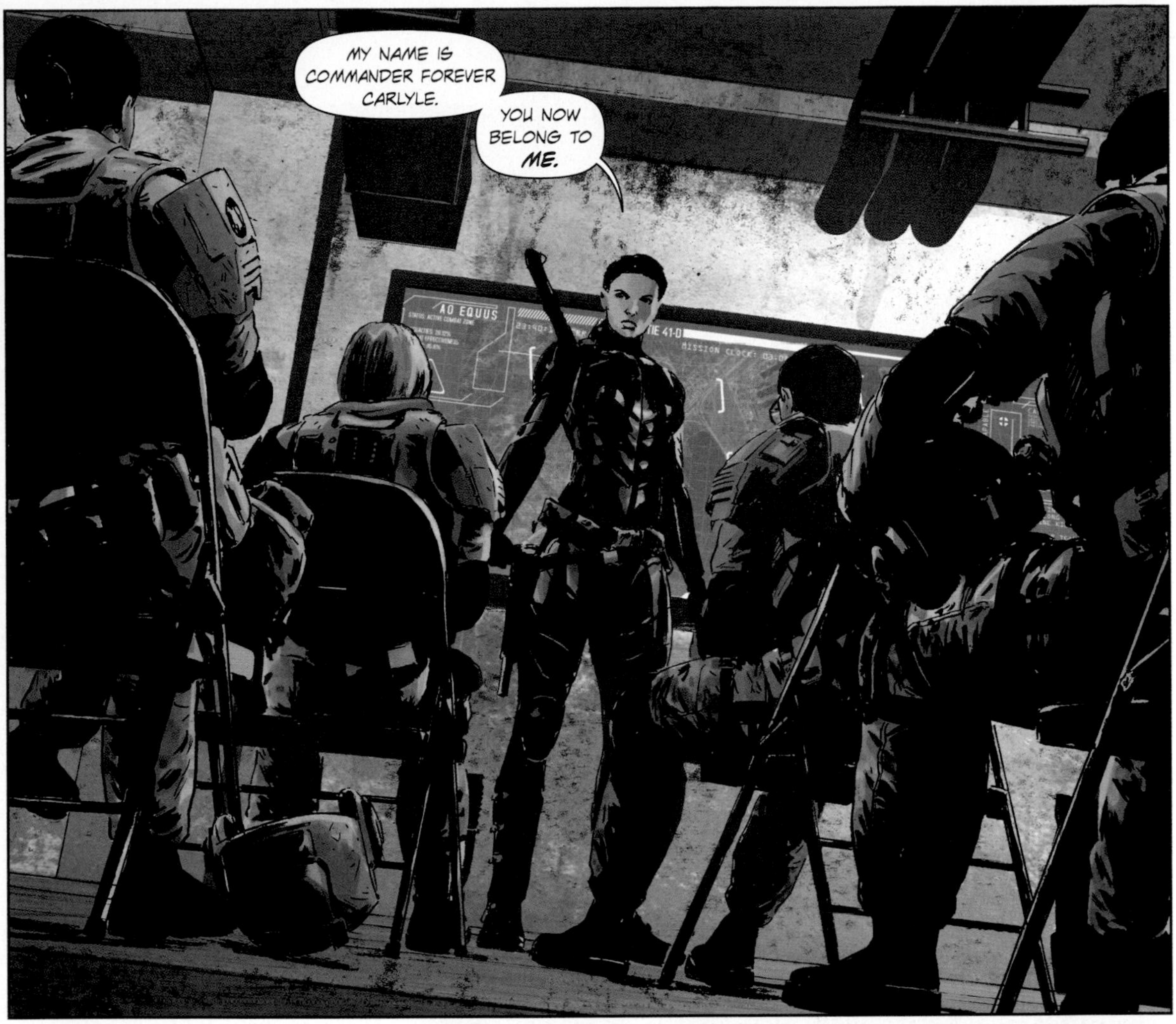
MY NAME IS COMMANDER FOREVER CARLYLE.
YOU NOW BELONG TO **ME.**
AO EQUUS

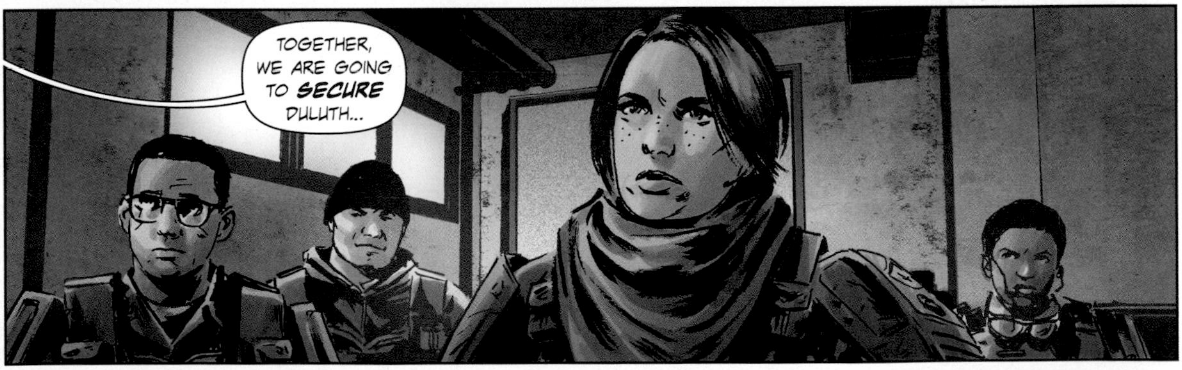
TOGETHER, WE ARE GOING TO **SECURE** DULUTH...

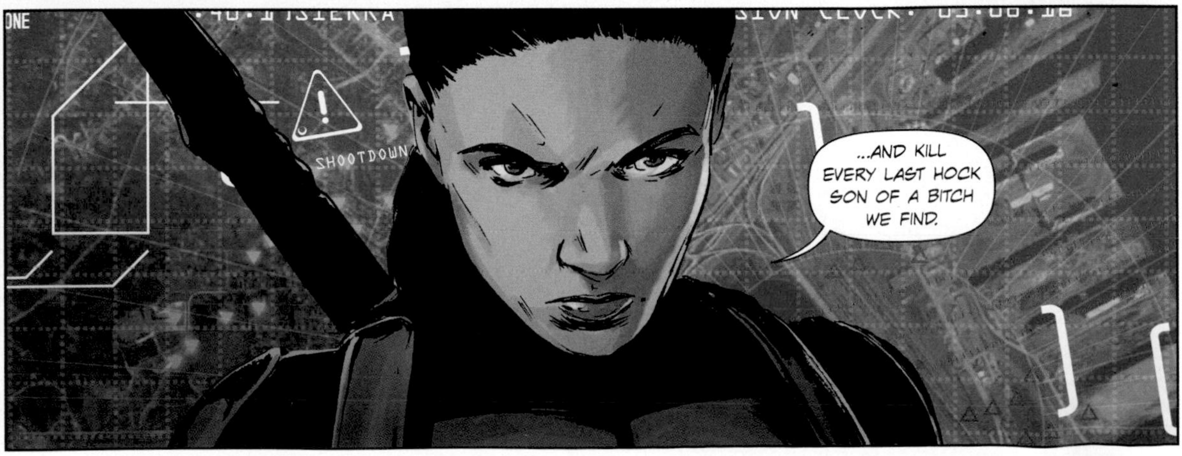
SHOOTDOWN
...AND KILL EVERY LAST HOCK SON OF A BITCH WE FIND.

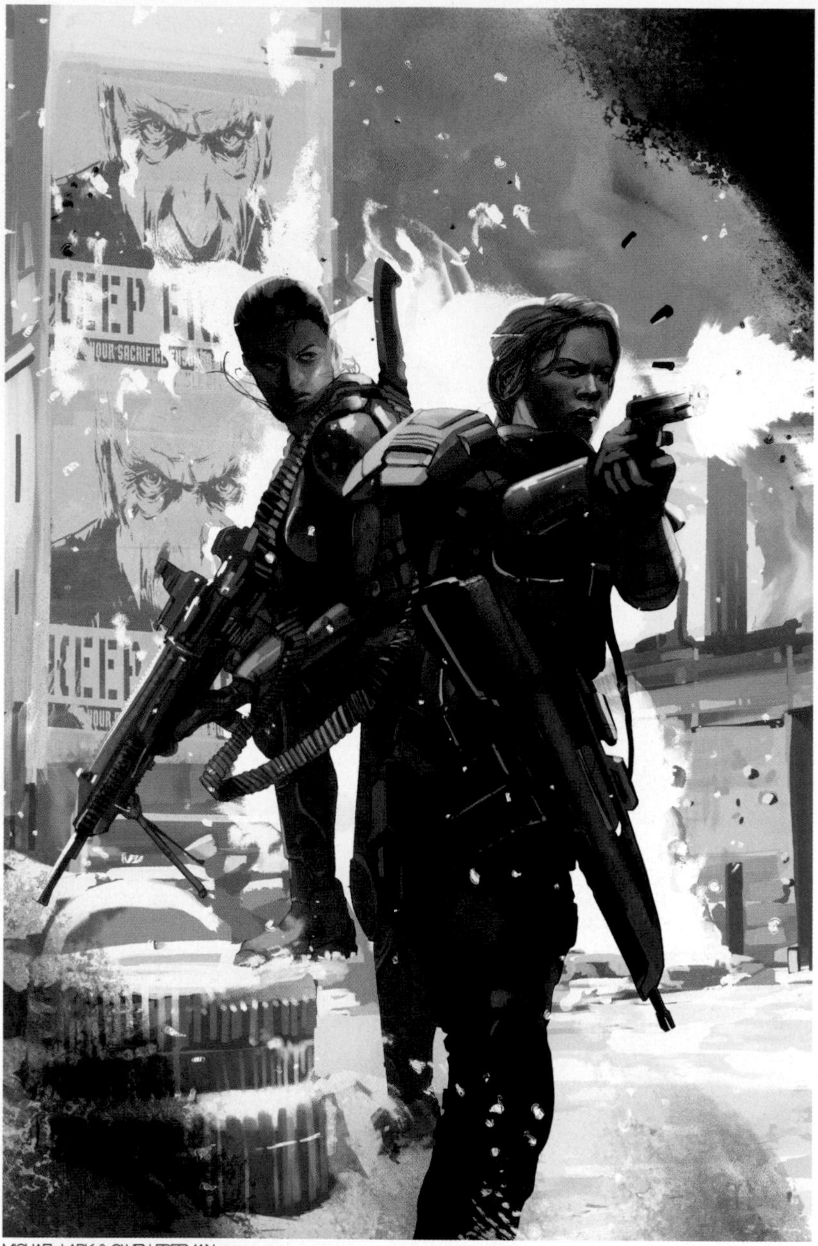
KEEP
KEEP

MICHAEL LARK & OWEN FREEMAN

POISON

CHAPTER TWO

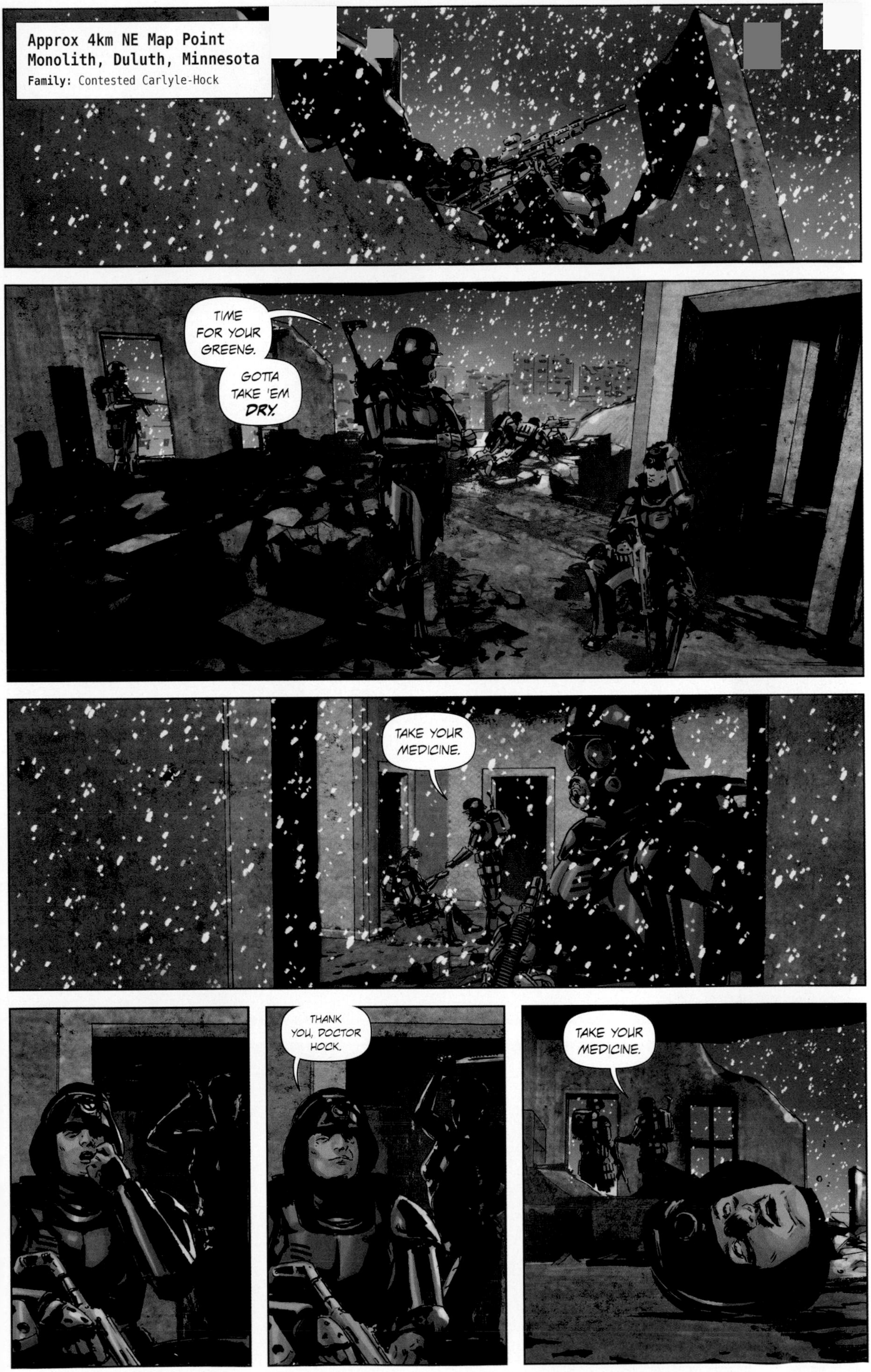
Approx 4km NE Map Point Monolith, Duluth, Minnesota
Family: Contested Carlyle-Hock
TIME FOR YOUR GREENS.
GOTTA TAKE 'EM DRY.
TAKE YOUR MEDICINE.
THANK YOU, DOCTOR HOCK.
TAKE YOUR MEDICINE.

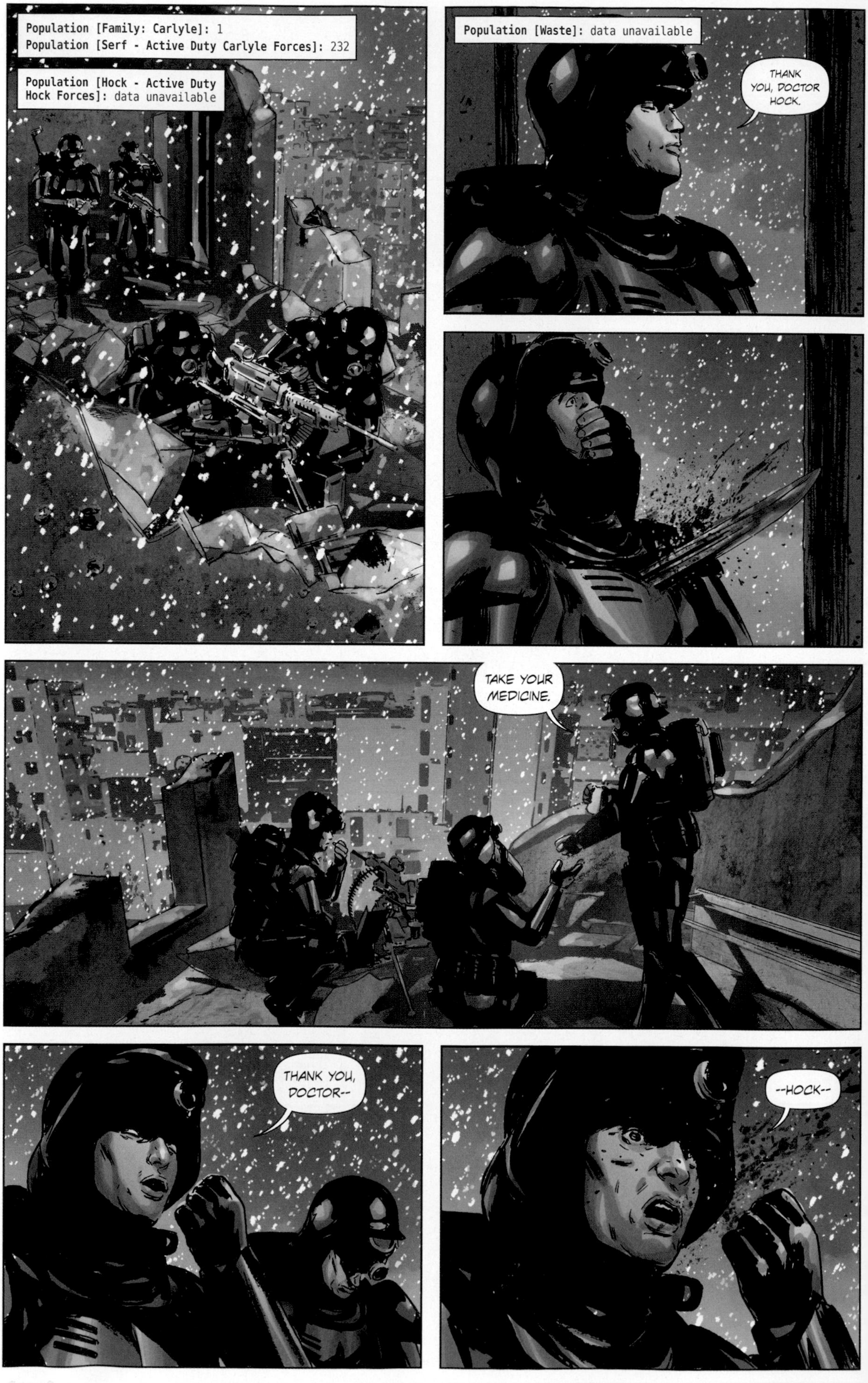
Population [Family: Carlyle]: 1
Population [Serf - Active Duty Carlyle Forces]: 232
Population [Hock - Active Duty Hock Forces]: data unavailable
Population [Waste]: data unavailable
THANK YOU, DOCTOR HOCK.
TAKE YOUR MEDICINE.
THANK YOU, DOCTOR--
--HOCK--

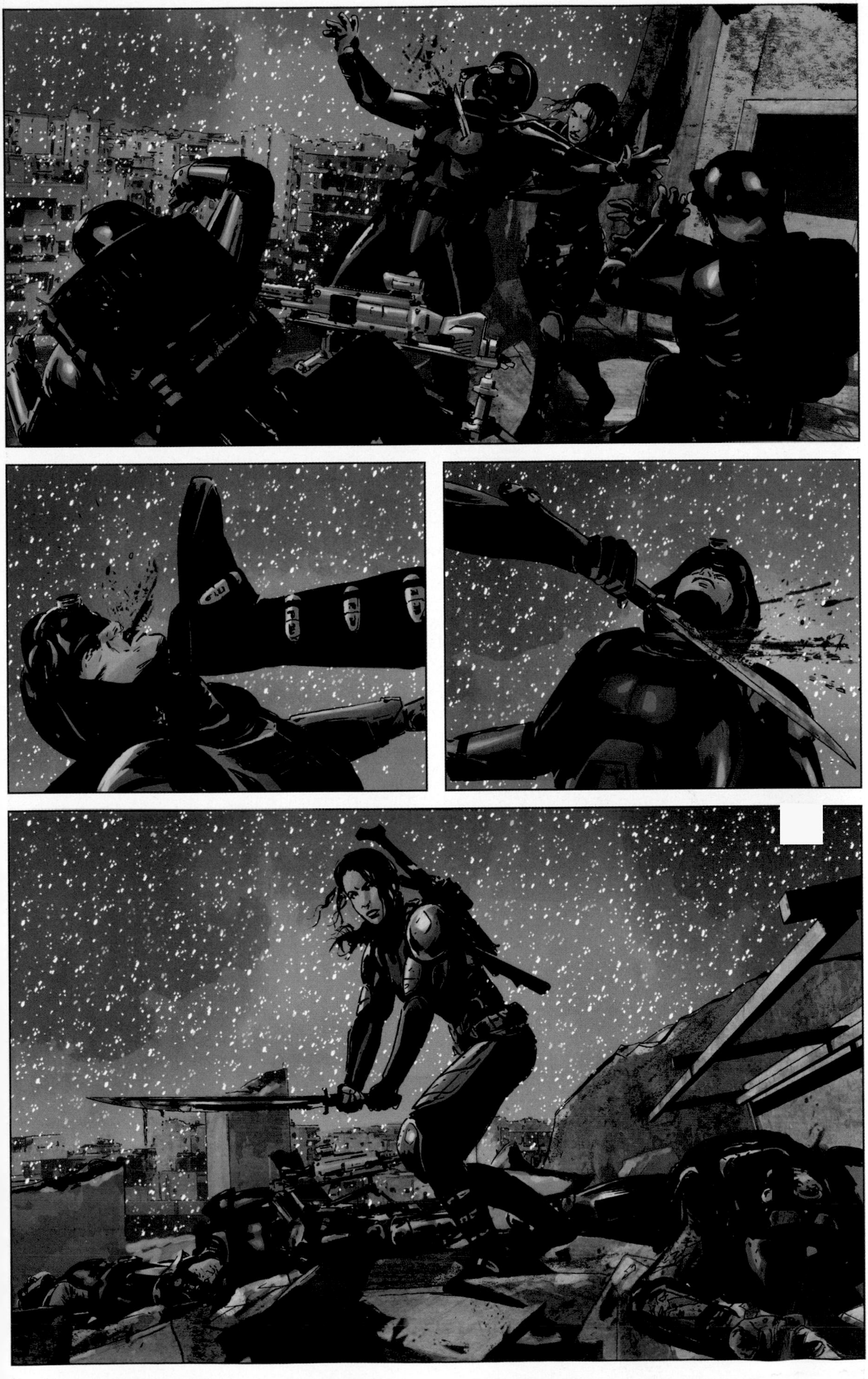

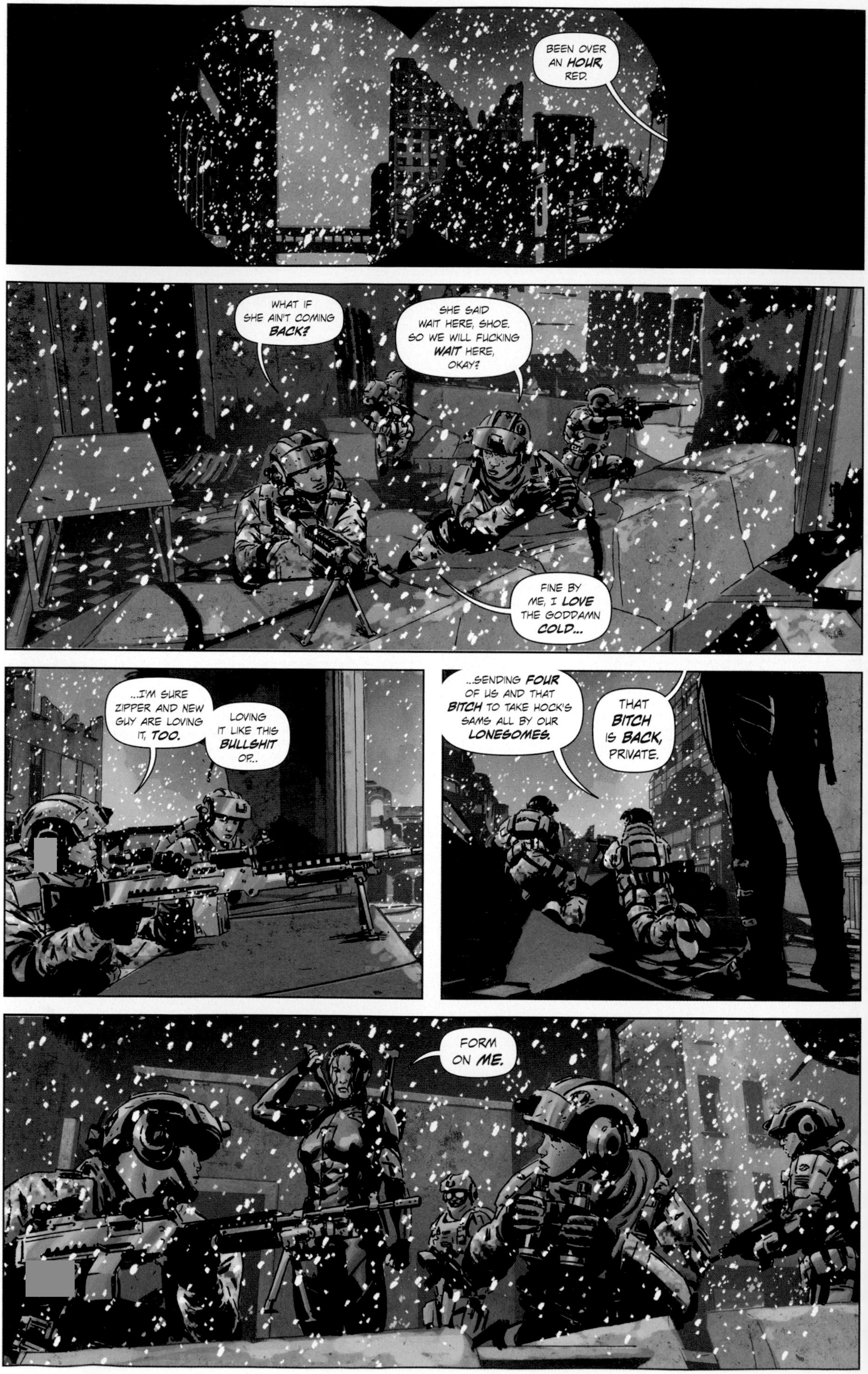
BEEN OVER AN HOUR, RED.
WHAT IF SHE AIN'T COMING BACK?
SHE SAID WAIT HERE, SHOE. SO WE WILL FUCKING WAIT HERE, OKAY?
FINE BY ME, I LOVE THE GODDAMN COLD...
...I'M SURE ZIPPER AND NEW GUY ARE LOVING IT, TOO.
LOVING IT LIKE THIS BULLSHIT OP...
...SENDING FOUR OF US AND THAT BITCH TO TAKE HOCK'S SAMS ALL BY OUR LONESOMES.
THAT BITCH IS BACK, PRIVATE.
FORM ON ME.

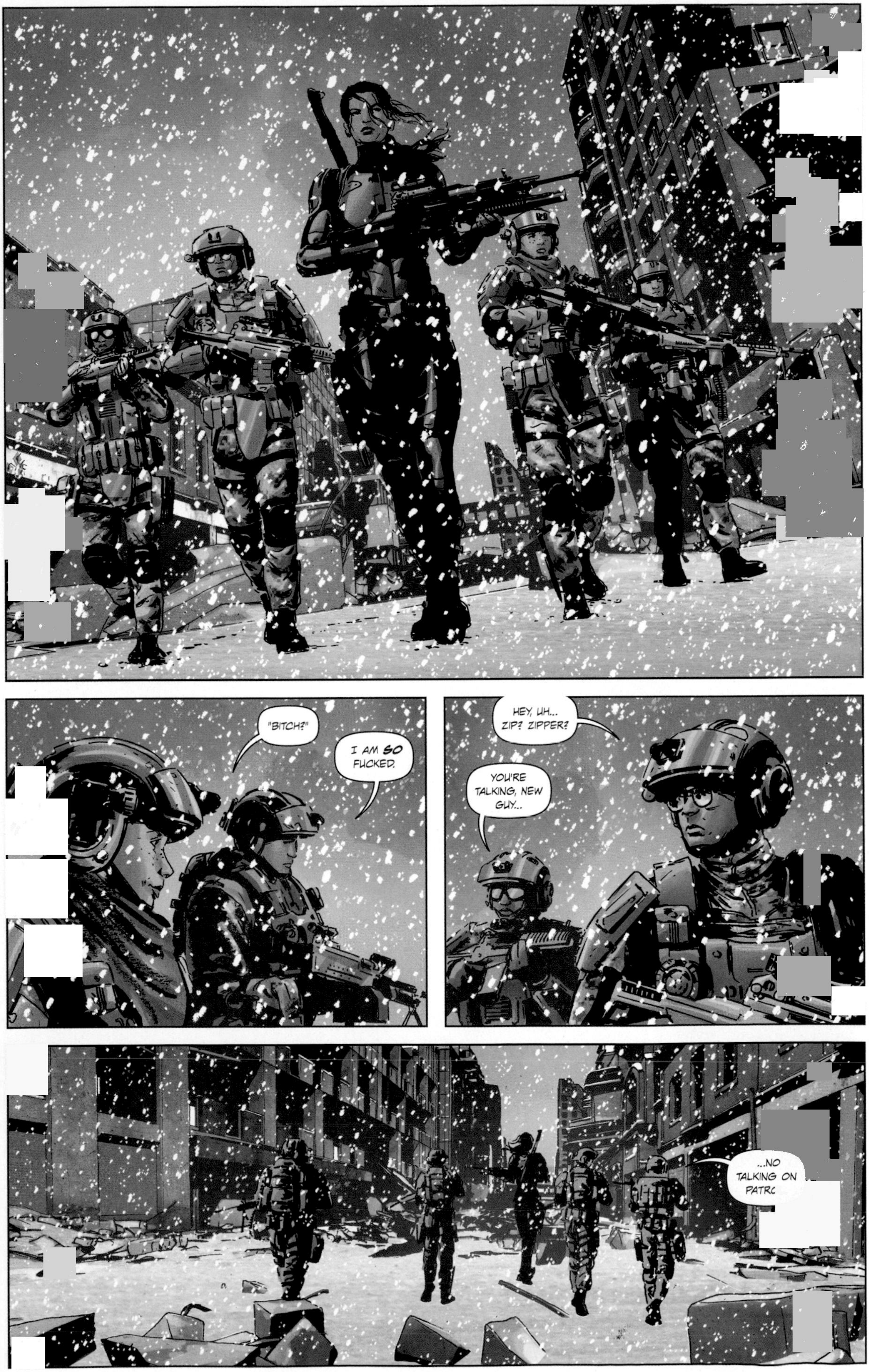
"BITCH?"
I AM SO FUCKED.
HEY, UH... ZIP? ZIPPER?
YOU'RE TALKING, NEW GUY...
...NO TALKING ON

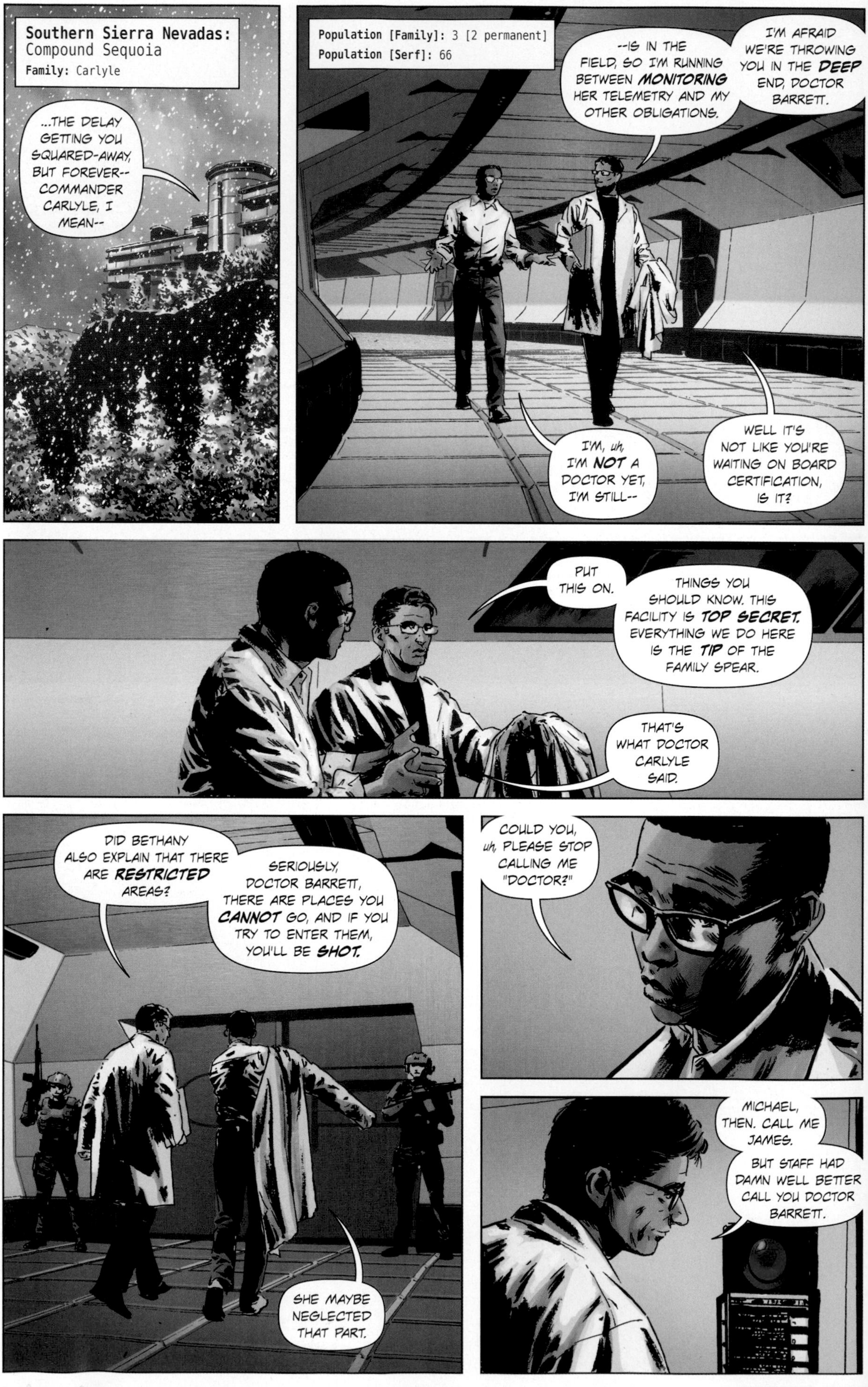
Southern Sierra Nevadas: Compound Sequoia
Family: Carlyle
...THE DELAY GETTING YOU SQUARED-AWAY, BUT FOREVER-- COMMANDER CARLYLE, I MEAN--
Population [Family]: 3 [2 permanent]
Population [Serf]: 66
I'M AFRAID WE'RE THROWING YOU IN THE DEEP END, DOCTOR BARRETT.
--IS IN THE FIELD, SO I'M RUNNING BETWEEN MONITORING HER TELEMETRY AND MY OTHER OBLIGATIONS.
I'M, uh, I'M NOT A DOCTOR YET, I'M STILL--
WELL IT'S NOT LIKE YOU'RE WAITING ON BOARD CERTIFICATION, IS IT?
PUT THIS ON.
THINGS YOU SHOULD KNOW. THIS FACILITY IS TOP SECRET. EVERYTHING WE DO HERE IS THE TIP OF THE FAMILY SPEAR.
THAT'S WHAT DOCTOR CARLYLE SAID.
DID BETHANY ALSO EXPLAIN THAT THERE ARE RESTRICTED AREAS?
SERIOUSLY, DOCTOR BARRETT, THERE ARE PLACES YOU CANNOT GO, AND IF YOU TRY TO ENTER THEM, YOU'LL BE SHOT.
SHE MAYBE NEGLECTED THAT PART.
COULD YOU, uh, PLEASE STOP CALLING ME "DOCTOR?"
MICHAEL, THEN. CALL ME JAMES.
BUT STAFF HAD DAMN WELL BETTER CALL YOU DOCTOR BARRETT.

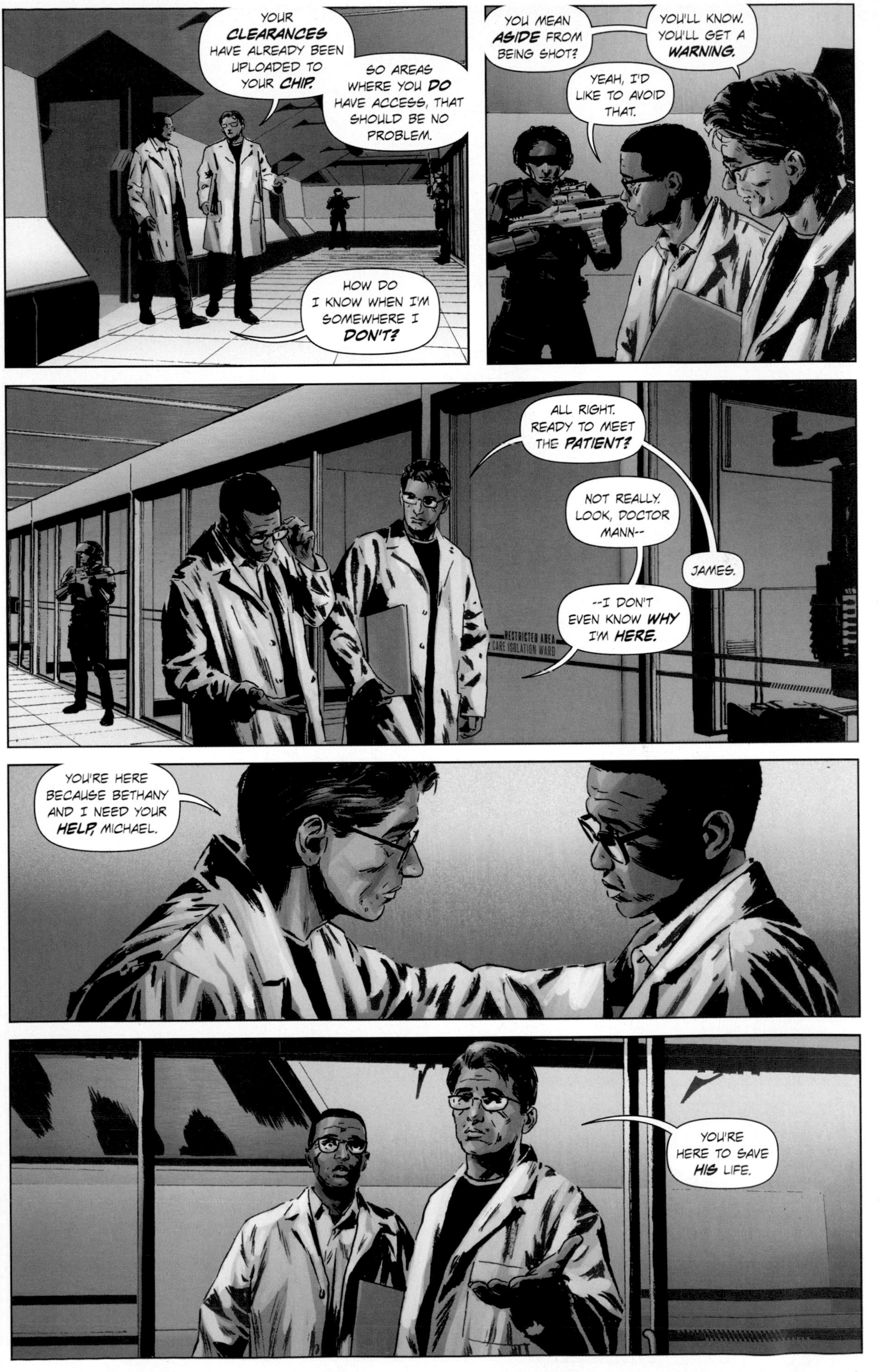

YOUR CLEARANCES HAVE ALREADY BEEN UPLOADED TO YOUR CHIP.
SO AREAS WHERE YOU DO HAVE ACCESS, THAT SHOULD BE NO PROBLEM.
HOW DO I KNOW WHEN I'M SOMEWHERE I DON'T?
YOU'LL KNOW. YOU'LL GET A WARNING.
YOU MEAN ASIDE FROM BEING SHOT?
YEAH, I'D LIKE TO AVOID THAT.
ALL RIGHT. READY TO MEET THE PATIENT?
NOT REALLY. LOOK, DOCTOR MANN--
JAMES.
--I DON'T EVEN KNOW WHY I'M HERE.
RESTRICTED AREA
CARE ISOLATION WARD
YOU'RE HERE BECAUSE BETHANY AND I NEED YOUR HELP, MICHAEL.
YOU'RE HERE TO SAVE HIS LIFE.

ANY CHANGE?

HIS SATS ARE AWFUL, BUT HIS BP HAS STABILIZED AGAIN, AT LEAST.

I'M GETTING VERY CONCERNED ABOUT THE POTENTIAL LONGTERM DAMAGE, THOUGH, JAMES.

JESUS CHRIST.

NO.

JUST MY FATHER.

MALCOLM CARLYLE.

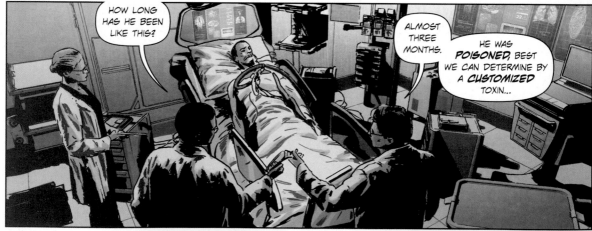

HOW LONG HAS HE BEEN LIKE THIS?

ALMOST THREE MONTHS.

HE WAS *POISONED,* BEST WE CAN DETERMINE BY A *CUSTOMIZED* TOXIN...

...CREATED BY JAKOB HOCK.

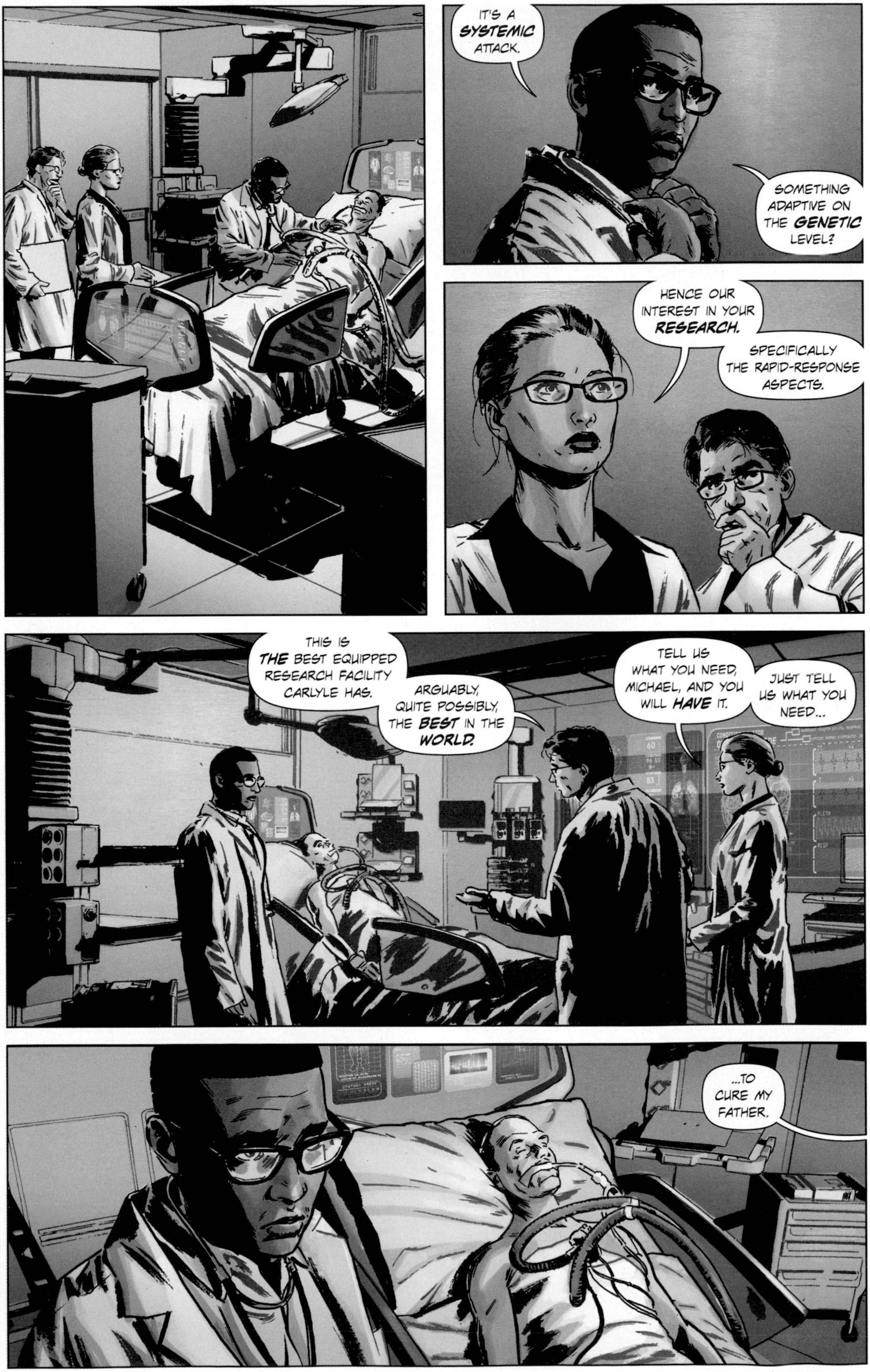

IT'S A SYSTEMIC ATTACK.
SOMETHING ADAPTIVE ON THE GENETIC LEVEL?
HENCE OUR INTEREST IN YOUR RESEARCH.
SPECIFICALLY THE RAPID-RESPONSE ASPECTS.
THIS IS THE BEST EQUIPPED RESEARCH FACILITY CARLYLE HAS.
ARGUABLY, QUITE POSSIBLY, THE BEST IN THE WORLD.
TELL US WHAT YOU NEED, MICHAEL, AND YOU WILL HAVE IT.
JUST TELL US WHAT YOU NEED...
...TO CURE MY FATHER.

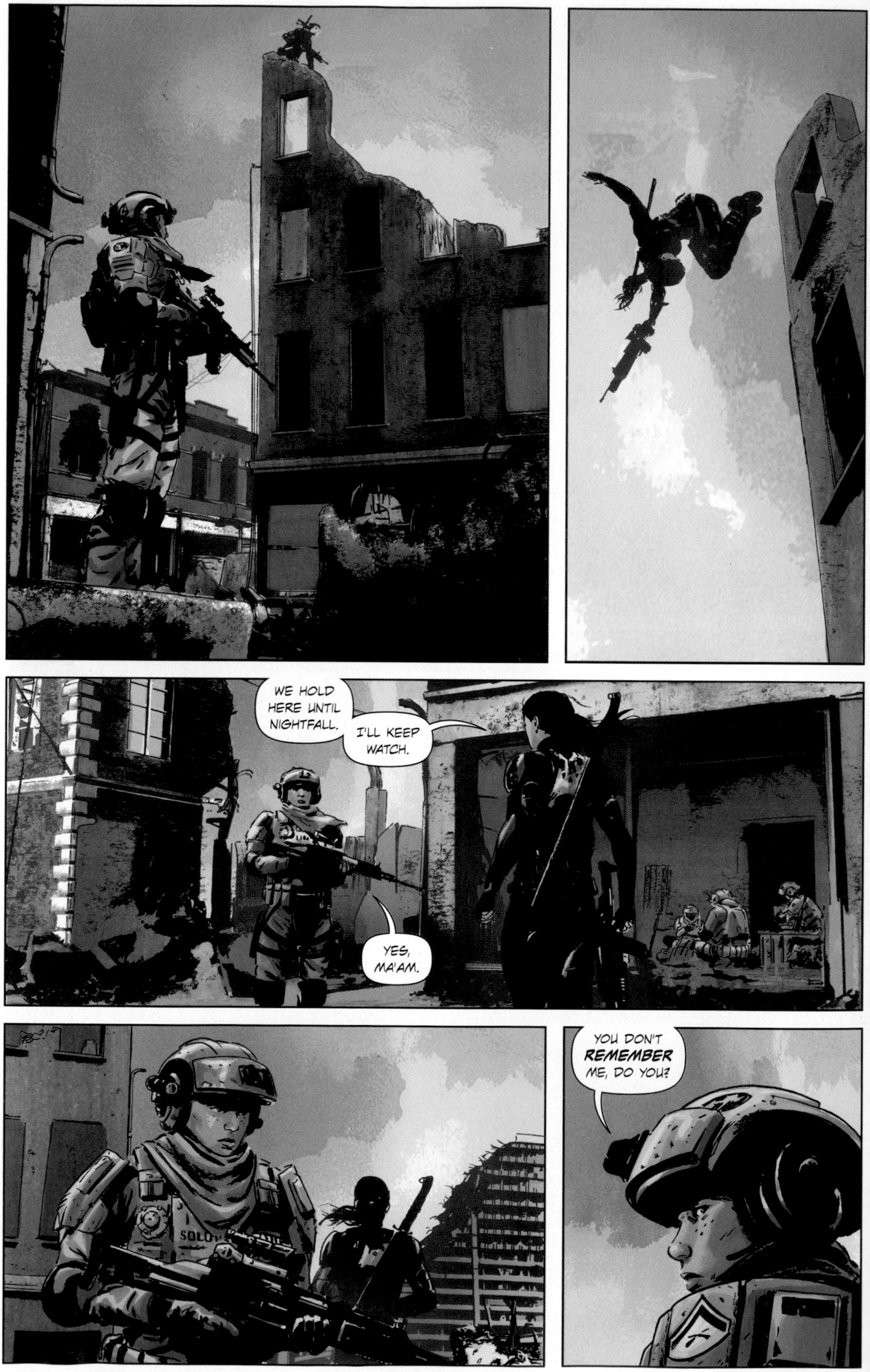
WE HOLD HERE UNTIL NIGHTFALL.
I'LL KEEP WATCH.
YES, MA'AM.
YOU DON'T REMEMBER ME, DO YOU?

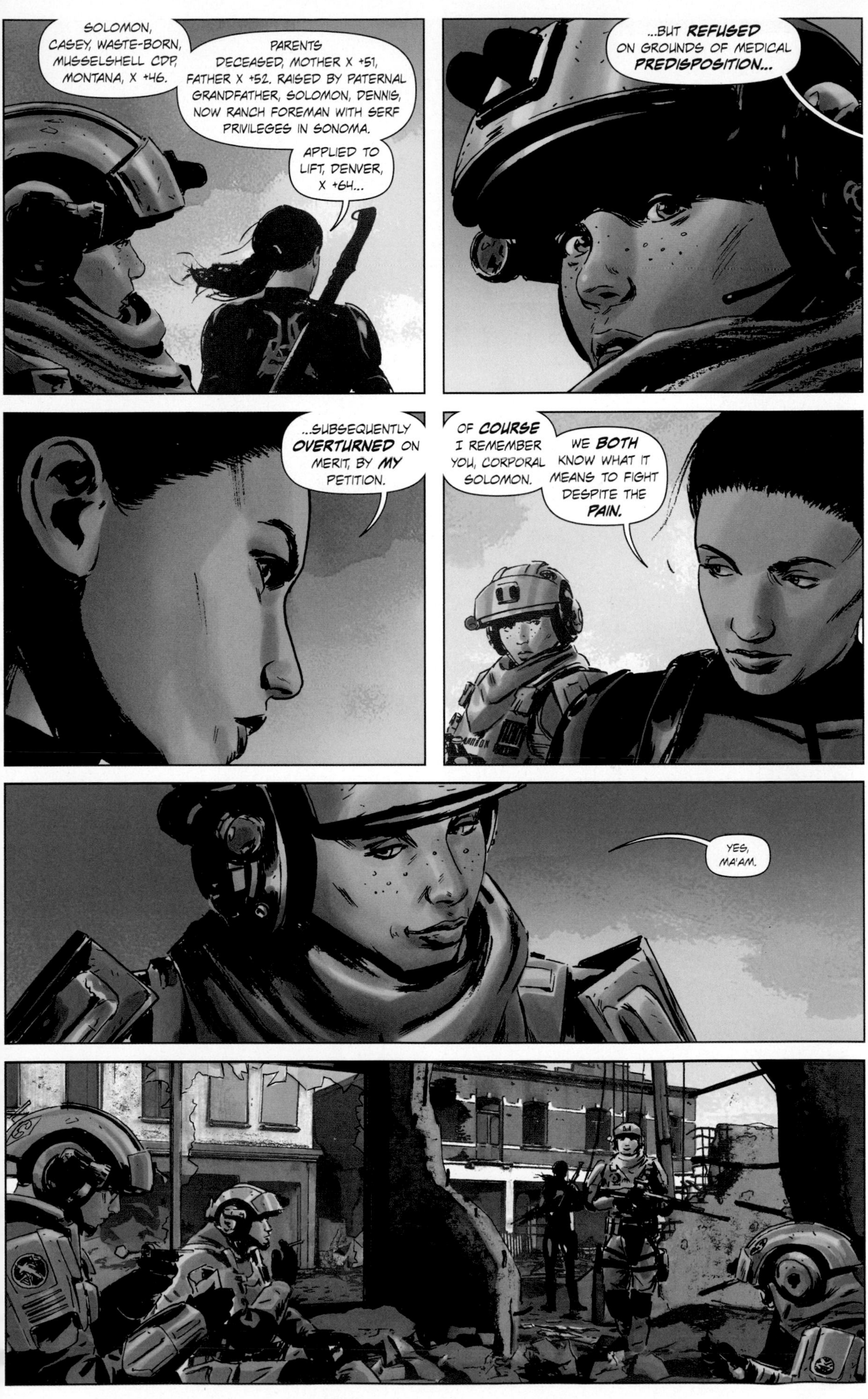
SOLOMON, CASEY, WASTE-BORN, MUSSELSHELL CDP, MONTANA, X +46.
PARENTS DECEASED, MOTHER X +51, FATHER X +52. RAISED BY PATERNAL GRANDFATHER, SOLOMON, DENNIS, NOW RANCH FOREMAN WITH SERF PRIVILEGES IN SONOMA.
APPLIED TO LIFT, DENVER, X +64...
...BUT REFUSED ON GROUNDS OF MEDICAL PREDISPOSITION...
...SUBSEQUENTLY OVERTURNED ON MERIT, BY MY PETITION.
OF COURSE I REMEMBER YOU, CORPORAL SOLOMON.
WE BOTH KNOW WHAT IT MEANS TO FIGHT DESPITE THE PAIN.
YES, MA'AM.

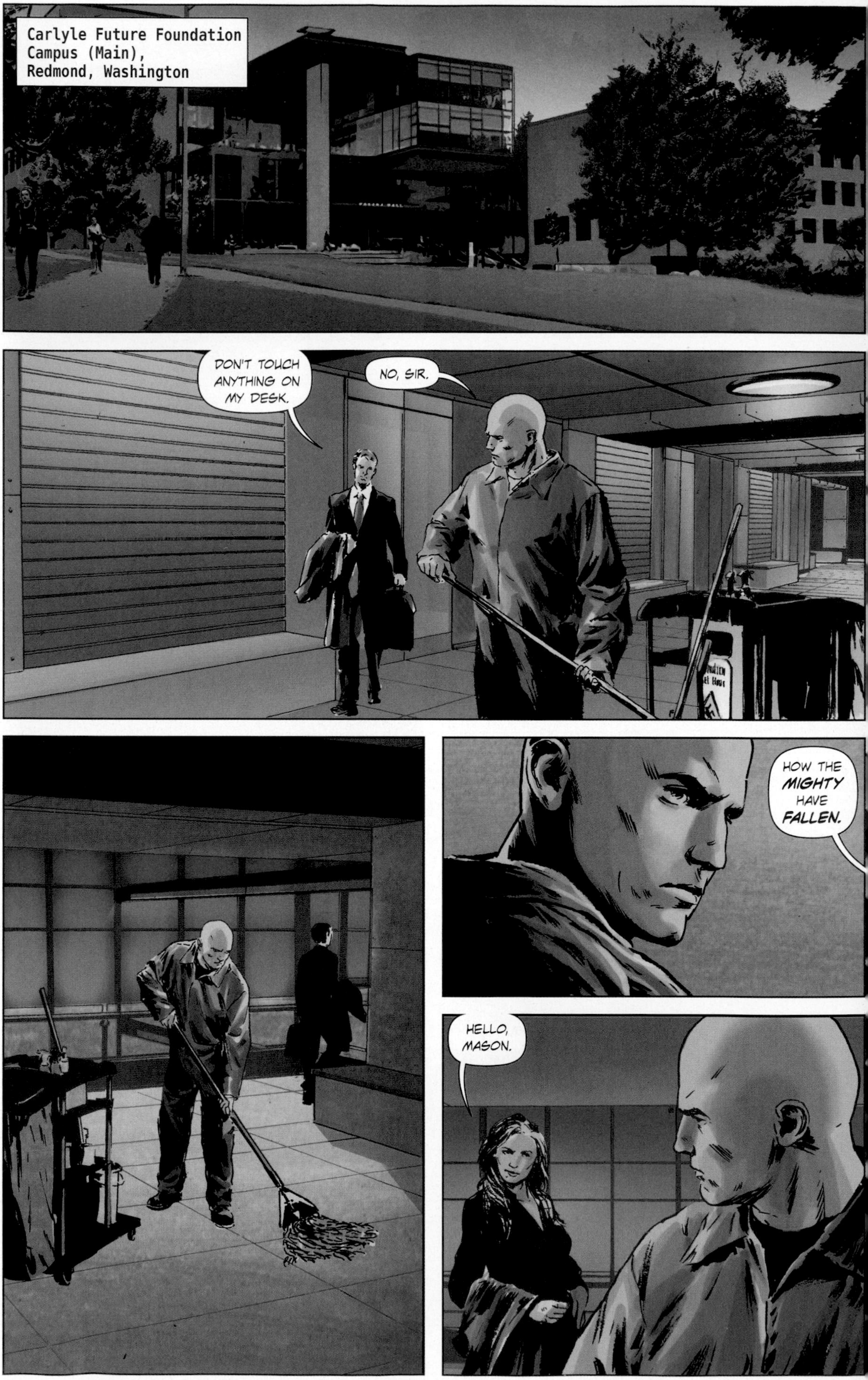
Carlyle Future Foundation Campus (Main), Redmond, Washington
DON'T TOUCH ANYTHING ON MY DESK.
NO, SIR.
HOW THE MIGHTY HAVE FALLEN.
HELLO, MASON.

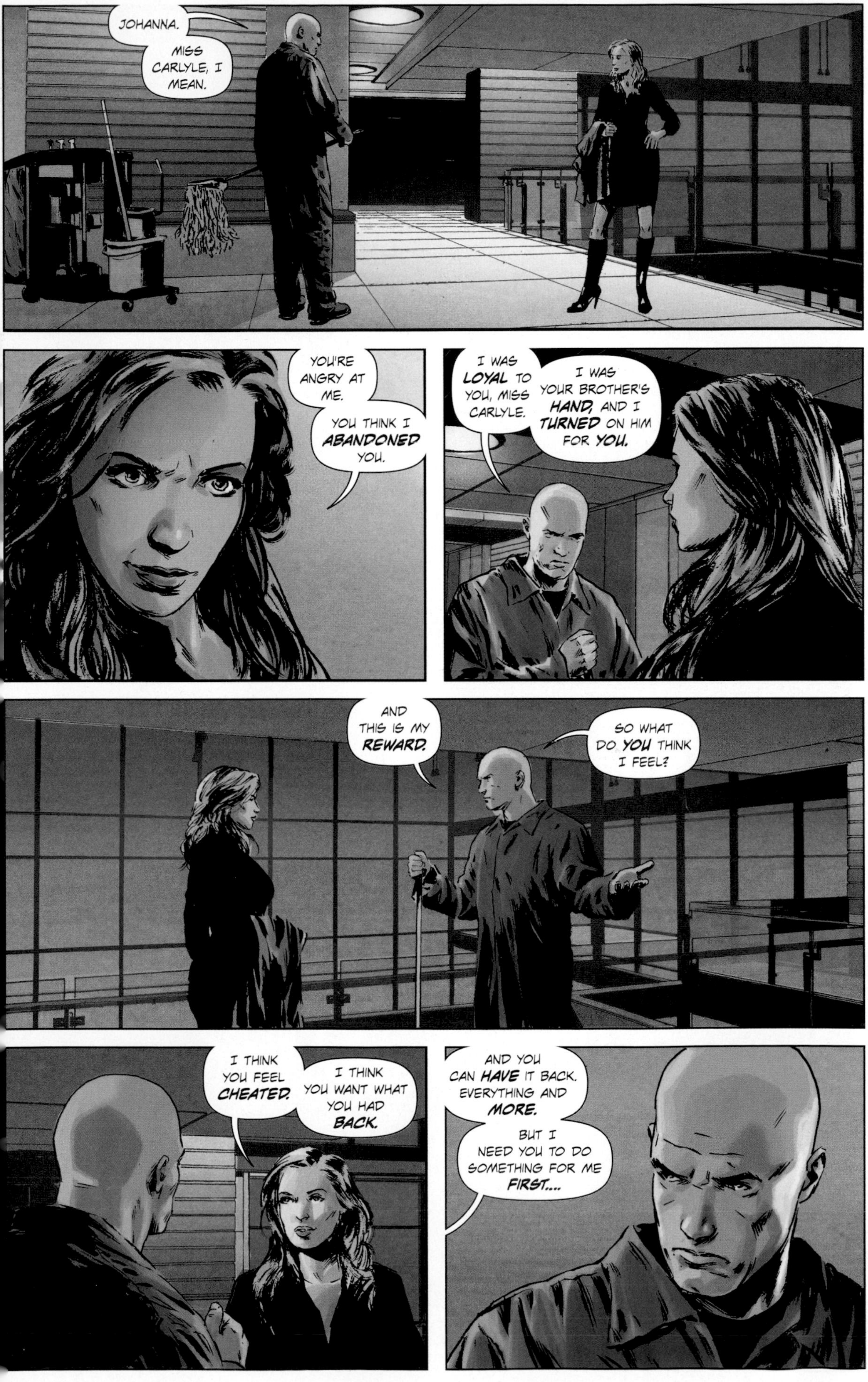
JOHANNA.
MISS CARLYLE, I MEAN.
YOU'RE ANGRY AT ME.
YOU THINK I ABANDONED YOU.
I WAS LOYAL TO YOU, MISS CARLYLE.
I WAS YOUR BROTHER'S HAND, AND I TURNED ON HIM FOR YOU.
AND THIS IS MY REWARD.
SO WHAT DO YOU THINK I FEEL?
I THINK YOU FEEL CHEATED.
I THINK YOU WANT WHAT YOU HAD BACK.
AND YOU CAN HAVE IT BACK. EVERYTHING AND MORE.
BUT I NEED YOU TO DO SOMETHING FOR ME FIRST....

Puget Sound
Family: Carlyle

--UNDERSTAND YOUR SITUATION, EDGAR, I REALLY *DO*...

Population [Family]: 4 [1 permanent]

...BUT *ALL* I CAN TELL YOU IS THAT WE'RE DOING *EVERYTHING* WE CAN.

AND I AM TELLING YOU THAT BY *MY* FAMILY'S AGREEMENT WITH YOUR *FATHER*, CARLYLE AND MORRAY ARE BOUND IN *MUTUAL* DEFENSE.

WITH BITTNER'S *COLLAPSE* IN WESTERN EUROPE, D'SOUZA HAS BEEN ABLE TO FOCUS HIS ATTENTION TO OUR *SOUTH.*

WE NEED *REINFORCEMENT.*

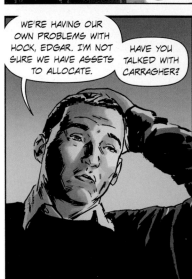

WE'RE HAVING OUR OWN PROBLEMS WITH HOCK, EDGAR. I'M NOT SURE WE HAVE ASSETS TO ALLOCATE.

HAVE YOU TALKED WITH CARRAGHER?

CARRAGHER HAS HIS *OWN* PROBLEMS.

YOUR FATHER HAD A *PLAN* FOR THIS CONTINGENCY, STEPHEN.

I'M *SURE* HE DID, BUT UNFORTUNATELY HE DIDN'T *SHARE* IT.

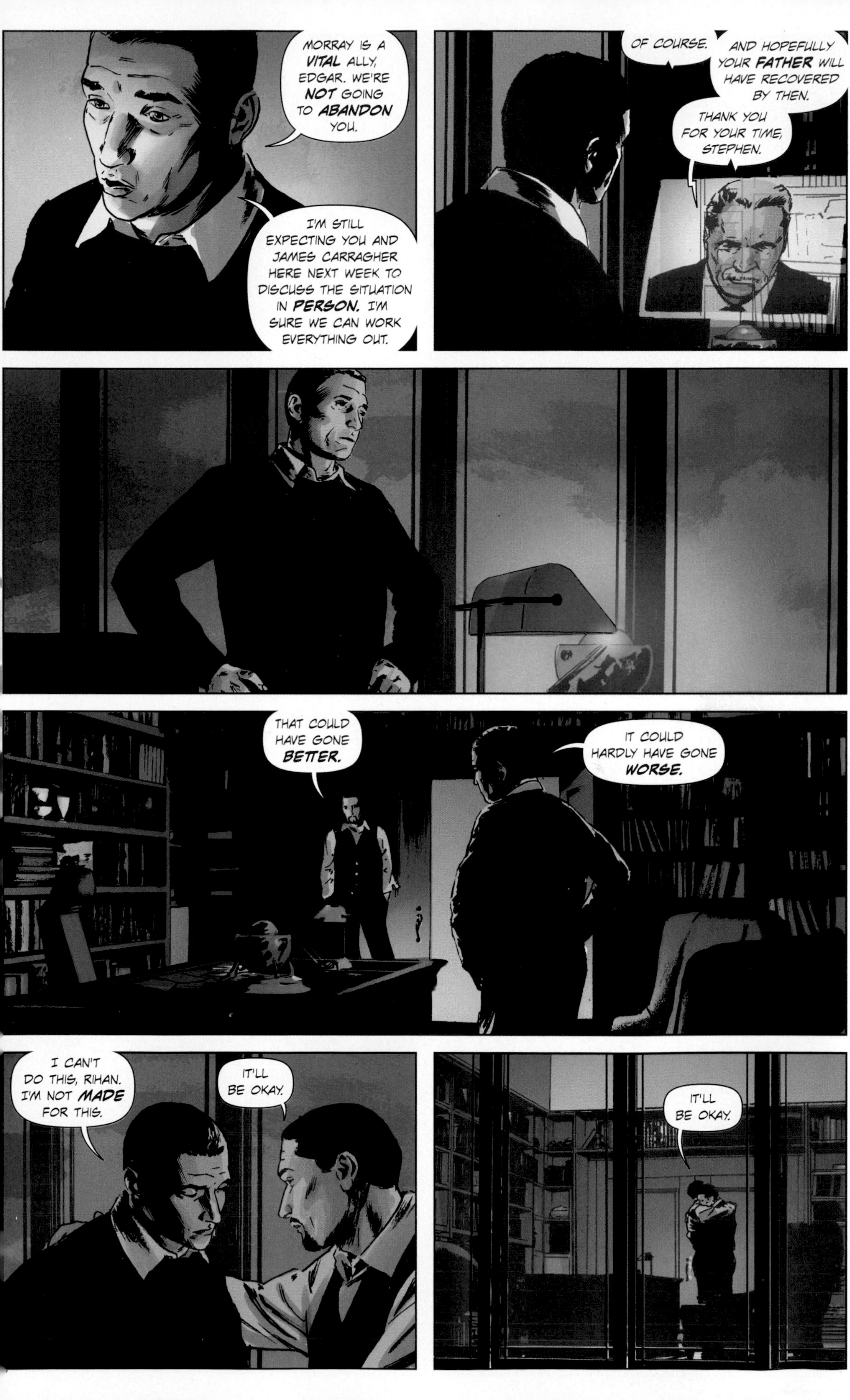

MORRAY IS A VITAL ALLY, EDGAR. WE'RE NOT GOING TO ABANDON YOU.
I'M STILL EXPECTING YOU AND JAMES CARRAGHER HERE NEXT WEEK TO DISCUSS THE SITUATION IN PERSON. I'M SURE WE CAN WORK EVERYTHING OUT.
OF COURSE.
AND HOPEFULLY YOUR FATHER WILL HAVE RECOVERED BY THEN.
THANK YOU FOR YOUR TIME, STEPHEN.
THAT COULD HAVE GONE BETTER.
IT COULD HARDLY HAVE GONE WORSE.
I CAN'T DO THIS, RIHAN. I'M NOT MADE FOR THIS.
IT'LL BE OKAY.
IT'LL BE OKAY.

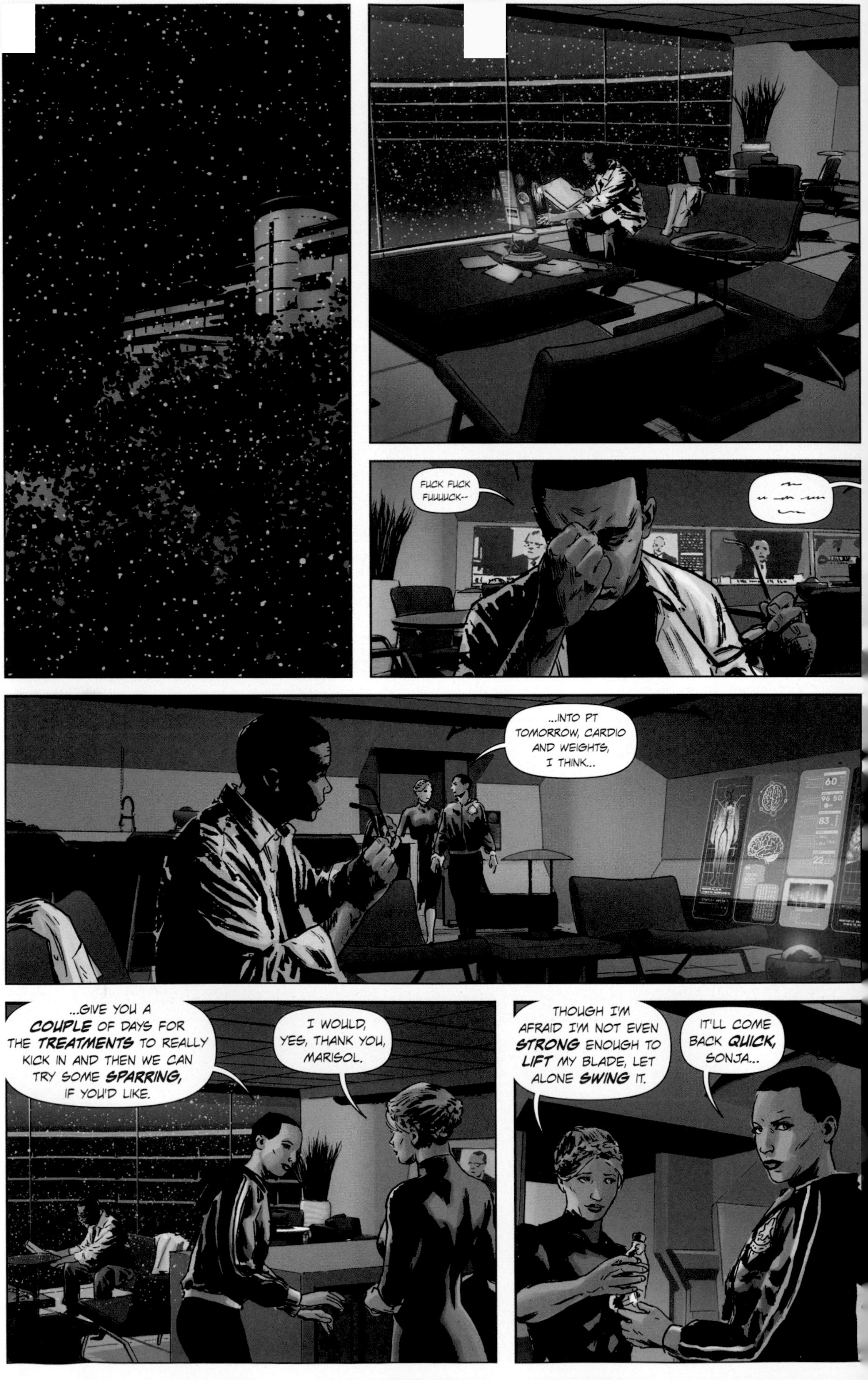
FUCK FUCK FUUUUCK--
...INTO PT TOMORROW, CARDIO AND WEIGHTS, I THINK...
...GIVE YOU A COUPLE OF DAYS FOR THE TREATMENTS TO REALLY KICK IN AND THEN WE CAN TRY SOME SPARRING, IF YOU'D LIKE.
I WOULD, YES, THANK YOU, MARISOL.
THOUGH I'M AFRAID I'M NOT EVEN STRONG ENOUGH TO LIFT MY BLADE, LET ALONE SWING IT.
IT'LL COME BACK QUICK, SONJA...

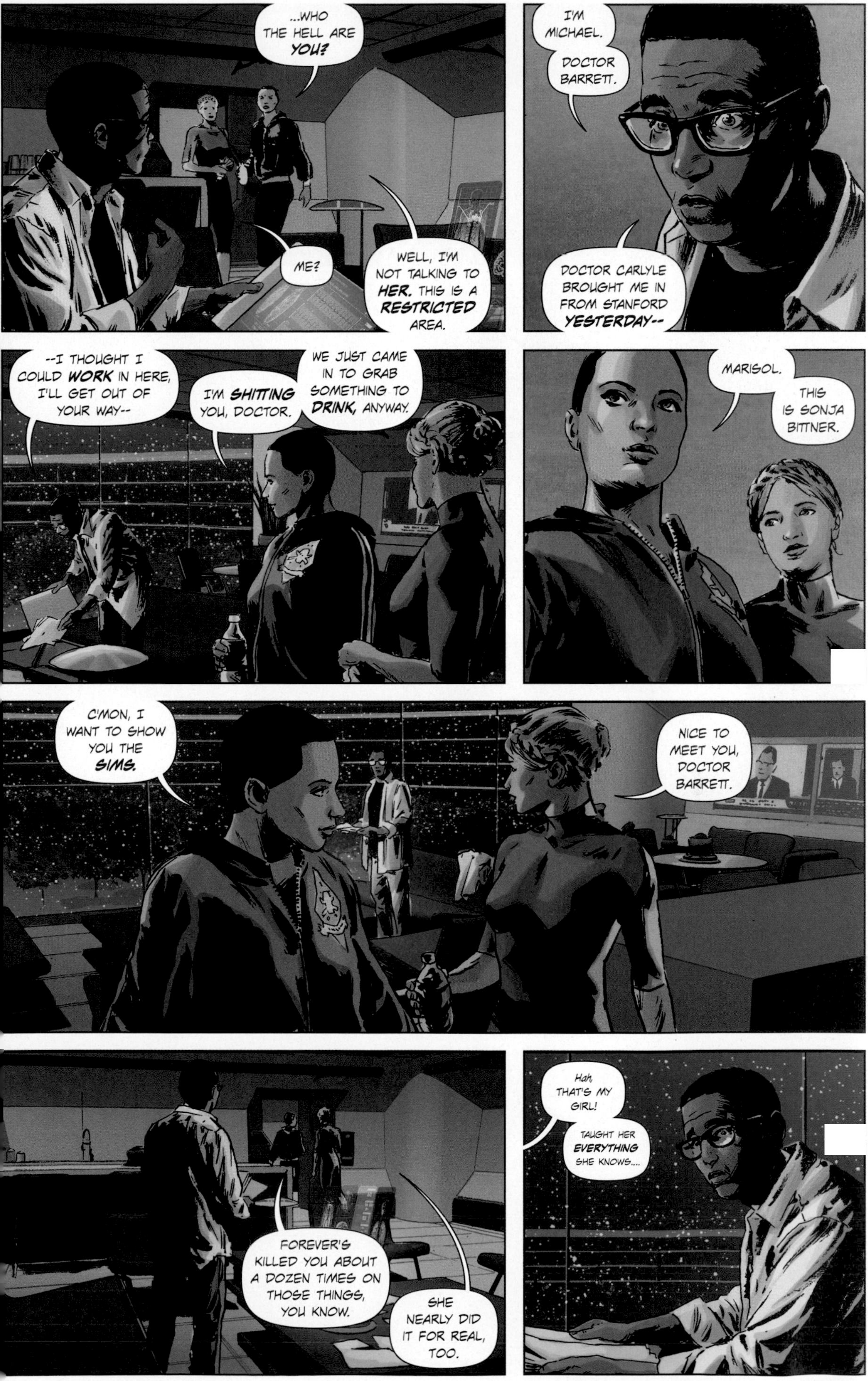
...WHO THE HELL ARE YOU?
ME?
WELL, I'M NOT TALKING TO HER. THIS IS A RESTRICTED AREA.
I'M MICHAEL.
DOCTOR BARRETT.
DOCTOR CARLYLE BROUGHT ME IN FROM STANFORD YESTERDAY--
--I THOUGHT I COULD WORK IN HERE, I'LL GET OUT OF YOUR WAY--
I'M SHITTING YOU, DOCTOR.
WE JUST CAME IN TO GRAB SOMETHING TO DRINK, ANYWAY.
MARISOL.
THIS IS SONJA BITTNER.
C'MON, I WANT TO SHOW YOU THE SIMS.
NICE TO MEET YOU, DOCTOR BARRETT.
FOREVER'S KILLED YOU ABOUT A DOZEN TIMES ON THOSE THINGS, YOU KNOW.
SHE NEARLY DID IT FOR REAL, TOO.
Hah, THAT'S MY GIRL!
TAUGHT HER EVERYTHING SHE KNOWS....

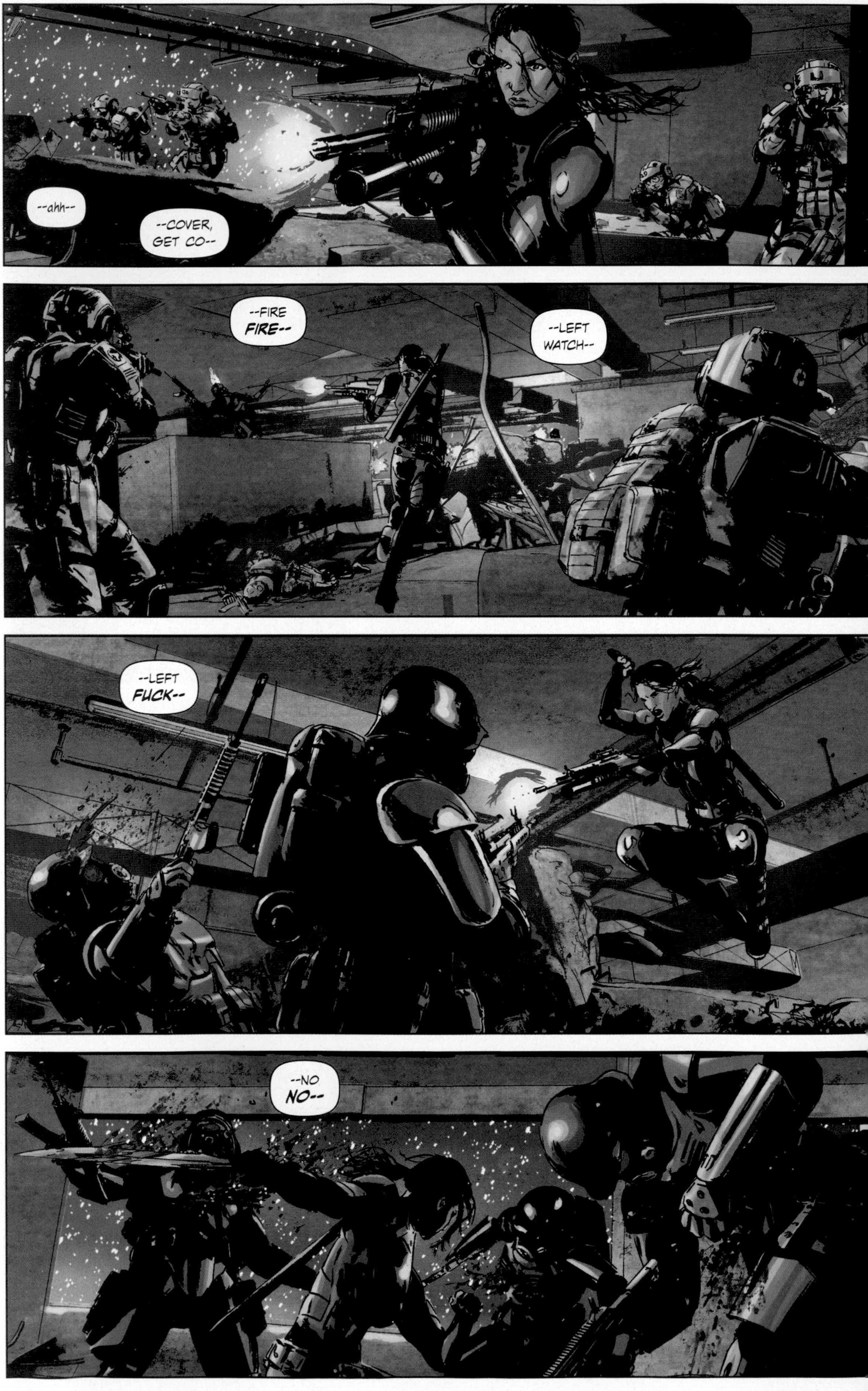
--ahh--
--COVER, GET CO--
--FIRE FIRE--
--LEFT WATCH--
--LEFT FUCK--
--NO NO--

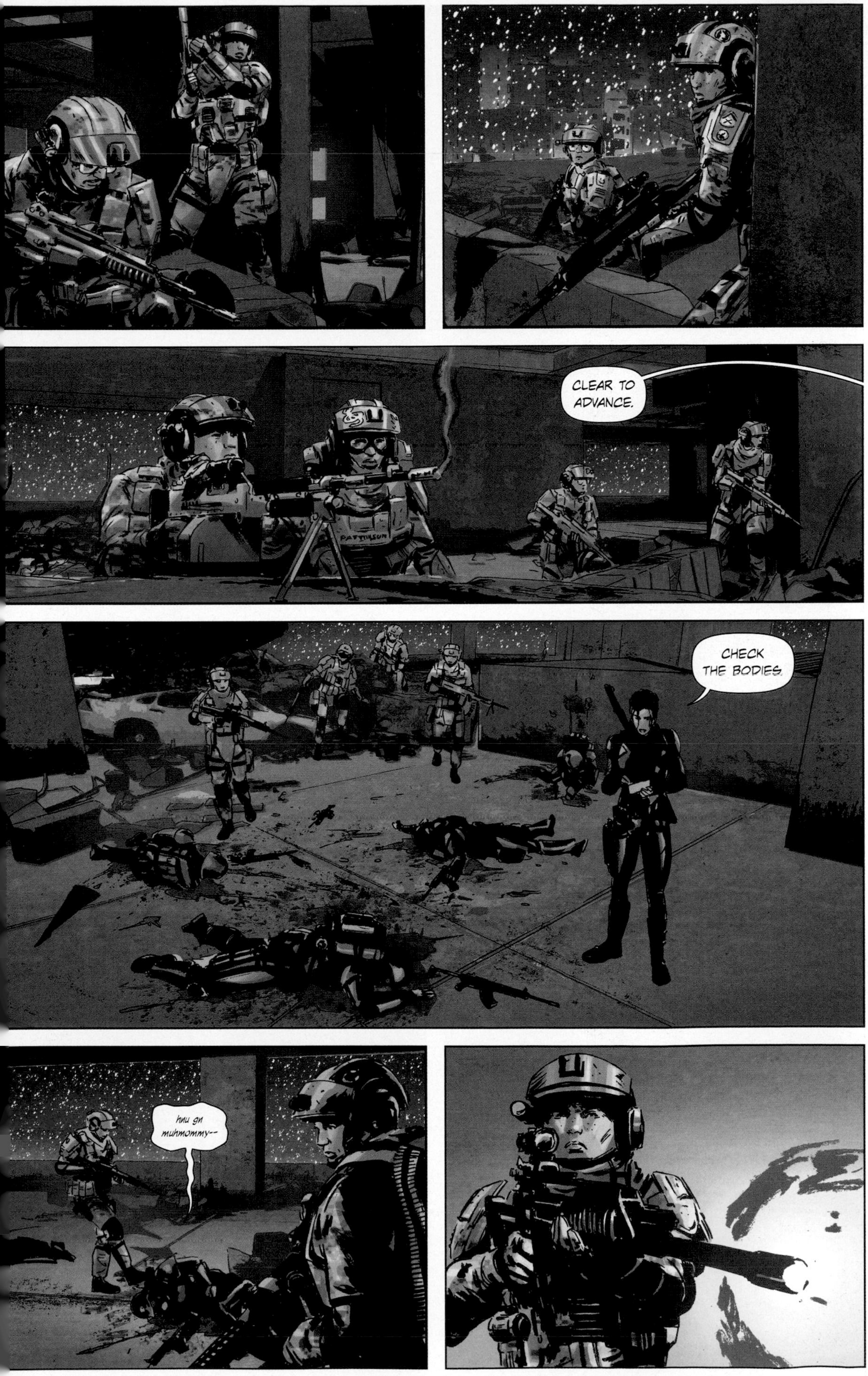
CLEAR TO ADVANCE.
CHECK THE BODIES.
hnu gn muhmommy--

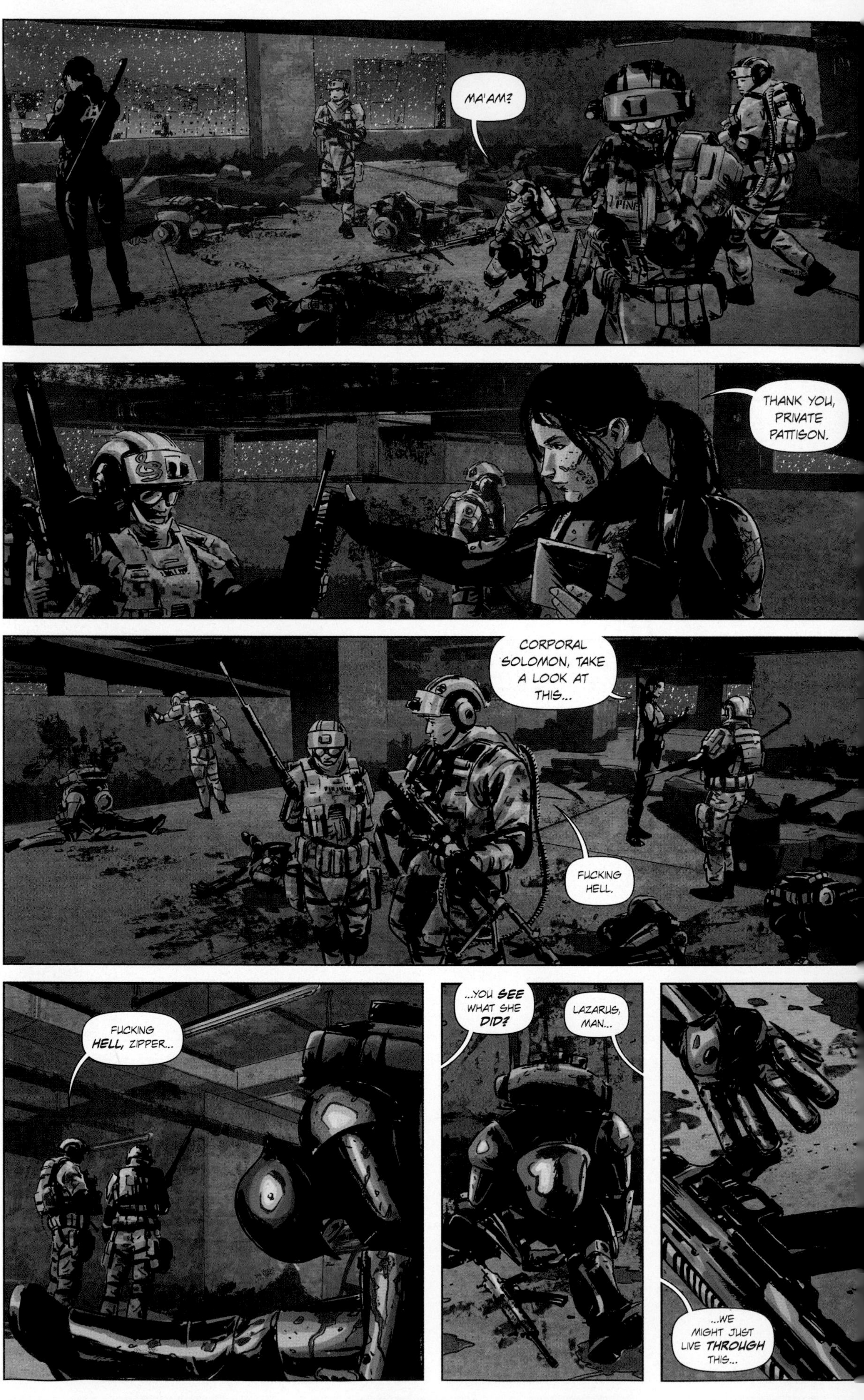
MA'AM?
THANK YOU, PRIVATE PATTISON.
CORPORAL SOLOMON, TAKE A LOOK AT THIS...
FUCKING HELL.
FUCKING HELL, ZIPPER...
...YOU SEE WHAT SHE DID?
LAZARUS, MAN...
...WE MIGHT JUST LIVE THROUGH THIS...

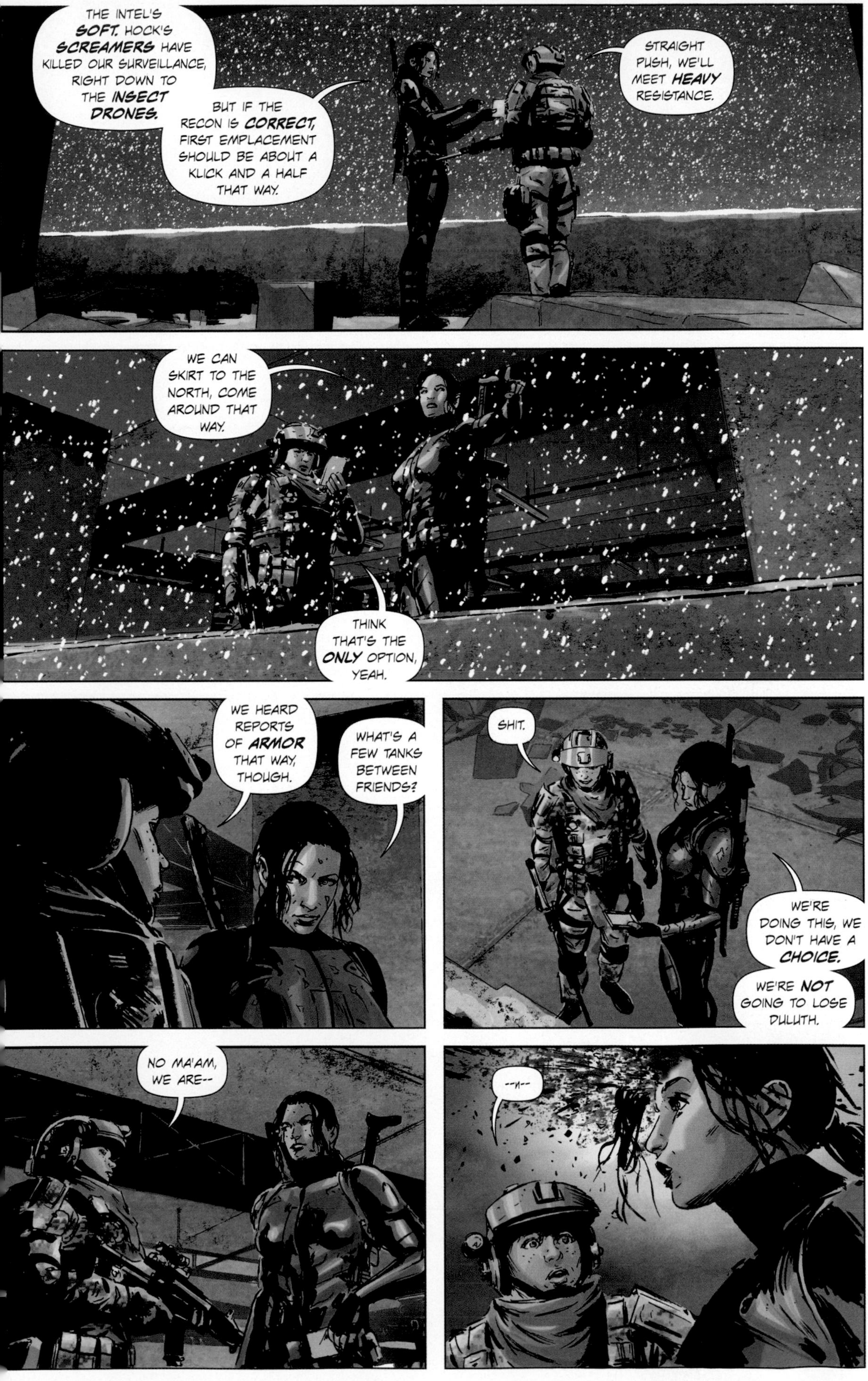
THE INTEL'S SOFT. HOCK'S SCREAMERS HAVE KILLED OUR SURVEILLANCE, RIGHT DOWN TO THE INSECT DRONES.
BUT IF THE RECON IS CORRECT, FIRST EMPLACEMENT SHOULD BE ABOUT A KLICK AND A HALF THAT WAY.
STRAIGHT PUSH, WE'LL MEET HEAVY RESISTANCE.
WE CAN SKIRT TO THE NORTH, COME AROUND THAT WAY.
THINK THAT'S THE ONLY OPTION, YEAH.
WE HEARD REPORTS OF ARMOR THAT WAY, THOUGH.
WHAT'S A FEW TANKS BETWEEN FRIENDS?
SHIT.
WE'RE DOING THIS, WE DON'T HAVE A CHOICE.
WE'RE NOT GOING TO LOSE DULUTH.
NO MA'AM, WE ARE--
--N--

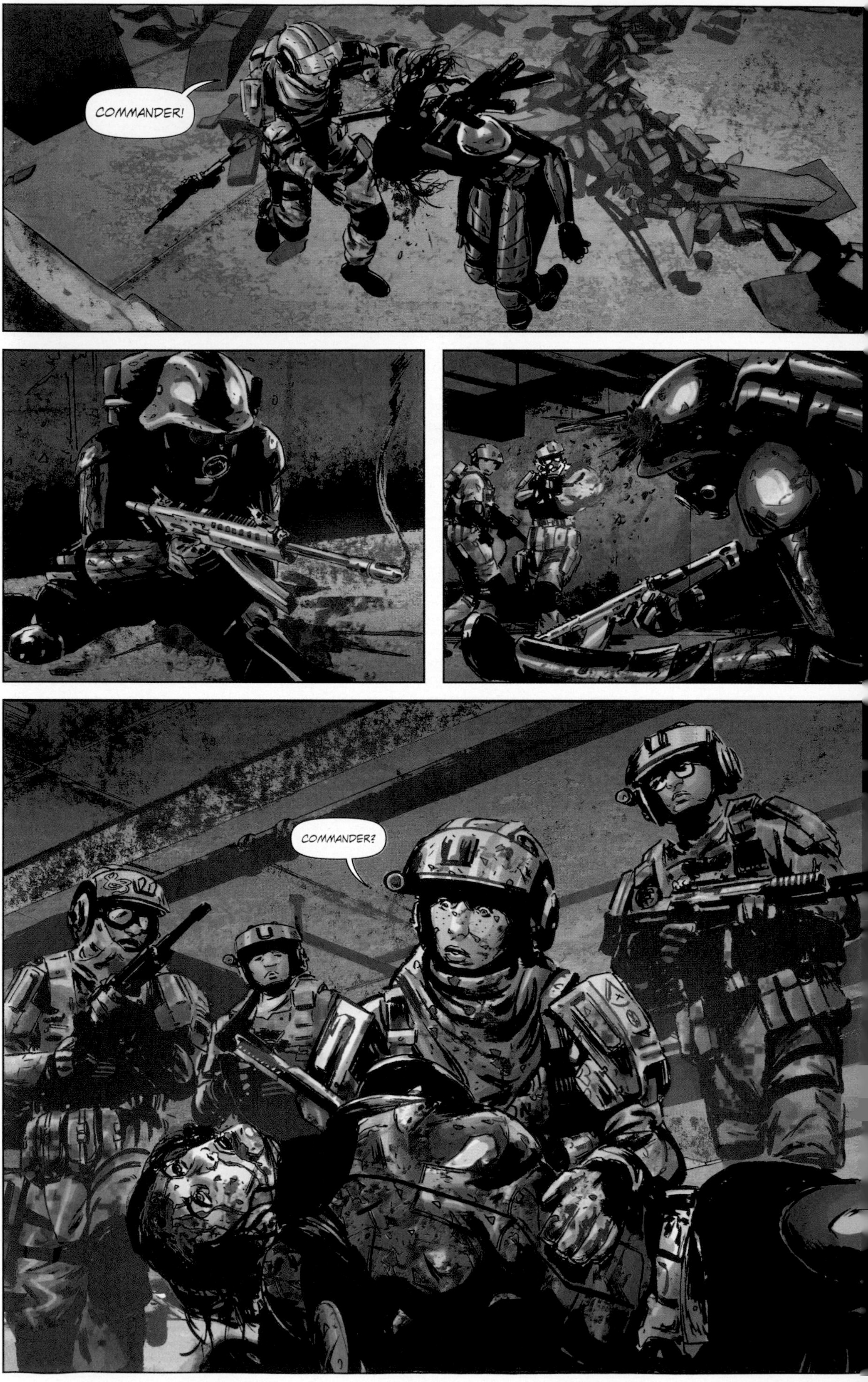
COMMANDER!
COMMANDER?

CARLYLE

ODERINT DUM METUANT

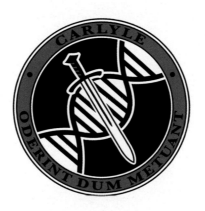

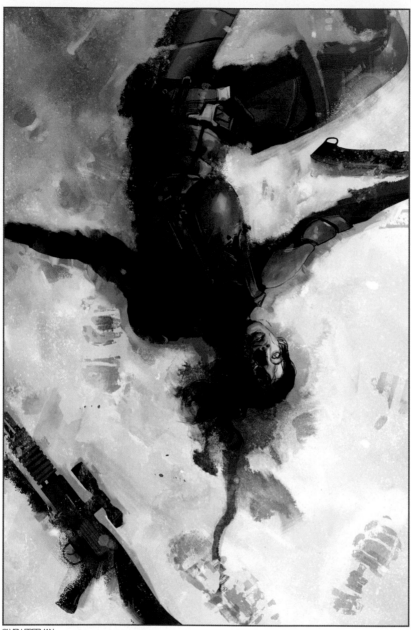

OWEN FREEMAN

POISON
CHAPTER THREE

Southern Sierra Nevadas:
Compound Sequoia
Family: Carlyle

THE SiRNA APPROACH DOESN'T *WORK*, MICHAEL.

HOCK'S POISON JUST *CHANGES* STRATEGY AND FINDS A *NEW* TARGET ON THE GENOME.

AND SETS OFF *ANOTHER* CYTOKINE STORM, YEAH.

THERE ARE *PROPRIETARY* SEQUENCES IN YOUR FATHER, CORRECT?

SPECIFIC ONLY TO *YOUR* FAMILY, I MEAN.

Population [Family]: 3
[2 permanent]
Population [Serf]: 66

OBVIOUSLY.

NO, I MEAN *ARTIFICIALLY* INTRODUCED--

DREETDREETDREETDREETDREE

SHIT!

WHAT IS IT?

DREETDREETDREETDREETDREETDREETDREETDREETDREE

THE TRAUMA ALERT FOR MY *SISTER*. SHE'S BEEN *INJURED*...

TDREETDREETDREETDREE ... ANDREETDREETDREE

...THIS...

...SOMETHING'S *WRONG*...

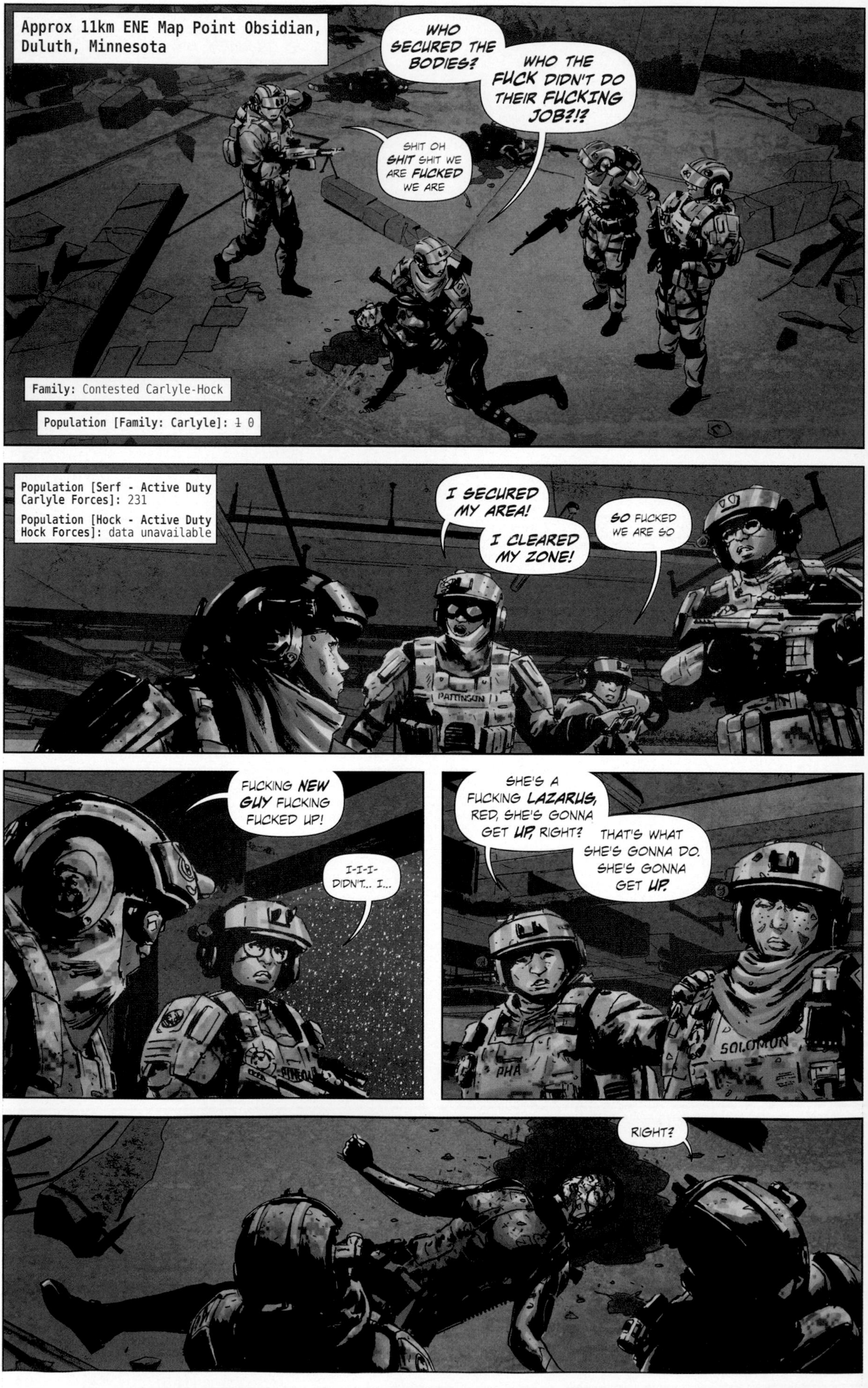

Approx 11km ENE Map Point Obsidian, Duluth, Minnesota
WHO SECURED THE BODIES?
WHO THE FUCK DIDN'T DO THEIR FUCKING JOB?!?
SHIT OH SHIT SHIT WE ARE FUCKED WE ARE
Family: Contested Carlyle-Hock
Population [Family: Carlyle]: ~~1~~ 0
Population [Serf - Active Duty Carlyle Forces]: 231
Population [Hock - Active Duty Hock Forces]: data unavailable
I SECURED MY AREA!
I CLEARED MY ZONE!
SO FUCKED WE ARE SO
FUCKING NEW GUY FUCKING FUCKED UP!
I-I-I-DIDN'T... I...
SHE'S A FUCKING LAZARUS, RED, SHE'S GONNA GET UP, RIGHT?
THAT'S WHAT SHE'S GONNA DO. SHE'S GONNA GET UP.
RIGHT?

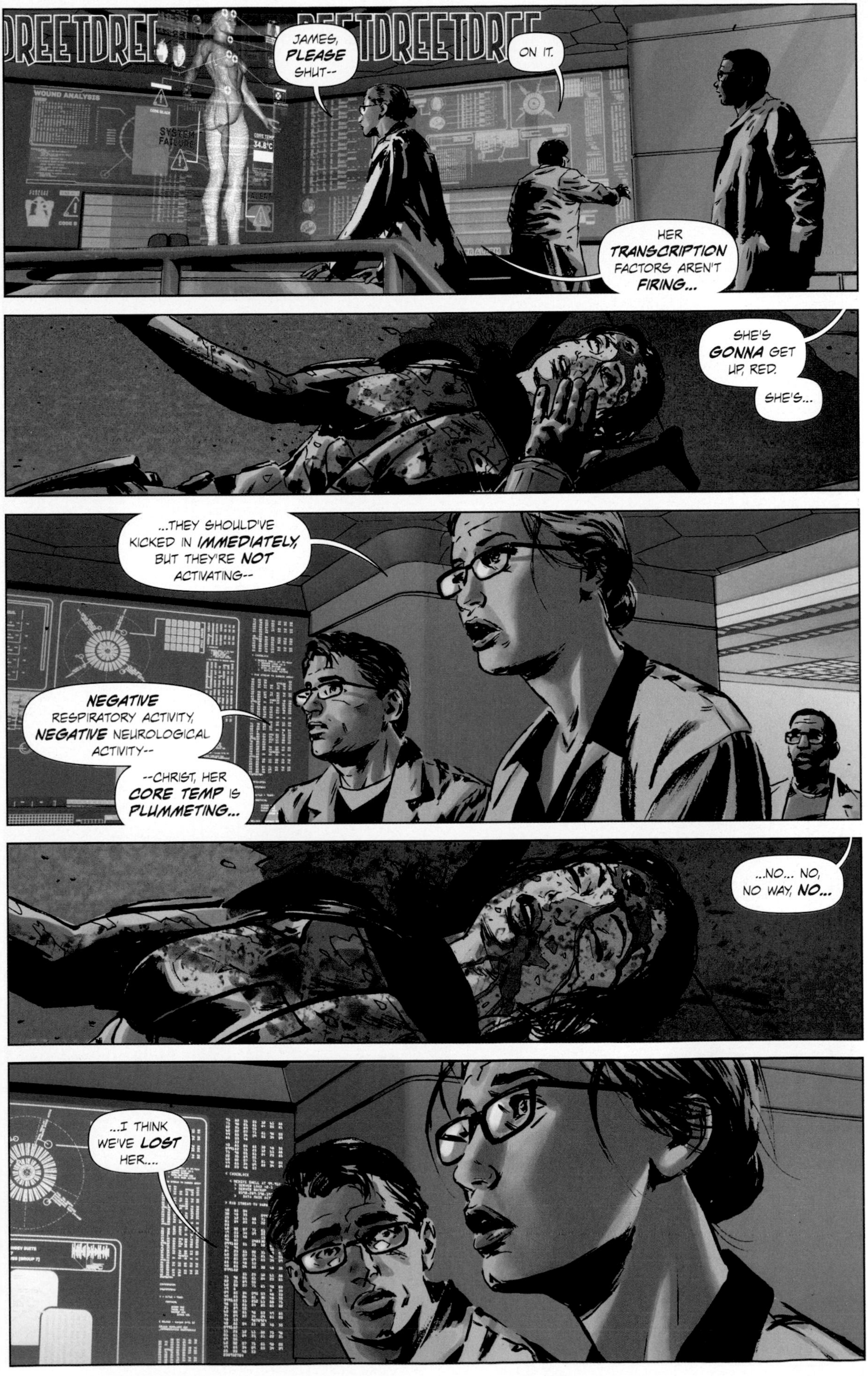

DREETDREE
JAMES, PLEASE SHUT--
ON IT.
HER TRANSCRIPTION FACTORS AREN'T FIRING...
SHE'S GONNA GET UP, RED.
SHE'S...
...THEY SHOULD'VE KICKED IN IMMEDIATELY, BUT THEY'RE NOT ACTIVATING--
NEGATIVE RESPIRATORY ACTIVITY, NEGATIVE NEUROLOGICAL ACTIVITY--
--CHRIST, HER CORE TEMP IS PLUMMETING...
...NO... NO, NO WAY, NO...
...I THINK WE'VE LOST HER...

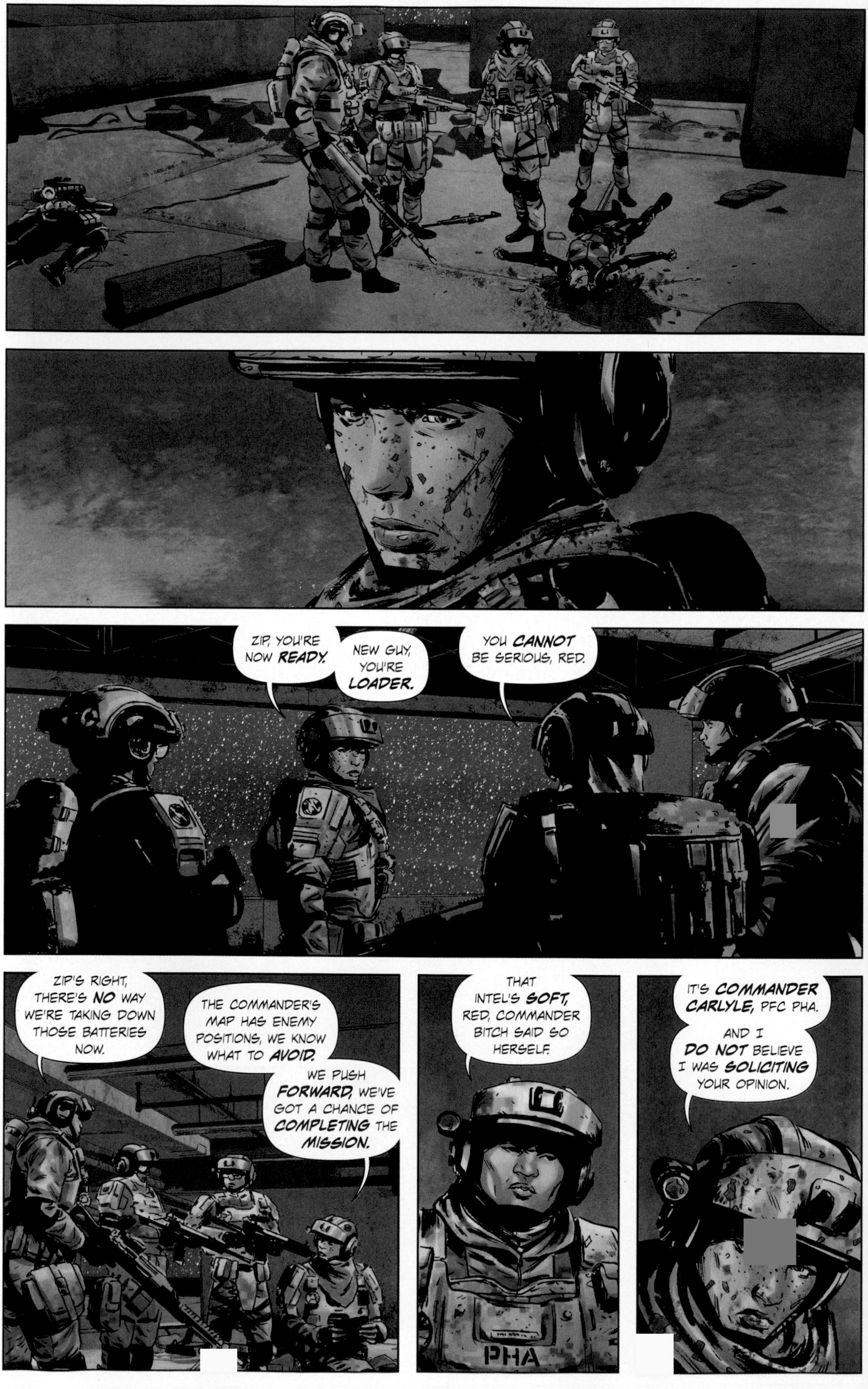
ZIP, YOU'RE NOW **READY.**
NEW GUY, YOU'RE **LOADER.**
YOU **CANNOT** BE SERIOUS, RED.
ZIP'S RIGHT, THERE'S **NO** WAY WE'RE TAKING DOWN THOSE BATTERIES NOW.
THE COMMANDER'S MAP HAS ENEMY POSITIONS, WE KNOW WHAT TO **AVOID.**
WE PUSH **FORWARD,** WE'VE GOT A CHANCE OF **COMPLETING** THE **MISSION.**
THAT INTEL'S **SOFT,** RED, COMMANDER BITCH SAID SO HERSELF.
PHA
IT'S **COMMANDER CARLYLE,** PFC PHA.
AND I **DO NOT** BELIEVE I WAS **SOLICITING** YOUR OPINION.

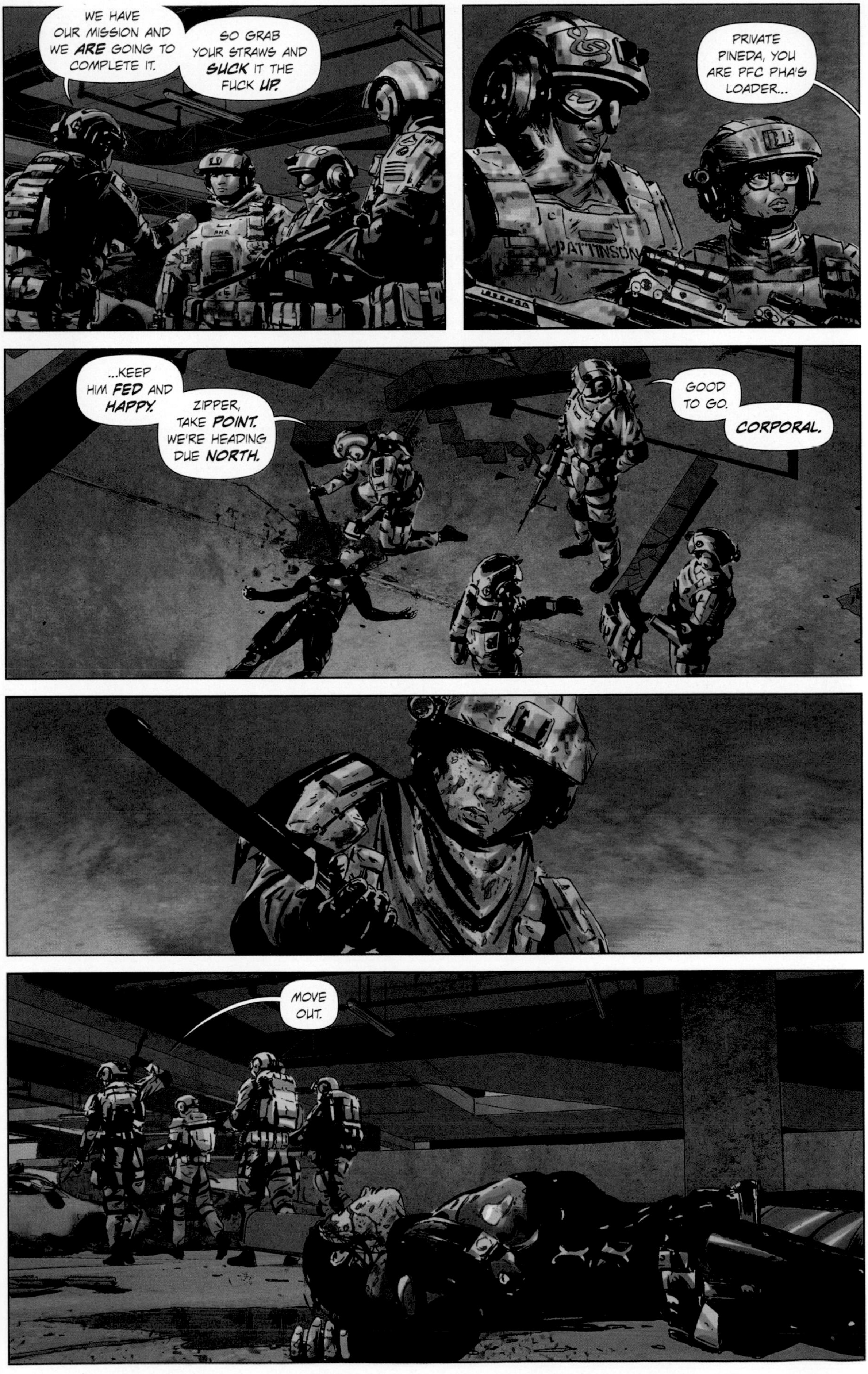
WE HAVE OUR MISSION AND WE ARE GOING TO COMPLETE IT.
SO GRAB YOUR STRAWS AND SUCK IT THE FUCK UP.
PRIVATE PINEDA, YOU ARE PFC PHA'S LOADER...
...KEEP HIM FED AND HAPPY.
ZIPPER, TAKE POINT. WE'RE HEADING DUE NORTH.
GOOD TO GO.
CORPORAL.
MOVE OUT.

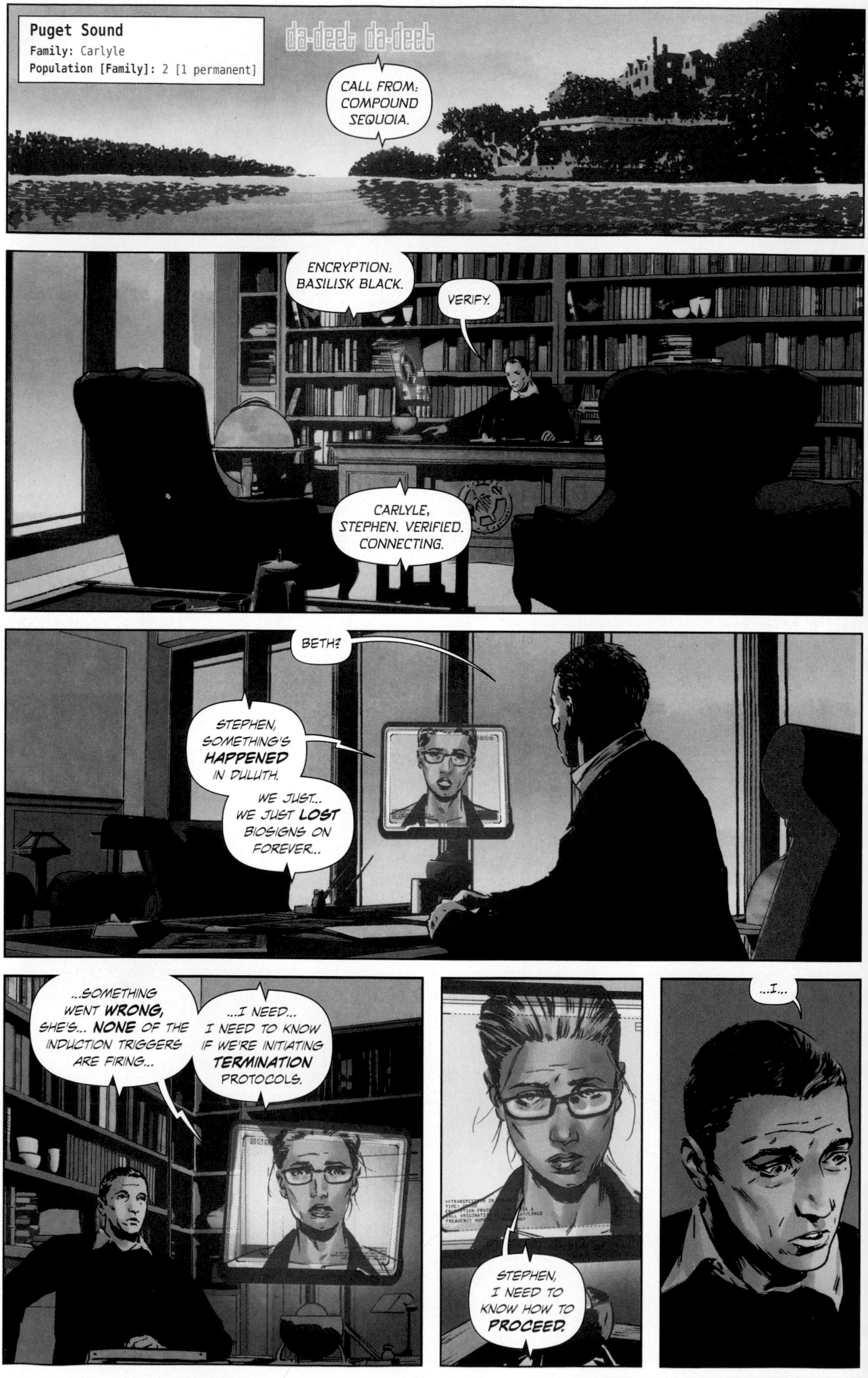
Puget Sound
Family: Carlyle
Population [Family]: 2 [1 permanent]
da-deet da-deet
CALL FROM: COMPOUND SEQUOIA.
ENCRYPTION: BASILISK BLACK.
VERIFY.
CARLYLE, STEPHEN. VERIFIED. CONNECTING.
BETH?
STEPHEN, SOMETHING'S HAPPENED IN DULUTH.
WE JUST... WE JUST LOST BIOSIGNS ON FOREVER...
...SOMETHING WENT WRONG, SHE'S... NONE OF THE INDUCTION TRIGGERS ARE FIRING...
...I NEED... I NEED TO KNOW IF WE'RE INITIATING TERMINATION PROTOCOLS.
STEPHEN, I NEED TO KNOW HOW TO PROCEED.
...I...

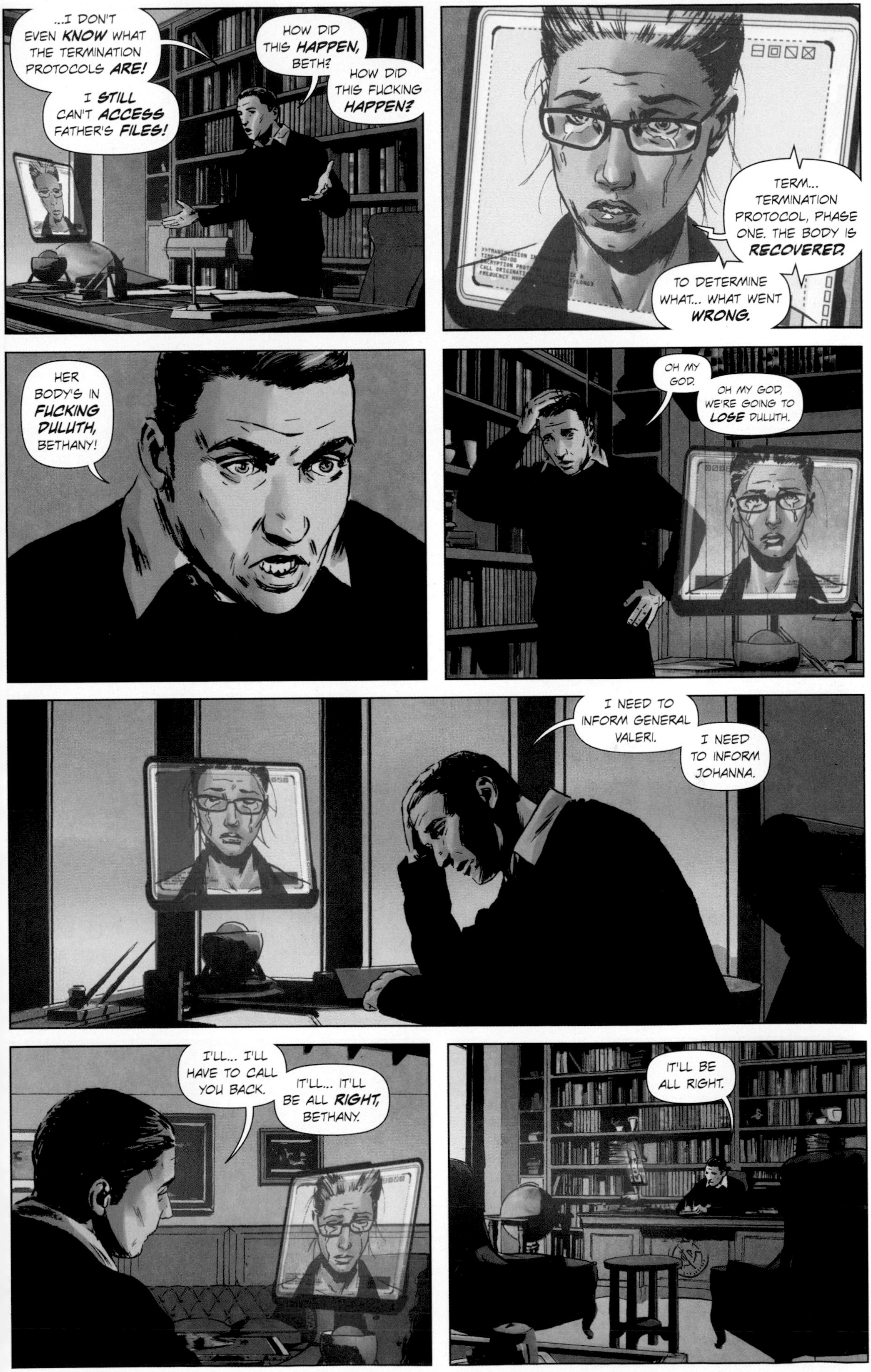
...I DON'T EVEN **KNOW** WHAT THE TERMINATION PROTOCOLS **ARE!**
I **STILL** CAN'T **ACCESS** FATHER'S **FILES!**
HOW DID THIS **HAPPEN,** BETH?
HOW DID THIS FUCKING **HAPPEN?**
TERM... TERMINATION PROTOCOL, PHASE ONE. THE BODY IS **RECOVERED.**
TO DETERMINE WHAT... WHAT WENT **WRONG.**
HER BODY'S IN **FUCKING DULUTH,** BETHANY!
OH MY GOD.
OH MY GOD, WE'RE GOING TO **LOSE** DULUTH.
I NEED TO INFORM GENERAL VALERI.
I NEED TO INFORM JOHANNA.
I'LL... I'LL HAVE TO CALL YOU BACK.
IT'LL... IT'LL BE ALL **RIGHT,** BETHANY.
IT'LL BE ALL RIGHT.

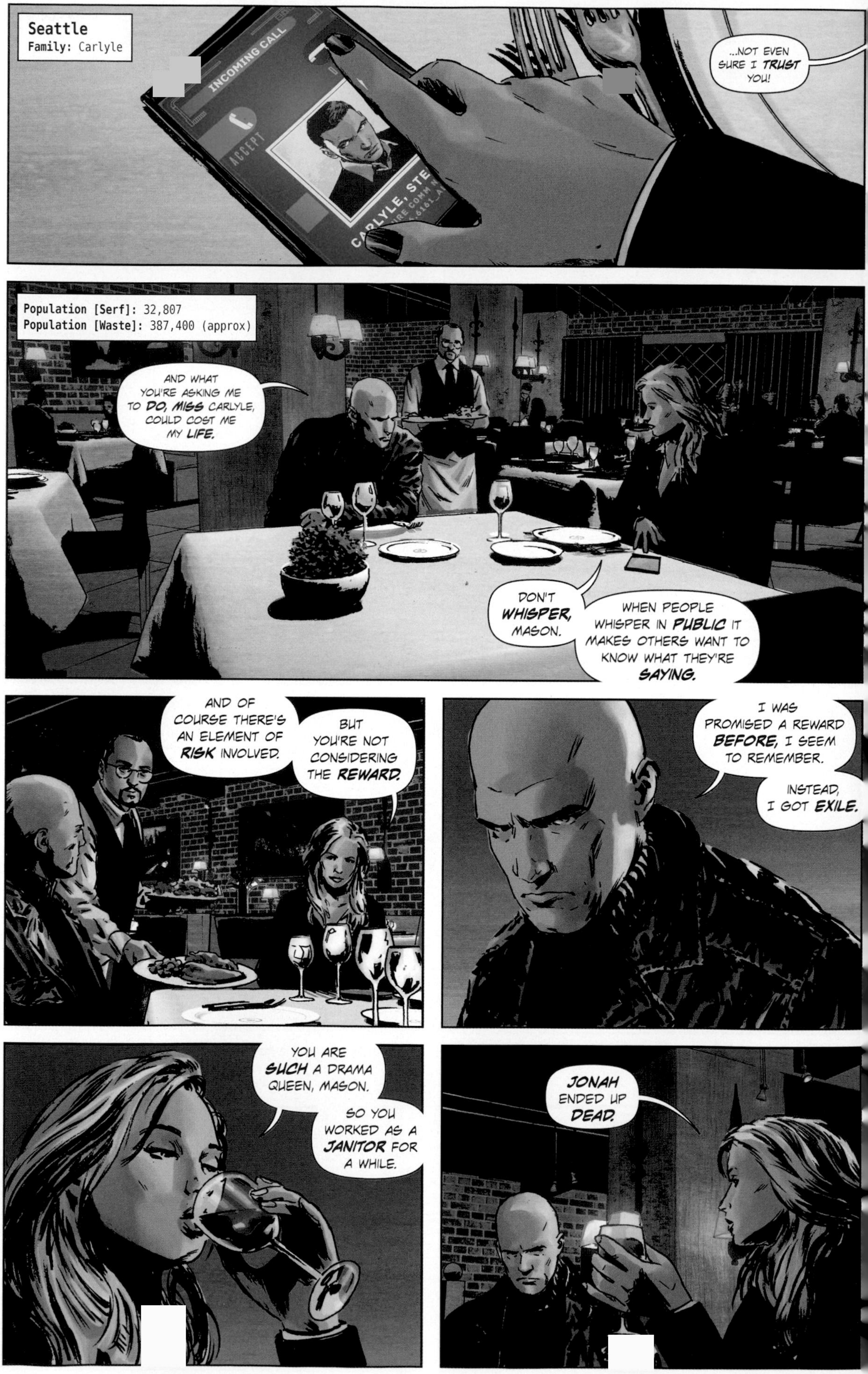
Seattle
Family: Carlyle
INCOMING CALL
ACCEPT
...NOT EVEN SURE I TRUST YOU!
Population [Serf]: 32,807
Population [Waste]: 387,400 (approx)
AND WHAT YOU'RE ASKING ME TO DO, MISS CARLYLE, COULD COST ME MY LIFE.
DON'T WHISPER, MASON.
WHEN PEOPLE WHISPER IN PUBLIC IT MAKES OTHERS WANT TO KNOW WHAT THEY'RE SAYING.
AND OF COURSE THERE'S AN ELEMENT OF RISK INVOLVED.
BUT YOU'RE NOT CONSIDERING THE REWARD.
I WAS PROMISED A REWARD BEFORE, I SEEM TO REMEMBER.
INSTEAD, I GOT EXILE.
YOU ARE SUCH A DRAMA QUEEN, MASON.
SO YOU WORKED AS A JANITOR FOR A WHILE.
JONAH ENDED UP DEAD.

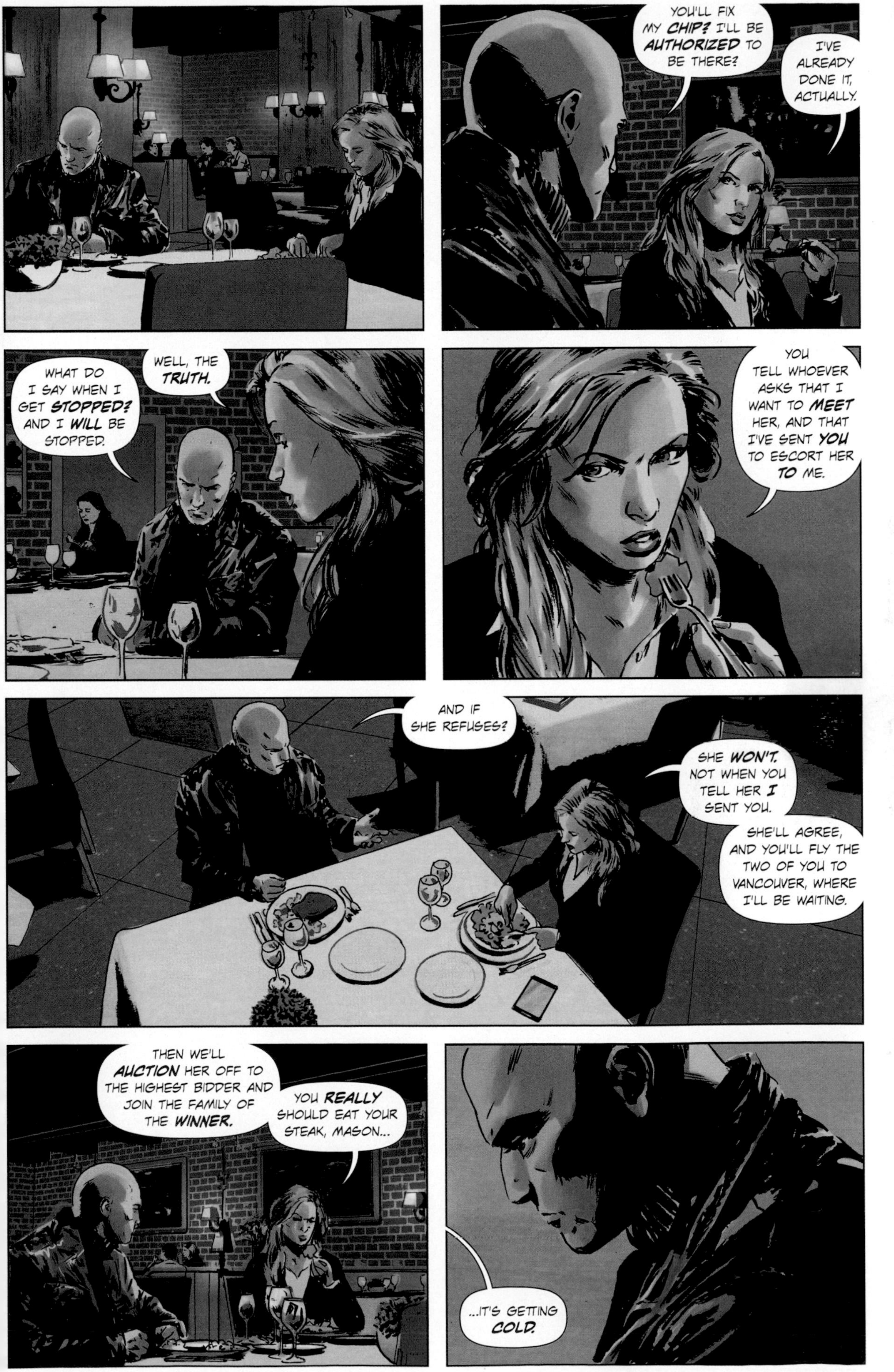
YOU'LL FIX MY CHIP? I'LL BE AUTHORIZED TO BE THERE?
I'VE ALREADY DONE IT, ACTUALLY.
WHAT DO I SAY WHEN I GET STOPPED? AND I WILL BE STOPPED.
WELL, THE TRUTH.
YOU TELL WHOEVER ASKS THAT I WANT TO MEET HER, AND THAT I'VE SENT YOU TO ESCORT HER TO ME.
AND IF SHE REFUSES?
SHE WON'T. NOT WHEN YOU TELL HER I SENT YOU.
SHE'LL AGREE, AND YOU'LL FLY THE TWO OF YOU TO VANCOUVER, WHERE I'LL BE WAITING.
THEN WE'LL AUCTION HER OFF TO THE HIGHEST BIDDER AND JOIN THE FAMILY OF THE WINNER.
YOU REALLY SHOULD EAT YOUR STEAK, MASON...
...IT'S GETTING COLD.

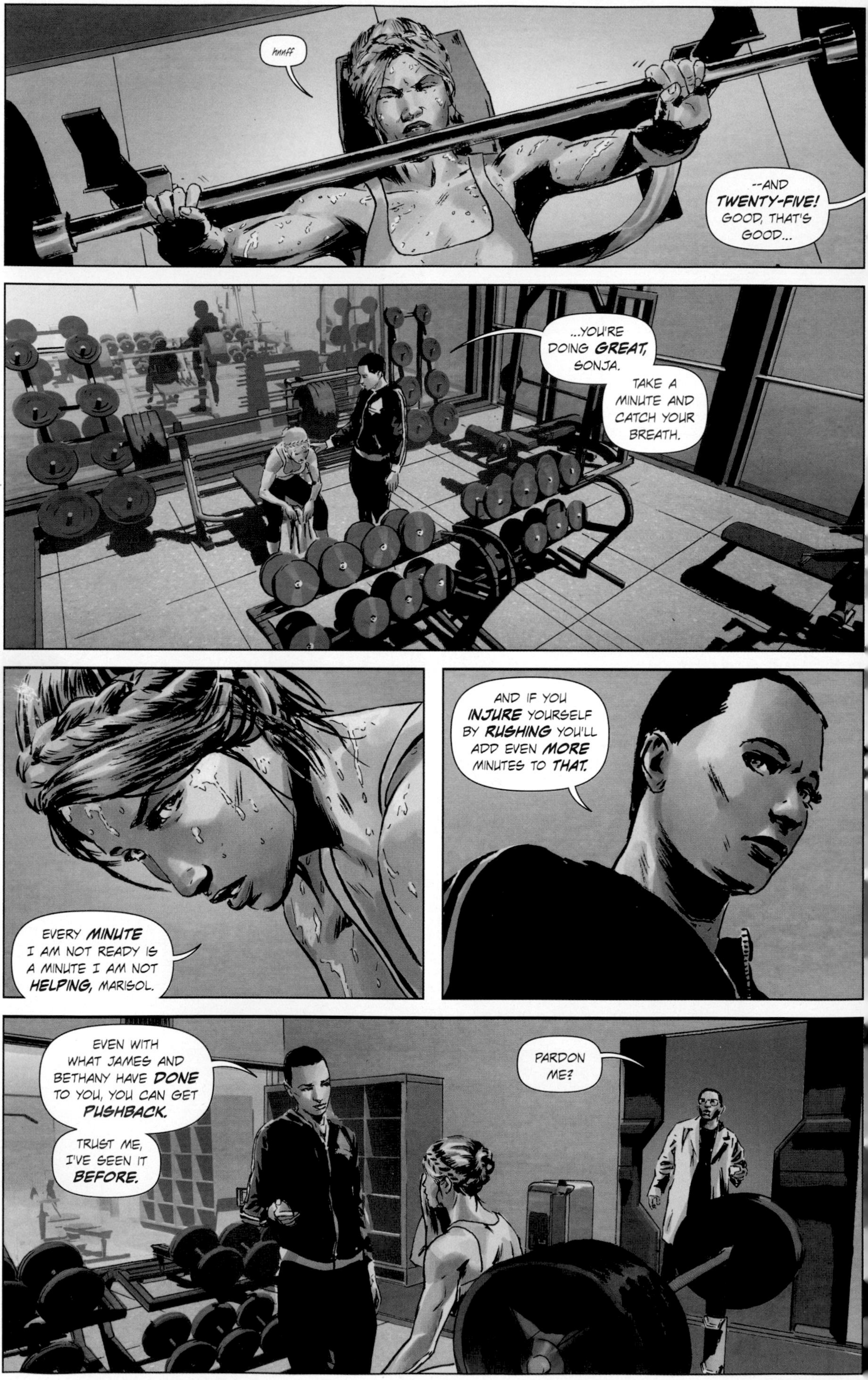
hnnff
--AND TWENTY-FIVE! GOOD, THAT'S GOOD...
...YOU'RE DOING GREAT, SONJA.
TAKE A MINUTE AND CATCH YOUR BREATH.
EVERY MINUTE I AM NOT READY IS A MINUTE I AM NOT HELPING, MARISOL.
AND IF YOU INJURE YOURSELF BY RUSHING YOU'LL ADD EVEN MORE MINUTES TO THAT.
EVEN WITH WHAT JAMES AND BETHANY HAVE DONE TO YOU, YOU CAN GET PUSHBACK.
TRUST ME, I'VE SEEN IT BEFORE.
PARDON ME?

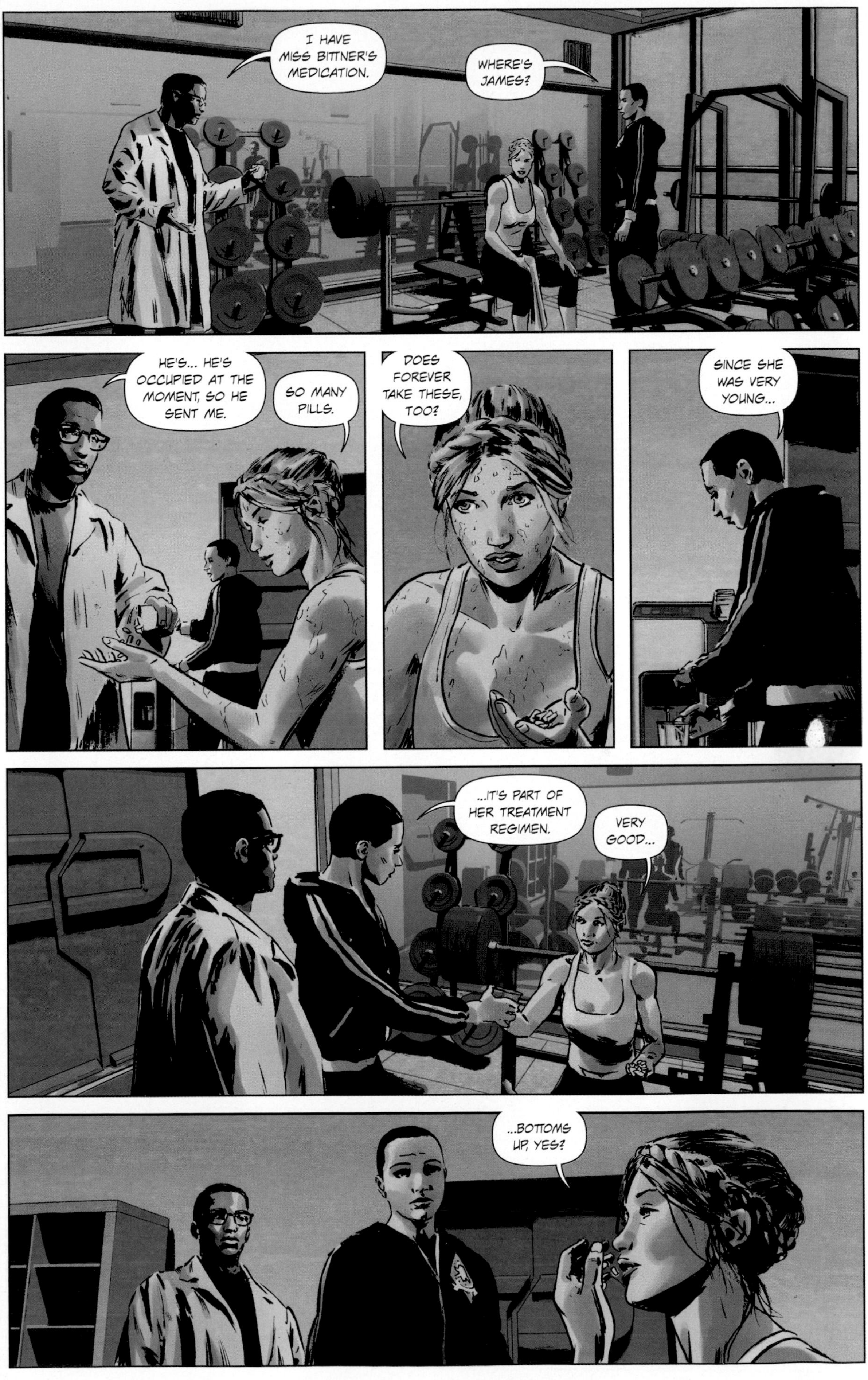
I HAVE MISS BITTNER'S MEDICATION.
WHERE'S JAMES?
HE'S... HE'S OCCUPIED AT THE MOMENT, SO HE SENT ME.
SO MANY PILLS.
DOES FOREVER TAKE THESE, TOO?
SINCE SHE WAS VERY YOUNG...
...IT'S PART OF HER TREATMENT REGIMEN.
VERY GOOD...
...BOTTOMS UP, YES?

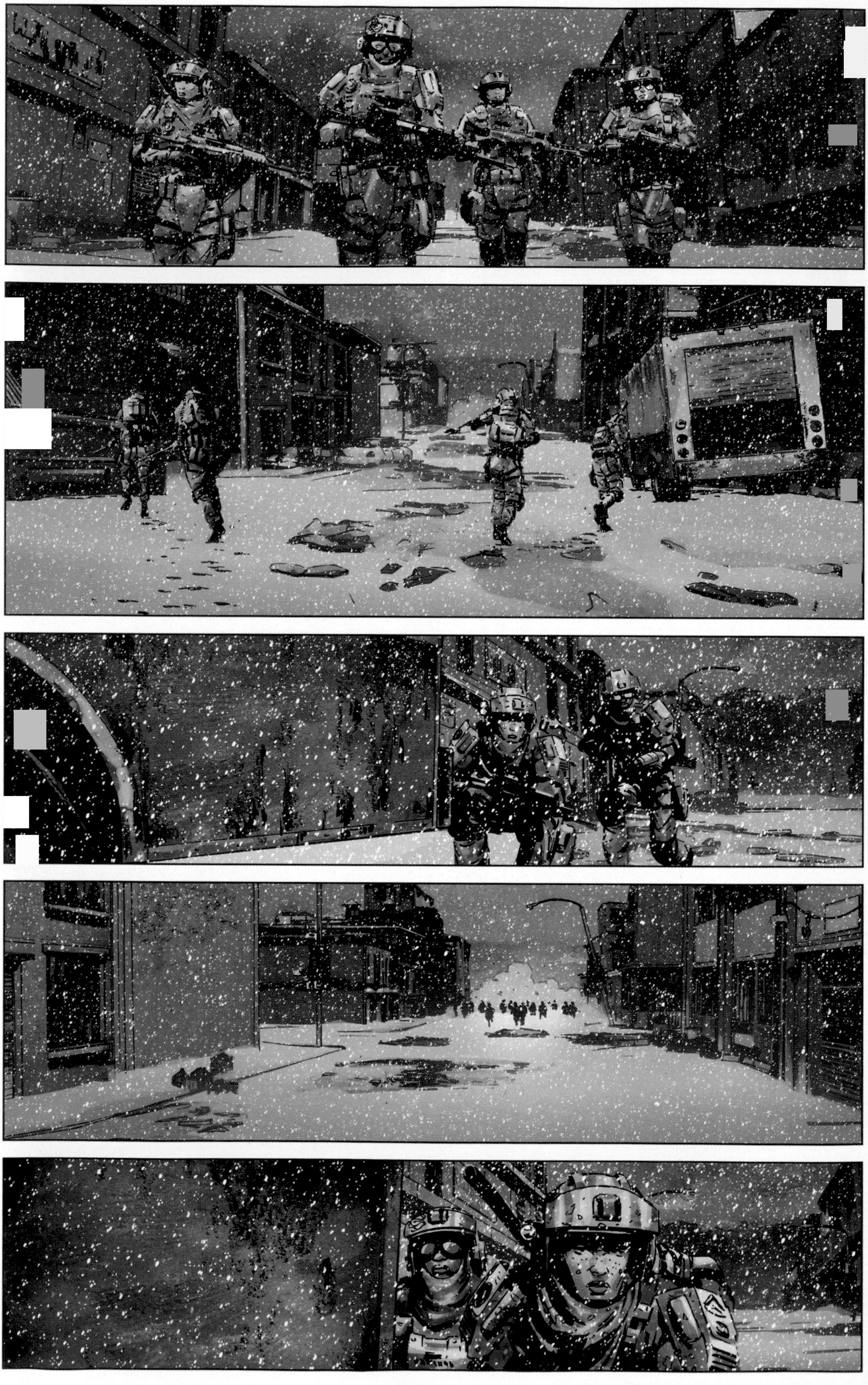

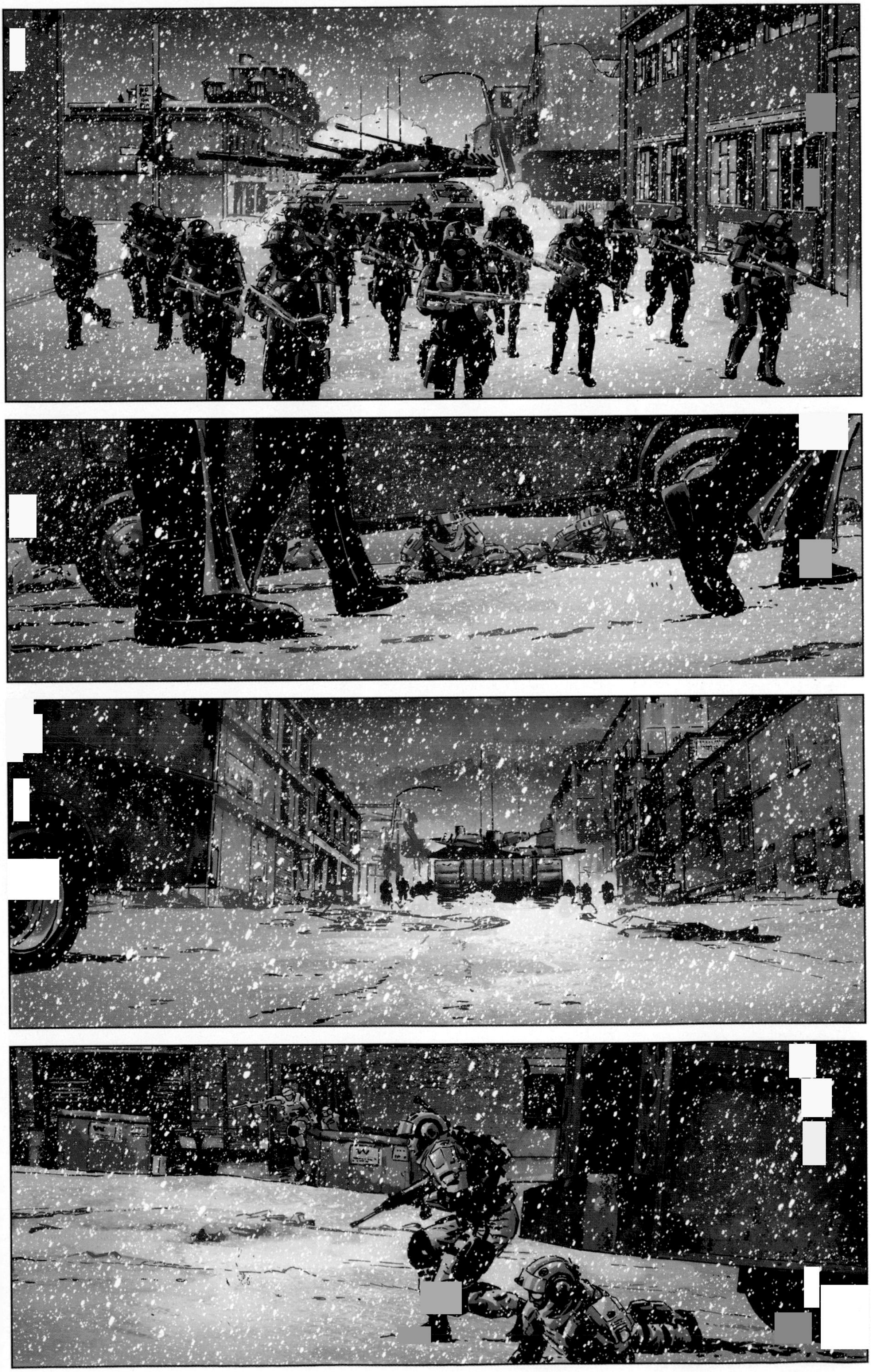

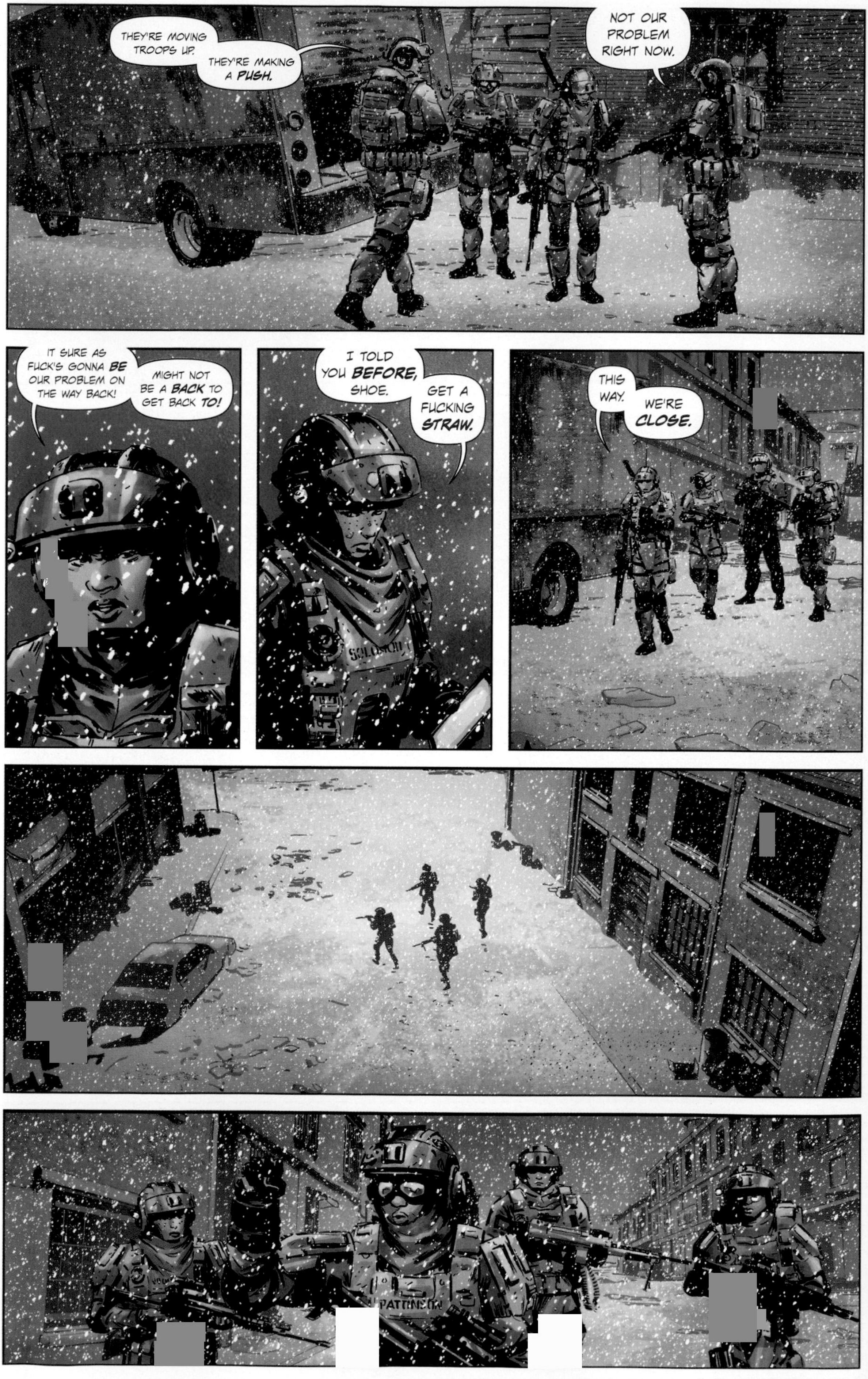
THEY'RE MOVING TROOPS UP.
THEY'RE MAKING A PUSH.
NOT OUR PROBLEM RIGHT NOW.
IT SURE AS FUCK'S GONNA BE OUR PROBLEM ON THE WAY BACK!
MIGHT NOT BE A BACK TO GET BACK TO!
I TOLD YOU BEFORE, SHOE.
GET A FUCKING STRAW.
THIS WAY.
WE'RE CLOSE.

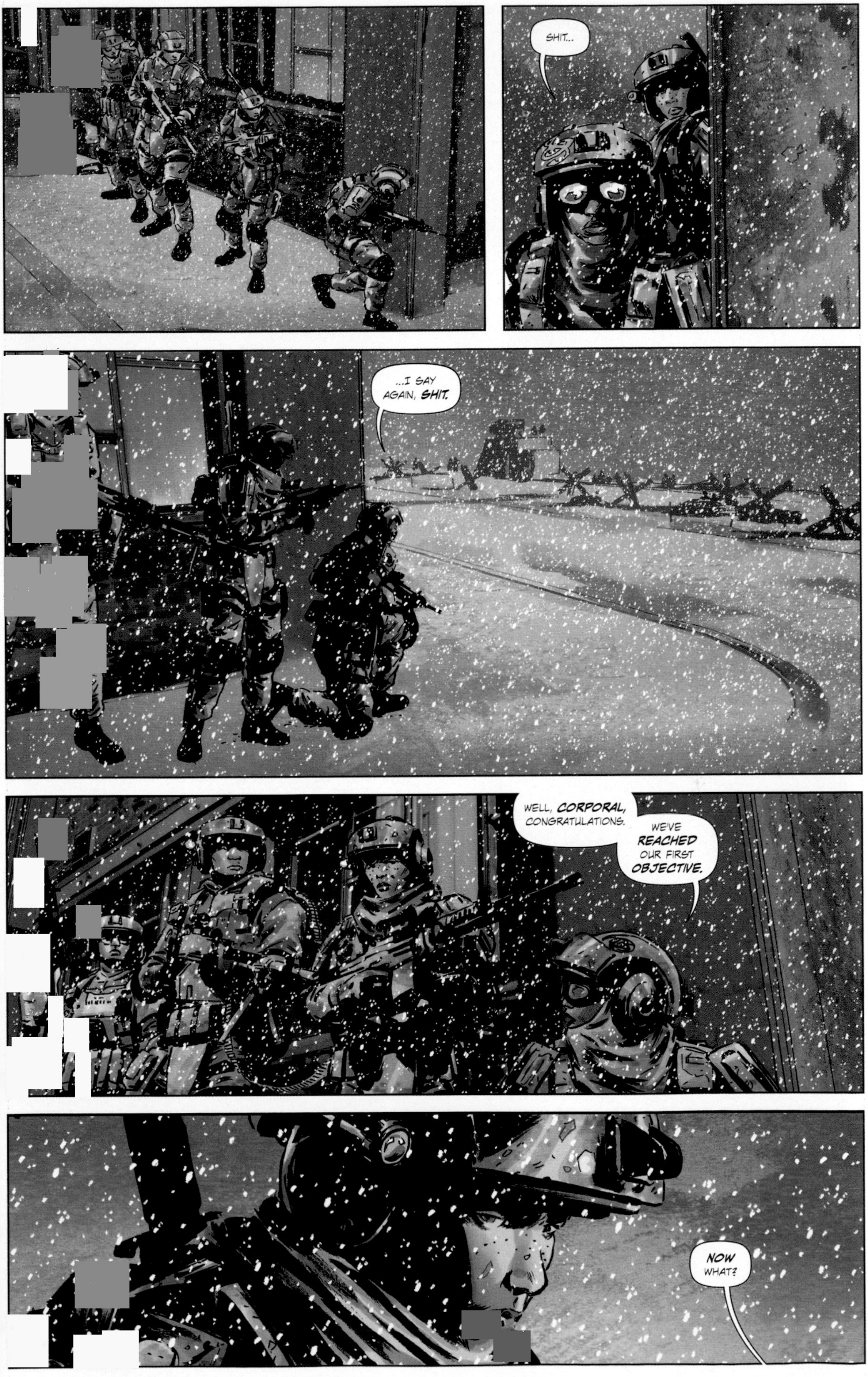
SHIT...
...I SAY AGAIN, SHIT.
WELL, CORPORAL, CONGRATULATIONS.
WE'VE REACHED OUR FIRST OBJECTIVE.
NOW WHAT?

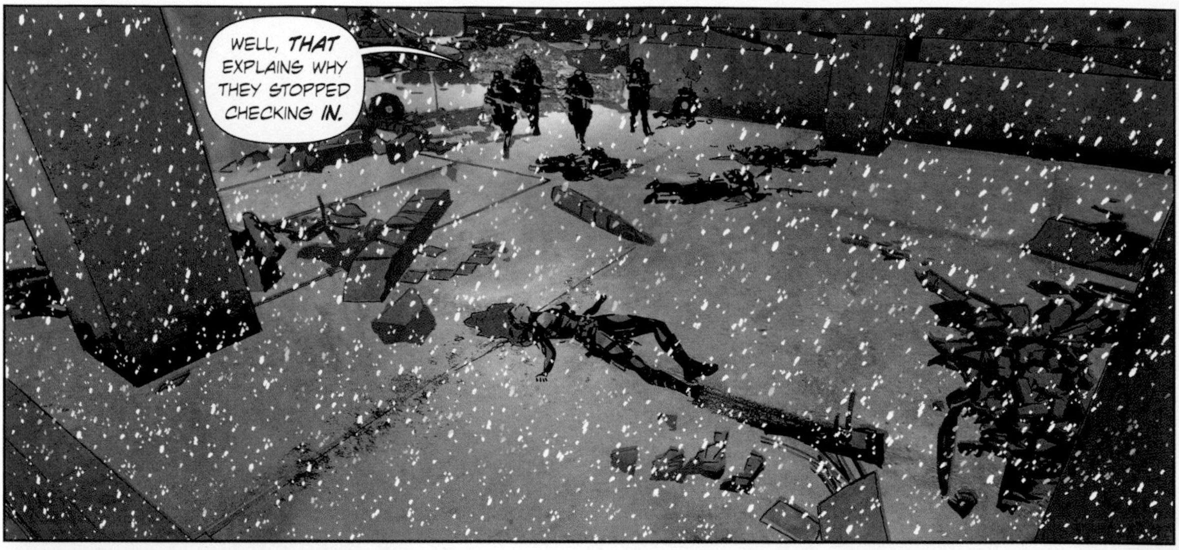
WELL, THAT EXPLAINS WHY THEY STOPPED CHECKING IN.
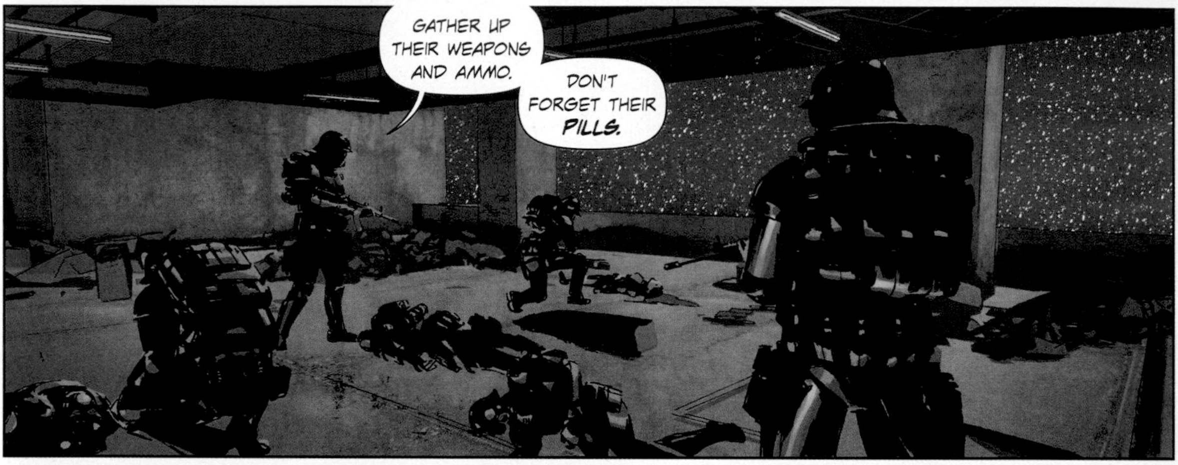
GATHER UP THEIR WEAPONS AND AMMO.
DON'T FORGET THEIR PILLS.
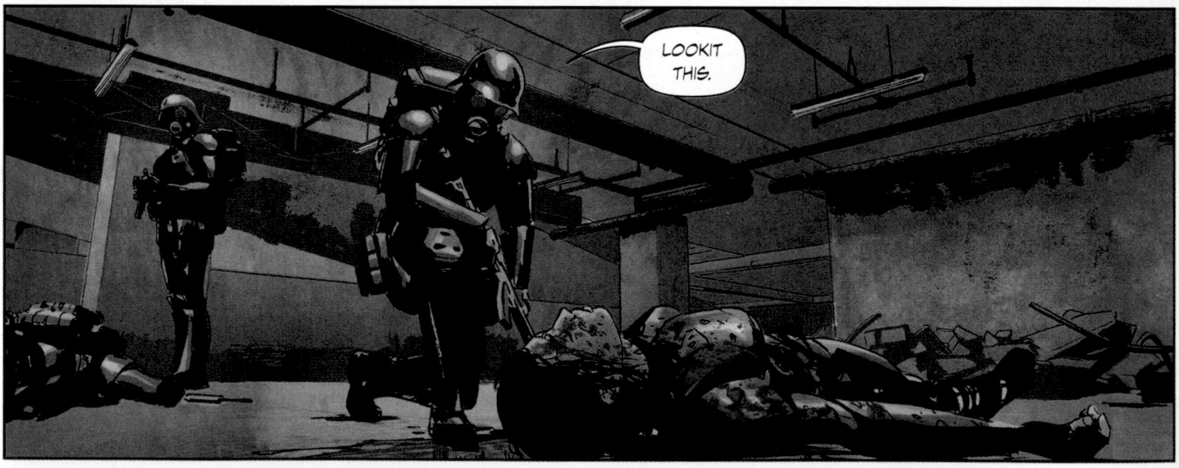
LOOKIT THIS.
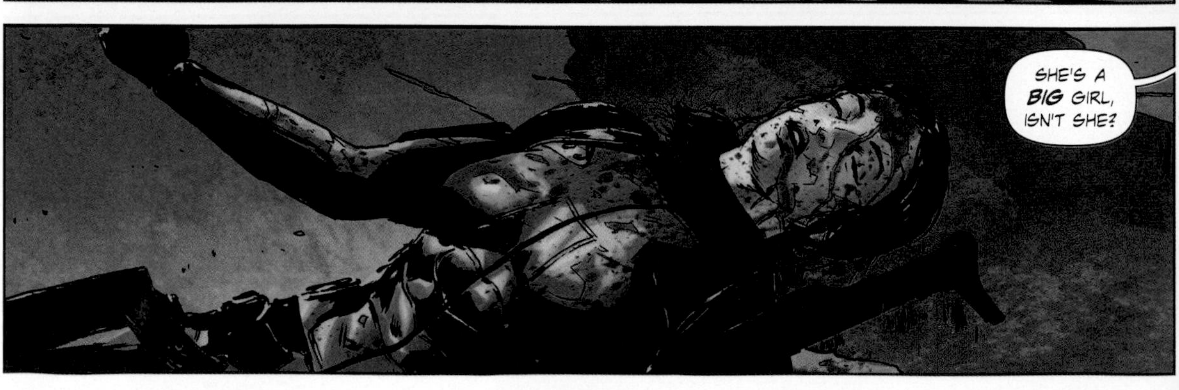
SHE'S A BIG GIRL, ISN'T SHE?

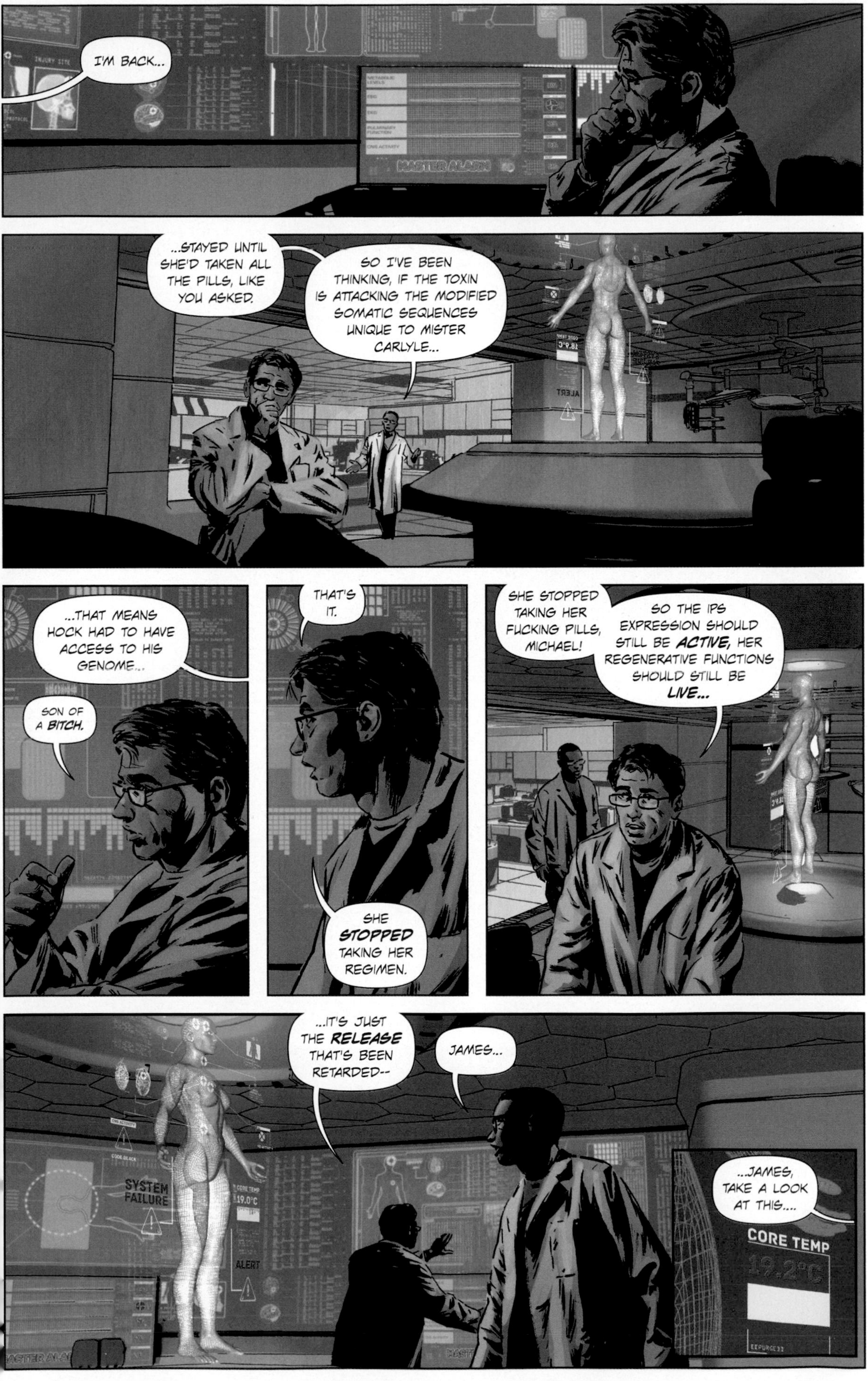
I'M BACK...
...STAYED UNTIL SHE'D TAKEN ALL THE PILLS, LIKE YOU ASKED.
SO I'VE BEEN THINKING, IF THE TOXIN IS ATTACKING THE MODIFIED SOMATIC SEQUENCES UNIQUE TO MISTER CARLYLE...
...THAT MEANS HOCK HAD TO HAVE ACCESS TO HIS GENOME...
SON OF A BITCH.
THAT'S IT.
SHE STOPPED TAKING HER REGIMEN.
SHE STOPPED TAKING HER FUCKING PILLS, MICHAEL!
SO THE IPS EXPRESSION SHOULD STILL BE ACTIVE, HER REGENERATIVE FUNCTIONS SHOULD STILL BE LIVE...
...IT'S JUST THE RELEASE THAT'S BEEN RETARDED--
JAMES...
...JAMES, TAKE A LOOK AT THIS....
SYSTEM FAILURE
ALERT
CORE TEMP
19.0°C
CORE TEMP
19.2°C

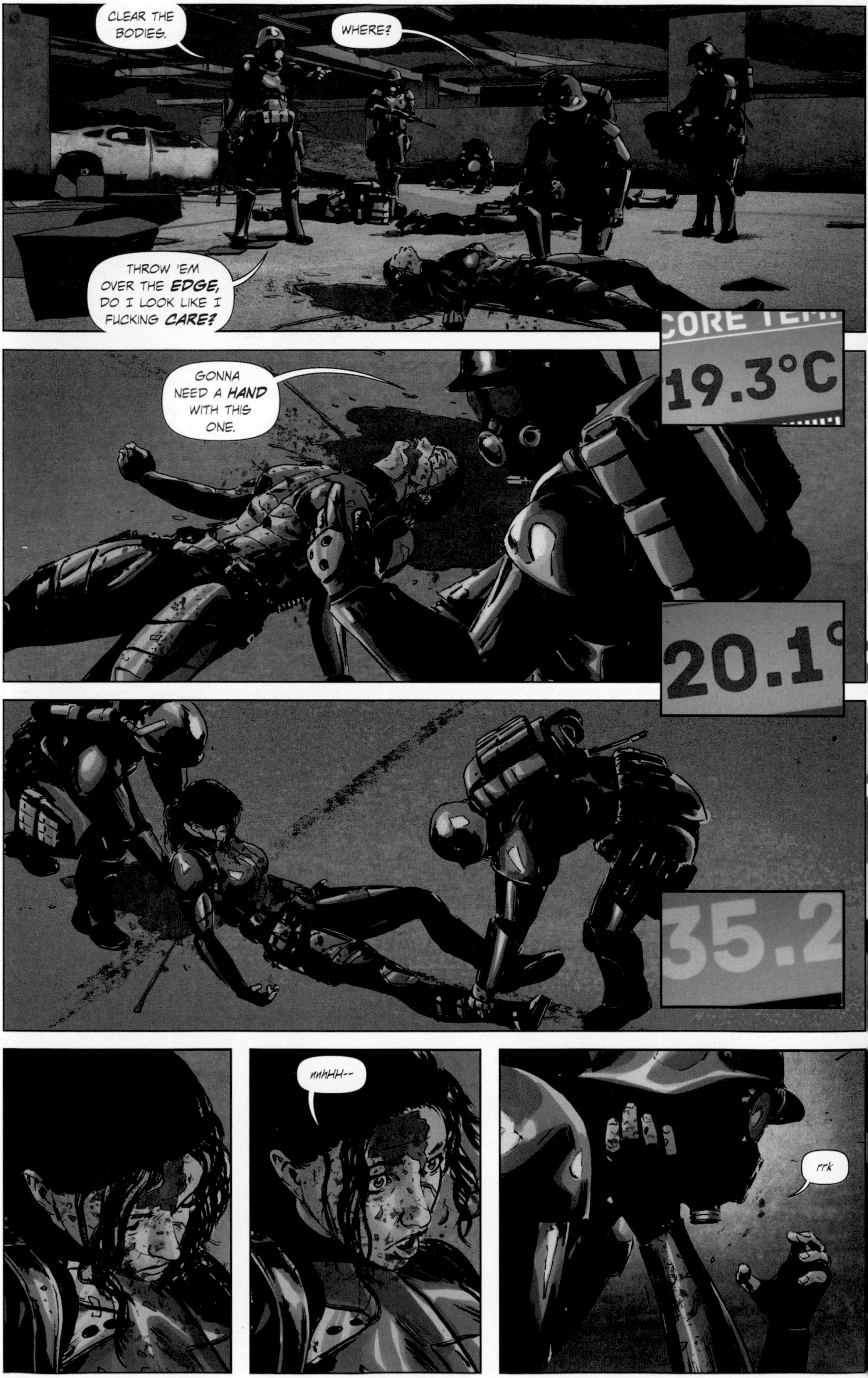
CLEAR THE BODIES.
WHERE?
THROW 'EM OVER THE EDGE, DO I LOOK LIKE I FUCKING CARE?
CORE TEM
19.3°C
GONNA NEED A HAND WITH THIS ONE.
20.1°
35.2
nnhHH--
rrk

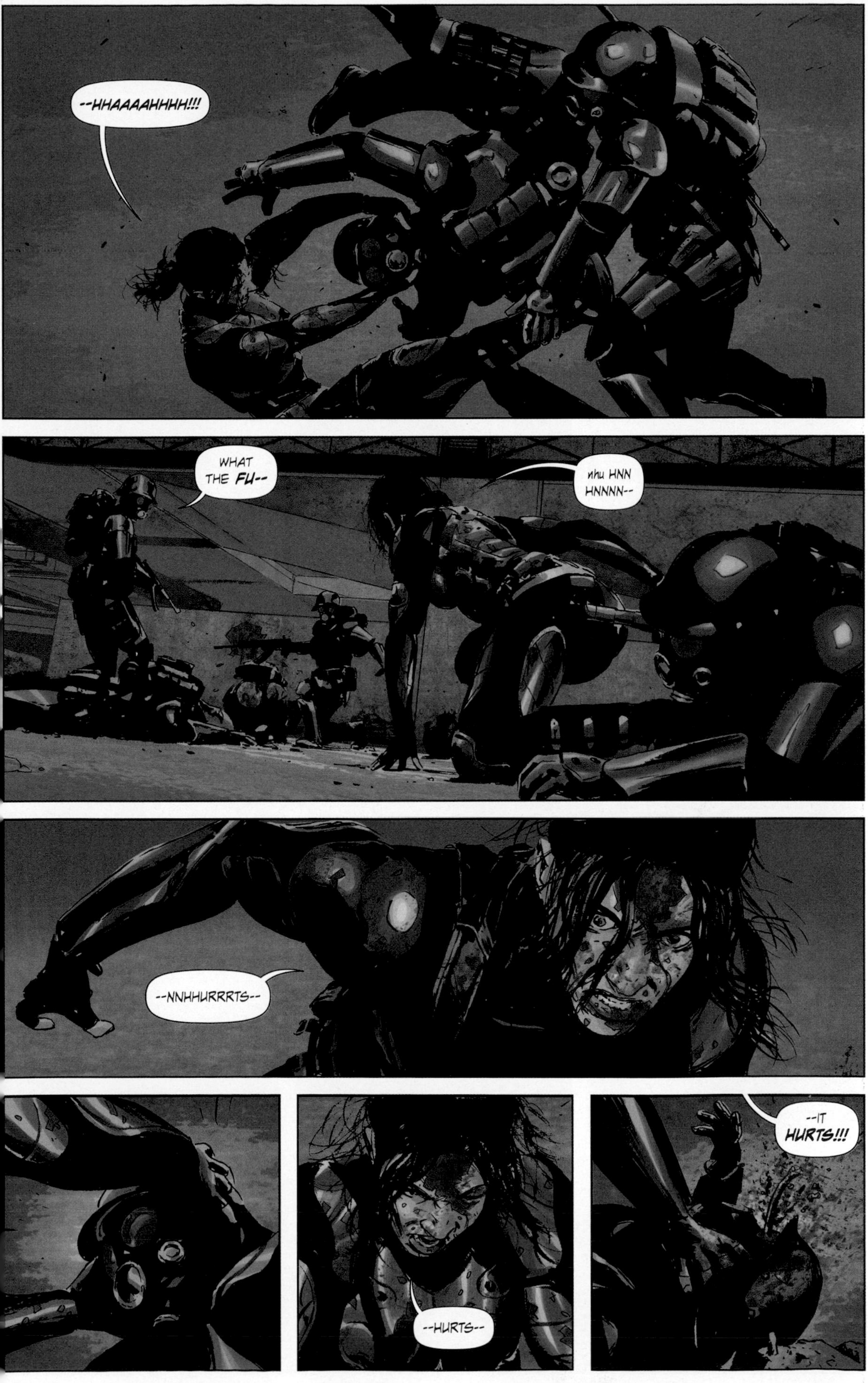
--HHAAAAHHHH!!!
WHAT THE FU--
nhu HNN HNNNN--
--NNHHURRRTS--
--HURTS--
--IT HURTS!!!

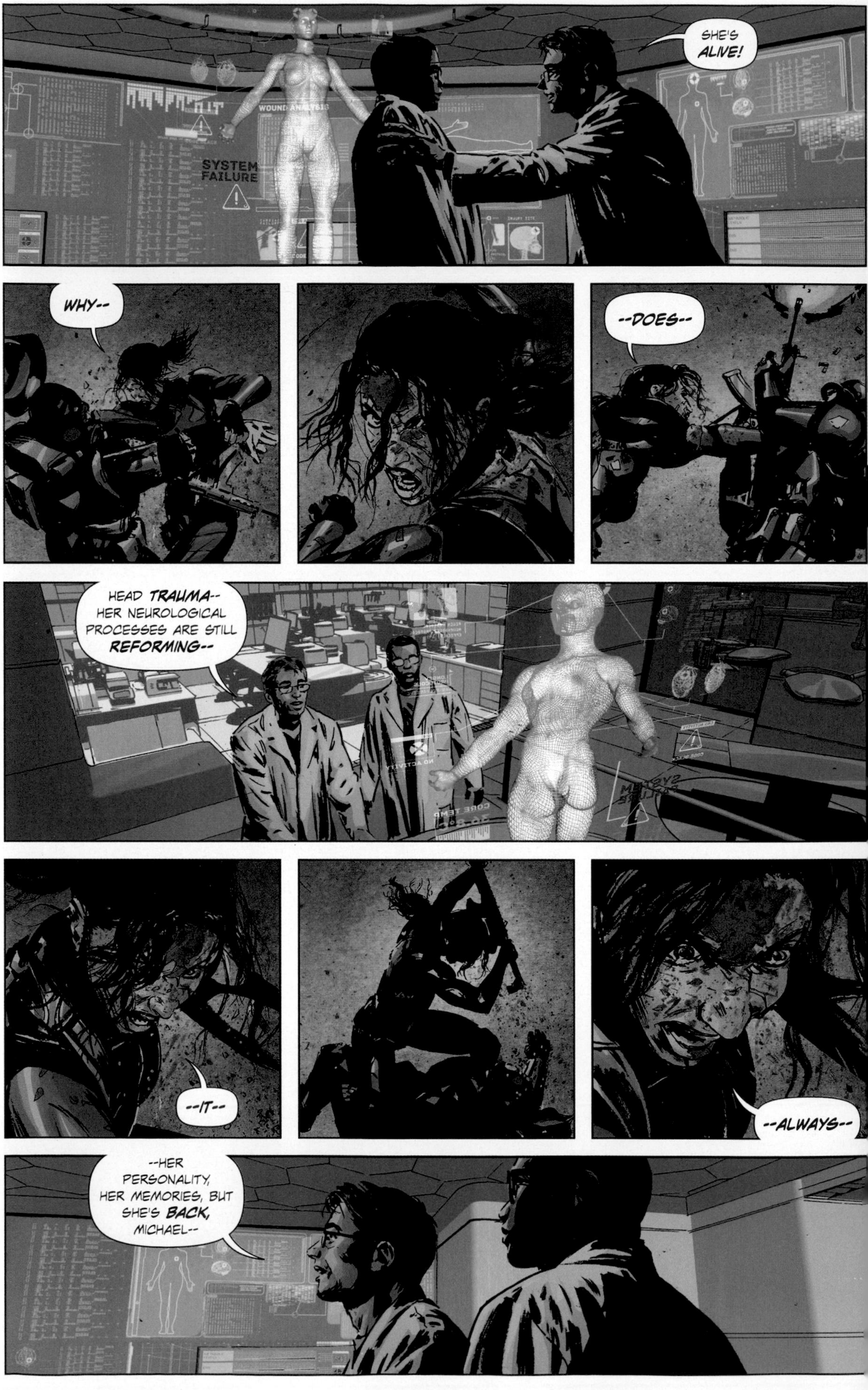
SHE'S ALIVE!
WOUND ANALYSIS
SYSTEM FAILURE
WHY--
--DOES--
HEAD TRAUMA-- HER NEUROLOGICAL PROCESSES ARE STILL REFORMING--
--IT--
--ALWAYS--
--HER PERSONALITY, HER MEMORIES, BUT SHE'S BACK, MICHAEL--

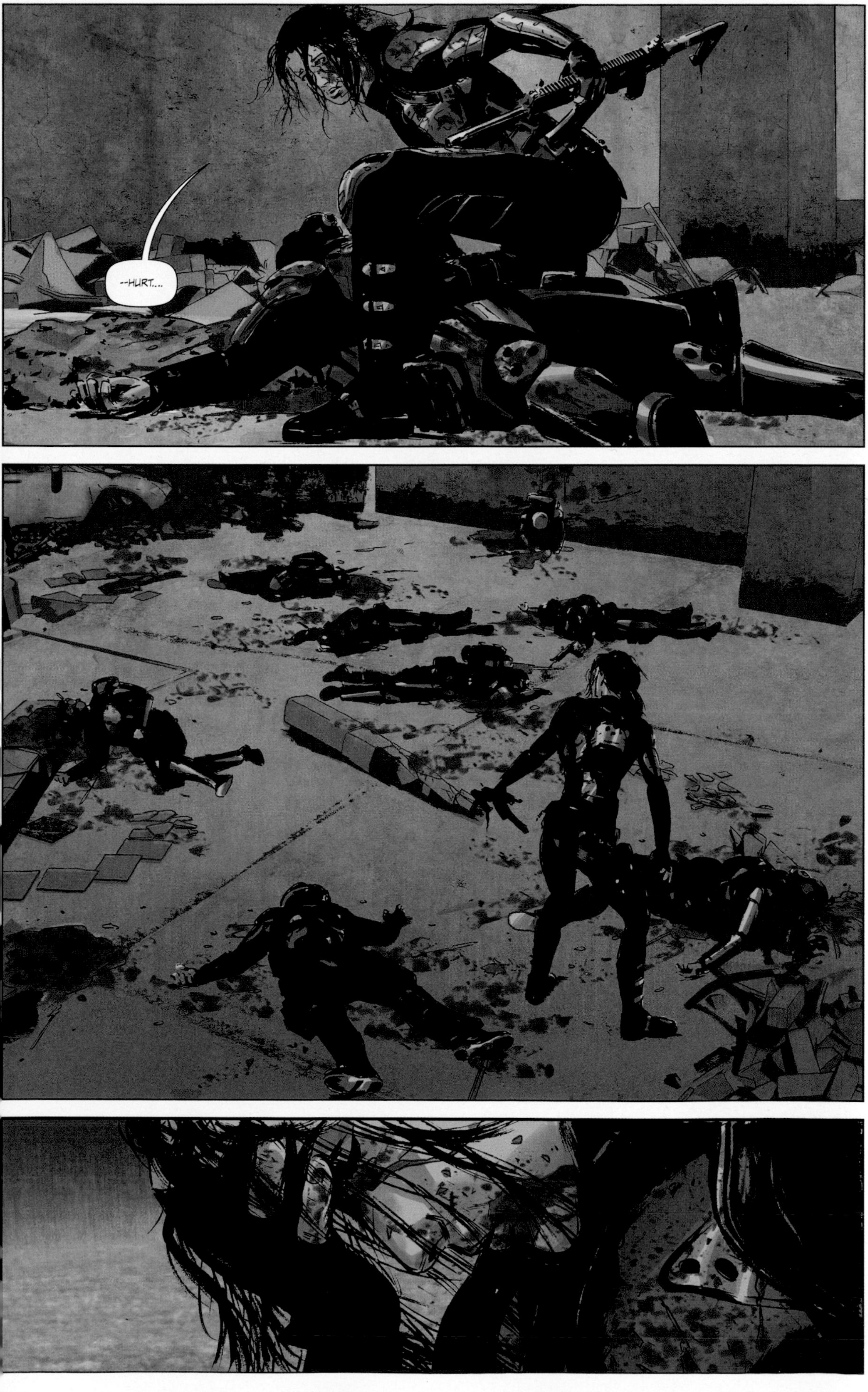
--HURT...

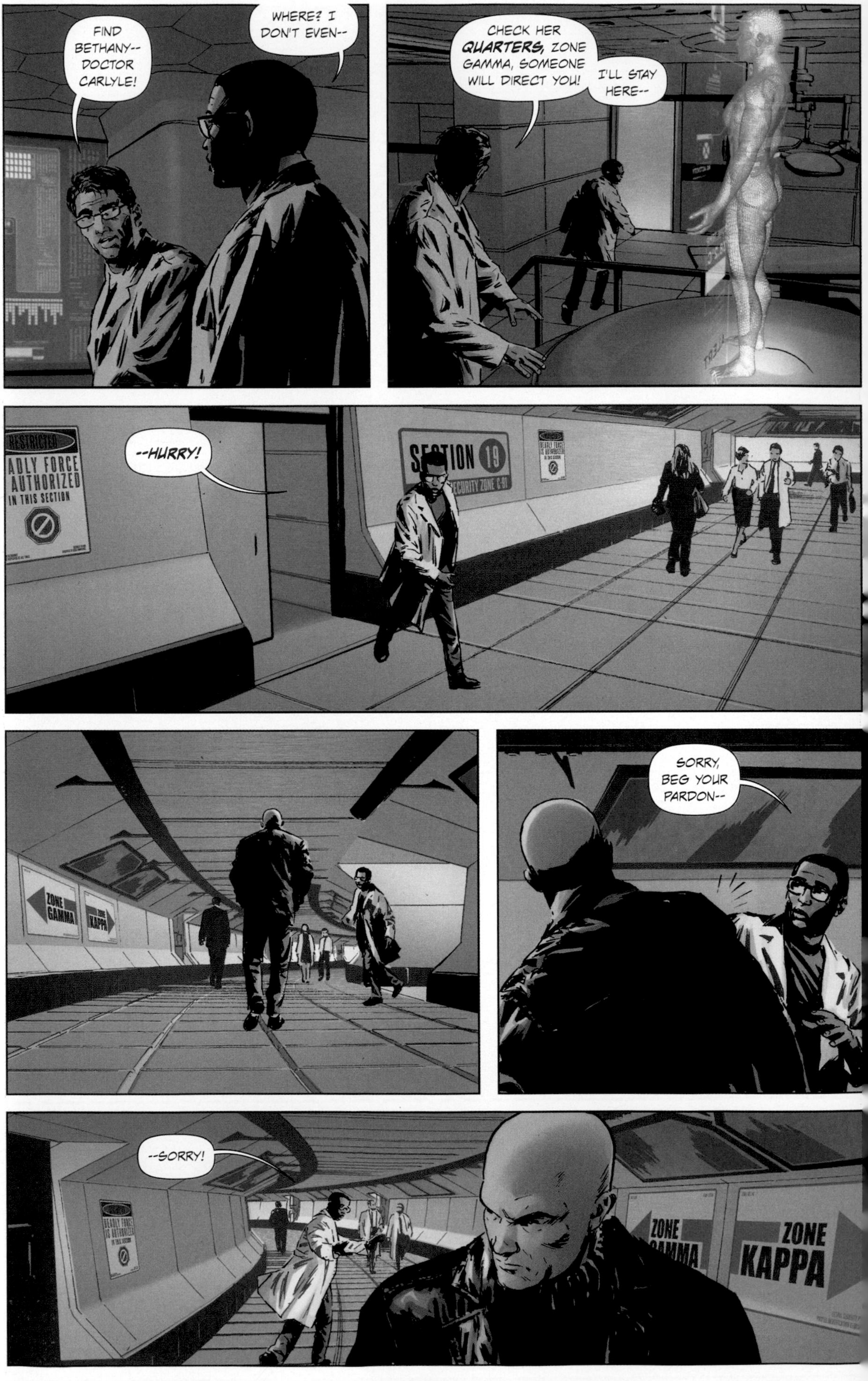
FIND BETHANY-- DOCTOR CARLYLE!
WHERE? I DON'T EVEN--
CHECK HER **QUARTERS,** ZONE GAMMA, SOMEONE WILL DIRECT YOU!
I'LL STAY HERE--
RESTRICTED
ADLY FORCE AUTHORIZED IN THIS SECTION
--HURRY!
SECTION 19
SECURITY ZONE C-91
ZONE GAMMA
ZONE KAPPA
SORRY, BEG YOUR PARDON--
--SORRY!
ZONE GAMMA
ZONE KAPPA

CARLYLE

ODERINT DUM METUANT

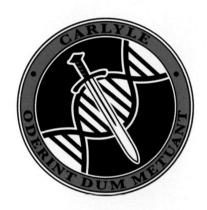

OWEN FREEMAN

POISON
CHAPTER FOUR

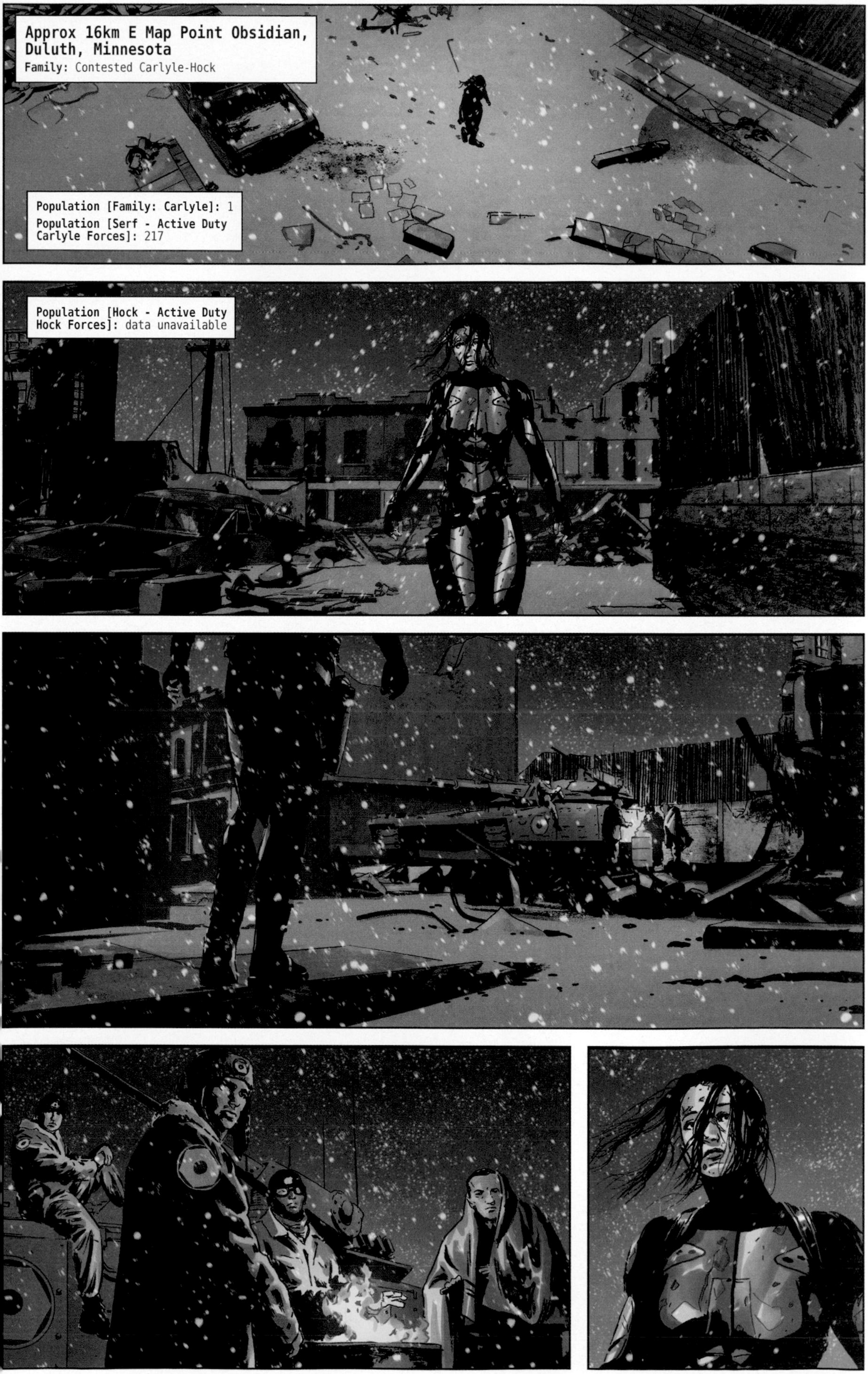

Approx 16km E Map Point Obsidian, Duluth, Minnesota
Family: Contested Carlyle-Hock
Population [Family: Carlyle]: 1
Population [Serf - Active Duty Carlyle Forces]: 217
Population [Hock - Active Duty Hock Forces]: data unavailable

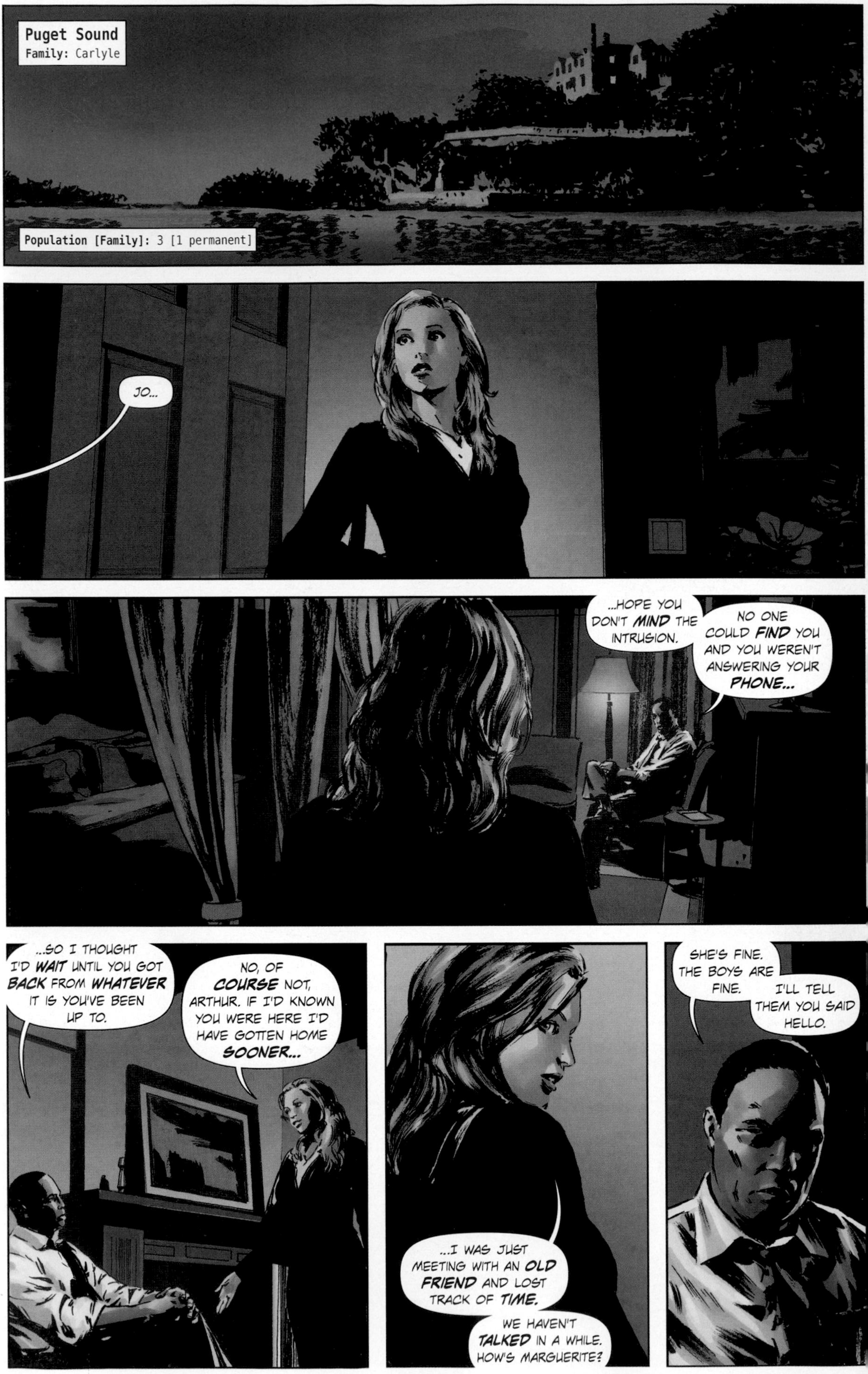

Puget Sound
Family: Carlyle
Population [Family]: 3 [1 permanent]
JO...
...HOPE YOU DON'T MIND THE INTRUSION.
NO ONE COULD FIND YOU AND YOU WEREN'T ANSWERING YOUR PHONE...
...SO I THOUGHT I'D WAIT UNTIL YOU GOT BACK FROM WHATEVER IT IS YOU'VE BEEN UP TO.
NO, OF COURSE NOT, ARTHUR. IF I'D KNOWN YOU WERE HERE I'D HAVE GOTTEN HOME SOONER...
...I WAS JUST MEETING WITH AN OLD FRIEND AND LOST TRACK OF TIME.
WE HAVEN'T TALKED IN A WHILE. HOW'S MARGUERITE?
SHE'S FINE. THE BOYS ARE FINE.
I'LL TELL THEM YOU SAID HELLO.

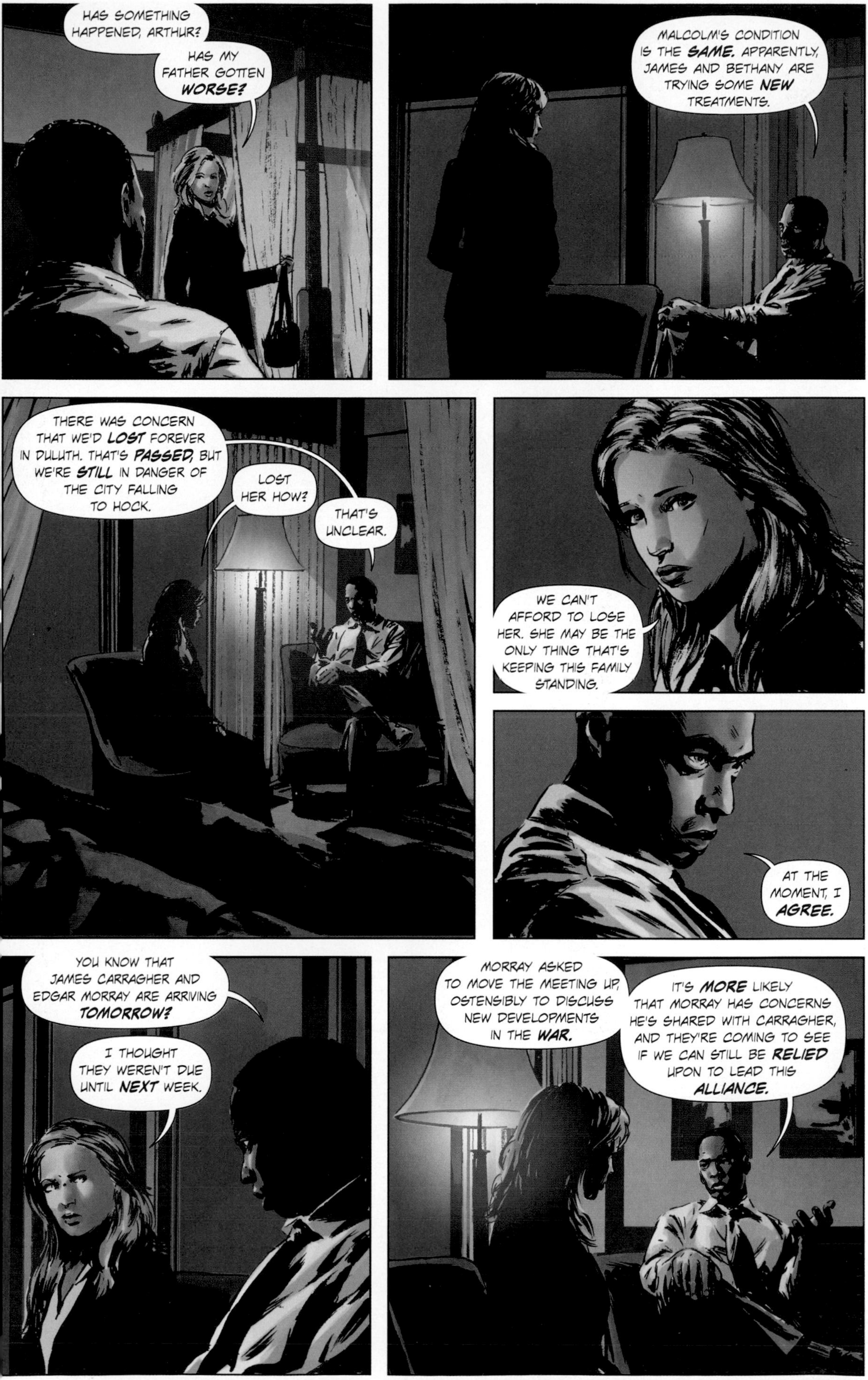
HAS SOMETHING HAPPENED, ARTHUR?
HAS MY FATHER GOTTEN WORSE?
MALCOLM'S CONDITION IS THE SAME. APPARENTLY, JAMES AND BETHANY ARE TRYING SOME NEW TREATMENTS.
THERE WAS CONCERN THAT WE'D LOST FOREVER IN DULUTH. THAT'S PASSED, BUT WE'RE STILL IN DANGER OF THE CITY FALLING TO HOCK.
LOST HER HOW?
THAT'S UNCLEAR.
WE CAN'T AFFORD TO LOSE HER. SHE MAY BE THE ONLY THING THAT'S KEEPING THIS FAMILY STANDING.
AT THE MOMENT, I AGREE.
YOU KNOW THAT JAMES CARRAGHER AND EDGAR MORRAY ARE ARRIVING TOMORROW?
I THOUGHT THEY WEREN'T DUE UNTIL NEXT WEEK.
MORRAY ASKED TO MOVE THE MEETING UP, OSTENSIBLY TO DISCUSS NEW DEVELOPMENTS IN THE WAR.
IT'S MORE LIKELY THAT MORRAY HAS CONCERNS HE'S SHARED WITH CARRAGHER, AND THEY'RE COMING TO SEE IF WE CAN STILL BE RELIED UPON TO LEAD THIS ALLIANCE.

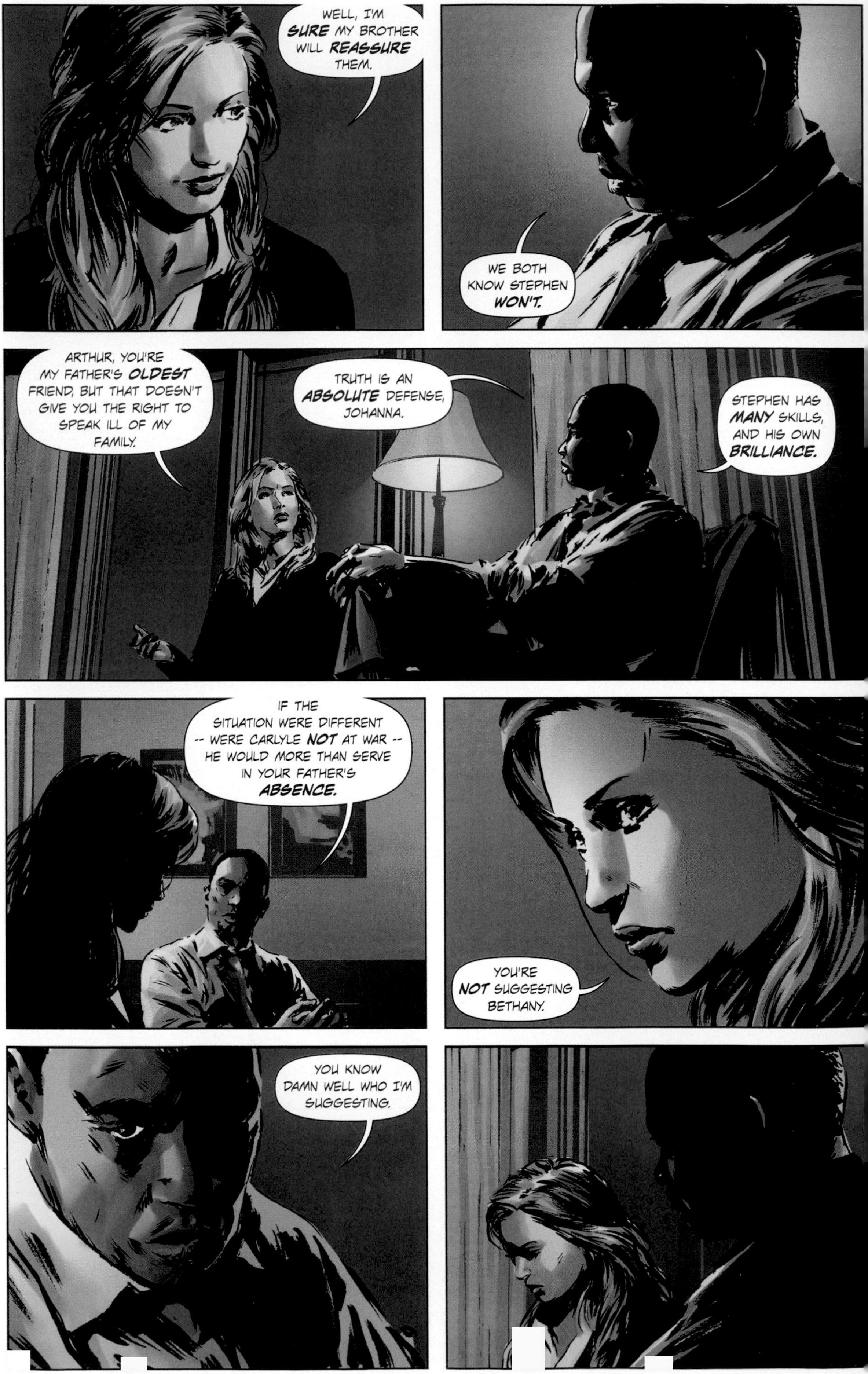
WELL, I'M SURE MY BROTHER WILL REASSURE THEM.
WE BOTH KNOW STEPHEN WON'T.
ARTHUR, YOU'RE MY FATHER'S OLDEST FRIEND, BUT THAT DOESN'T GIVE YOU THE RIGHT TO SPEAK ILL OF MY FAMILY.
TRUTH IS AN ABSOLUTE DEFENSE, JOHANNA.
STEPHEN HAS MANY SKILLS, AND HIS OWN BRILLIANCE.
IF THE SITUATION WERE DIFFERENT -- WERE CARLYLE NOT AT WAR -- HE WOULD MORE THAN SERVE IN YOUR FATHER'S ABSENCE.
YOU'RE NOT SUGGESTING BETHANY.
YOU KNOW DAMN WELL WHO I'M SUGGESTING.

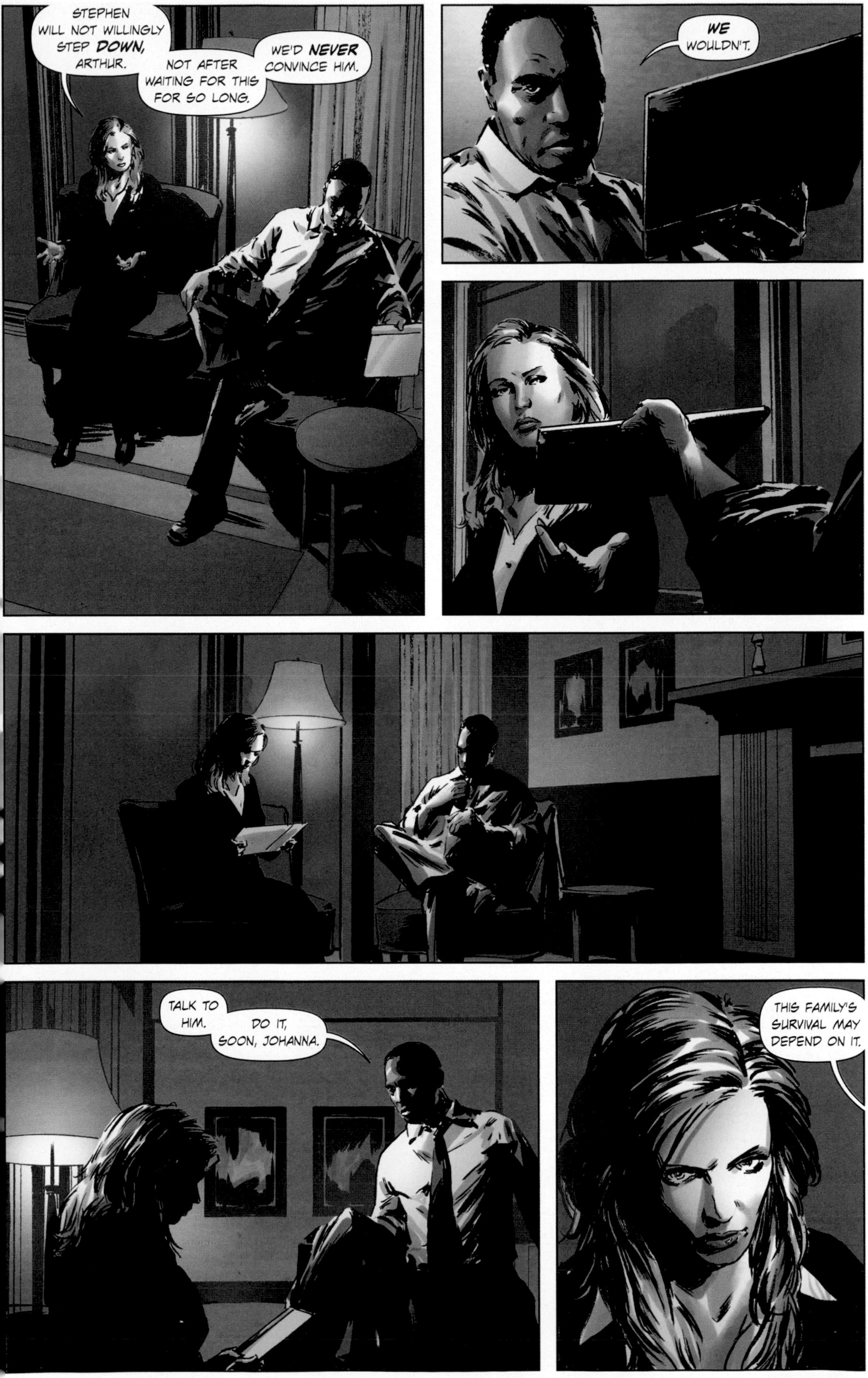
STEPHEN WILL NOT WILLINGLY STEP DOWN, ARTHUR.
NOT AFTER WAITING FOR THIS FOR SO LONG.
WE'D NEVER CONVINCE HIM.
WE WOULDN'T.
TALK TO HIM.
DO IT, SOON, JOHANNA.
THIS FAMILY'S SURVIVAL MAY DEPEND ON IT.

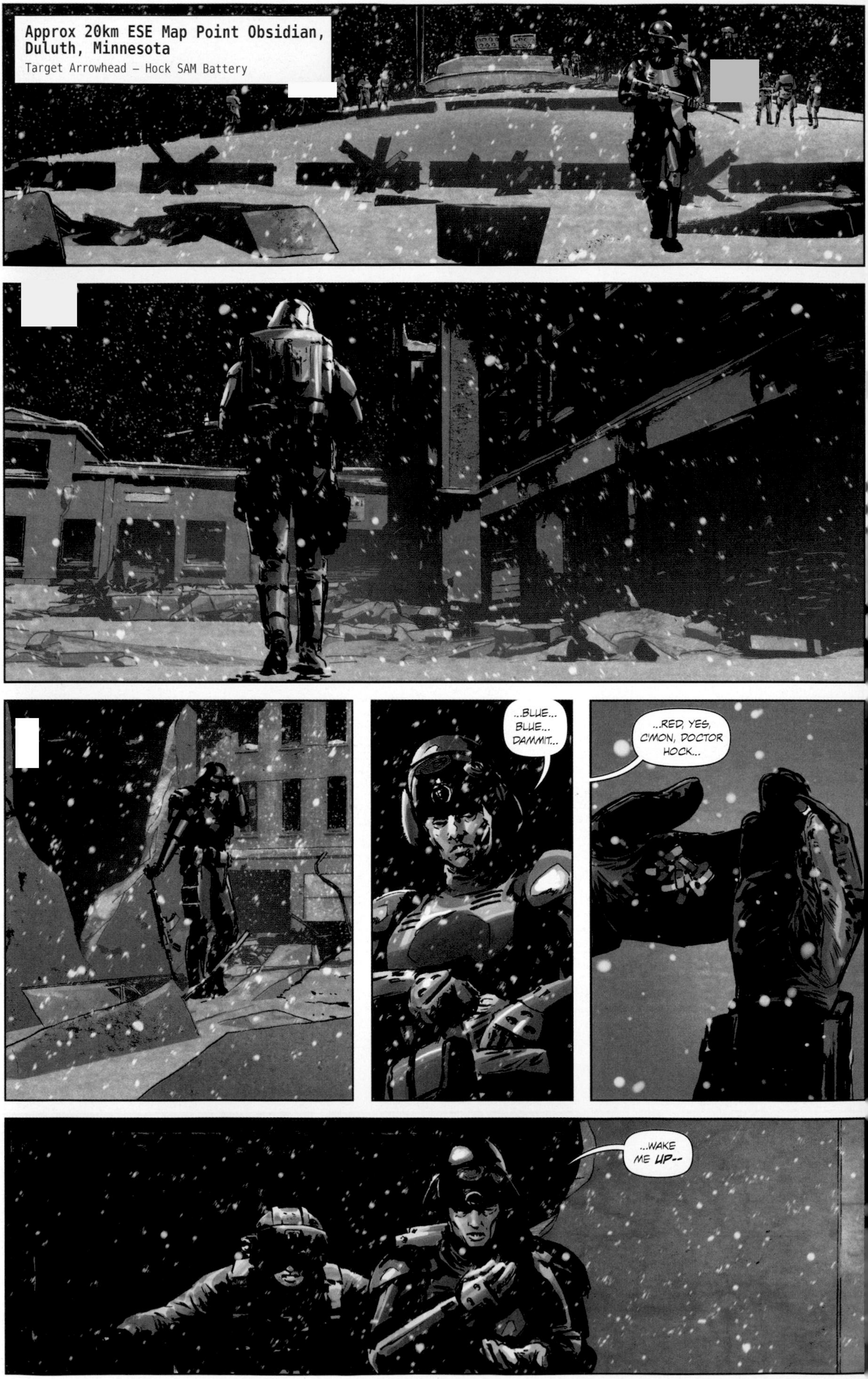
Approx 20km ESE Map Point Obsidian, Duluth, Minnesota
Target Arrowhead – Hock SAM Battery
...BLUE... BLUE... DAMMIT...
...RED, YES, C'MON, DOCTOR HOCK...
...WAKE ME UP--

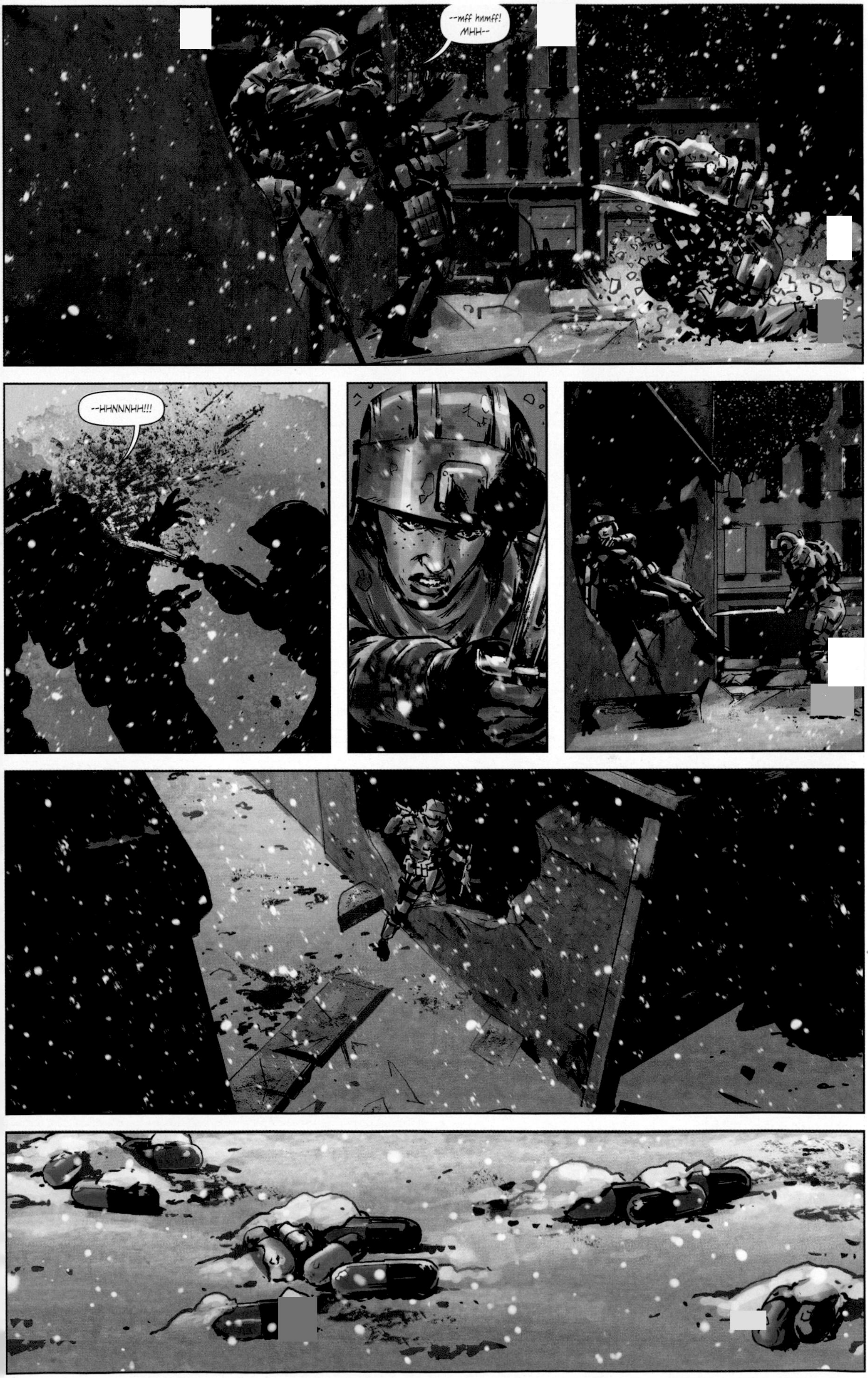
--mff hnmff! MHH--
--HHNNNHH!!!

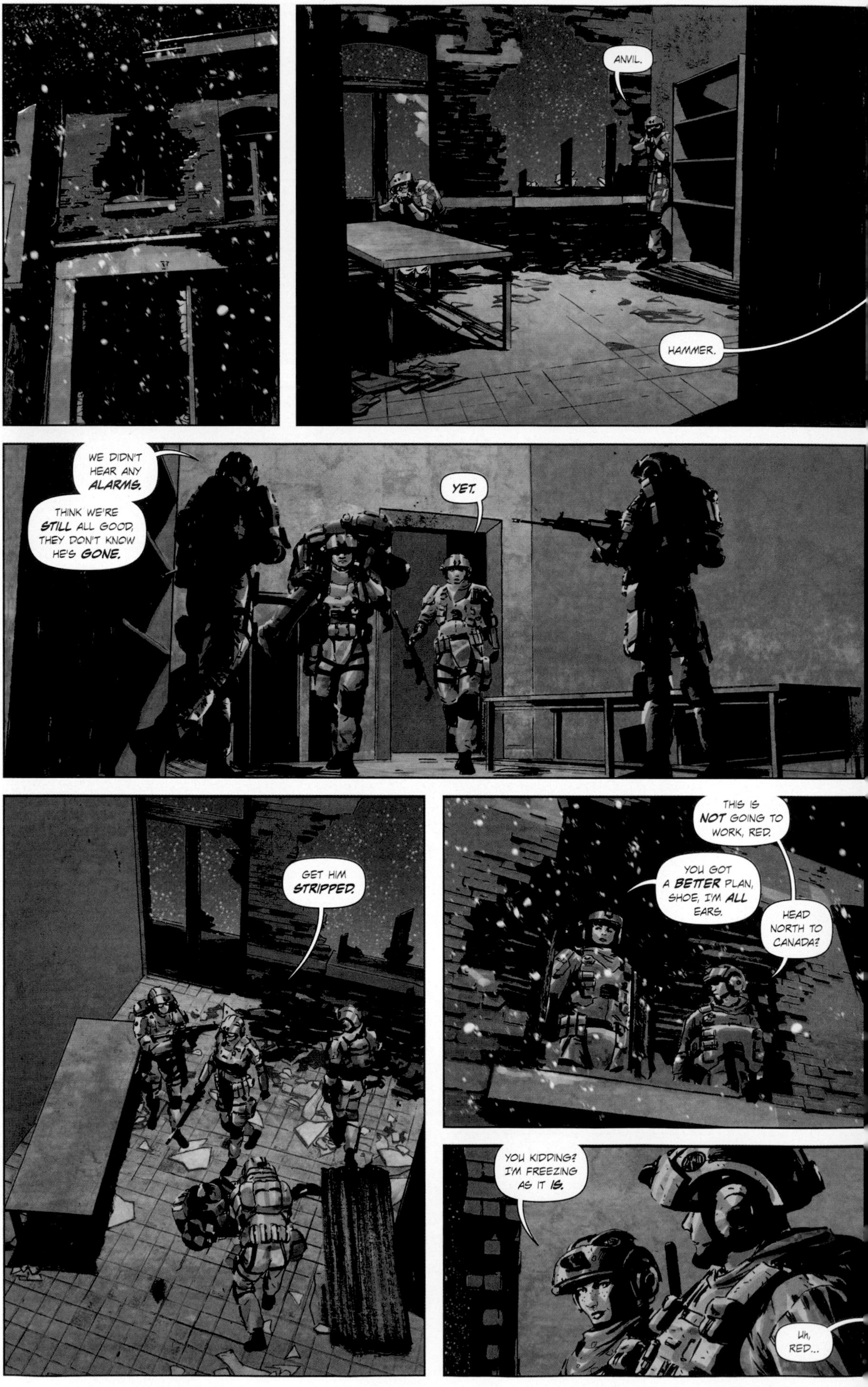
ANVIL.
HAMMER.
WE DIDN'T HEAR ANY ALARMS.
THINK WE'RE STILL ALL GOOD, THEY DON'T KNOW HE'S GONE.
YET.
GET HIM STRIPPED.
THIS IS NOT GOING TO WORK, RED.
YOU GOT A BETTER PLAN, SHOE, I'M ALL EARS.
HEAD NORTH TO CANADA?
YOU KIDDING? I'M FREEZING AS IT IS.
UH, RED...

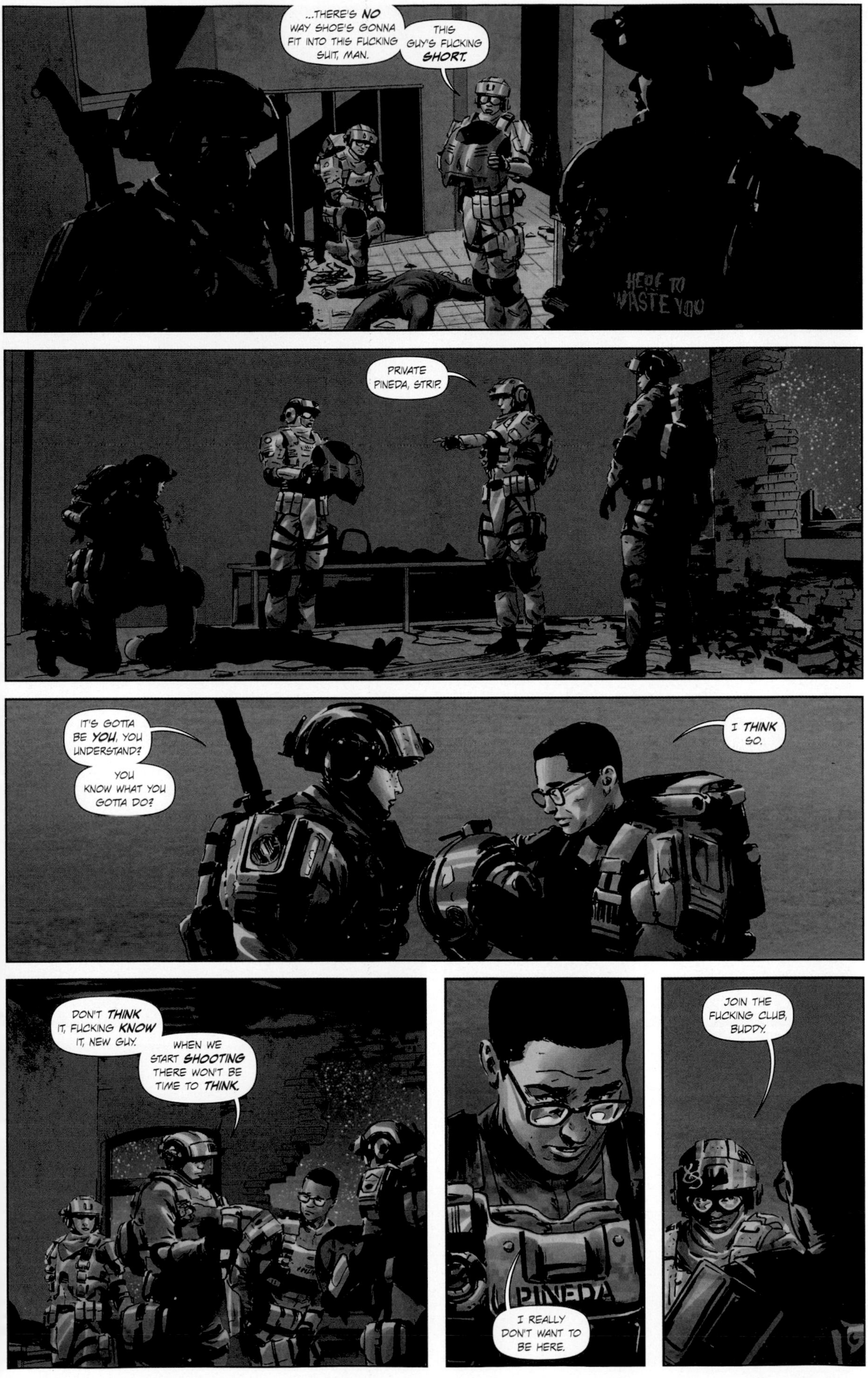
...THERE'S NO WAY SHOE'S GONNA FIT INTO THIS FUCKING SUIT, MAN.
THIS GUY'S FUCKING SHORT.
HE'OF TO WASTE YOU
PRIVATE PINEDA, STRIP.
IT'S GOTTA BE YOU, YOU UNDERSTAND?
YOU KNOW WHAT YOU GOTTA DO?
I THINK SO.
DON'T THINK IT, FUCKING KNOW IT, NEW GUY.
WHEN WE START SHOOTING THERE WON'T BE TIME TO THINK.
PINEDA
I REALLY DON'T WANT TO BE HERE.
JOIN THE FUCKING CLUB, BUDDY.

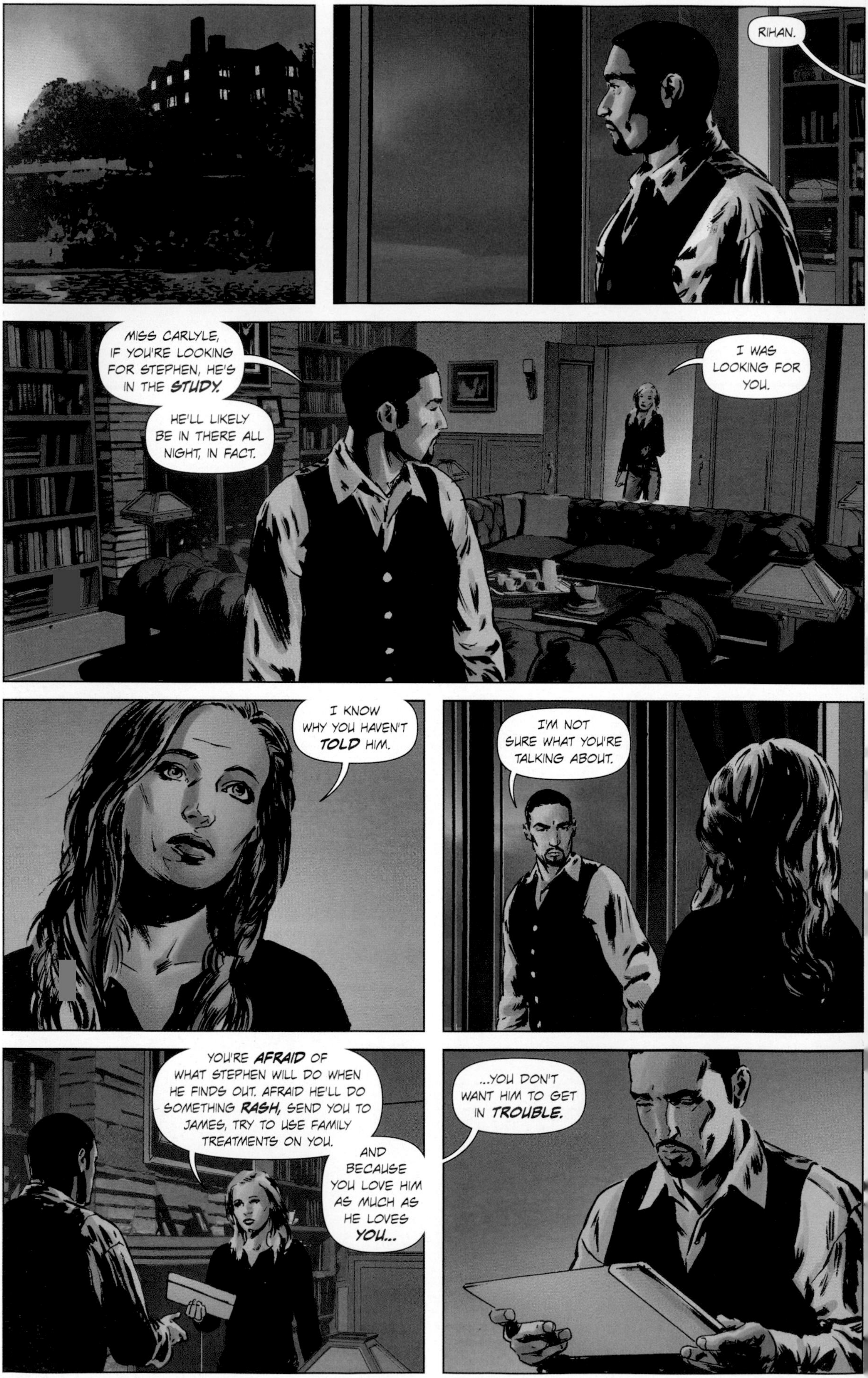
RIHAN.
MISS CARLYLE, IF YOU'RE LOOKING FOR STEPHEN, HE'S IN THE STUDY.
HE'LL LIKELY BE IN THERE ALL NIGHT, IN FACT.
I WAS LOOKING FOR YOU.
I KNOW WHY YOU HAVEN'T TOLD HIM.
I'M NOT SURE WHAT YOU'RE TALKING ABOUT.
YOU'RE AFRAID OF WHAT STEPHEN WILL DO WHEN HE FINDS OUT. AFRAID HE'LL DO SOMETHING RASH, SEND YOU TO JAMES, TRY TO USE FAMILY TREATMENTS ON YOU.
AND BECAUSE YOU LOVE HIM AS MUCH AS HE LOVES YOU...
...YOU DON'T WANT HIM TO GET IN TROUBLE.

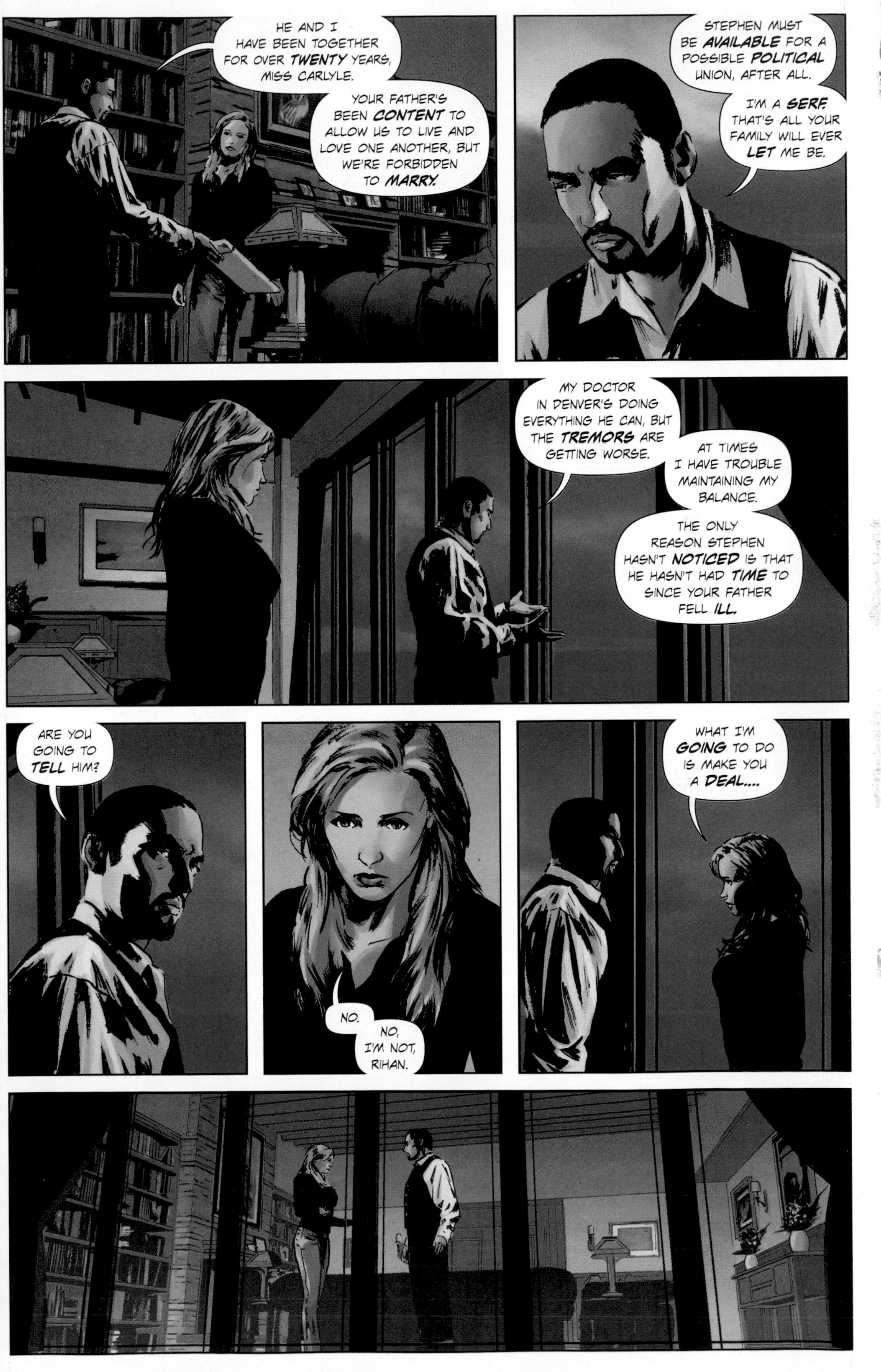
HE AND I HAVE BEEN TOGETHER FOR OVER TWENTY YEARS, MISS CARLYLE.
YOUR FATHER'S BEEN CONTENT TO ALLOW US TO LIVE AND LOVE ONE ANOTHER, BUT WE'RE FORBIDDEN TO MARRY.
STEPHEN MUST BE AVAILABLE FOR A POSSIBLE POLITICAL UNION, AFTER ALL.
I'M A SERF. THAT'S ALL YOUR FAMILY WILL EVER LET ME BE.
MY DOCTOR IN DENVER'S DOING EVERYTHING HE CAN, BUT THE TREMORS ARE GETTING WORSE.
AT TIMES I HAVE TROUBLE MAINTAINING MY BALANCE.
THE ONLY REASON STEPHEN HASN'T NOTICED IS THAT HE HASN'T HAD TIME TO SINCE YOUR FATHER FELL ILL.
ARE YOU GOING TO TELL HIM?
NO.
NO, I'M NOT, RIHAN.
WHAT I'M GOING TO DO IS MAKE YOU A DEAL....

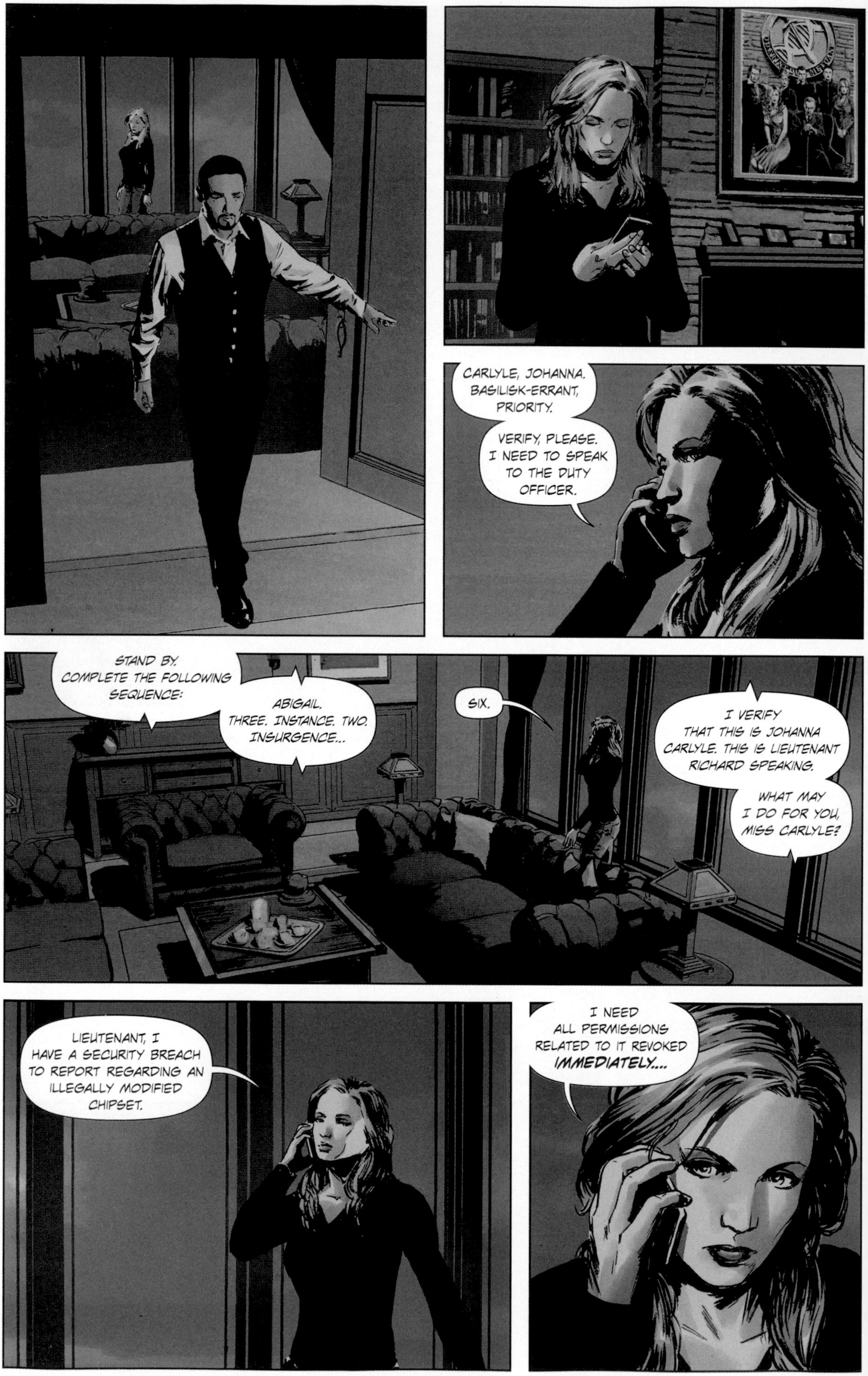
CARLYLE, JOHANNA. BASILISK-ERRANT, PRIORITY.
VERIFY, PLEASE. I NEED TO SPEAK TO THE DUTY OFFICER.
STAND BY. COMPLETE THE FOLLOWING SEQUENCE:
ABIGAIL. THREE. INSTANCE. TWO. INSURGENCE...
SIX.
I VERIFY THAT THIS IS JOHANNA CARLYLE. THIS IS LIEUTENANT RICHARD SPEAKING.
WHAT MAY I DO FOR YOU, MISS CARLYLE?
LIEUTENANT, I HAVE A SECURITY BREACH TO REPORT REGARDING AN ILLEGALLY MODIFIED CHIPSET.
I NEED ALL PERMISSIONS RELATED TO IT REVOKED *IMMEDIATELY....*

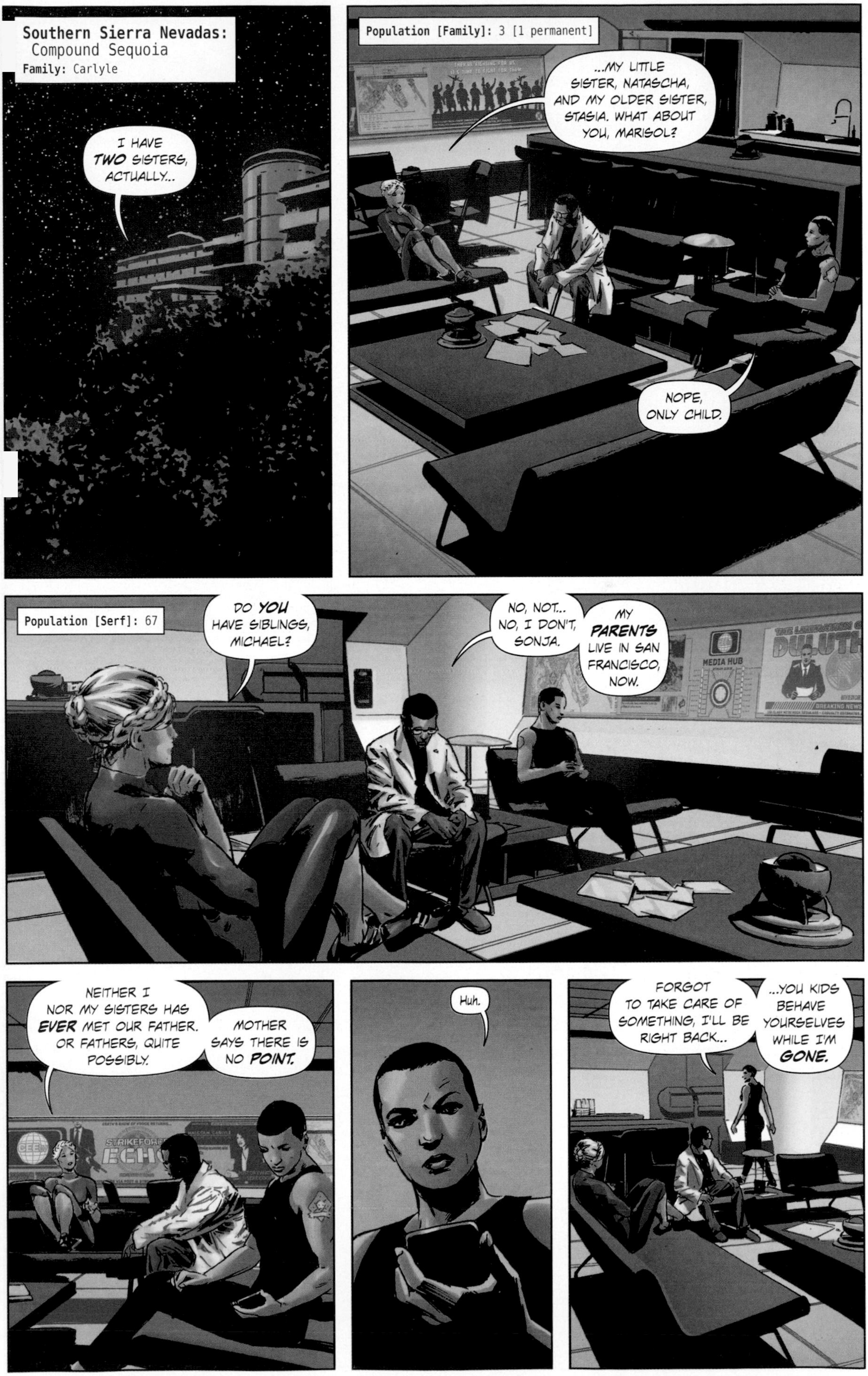
Southern Sierra Nevadas: Compound Sequoia
Family: Carlyle
I HAVE TWO SISTERS, ACTUALLY...
Population [Family]: 3 [1 permanent]
...MY LITTLE SISTER, NATASCHA, AND MY OLDER SISTER, STASIA. WHAT ABOUT YOU, MARISOL?
NOPE, ONLY CHILD.
Population [Serf]: 67
DO YOU HAVE SIBLINGS, MICHAEL?
NO, NOT... NO, I DON'T, SONJA.
MY PARENTS LIVE IN SAN FRANCISCO, NOW.
MEDIA HUB
NEITHER I NOR MY SISTERS HAS EVER MET OUR FATHER. OR FATHERS, QUITE POSSIBLY.
MOTHER SAYS THERE IS NO POINT.
Huh.
FORGOT TO TAKE CARE OF SOMETHING, I'LL BE RIGHT BACK...
...YOU KIDS BEHAVE YOURSELVES WHILE I'M GONE.

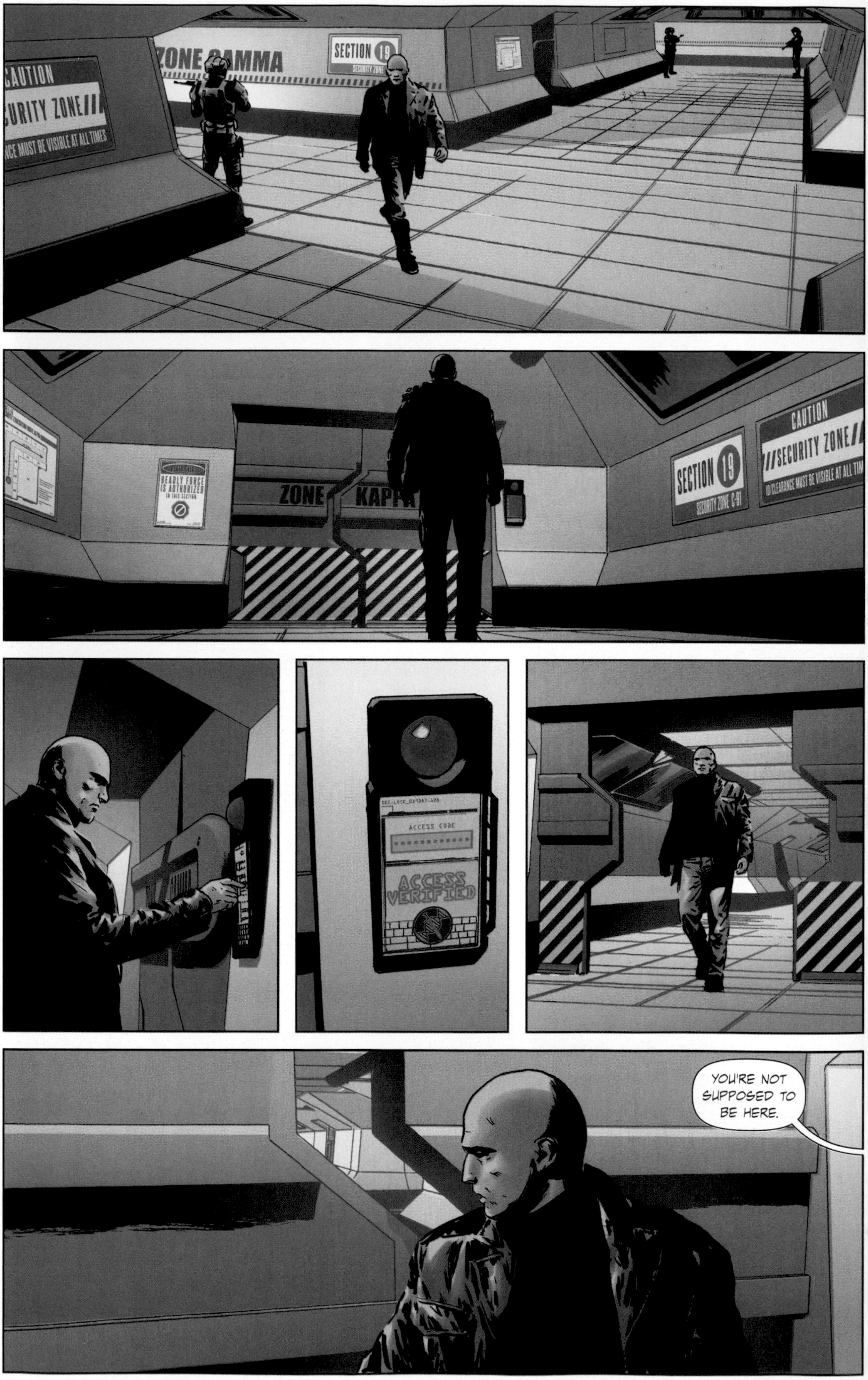
CAUTION
CURITY ZONE//
NCE MUST BE VISIBLE AT ALL TIMES
ZONE GAMMA
SECTION 19
SECURITY ZONE
DEADLY FORCE IS AUTHORIZED
IN THIS SECTION
ZONE KAPP
SECTION 19
SECURITY ZONE C-91
CAUTION
//SECURITY ZONE//
ID/CLEARANCE MUST BE VISIBLE AT ALL TIM
ACCESS CODE
ACCESS VERIFIED
YOU'RE NOT SUPPOSED TO BE HERE.

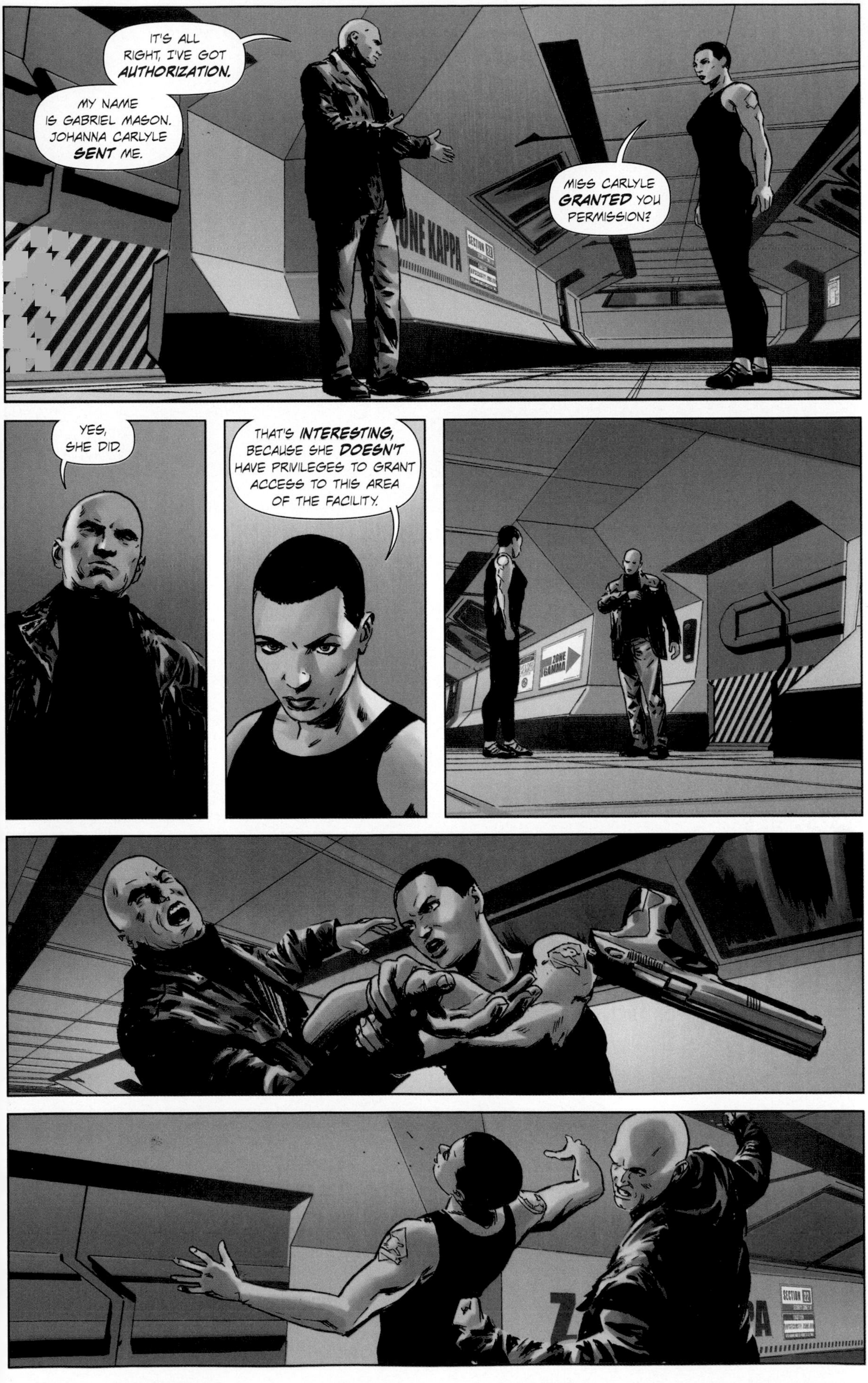
IT'S ALL RIGHT, I'VE GOT AUTHORIZATION.
MY NAME IS GABRIEL MASON. JOHANNA CARLYLE SENT ME.
MISS CARLYLE GRANTED YOU PERMISSION?
YES, SHE DID.
THAT'S INTERESTING, BECAUSE SHE DOESN'T HAVE PRIVILEGES TO GRANT ACCESS TO THIS AREA OF THE FACILITY.
ZONE GAMMA

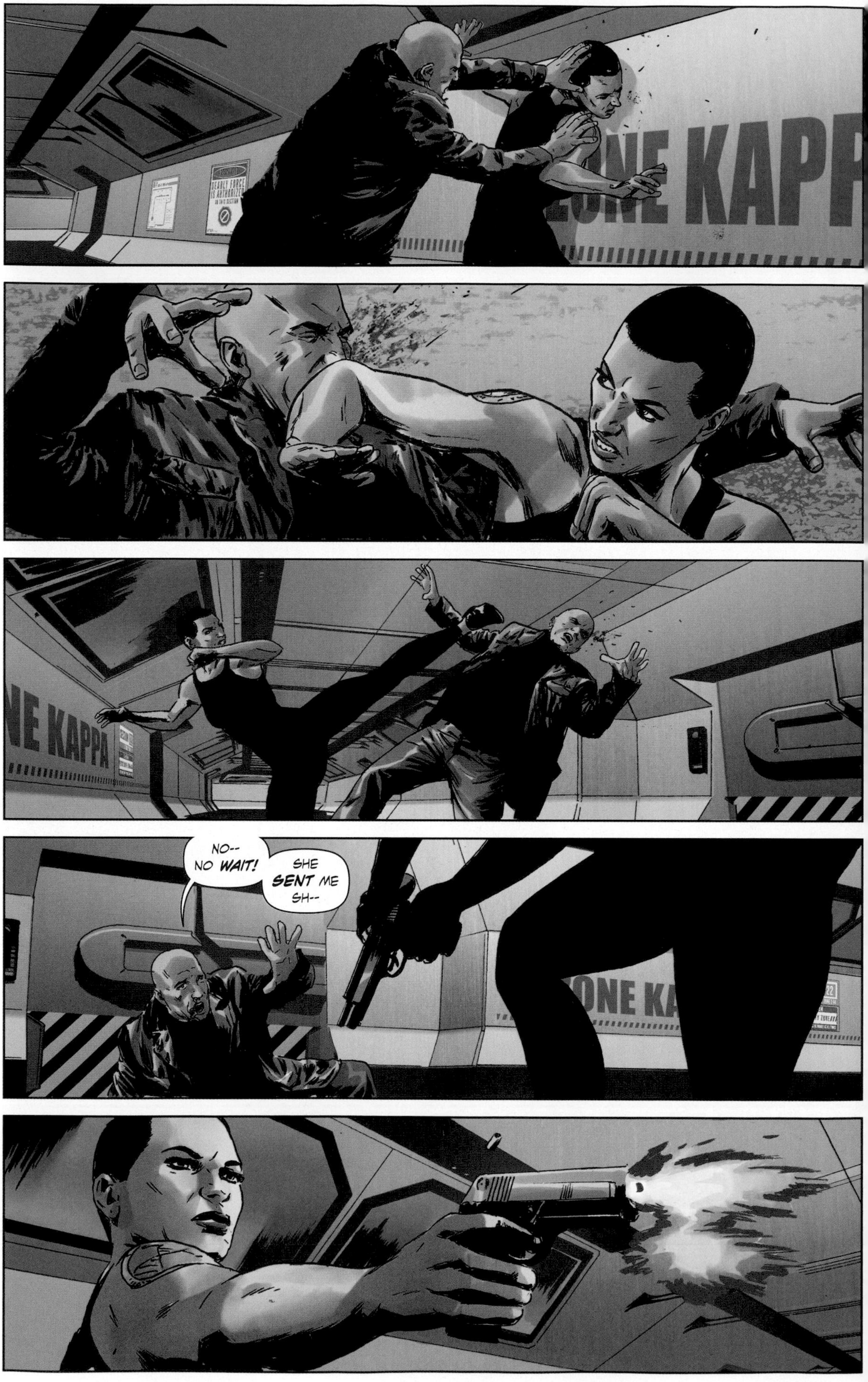
NO-- NO *WAIT!*
SHE *SENT* ME SH--

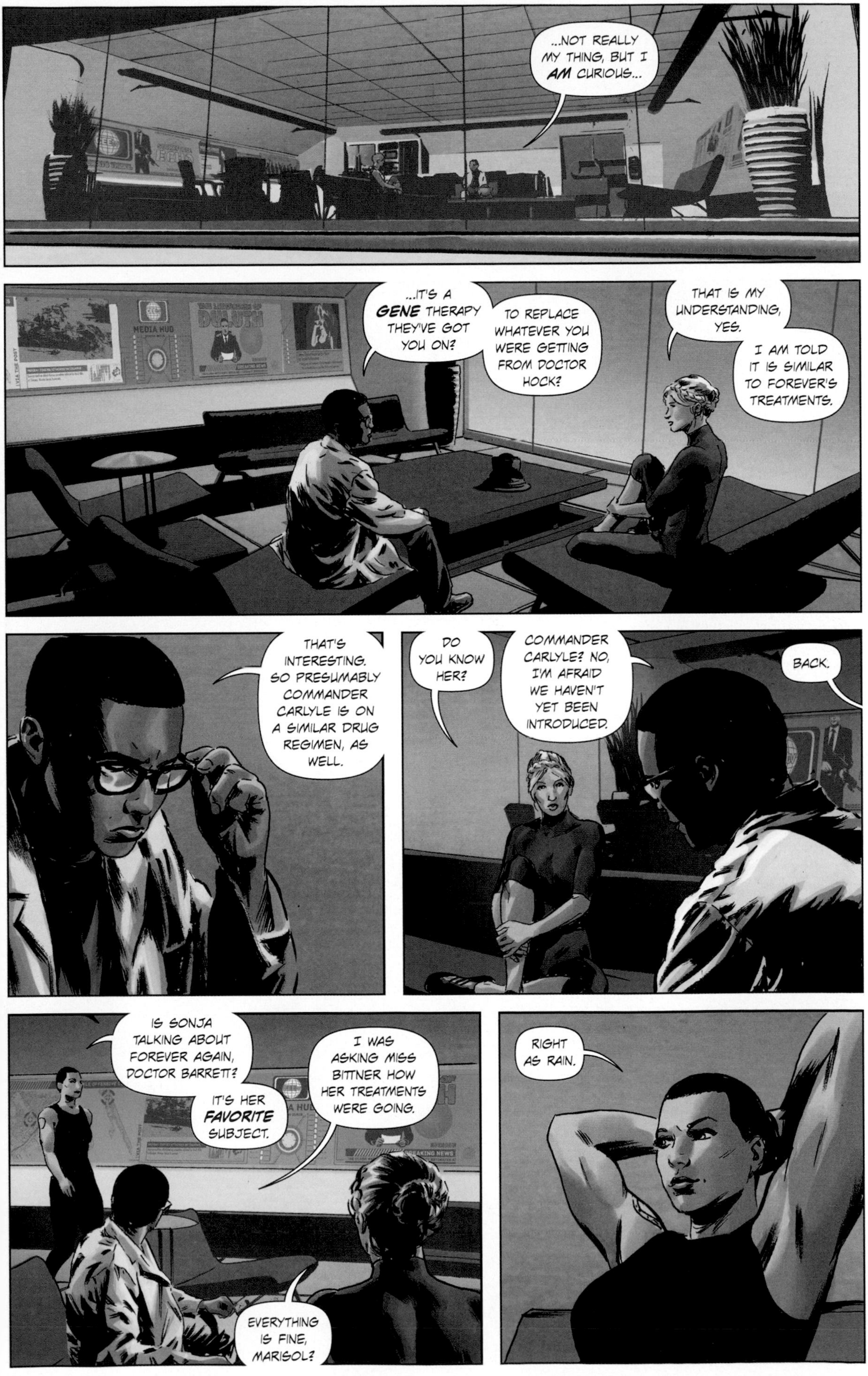
...NOT REALLY MY THING, BUT I AM CURIOUS...
...IT'S A GENE THERAPY THEY'VE GOT YOU ON?
TO REPLACE WHATEVER YOU WERE GETTING FROM DOCTOR HOCK?
THAT IS MY UNDERSTANDING, YES.
I AM TOLD IT IS SIMILAR TO FOREVER'S TREATMENTS.
THAT'S INTERESTING. SO PRESUMABLY COMMANDER CARLYLE IS ON A SIMILAR DRUG REGIMEN, AS WELL.
DO YOU KNOW HER?
COMMANDER CARLYLE? NO, I'M AFRAID WE HAVEN'T YET BEEN INTRODUCED.
BACK.
IS SONJA TALKING ABOUT FOREVER AGAIN, DOCTOR BARRETT?
IT'S HER FAVORITE SUBJECT.
I WAS ASKING MISS BITTNER HOW HER TREATMENTS WERE GOING.
EVERYTHING IS FINE, MARISOL?
RIGHT AS RAIN.

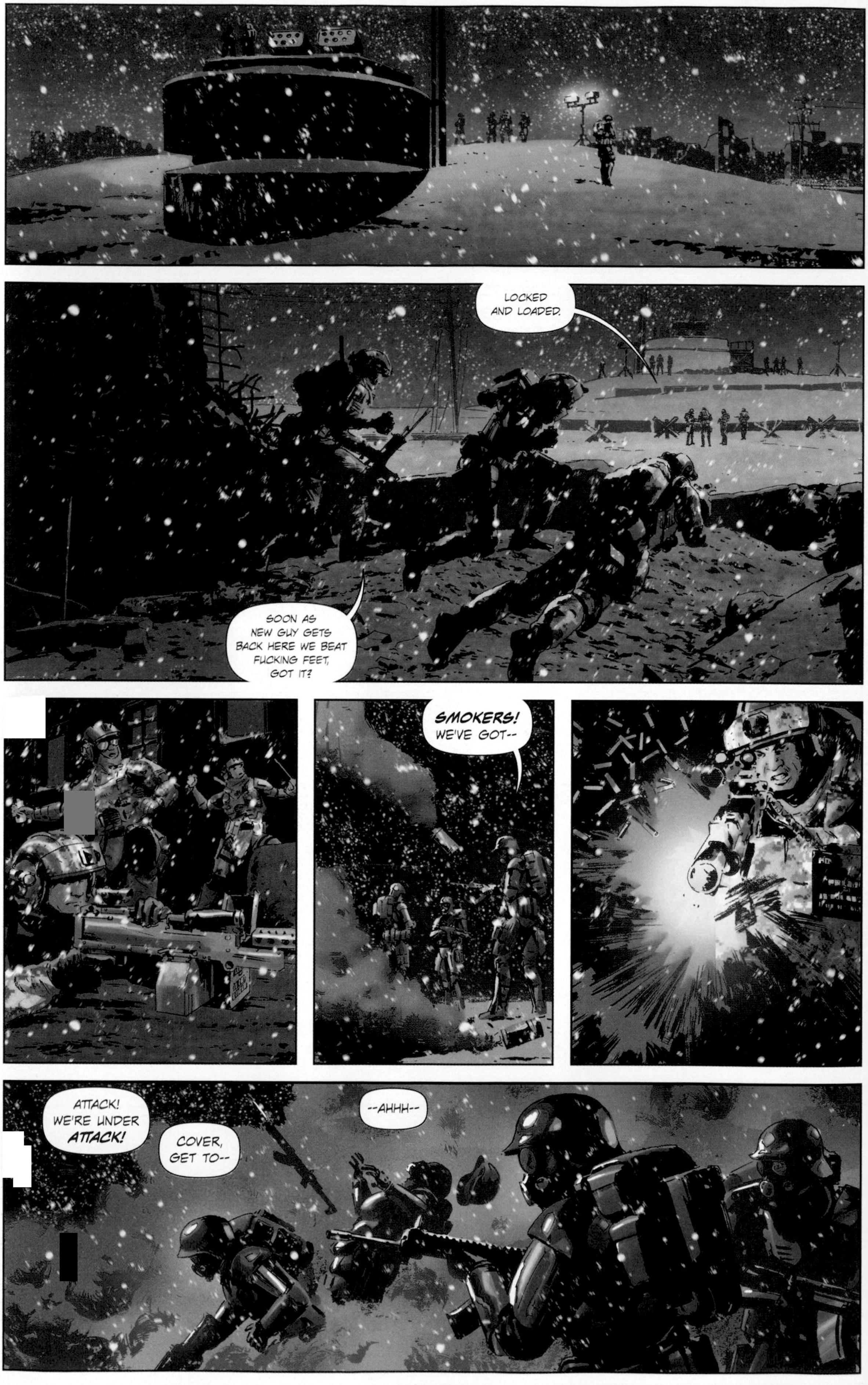
LOCKED AND LOADED.
SOON AS NEW GUY GETS BACK HERE WE BEAT FUCKING FEET, GOT IT?
SMOKERS! WE'VE GOT--
ATTACK! WE'RE UNDER ATTACK!
COVER, GET TO--
--AHHH--

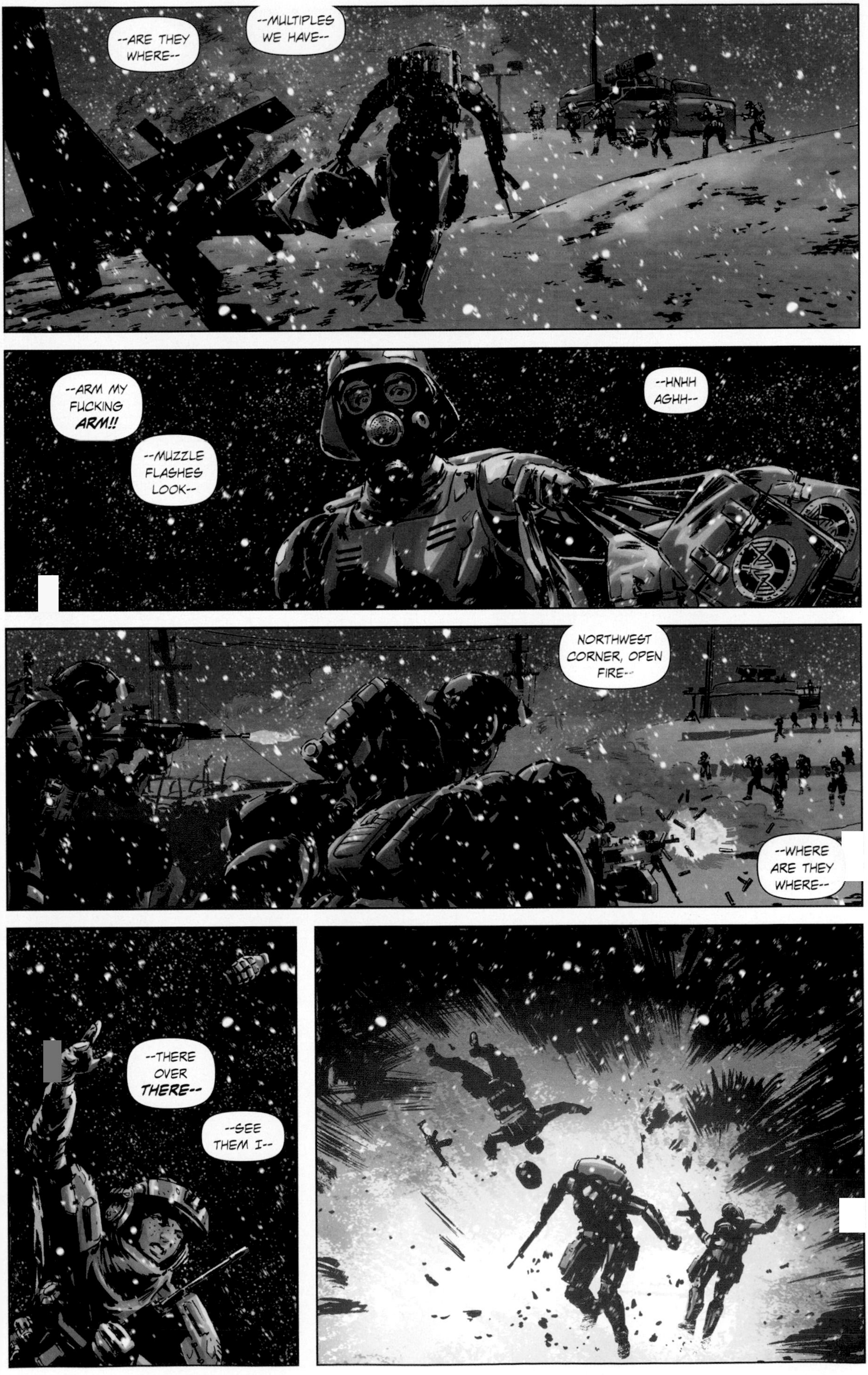

--ARE THEY WHERE--
--MULTIPLES WE HAVE--
--ARM MY FUCKING ARM!!
--MUZZLE FLASHES LOOK--
--HNHH AGHH--
NORTHWEST CORNER, OPEN FIRE--
--WHERE ARE THEY WHERE--
--THERE OVER THERE--
--SEE THEM I--

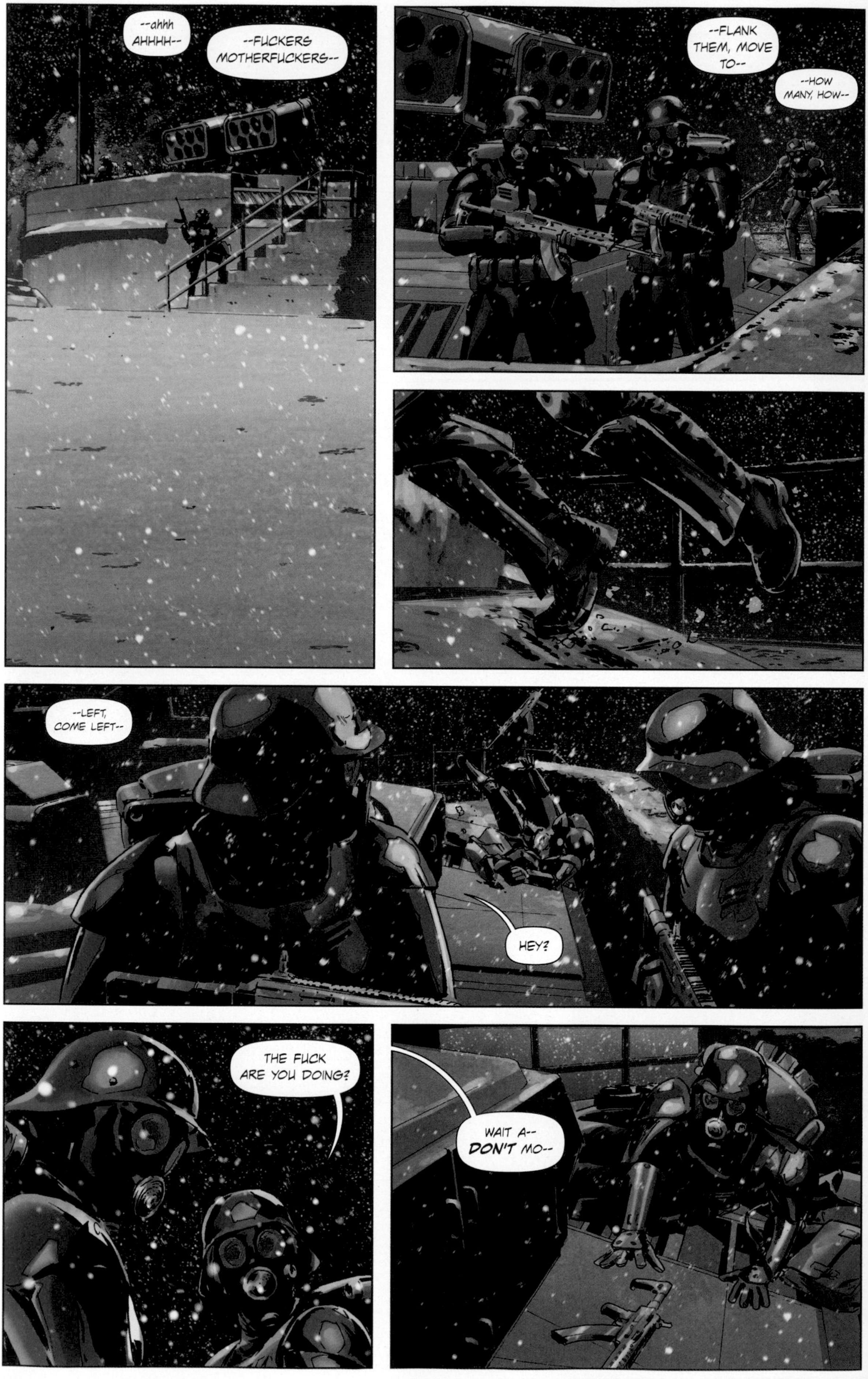
--ahhh AHHHH--
--FUCKERS MOTHERFUCKERS--
--FLANK THEM, MOVE TO--
--HOW MANY, HOW--
--LEFT, COME LEFT--
HEY?
THE FUCK ARE YOU DOING?
WAIT A--
DON'T MO--

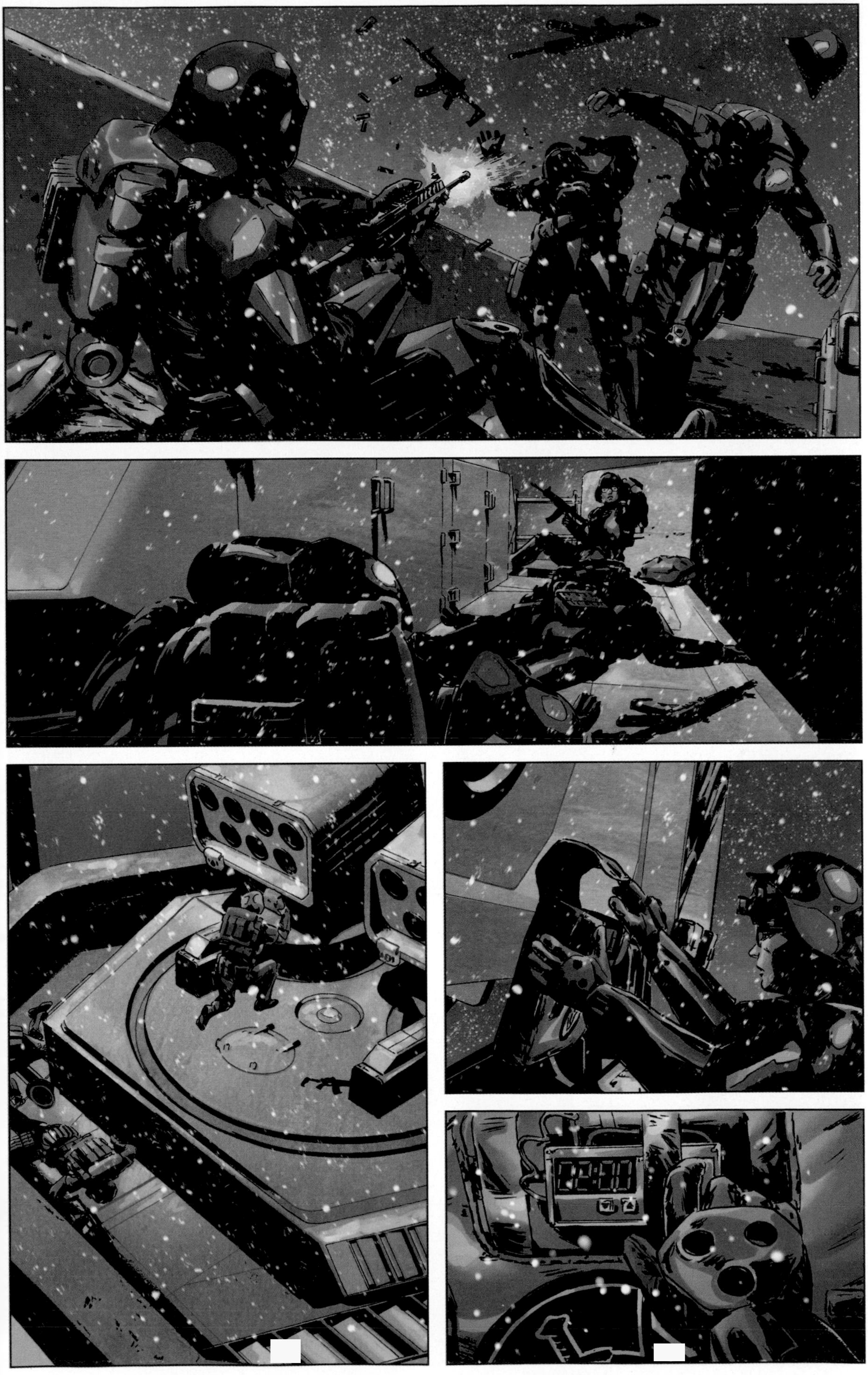

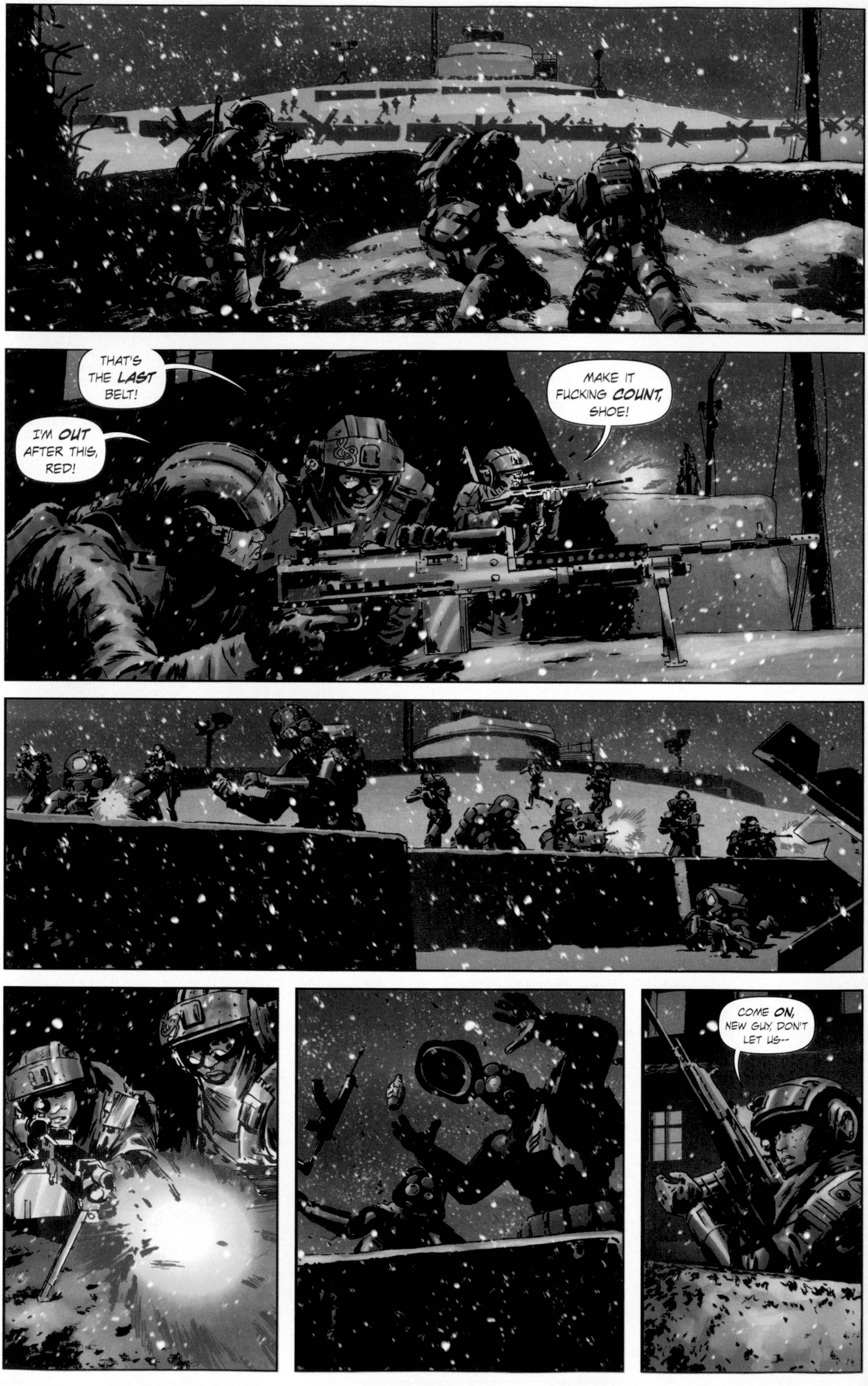
THAT'S THE LAST BELT!
I'M OUT AFTER THIS, RED!
MAKE IT FUCKING COUNT, SHOE!
COME ON, NEW GUY, DON'T LET US--

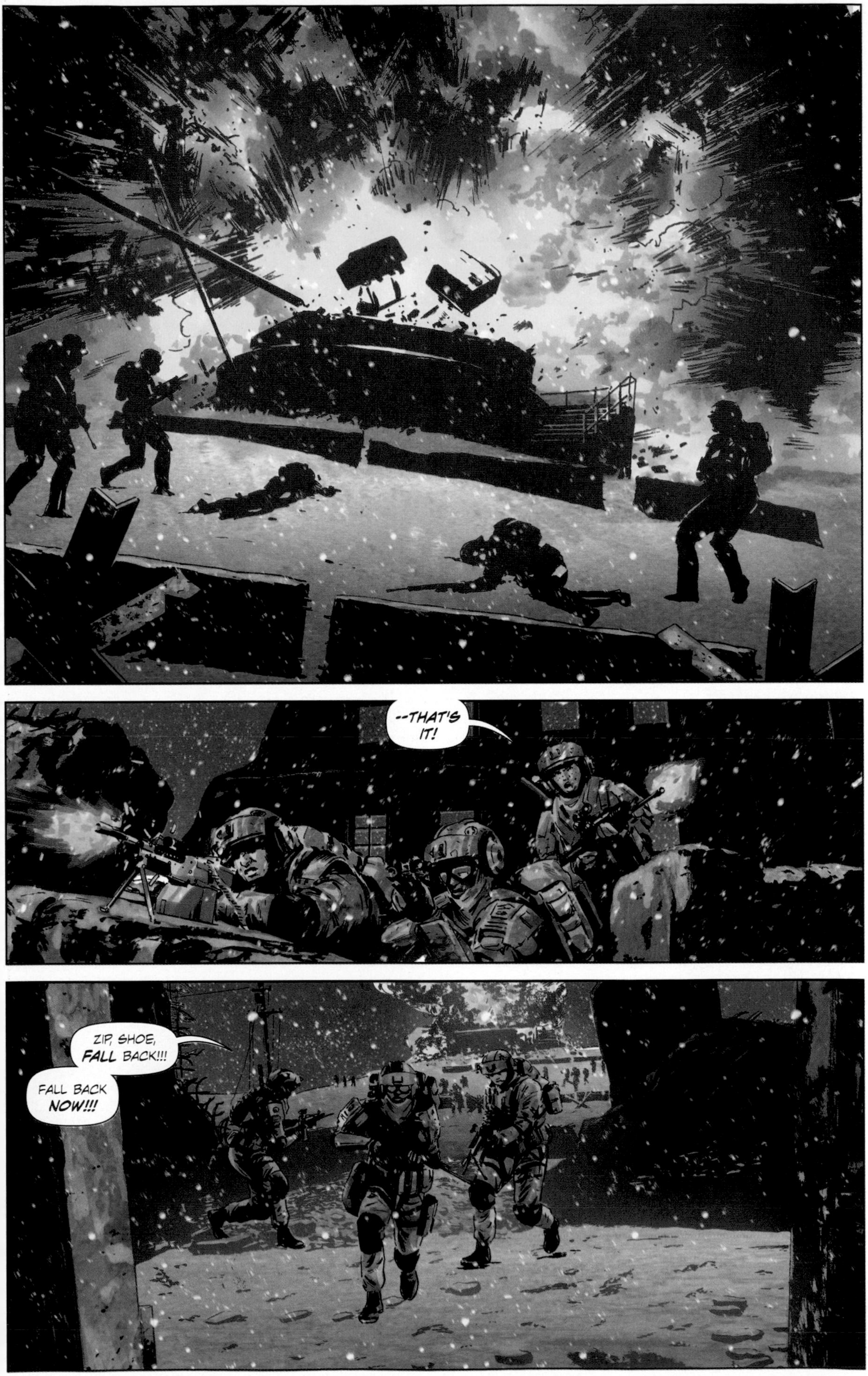
--THAT'S IT!
ZIP, SHOE, FALL BACK!!!
FALL BACK NOW!!!

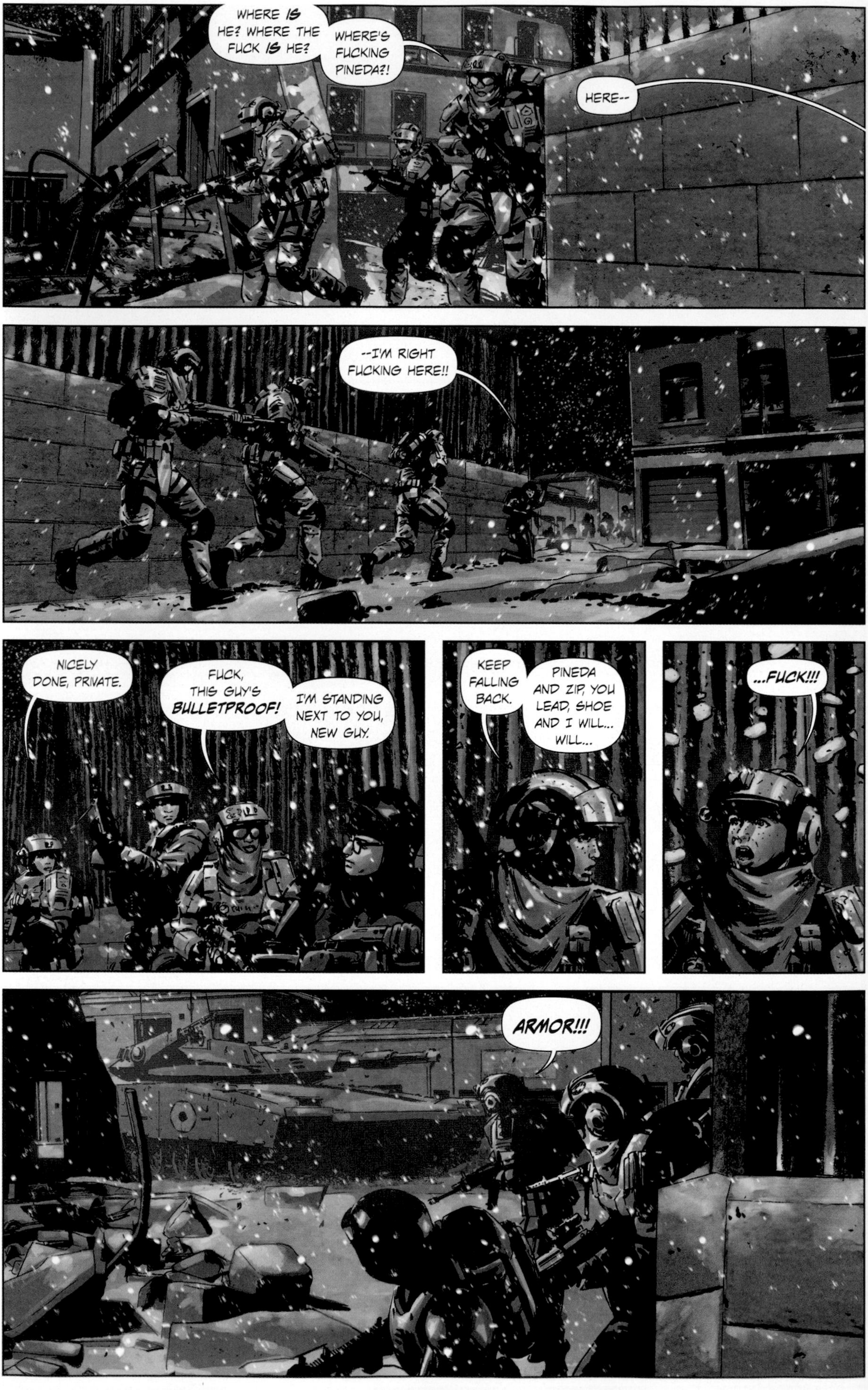
WHERE IS HE? WHERE THE FUCK IS HE?
WHERE'S FUCKING PINEDA?!
HERE--
--I'M RIGHT FUCKING HERE!!
NICELY DONE, PRIVATE.
FUCK, THIS GUY'S BULLETPROOF!
I'M STANDING NEXT TO YOU, NEW GUY.
KEEP FALLING BACK.
PINEDA AND ZIP, YOU LEAD, SHOE AND I WILL... WILL...
...FUCK!!!
ARMOR!!!

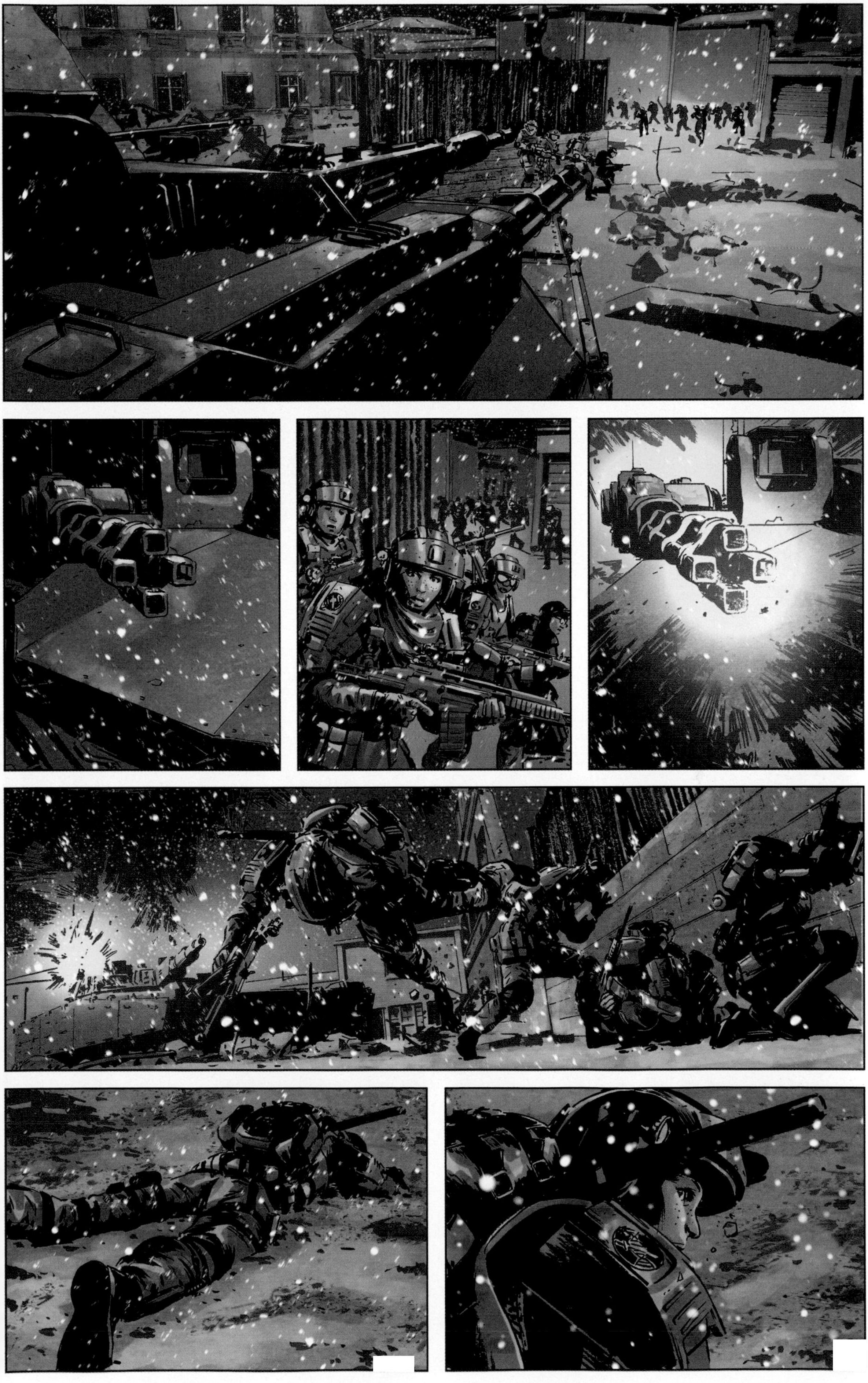

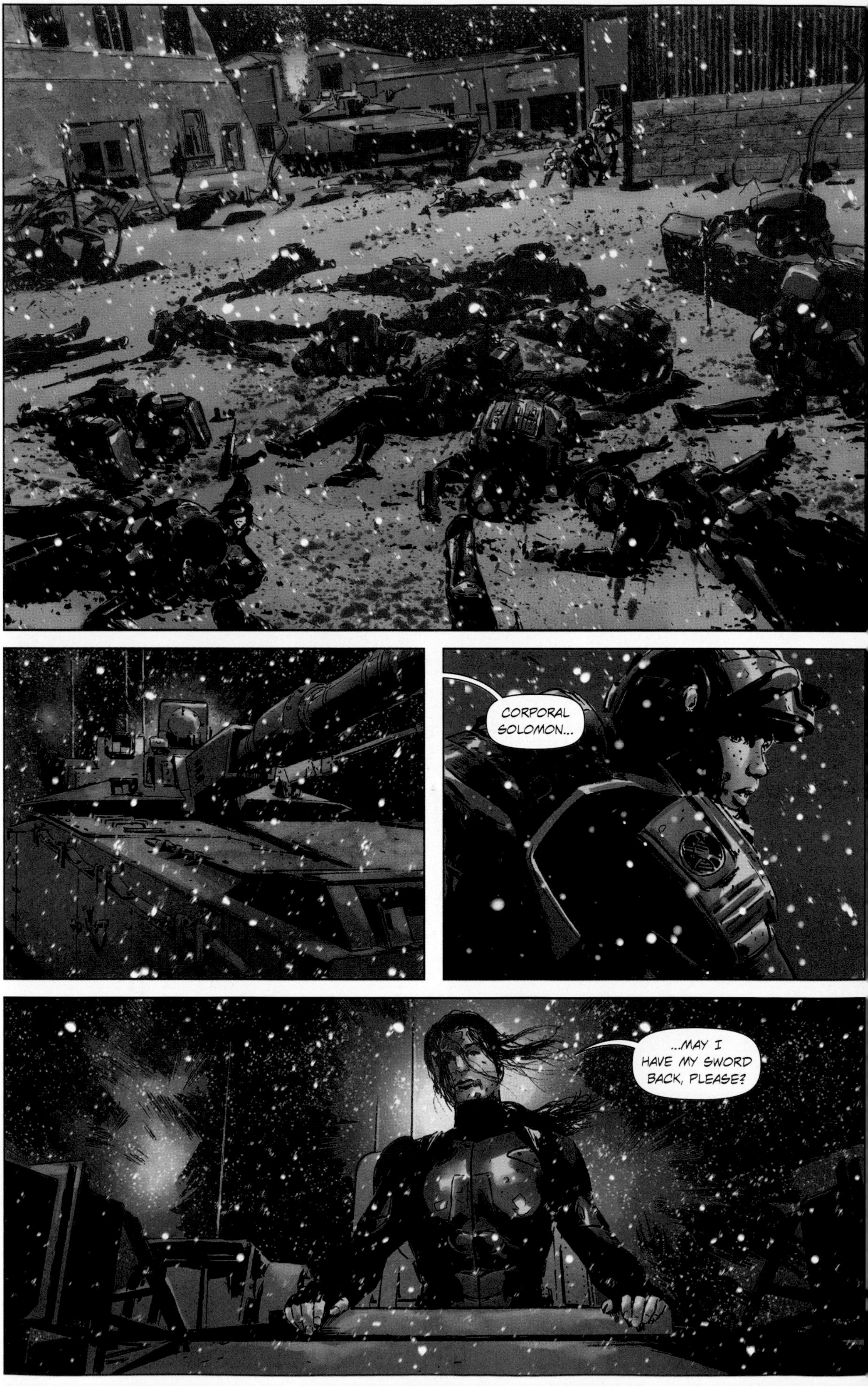
CORPORAL SOLOMON...
...MAY I HAVE MY SWORD BACK, PLEASE?

CARLYLE

ODERINT DUM METUANT

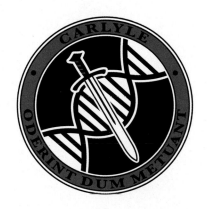

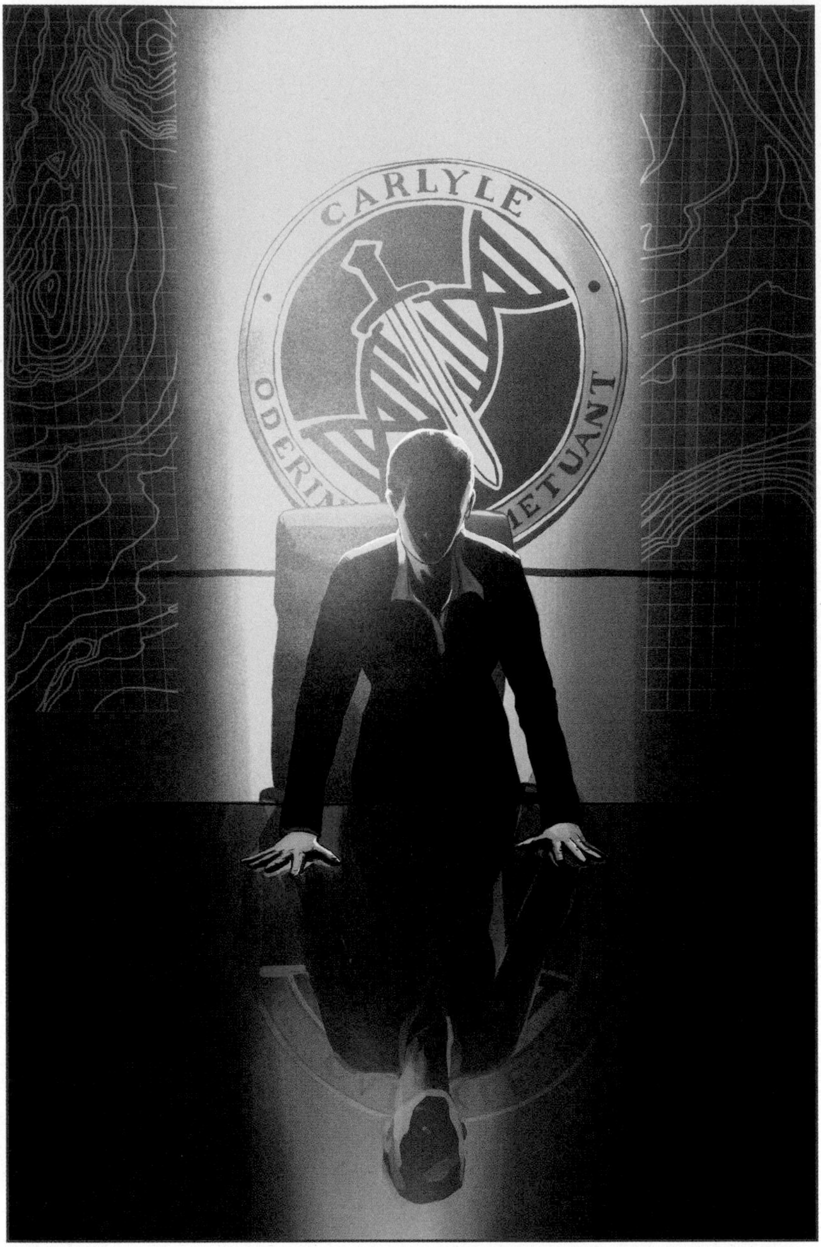
CARLYLE
ODERINT DUM METUANT
OWEN FREEMAN

POISON
CHAPTER FIVE

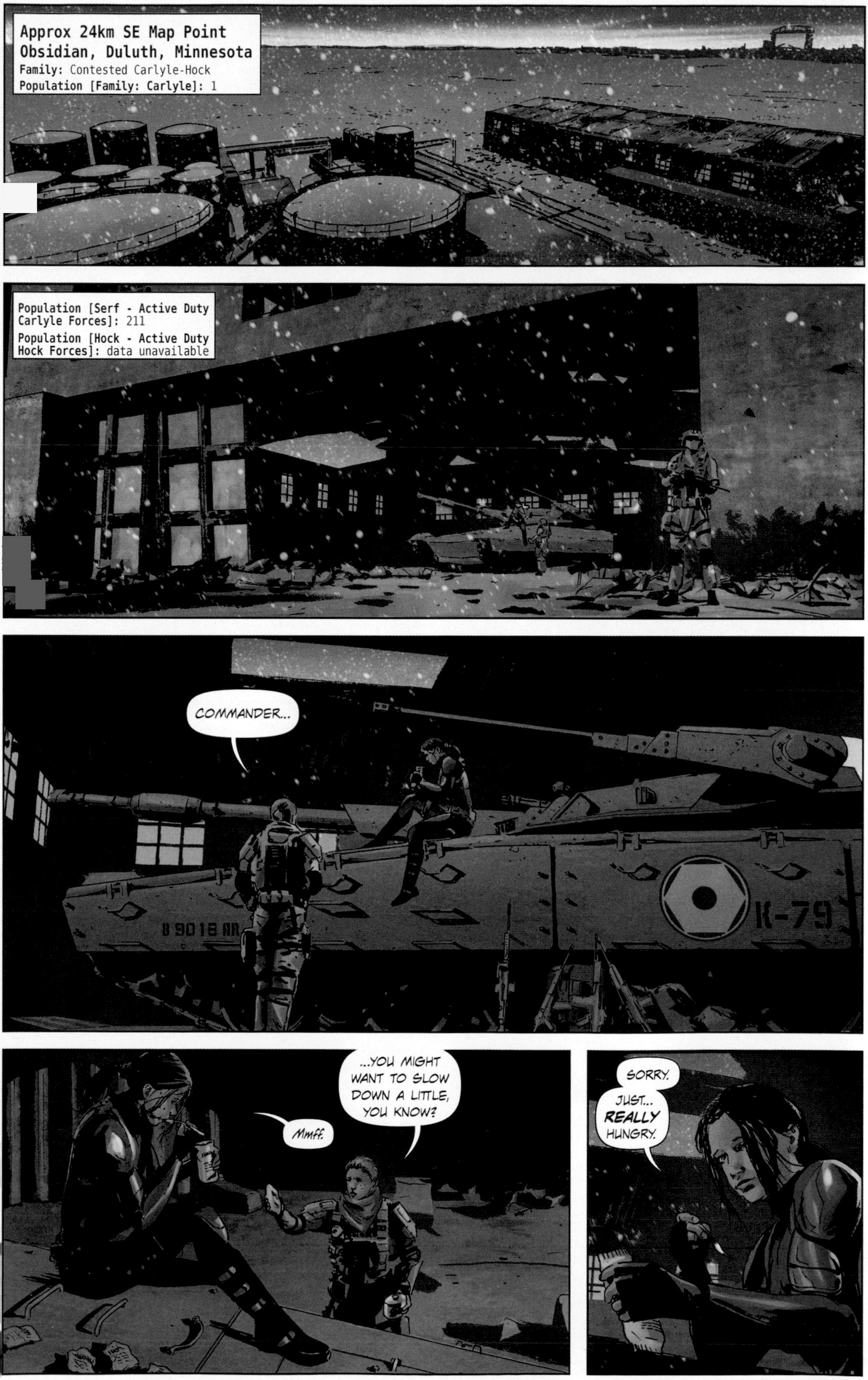
Approx 24km SE Map Point Obsidian, Duluth, Minnesota
Family: Contested Carlyle-Hock
Population [Family: Carlyle]: 1
Population [Serf - Active Duty Carlyle Forces]: 211
Population [Hock - Active Duty Hock Forces]: data unavailable
COMMANDER...
K-79
Mmff.
...YOU MIGHT WANT TO SLOW DOWN A LITTLE, YOU KNOW?
SORRY.
JUST... REALLY HUNGRY.

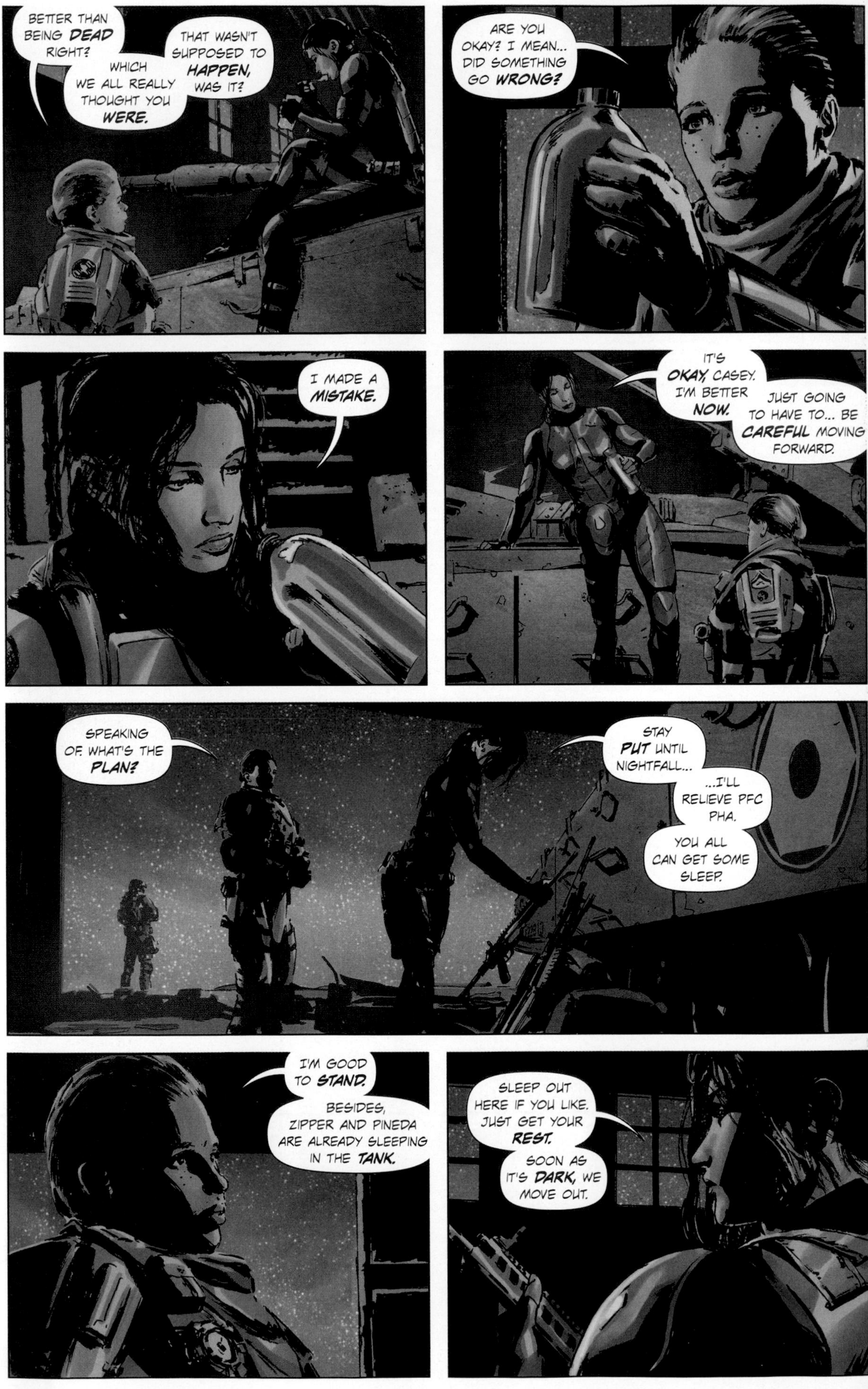
BETTER THAN BEING DEAD RIGHT?
WHICH WE ALL REALLY THOUGHT YOU WERE.
THAT WASN'T SUPPOSED TO HAPPEN, WAS IT?
ARE YOU OKAY? I MEAN... DID SOMETHING GO WRONG?
I MADE A MISTAKE.
IT'S OKAY, CASEY. I'M BETTER NOW.
JUST GOING TO HAVE TO... BE CAREFUL MOVING FORWARD.
SPEAKING OF. WHAT'S THE PLAN?
STAY PUT UNTIL NIGHTFALL...
...I'LL RELIEVE PFC PHA.
YOU ALL CAN GET SOME SLEEP.
I'M GOOD TO STAND.
BESIDES, ZIPPER AND PINEDA ARE ALREADY SLEEPING IN THE TANK.
SLEEP OUT HERE IF YOU LIKE. JUST GET YOUR REST.
SOON AS IT'S DARK, WE MOVE OUT.

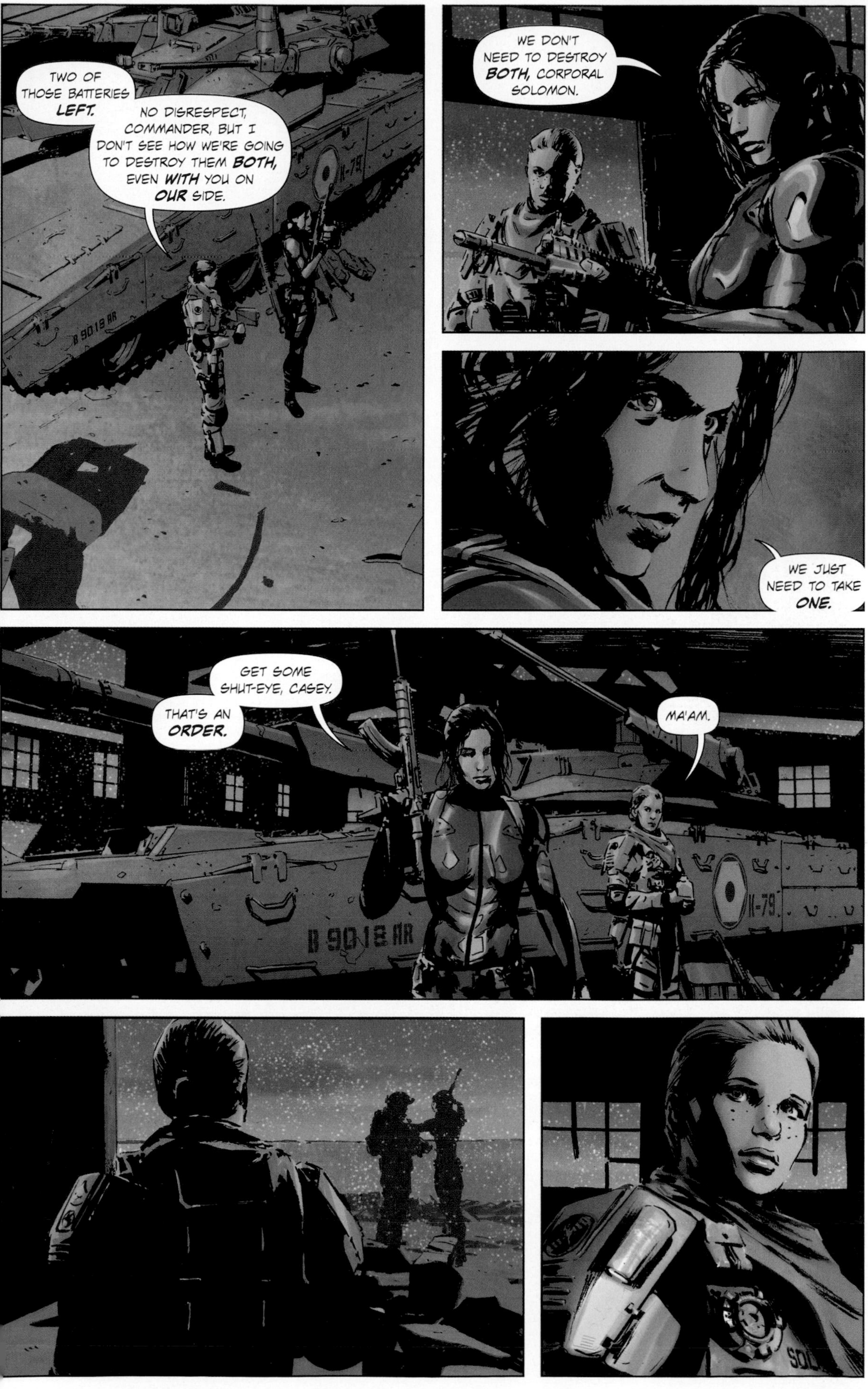
TWO OF THOSE BATTERIES LEFT.
NO DISRESPECT, COMMANDER, BUT I DON'T SEE HOW WE'RE GOING TO DESTROY THEM BOTH, EVEN WITH YOU ON OUR SIDE.
WE DON'T NEED TO DESTROY BOTH, CORPORAL SOLOMON.
WE JUST NEED TO TAKE ONE.
GET SOME SHUT-EYE, CASEY.
THAT'S AN ORDER.
MA'AM.

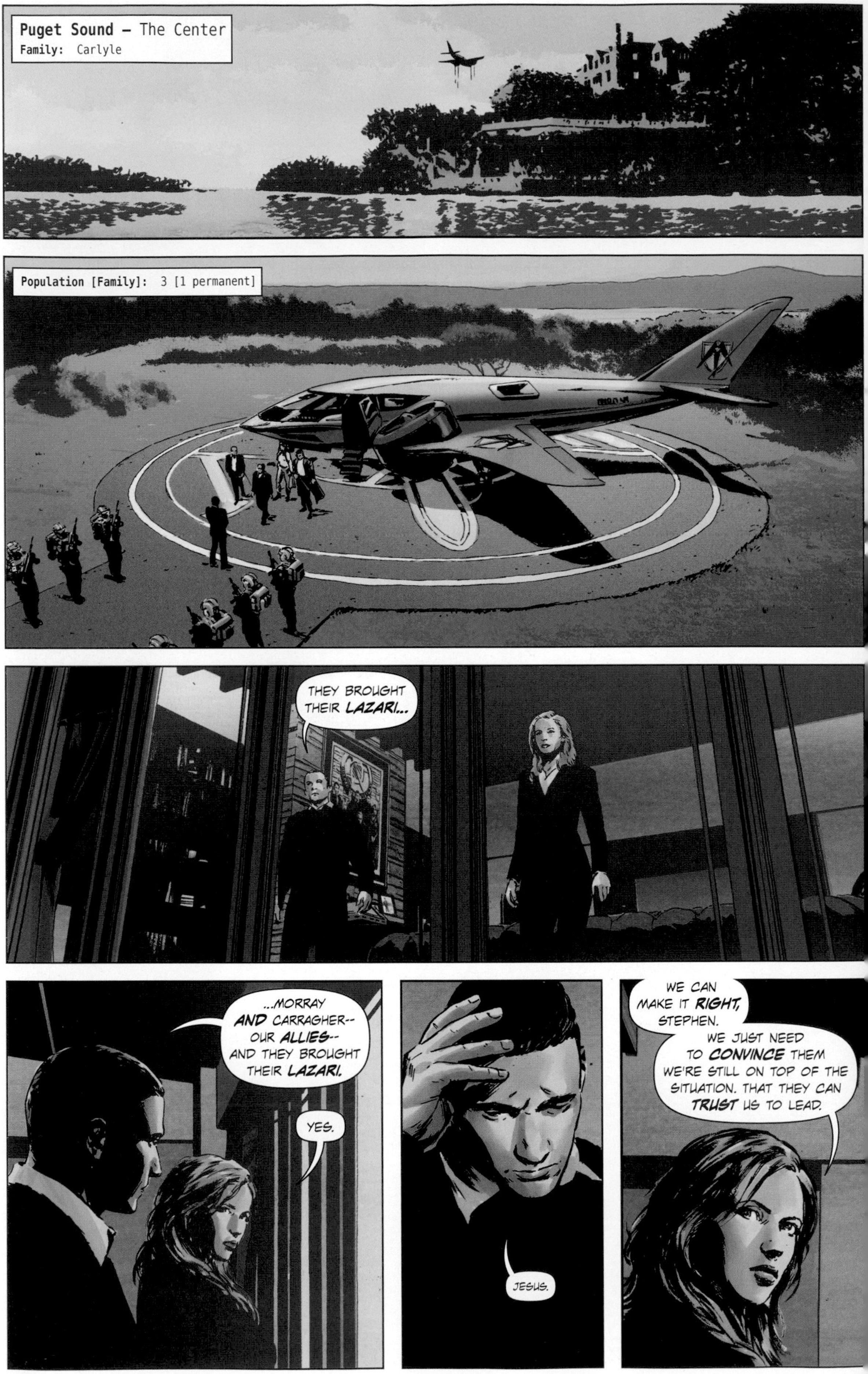

Puget Sound – The Center
Family: Carlyle
Population [Family]: 3 [1 permanent]
THEY BROUGHT THEIR LAZARI...
...MORRAY AND CARRAGHER-- OUR ALLIES-- AND THEY BROUGHT THEIR LAZARI.
YES.
JESUS.
WE CAN MAKE IT RIGHT, STEPHEN.
WE JUST NEED TO CONVINCE THEM WE'RE STILL ON TOP OF THE SITUATION. THAT THEY CAN TRUST US TO LEAD.

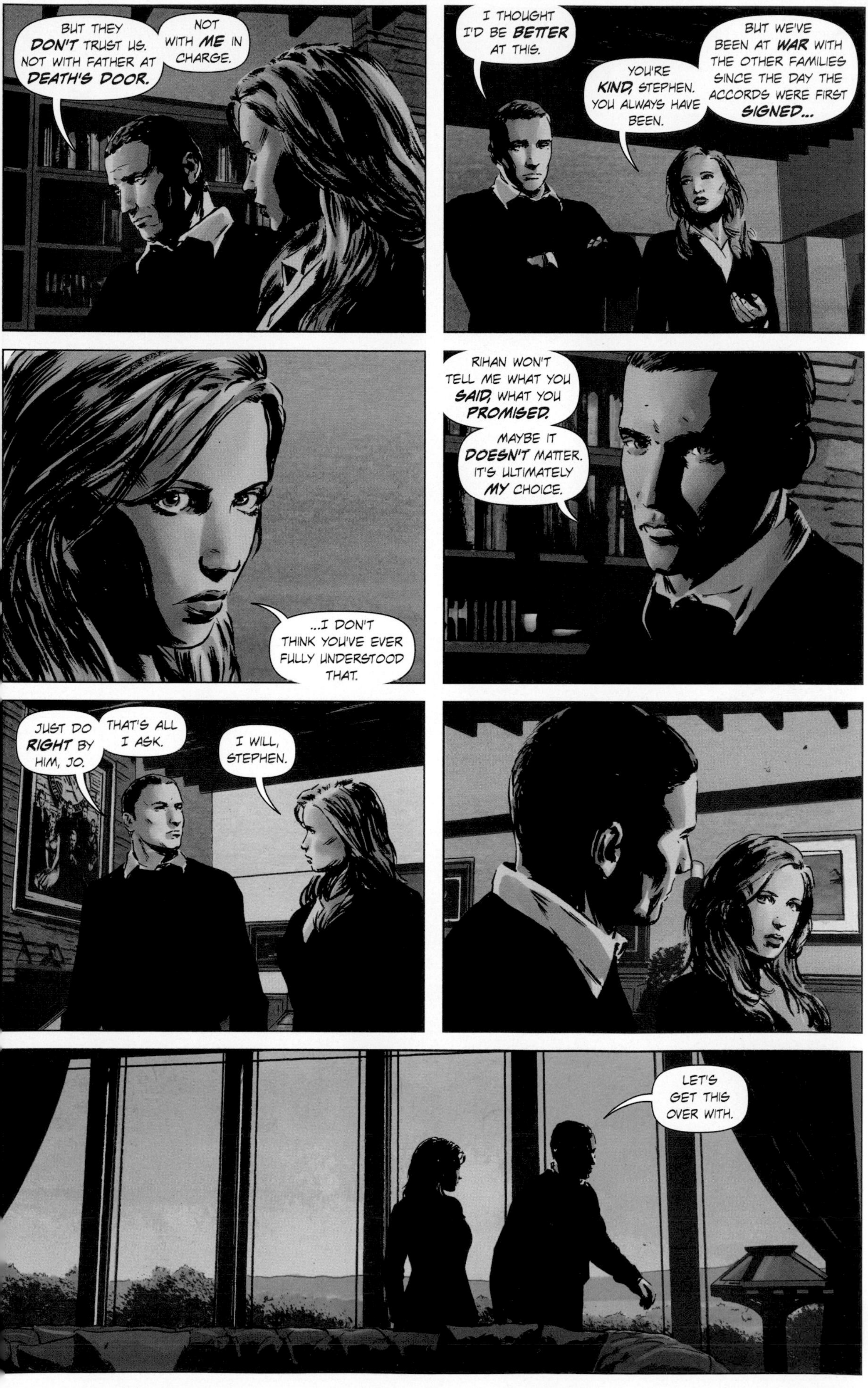
BUT THEY DON'T TRUST US. NOT WITH FATHER AT DEATH'S DOOR.
NOT WITH ME IN CHARGE.
I THOUGHT I'D BE BETTER AT THIS.
YOU'RE KIND, STEPHEN. YOU ALWAYS HAVE BEEN.
BUT WE'VE BEEN AT WAR WITH THE OTHER FAMILIES SINCE THE DAY THE ACCORDS WERE FIRST SIGNED...
...I DON'T THINK YOU'VE EVER FULLY UNDERSTOOD THAT.
RIHAN WON'T TELL ME WHAT YOU SAID, WHAT YOU PROMISED.
MAYBE IT DOESN'T MATTER. IT'S ULTIMATELY MY CHOICE.
JUST DO RIGHT BY HIM, JO.
THAT'S ALL I ASK.
I WILL, STEPHEN.
LET'S GET THIS OVER WITH.

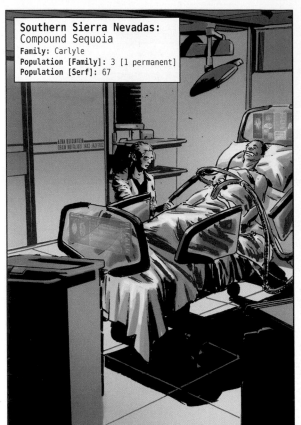

Southern Sierra Nevadas:
Compound Sequoia
Family: Carlyle
Population [Family]: 3 [1 permanent]
Population [Serf]: 67

DOCTOR CARLYLE?

I'M SORRY TO BOTHER YOU.

DOCTOR BARRETT. MICHAEL.

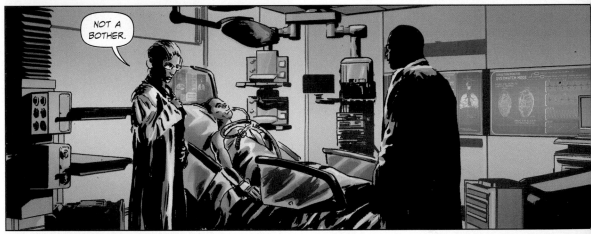

NOT A BOTHER.

FATHER IS STILL *DECLINING*. WE'VE SLOWED IT, BUT I DON'T THINK HE HAS MUCH TIME *LEFT*.

WAS THERE SOMETHING YOU NEEDED?

YES, ACTUALLY.

CAN I HAVE SOME OF YOUR DNA?

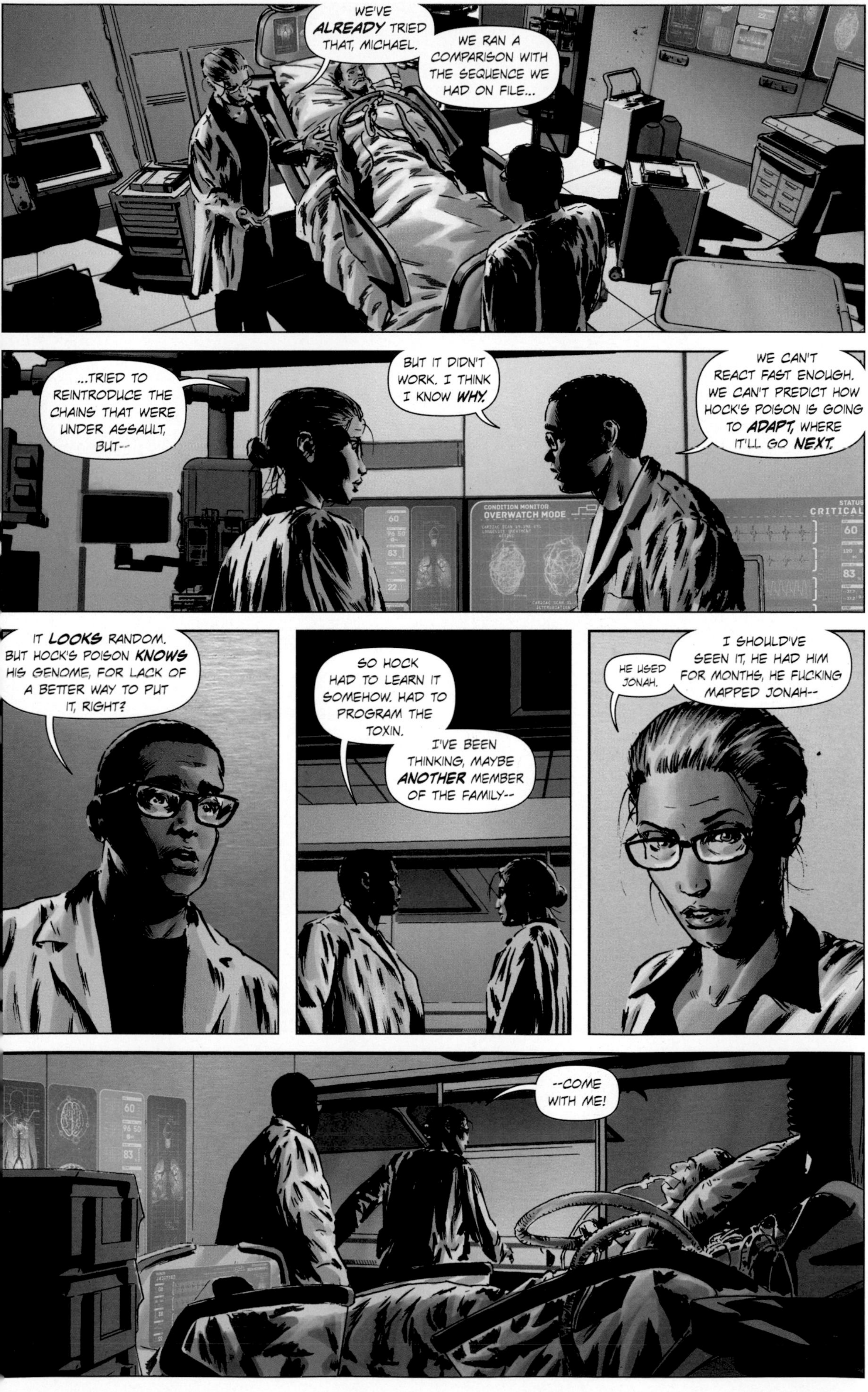
WE'VE ALREADY TRIED THAT, MICHAEL.
WE RAN A COMPARISON WITH THE SEQUENCE WE HAD ON FILE...
...TRIED TO REINTRODUCE THE CHAINS THAT WERE UNDER ASSAULT, BUT--
BUT IT DIDN'T WORK. I THINK I KNOW WHY.
WE CAN'T REACT FAST ENOUGH. WE CAN'T PREDICT HOW HOCK'S POISON IS GOING TO ADAPT, WHERE IT'LL GO NEXT.
CONDITION MONITOR
OVERWATCH MODE
STATUS
CRITICAL
IT LOOKS RANDOM. BUT HOCK'S POISON KNOWS HIS GENOME, FOR LACK OF A BETTER WAY TO PUT IT, RIGHT?
SO HOCK HAD TO LEARN IT SOMEHOW. HAD TO PROGRAM THE TOXIN.
I'VE BEEN THINKING, MAYBE ANOTHER MEMBER OF THE FAMILY--
HE USED JONAH.
I SHOULD'VE SEEN IT, HE HAD HIM FOR MONTHS, HE FUCKING MAPPED JONAH--
--COME WITH ME!

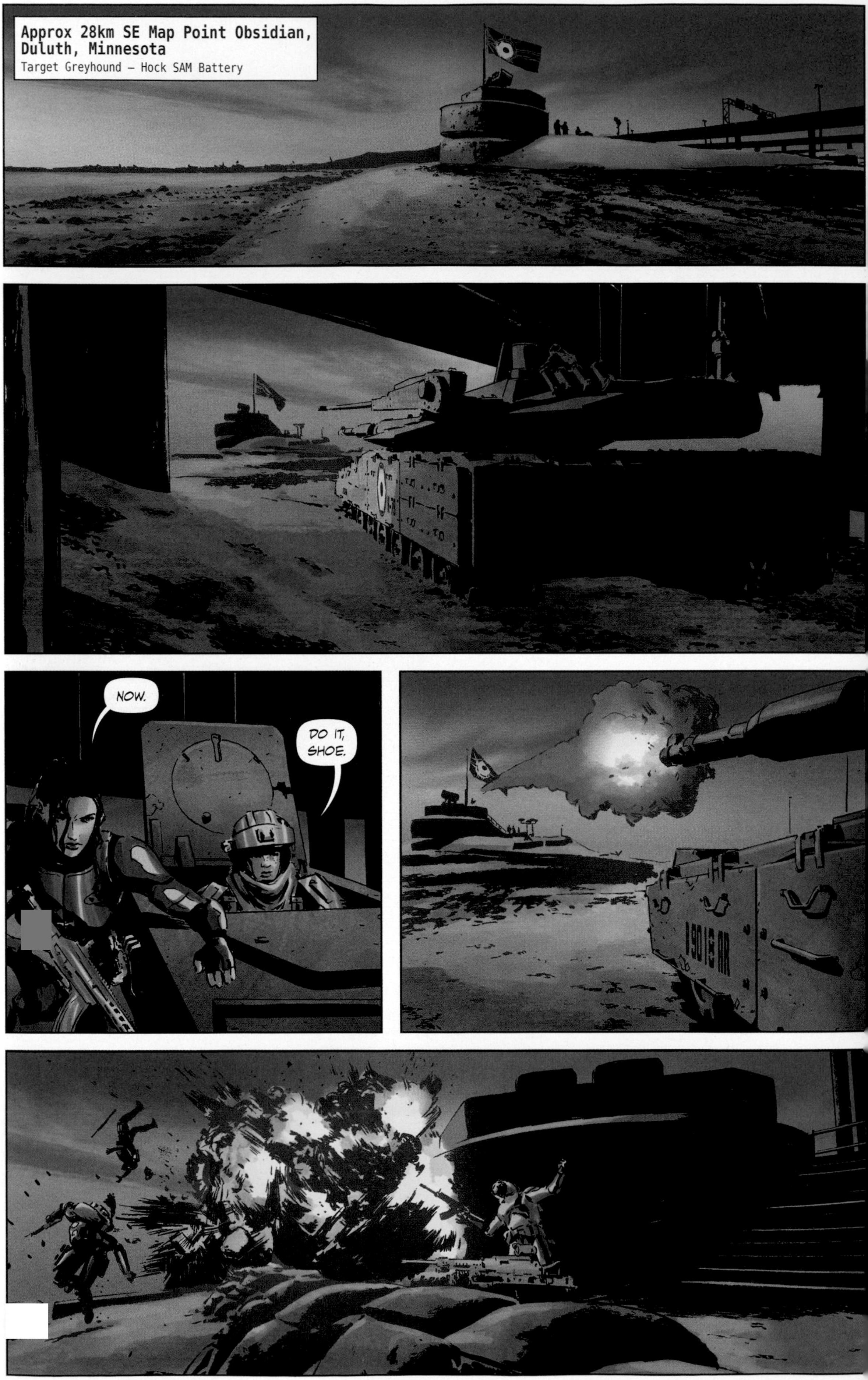
Approx 28km SE Map Point Obsidian, Duluth, Minnesota
Target Greyhound – Hock SAM Battery
NOW.
DO IT, SHOE.

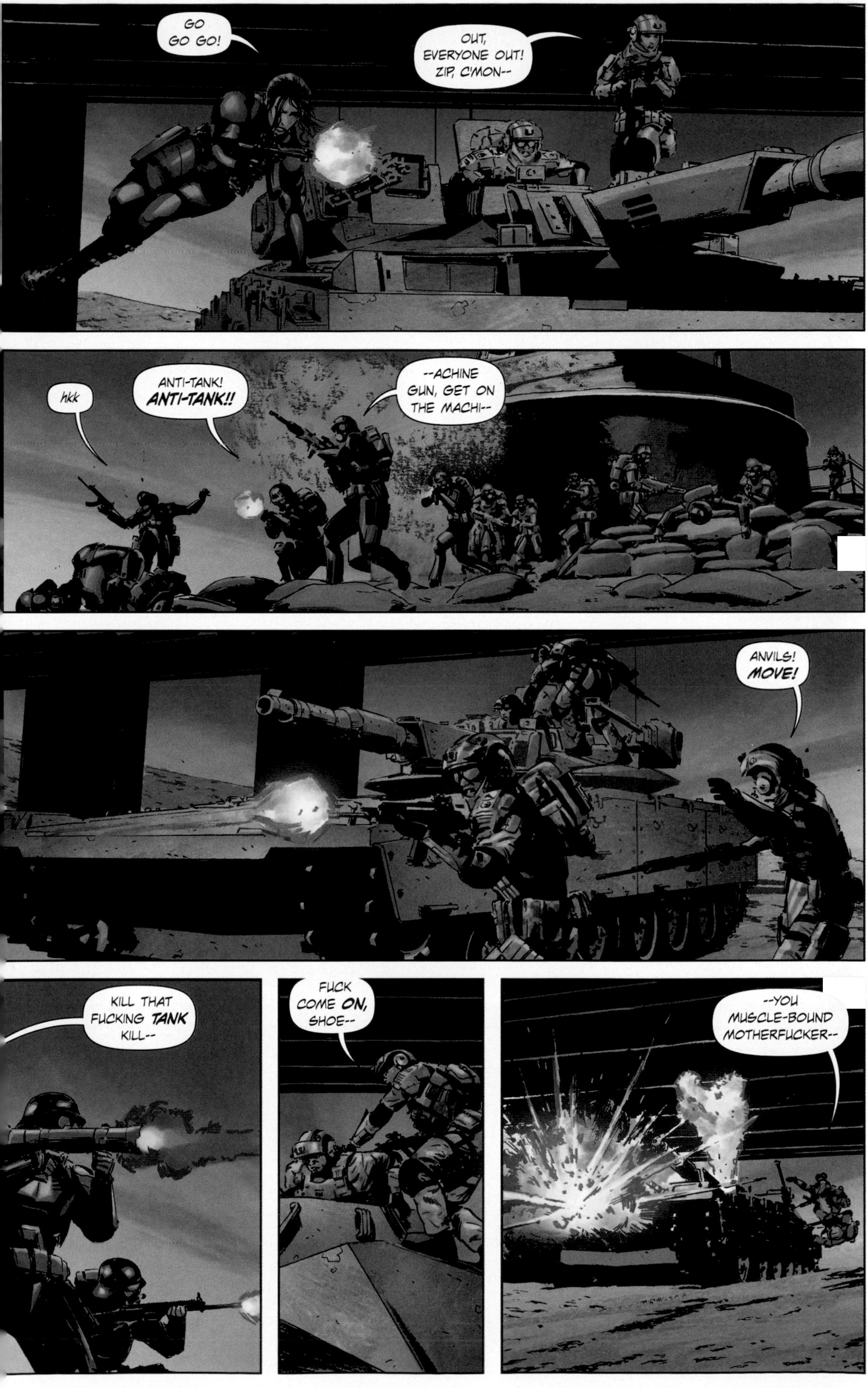
GO
GO GO!
OUT,
EVERYONE OUT!
ZIP, C'MON--
hkk
ANTI-TANK!
ANTI-TANK!!
--ACHINE
GUN, GET ON
THE MACHI--
ANVILS!
MOVE!
KILL THAT
FUCKING **TANK**
KILL--
FUCK
COME **ON**,
SHOE--
--YOU
MUSCLE-BOUND
MOTHERFUCKER--

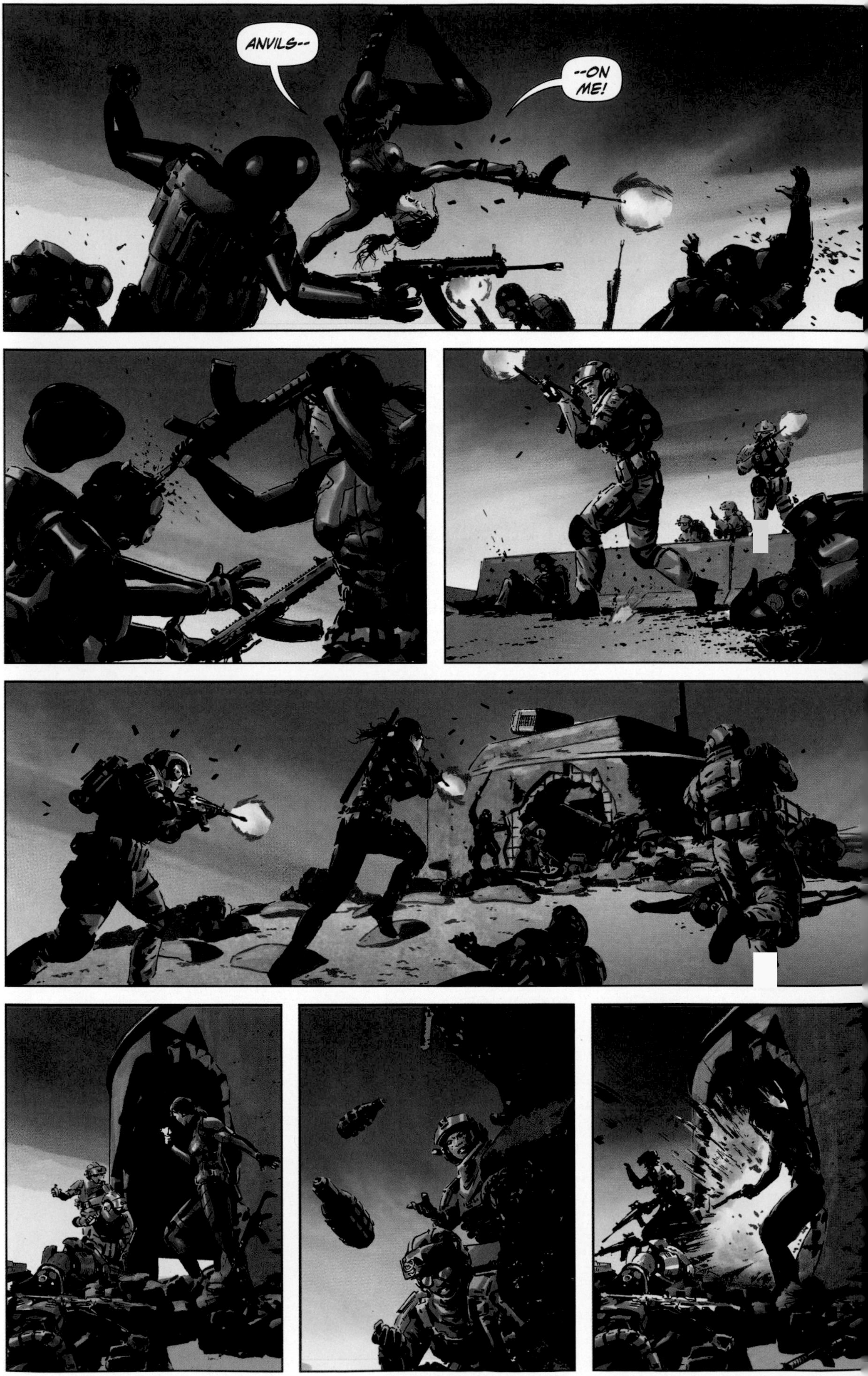
ANVILS--
--ON ME!

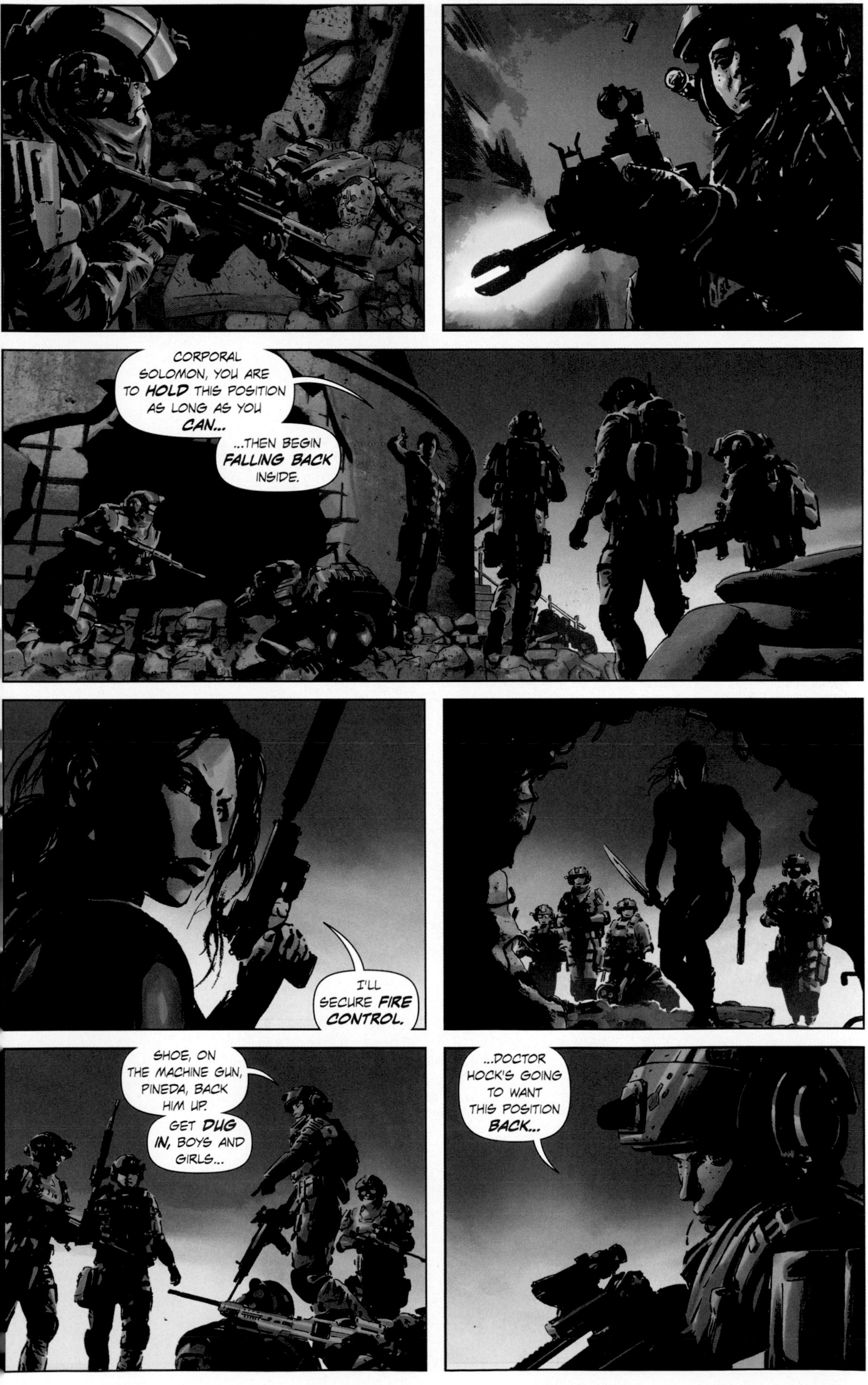
CORPORAL SOLOMON, YOU ARE TO HOLD THIS POSITION AS LONG AS YOU CAN...
...THEN BEGIN FALLING BACK INSIDE.
I'LL SECURE FIRE CONTROL.
SHOE, ON THE MACHINE GUN, PINEDA, BACK HIM UP.
GET DUG IN, BOYS AND GIRLS...
...DOCTOR HOCK'S GOING TO WANT THIS POSITION BACK...

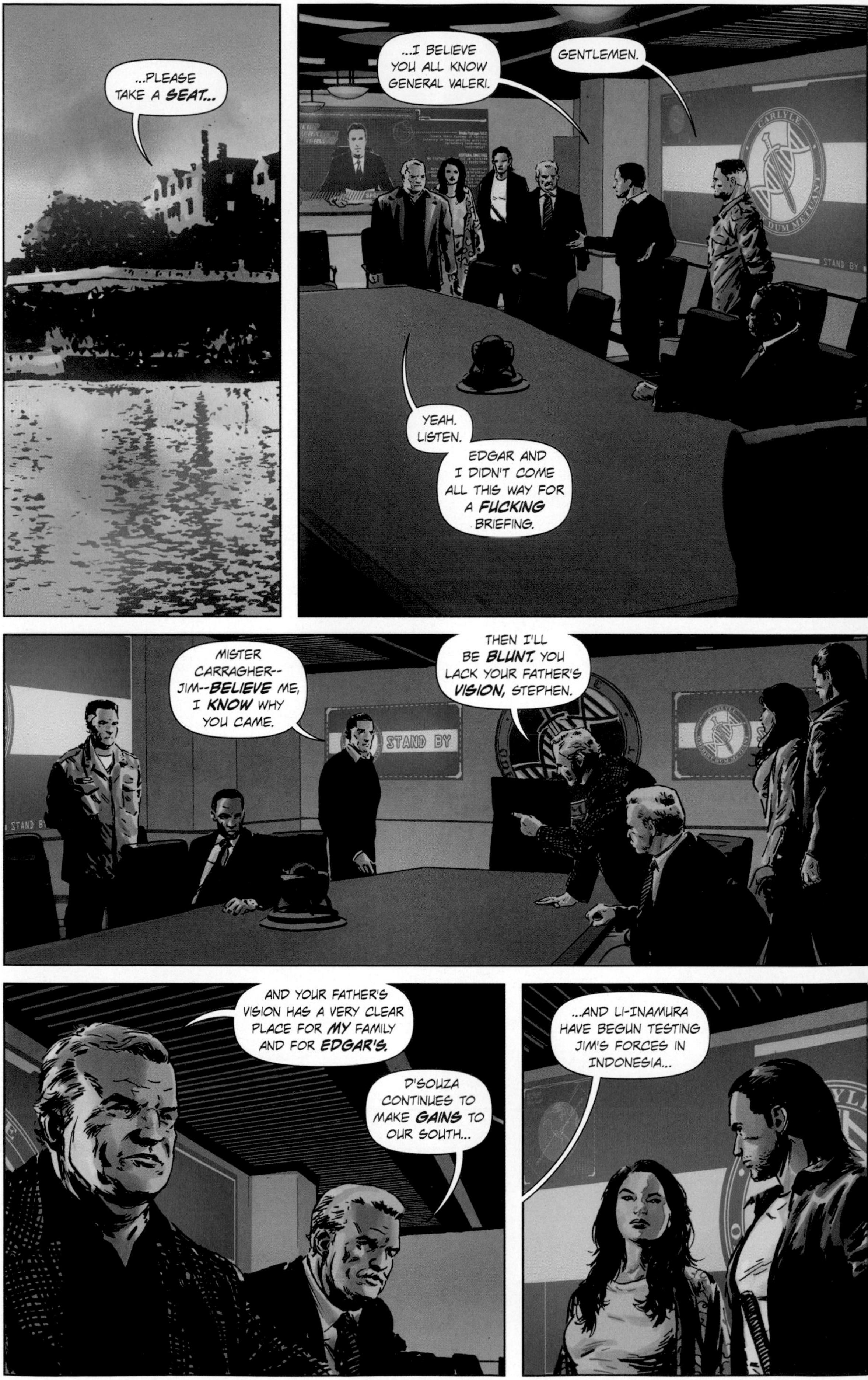
...PLEASE TAKE A SEAT...
...I BELIEVE YOU ALL KNOW GENERAL VALERI.
GENTLEMEN.
CARLYLE
YEAH. LISTEN.
EDGAR AND I DIDN'T COME ALL THIS WAY FOR A FUCKING BRIEFING.
MISTER CARRAGHER-- JIM--BELIEVE ME, I KNOW WHY YOU CAME.
STAND BY
THEN I'LL BE BLUNT. YOU LACK YOUR FATHER'S VISION, STEPHEN.
AND YOUR FATHER'S VISION HAS A VERY CLEAR PLACE FOR MY FAMILY AND FOR EDGAR'S.
D'SOUZA CONTINUES TO MAKE GAINS TO OUR SOUTH...
...AND LI-INAMURA HAVE BEGUN TESTING JIM'S FORCES IN INDONESIA...

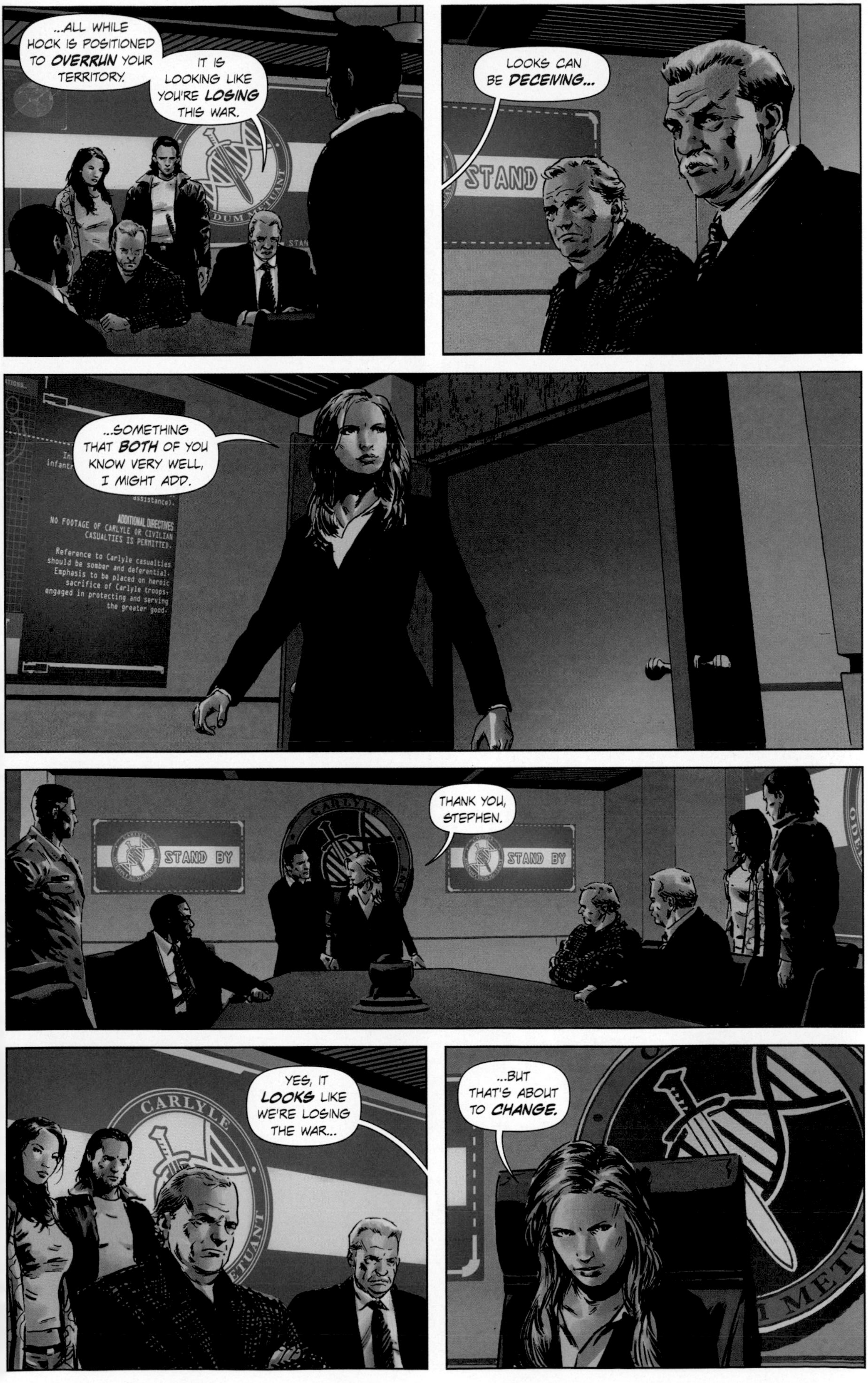
...ALL WHILE HOCK IS POSITIONED TO **OVERRUN** YOUR TERRITORY.
IT IS LOOKING LIKE YOU'RE **LOSING** THIS WAR.
LOOKS CAN BE **DECEIVING...**
STAND
...SOMETHING THAT **BOTH** OF YOU KNOW VERY WELL, I MIGHT ADD.
ADDITIONAL DIRECTIVES
NO FOOTAGE OF CARLYLE OR CIVILIAN CASUALTIES IS PERMITTED.
Reference to Carlyle casualties should be somber and deferential. Emphasis to be placed on heroic sacrifice of Carlyle troops, engaged in protecting and serving the greater good.
STAND BY
CARLYLE
STAND BY
THANK YOU, STEPHEN.
CARLYLE
YES, IT **LOOKS** LIKE WE'RE LOSING THE WAR...
...BUT THAT'S ABOUT TO **CHANGE.**

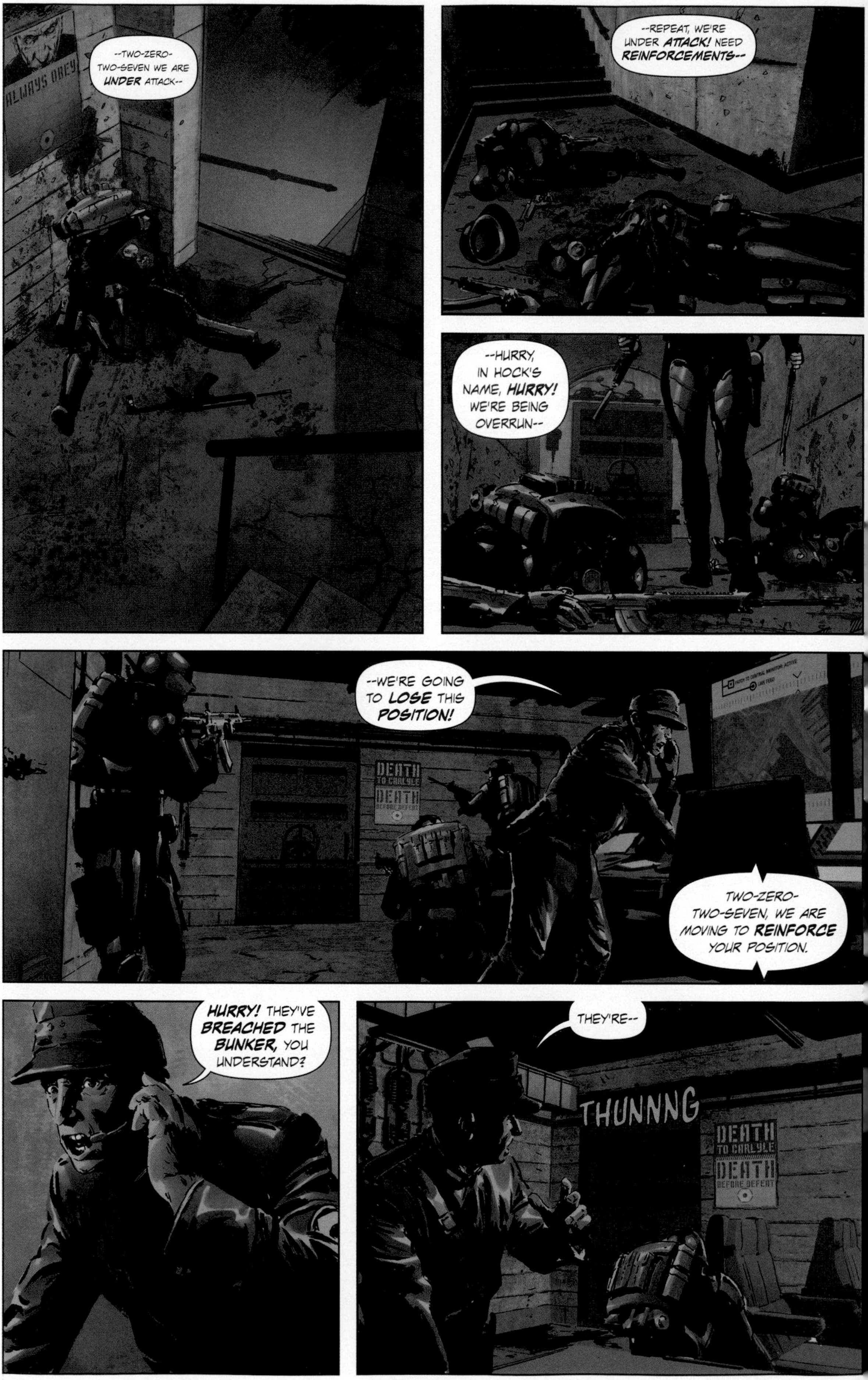
ALWAYS OBEY
--TWO-ZERO-TWO-SEVEN WE ARE **UNDER** ATTACK--
--REPEAT, WE'RE UNDER **ATTACK!** NEED **REINFORCEMENTS**--
--HURRY, IN HOCK'S NAME, **HURRY!** WE'RE BEING OVERRUN--
--WE'RE GOING TO **LOSE** THIS **POSITION!**
DEATH TO CARLYLE
DEATH BEFORE DEFEAT
TWO-ZERO-TWO-SEVEN, WE ARE MOVING TO **REINFORCE** YOUR POSITION.
HURRY! THEY'VE **BREACHED** THE **BUNKER,** YOU UNDERSTAND?
THEY'RE--
THUNNNG
DEATH TO CARLYLE
DEATH BEFORE DEFEAT

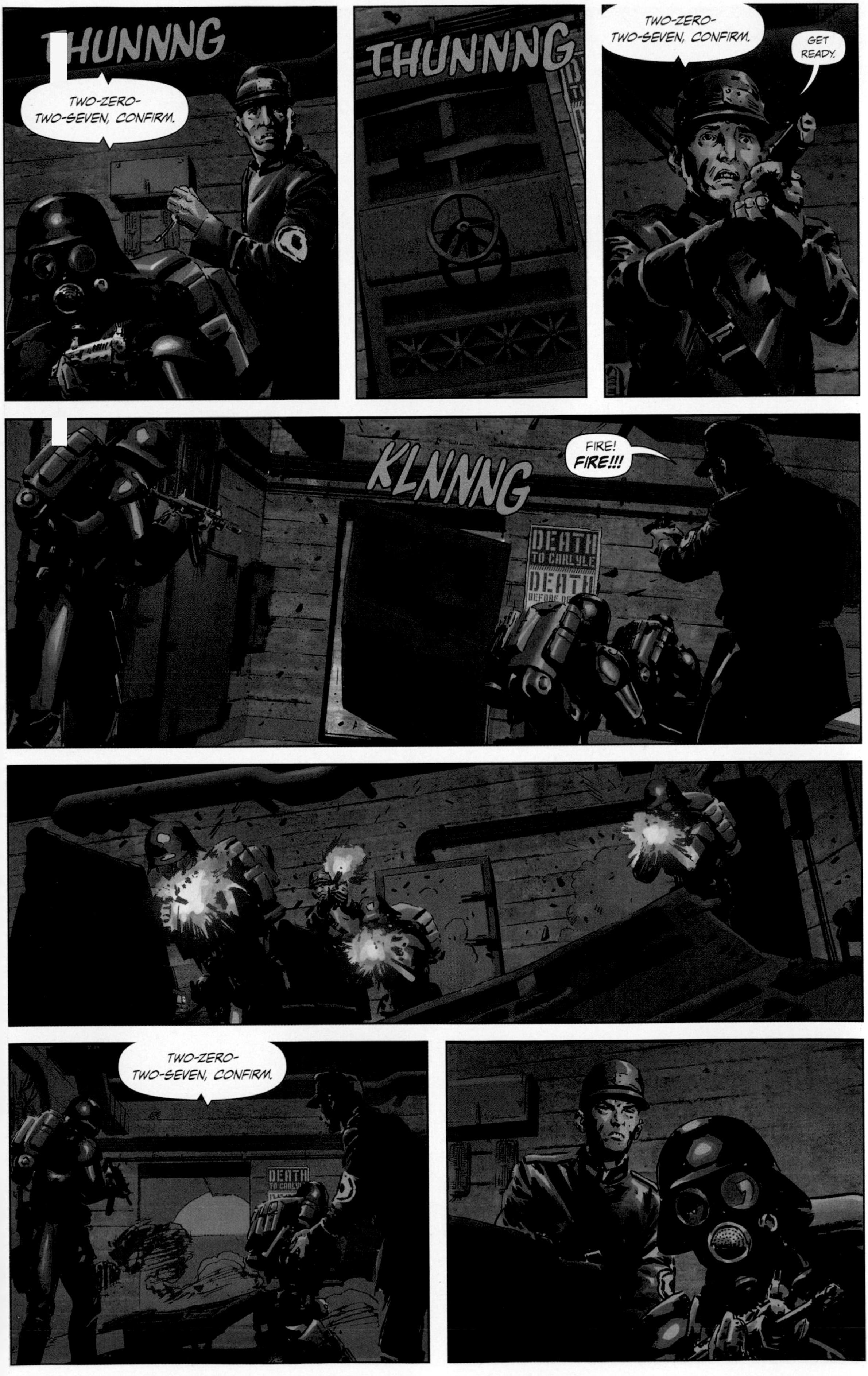
THUNNNG
TWO-ZERO-TWO-SEVEN, CONFIRM.
THUNNNG
TWO-ZERO-TWO-SEVEN, CONFIRM.
GET READY.
KLNNNG
FIRE! FIRE!!!
DEATH TO CARLYLE
DEATH
TWO-ZERO-TWO-SEVEN, CONFIRM.
DEATH

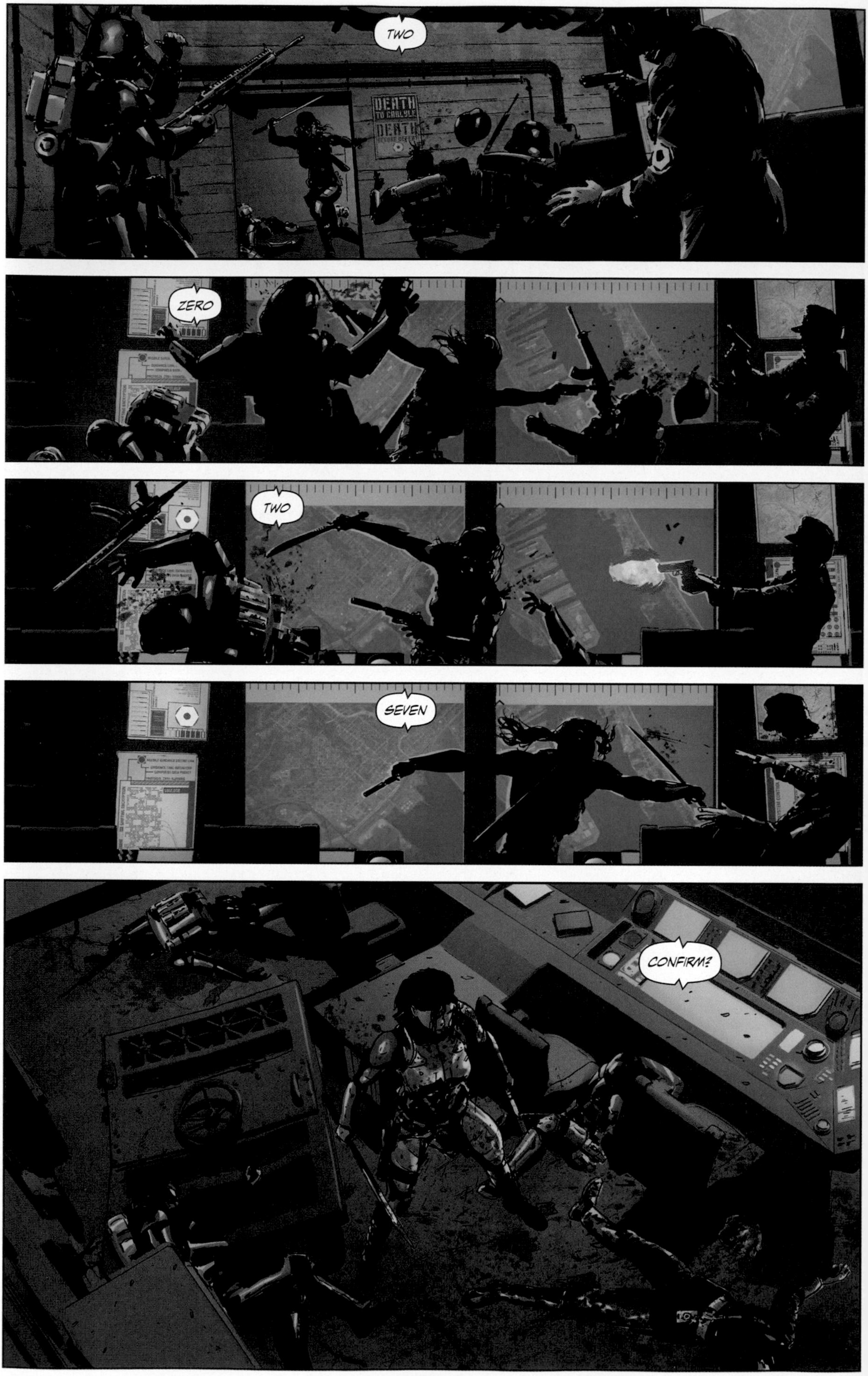
TWO
DEATH TO CARLYLE
DEATH
ZERO
TWO
SEVEN
CONFIRM?

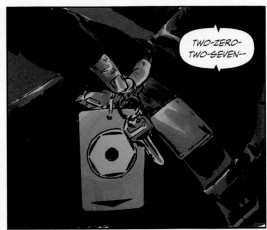

TWO-ZERO-TWO-SEVEN, PLEASE CONFIRM.

TWO-ZERO-TWO-SEVEN--

--PLEASE CONFIRM--

skkkkshsHHHHSsssss

deet

THIS IS GORGON-SIX ACTUAL ON OPEN CHANNEL TO ANY CARLYLE FORCES RECEIVING.

AUTHORIZING, BRAVO-TANGO-TANGO-CHARLIE, FOUR-FOUR-ECHO-X-RAY-ECHO-ZERO. THE WORD OF THE DAY IS, "FAULT-LINE."

I REPEAT, GORGON-SIX ACTUAL BROADCASTING IN THE OPEN, TO ANY CARLYLE FORCES RECEIVING--

skkkkshss

FOXTROT-OSCAR MACINTYRE-OH-ONE, WE RECEIVE AND CONFIRM, GORGON-SIX.

MACINTYRE-OH-ONE, GORGON-SIX ACTUAL...

...WE ARE IN **CONTROL** OF TARGET GREYHOUND...

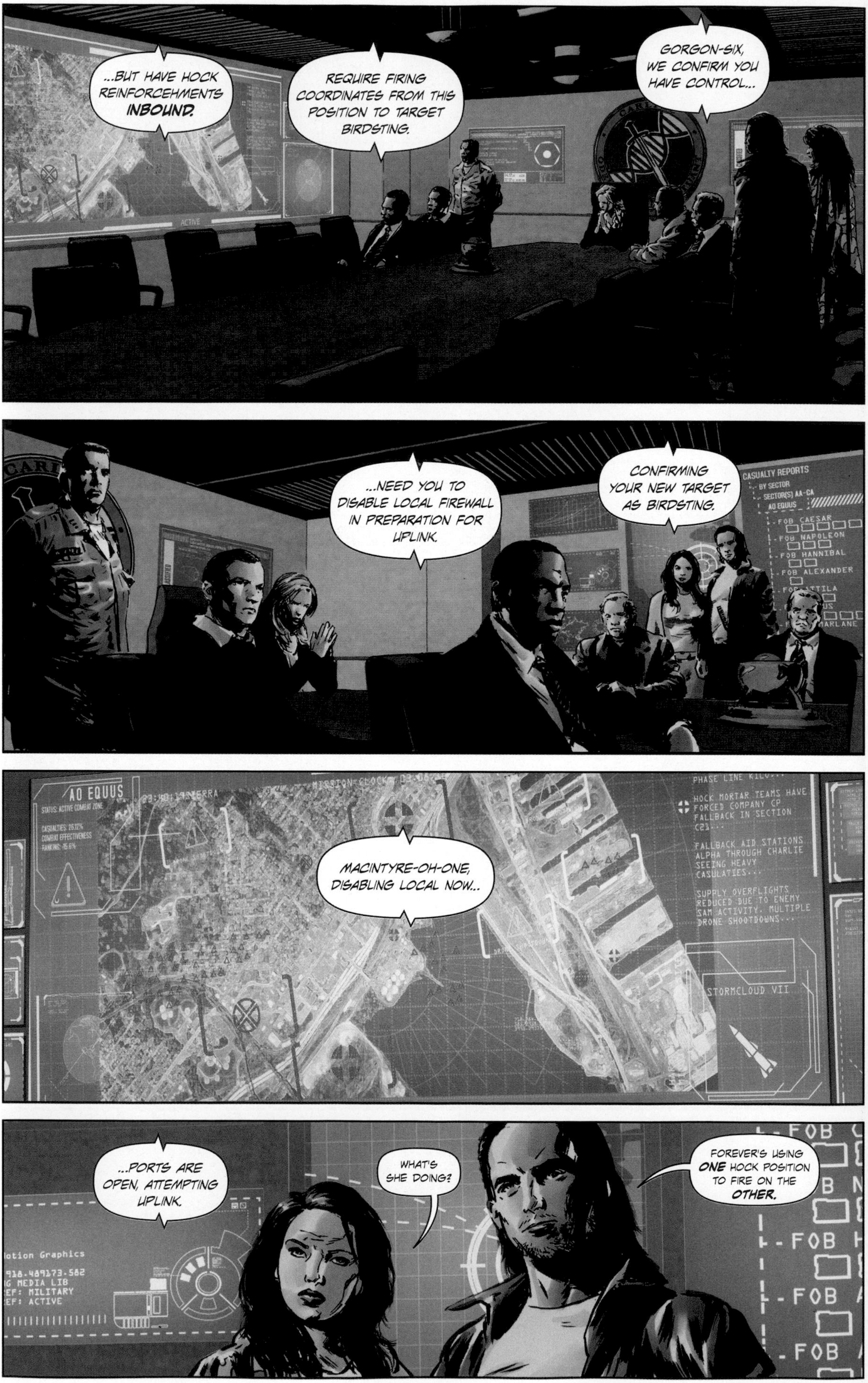
...BUT HAVE HOCK REINFORCEHMENTS INBOUND.
REQUIRE FIRING COORDINATES FROM THIS POSITION TO TARGET BIRDSTING.
GORGON-SIX, WE CONFIRM YOU HAVE CONTROL...
ACTIVE
...NEED YOU TO DISABLE LOCAL FIREWALL IN PREPARATION FOR UPLINK.
CONFIRMING YOUR NEW TARGET AS BIRDSTING.
CASUALTY REPORTS
BY SECTOR
SECTOR(S) AA-CA
AO EQUUS
FOB CAESAR
FOB NAPOLEON
FOB HANNIBAL
FOB ALEXANDER
AO EQUUS
STATUS: ACTIVE COMBAT ZONE
MACINTYRE-OH-ONE, DISABLING LOCAL NOW...
HOCK MORTAR TEAMS HAVE FORCED COMPANY CP FALLBACK IN SECTION C21...
FALLBACK AID STATIONS ALPHA THROUGH CHARLIE SEEING HEAVY CASULATIES...
SUPPLY OVERFLIGHTS REDUCED DUE TO ENEMY SAM ACTIVITY. MULTIPLE DRONE SHOOTDOWNS...
STORMCLOUD VII
...PORTS ARE OPEN, ATTEMPTING UPLINK.
WHAT'S SHE DOING?
FOREVER'S USING ONE HOCK POSITION TO FIRE ON THE OTHER.

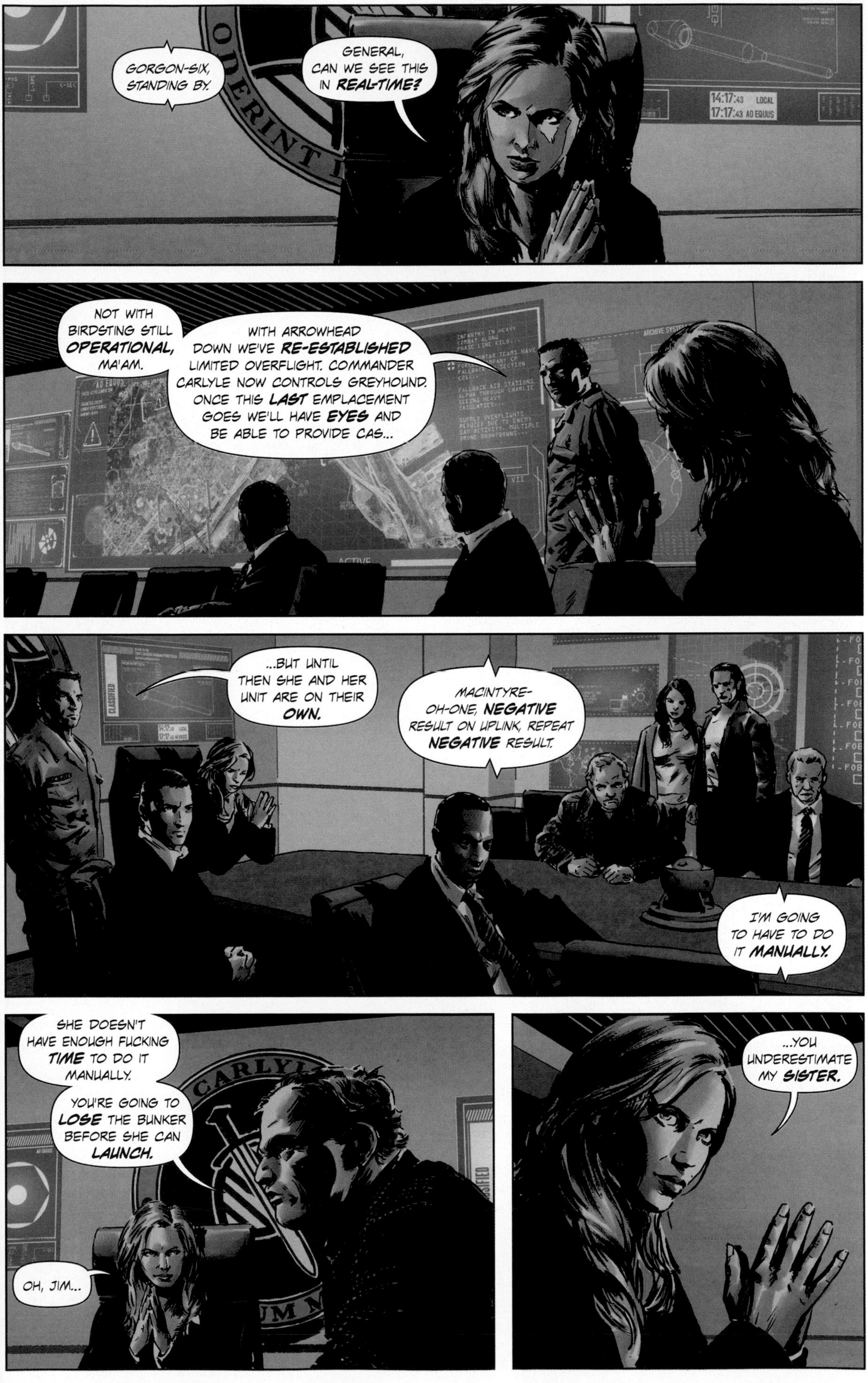
GORGON-SIX, STANDING BY.
GENERAL, CAN WE SEE THIS IN REAL-TIME?
NOT WITH BIRDSTING STILL OPERATIONAL, MA'AM.
WITH ARROWHEAD DOWN WE'VE RE-ESTABLISHED LIMITED OVERFLIGHT. COMMANDER CARLYLE NOW CONTROLS GREYHOUND. ONCE THIS LAST EMPLACEMENT GOES WE'LL HAVE EYES AND BE ABLE TO PROVIDE CAS...
...BUT UNTIL THEN SHE AND HER UNIT ARE ON THEIR OWN.
MACINTYRE-OH-ONE, NEGATIVE RESULT ON UPLINK, REPEAT NEGATIVE RESULT.
I'M GOING TO HAVE TO DO IT MANUALLY.
SHE DOESN'T HAVE ENOUGH FUCKING TIME TO DO IT MANUALLY.
YOU'RE GOING TO LOSE THE BUNKER BEFORE SHE CAN LAUNCH.
OH, JIM...
...YOU UNDERESTIMATE MY SISTER.

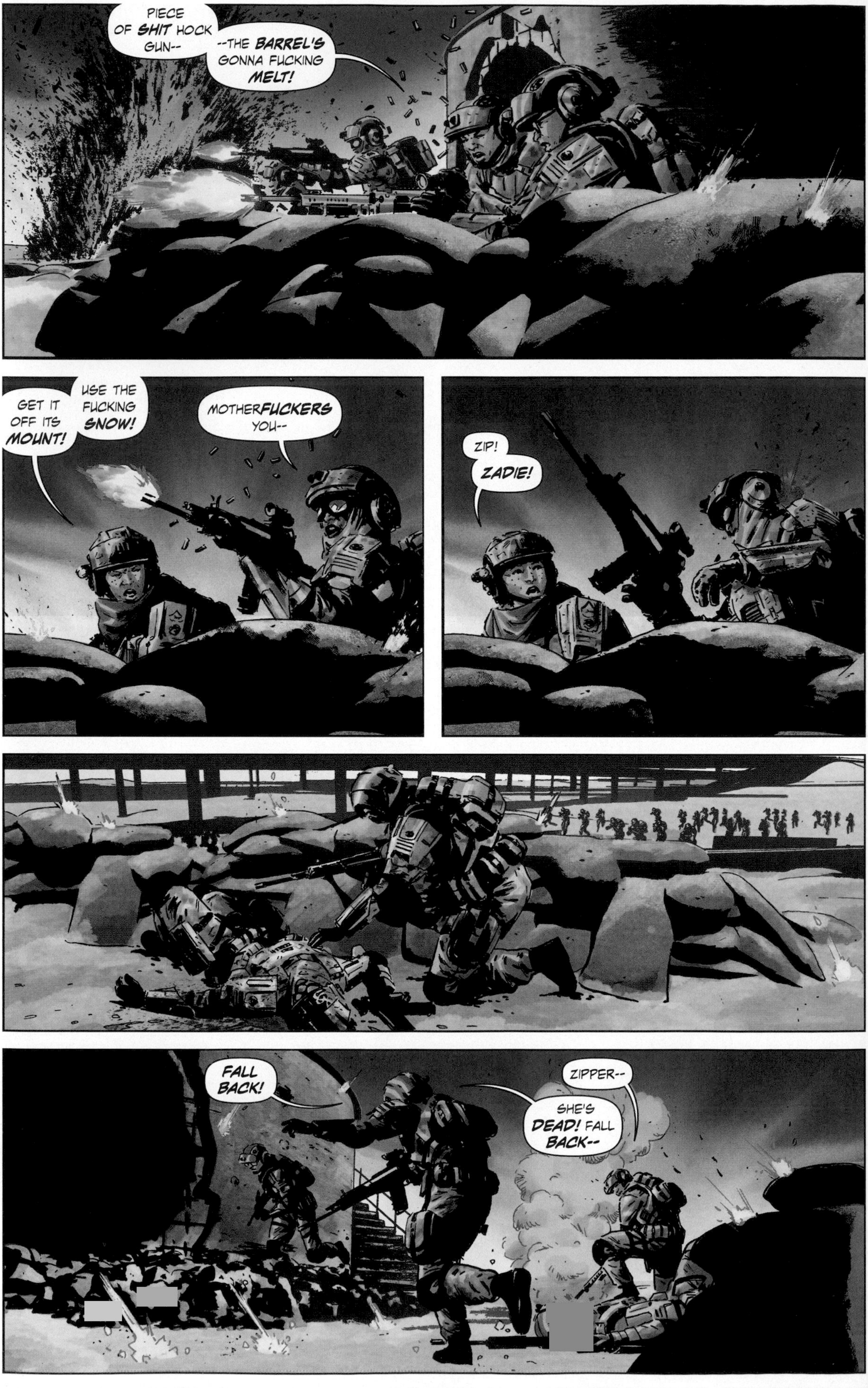
PIECE OF SHIT HOCK GUN--
--THE BARREL'S GONNA FUCKING MELT!
GET IT OFF ITS MOUNT!
USE THE FUCKING SNOW!
MOTHERFUCKERS YOU--
ZIP!
ZADIE!
FALL BACK!
ZIPPER--
SHE'S DEAD! FALL BACK--

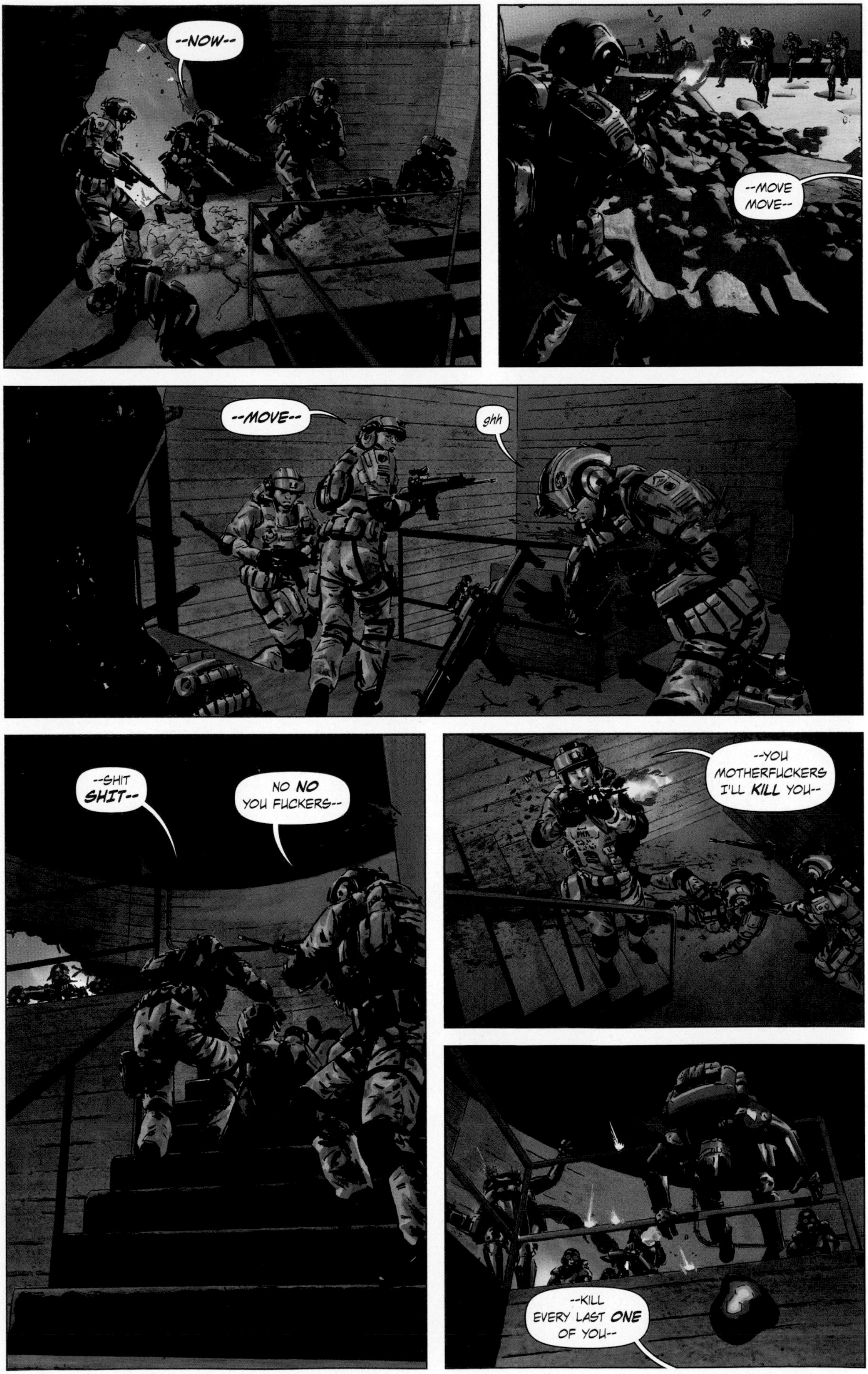
--NOW--
--MOVE MOVE--
--MOVE--
ghh
--SHIT SHIT--
NO NO YOU FUCKERS--
--YOU MOTHERFUCKERS I'LL KILL YOU--
--KILL EVERY LAST ONE OF YOU--

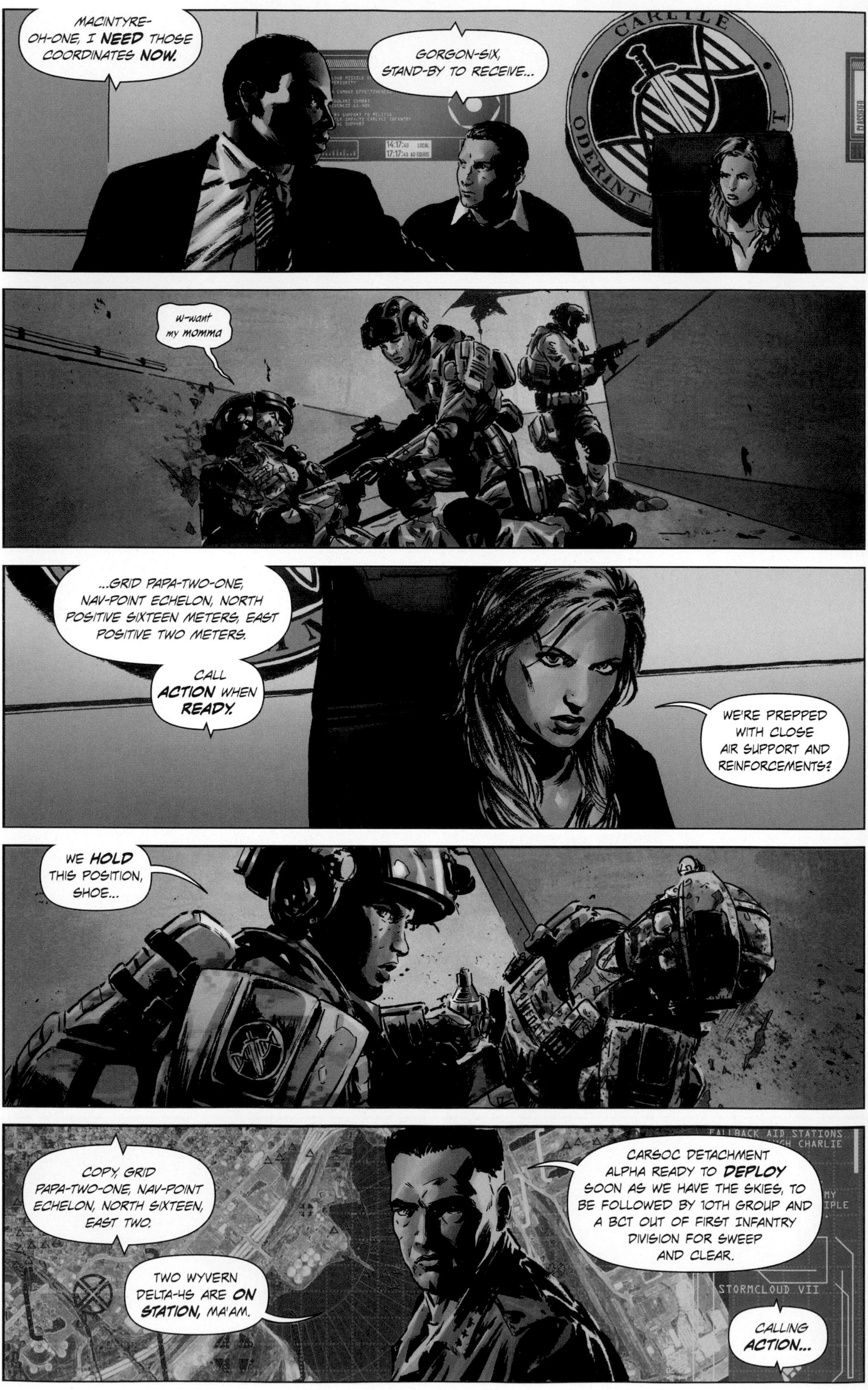
MACINTYRE-OH-ONE, I **NEED** THOSE COORDINATES **NOW.**
GORGON-SIX, STAND-BY TO RECEIVE...
w-want my momma
...GRID PAPA-TWO-ONE, NAV-POINT ECHELON, NORTH POSITIVE SIXTEEN METERS, EAST POSITIVE TWO METERS.
CALL **ACTION** WHEN **READY.**
WE'RE PREPPED WITH CLOSE AIR SUPPORT AND REINFORCEMENTS?
WE **HOLD** THIS POSITION, SHOE...
FALLBACK AID STATIONS
COPY, GRID PAPA-TWO-ONE, NAV-POINT ECHELON, NORTH SIXTEEN, EAST TWO.
TWO WYVERN DELTA-HS ARE **ON STATION,** MA'AM.
CARSOC DETACHMENT ALPHA READY TO **DEPLOY** SOON AS WE HAVE THE SKIES, TO BE FOLLOWED BY 10TH GROUP AND A BCT OUT OF FIRST INFANTRY DIVISION FOR SWEEP AND CLEAR.
STORMCLOUD VII
CALLING **ACTION...**

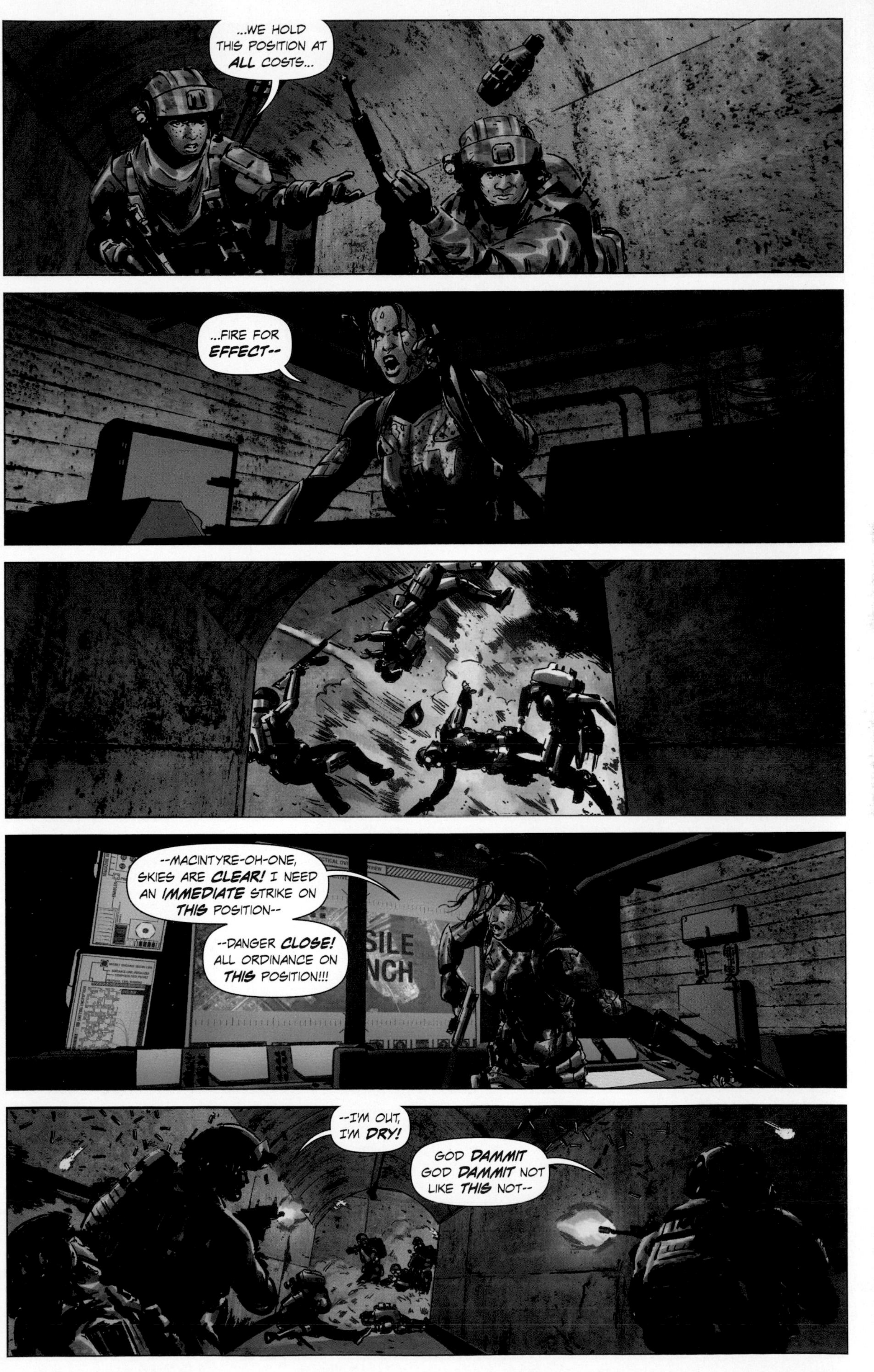
...WE HOLD THIS POSITION AT ALL COSTS...
...FIRE FOR EFFECT--
--MACINTYRE-OH-ONE, SKIES ARE CLEAR! I NEED AN IMMEDIATE STRIKE ON THIS POSITION--
--DANGER CLOSE! ALL ORDINANCE ON THIS POSITION!!!
SILE
NCH
--I'M OUT, I'M DRY!
GOD DAMMIT GOD DAMMIT NOT LIKE THIS NOT--

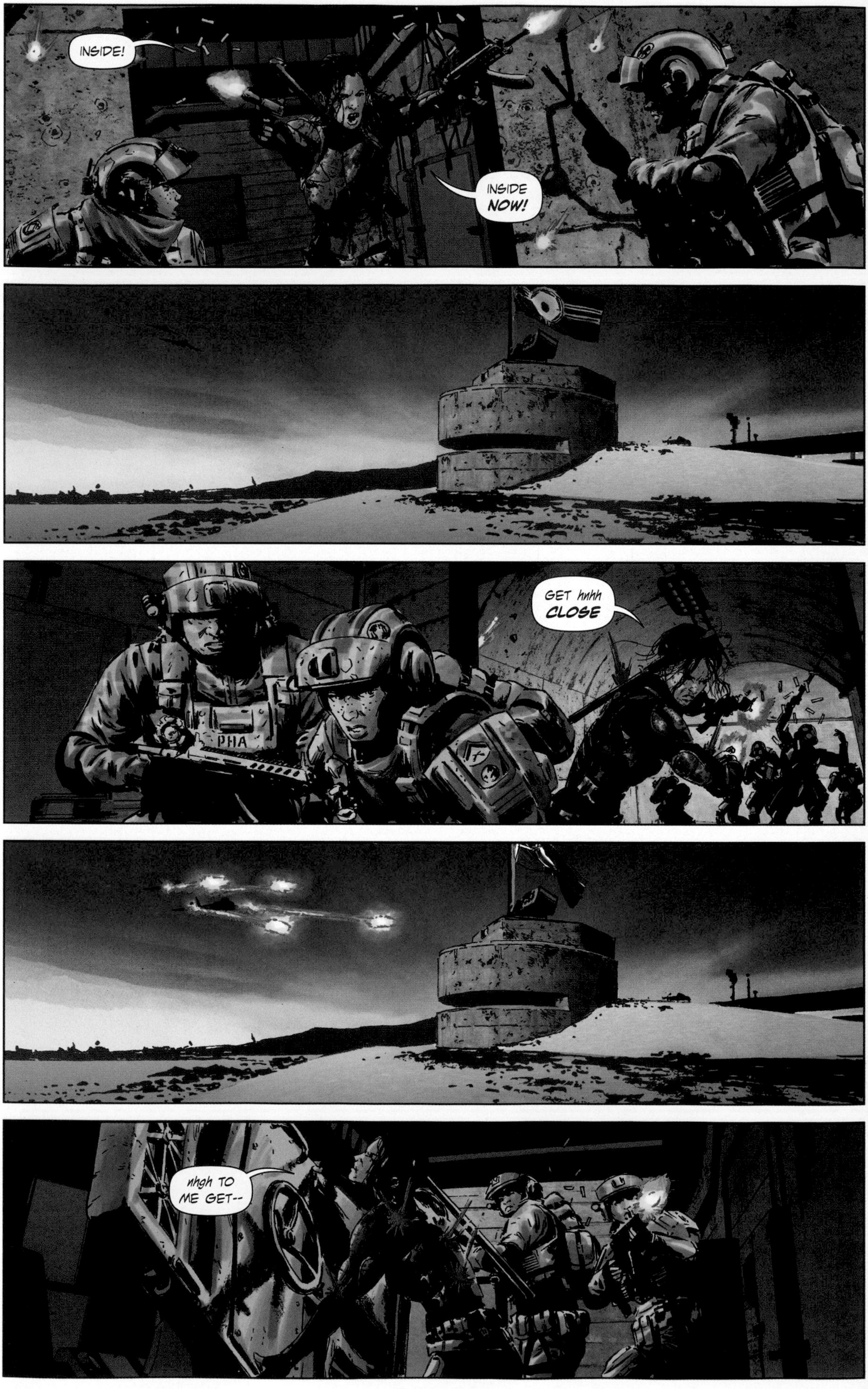
INSIDE!
INSIDE NOW!
GET hnhh CLOSE
nhgh TO ME GET--
PHA

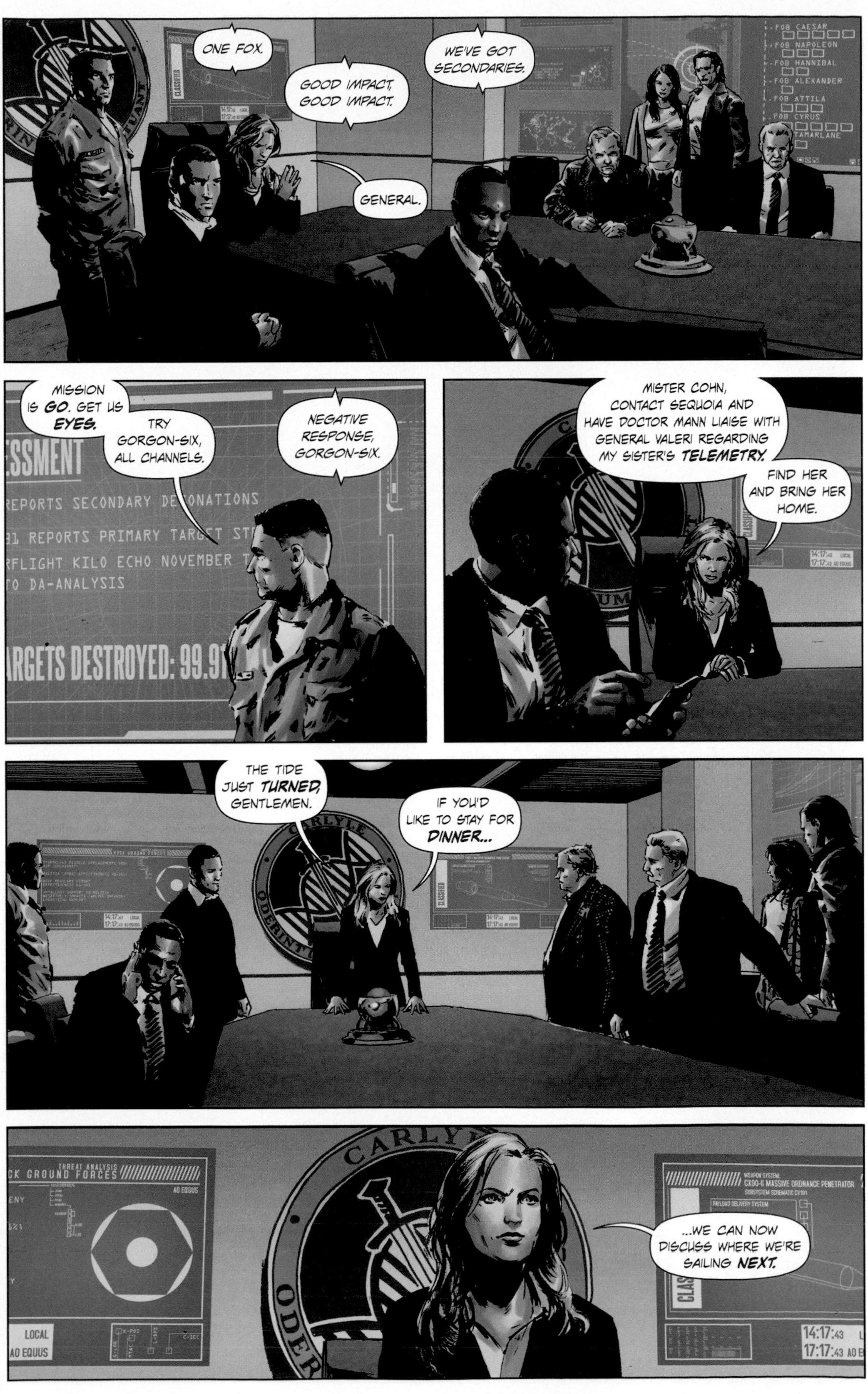
ONE FOX.
GOOD IMPACT, GOOD IMPACT.
WE'VE GOT SECONDARIES.
GENERAL.
MISSION IS GO. GET US EYES.
TRY GORGON-SIX, ALL CHANNELS.
NEGATIVE RESPONSE, GORGON-SIX.
MISTER COHN, CONTACT SEQUOIA AND HAVE DOCTOR MANN LIAISE WITH GENERAL VALERI REGARDING MY SISTER'S TELEMETRY.
FIND HER AND BRING HER HOME.
THE TIDE JUST TURNED, GENTLEMEN.
IF YOU'D LIKE TO STAY FOR DINNER...
...WE CAN NOW DISCUSS WHERE WE'RE SAILING NEXT.

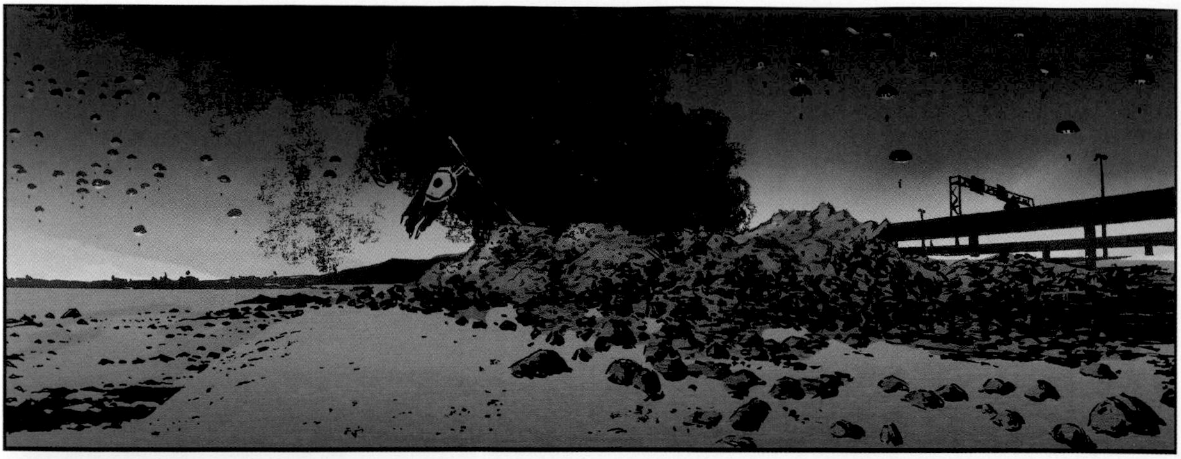

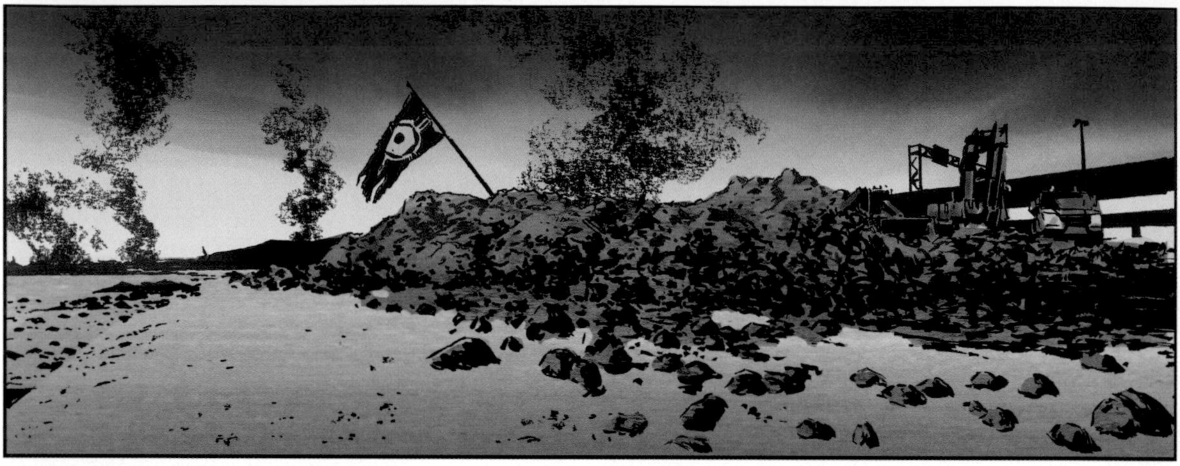

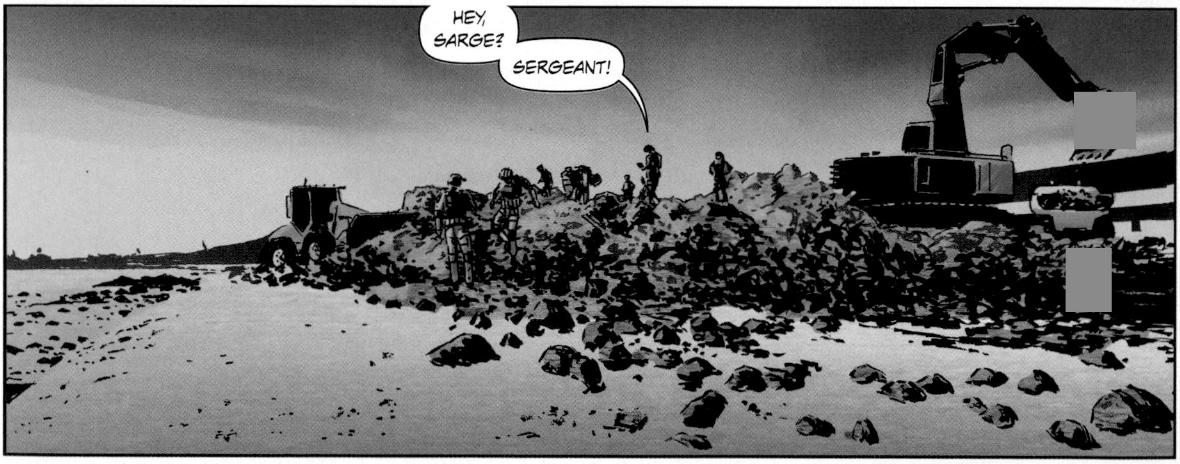
HEY, SARGE?
SERGEANT!

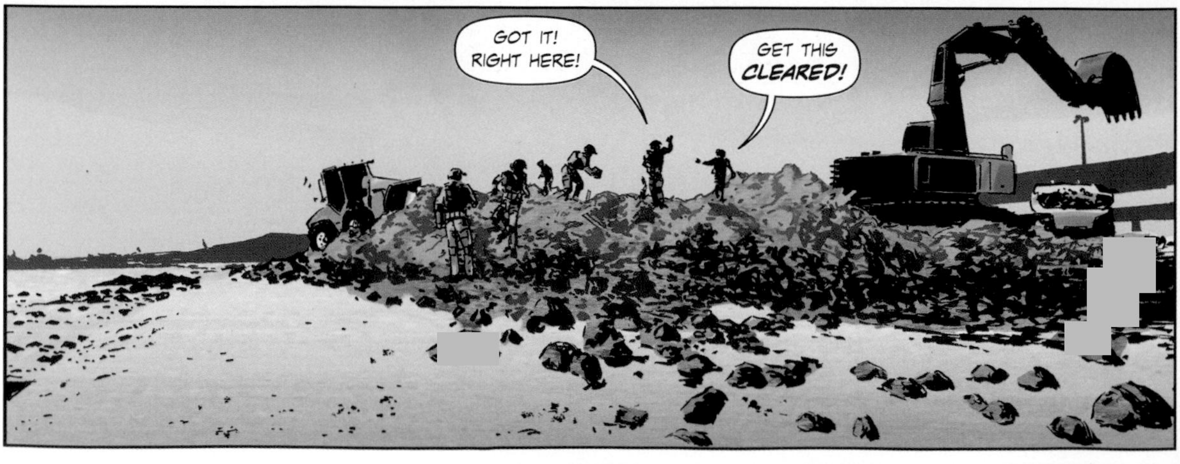
GOT IT! RIGHT HERE!
GET THIS *CLEARED!*

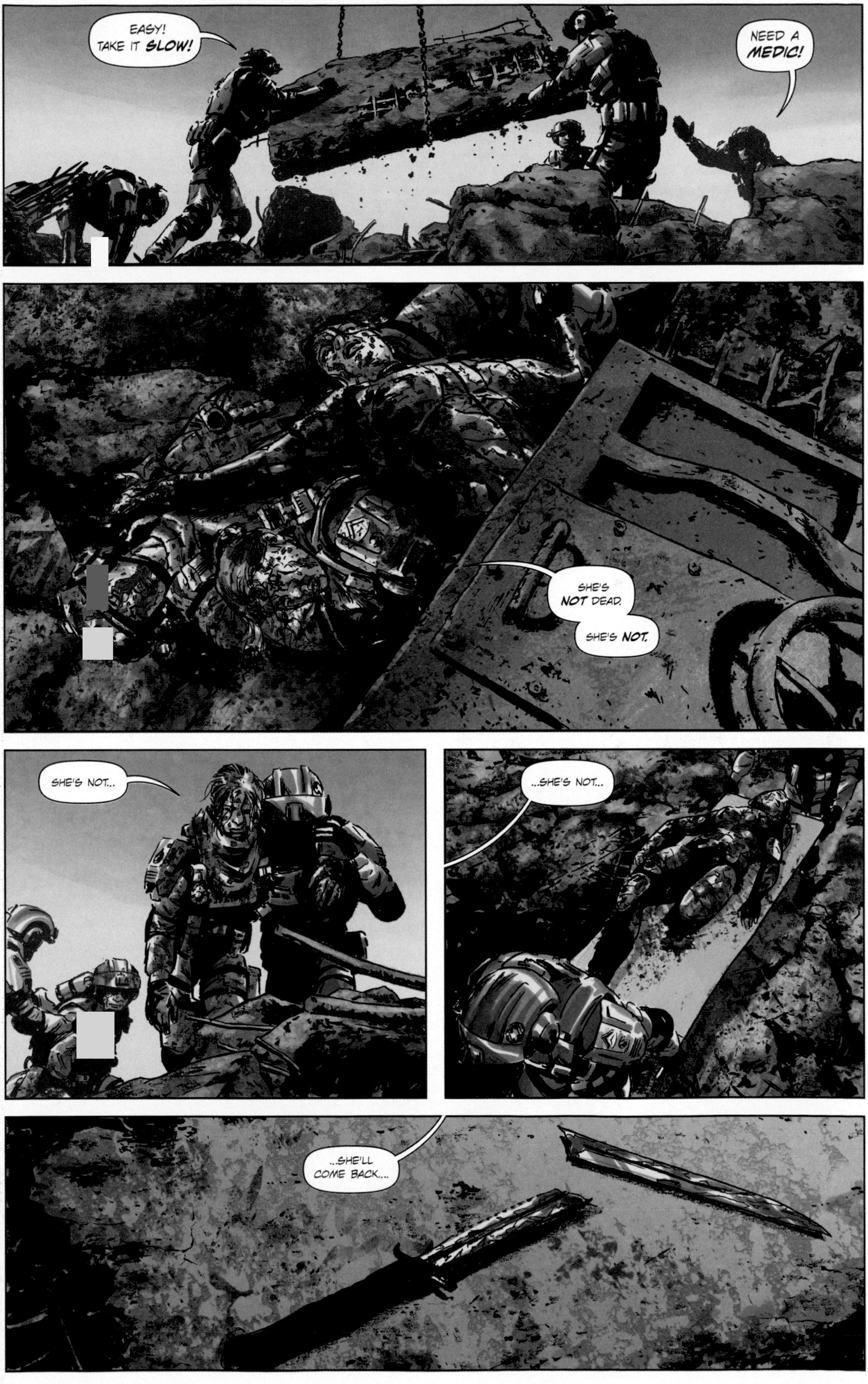
EASY! TAKE IT SLOW!
NEED A MEDIC!
SHE'S NOT DEAD.
SHE'S NOT.
SHE'S NOT...
...SHE'S NOT...
...SHE'LL COME BACK...

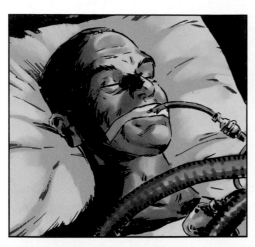

WHAT DO YOU THINK?

HE'S *STABLE*.

HE'S *STABLE*, MICHAEL.

YOU *DID* IT.

JUST A SECOND.

THEY FOUND FOREVER IN DULUTH, SHE'S BEING TRANSPORTED BACK HERE--

I CAN'T *FIND* HER, JAMES.

SHE'S GONE *WALKABOUT*.

WHAT? HOW?

DO I LOOK LIKE *I* KNOW? SHE'S A FUCKING LAZARUS.

IT WAS ONLY A MATTER OF *TIME* BEFORE SHE SLIPPED THE *LEASH*.

I'M INITIATING A *LOCKDOWN*.

I'LL ACTIVATE *TELEMETRY*...

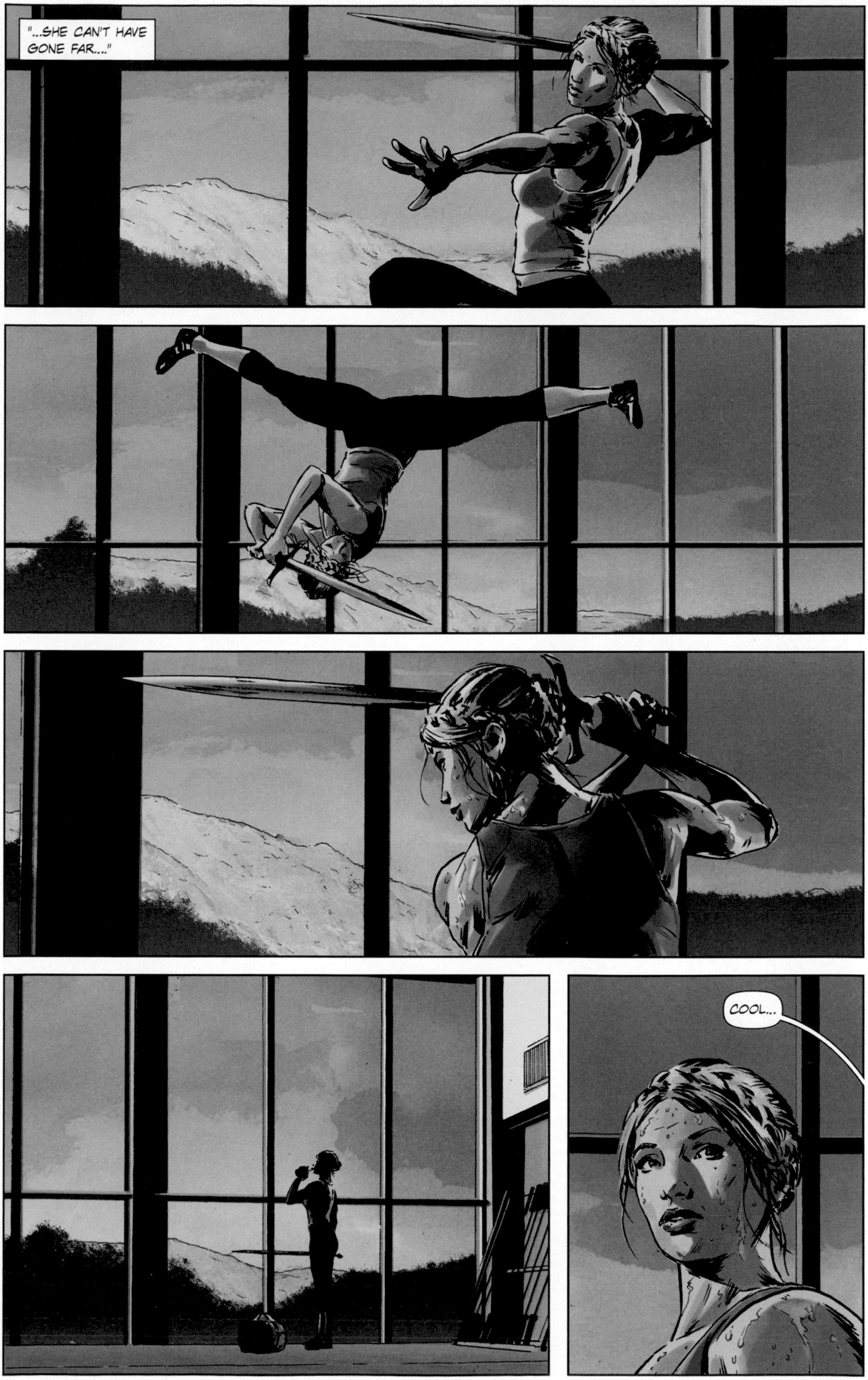
"...SHE CAN'T HAVE GONE FAR..."
COOL...

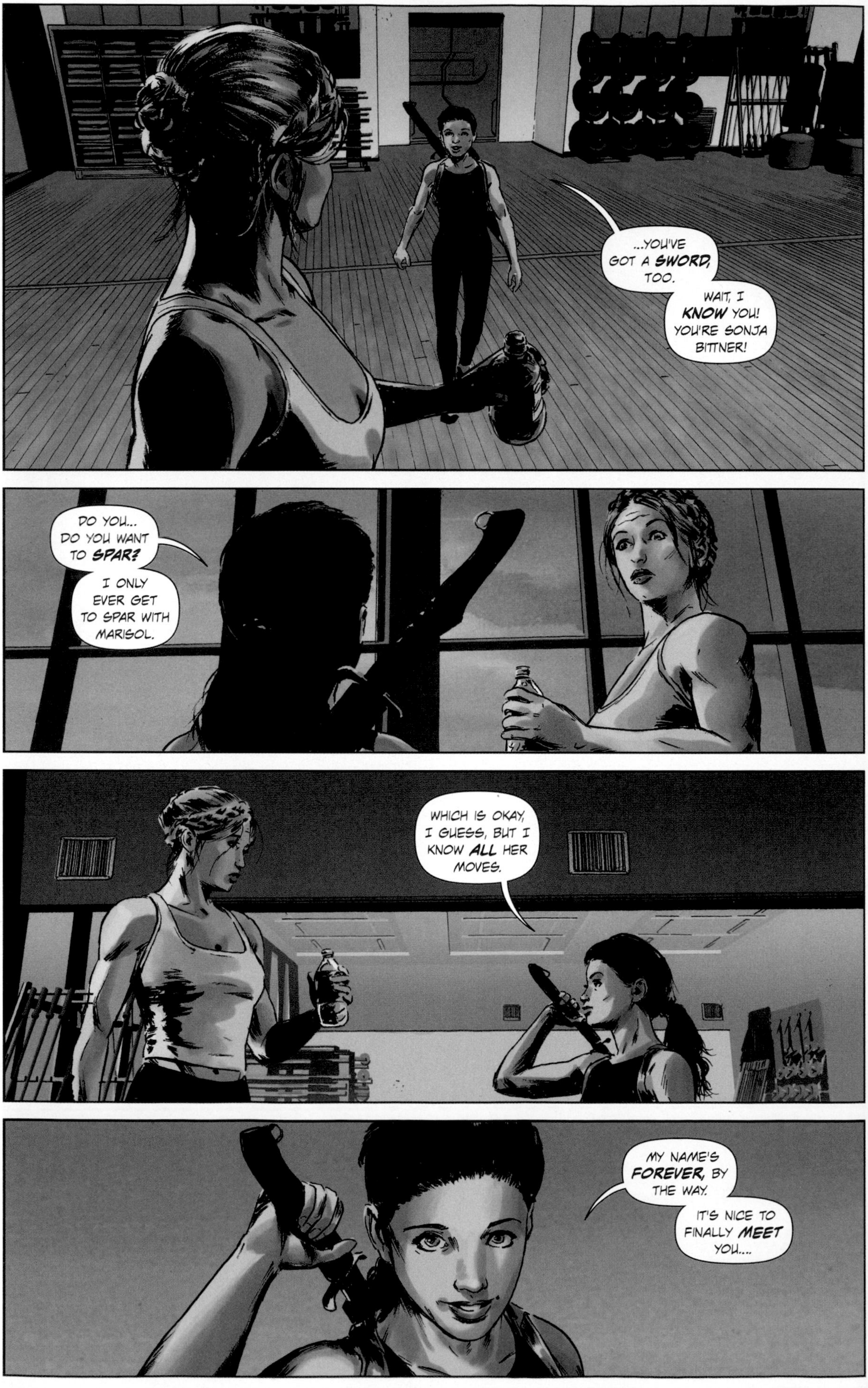
...YOU'VE GOT A **SWORD,** TOO.
WAIT, I **KNOW** YOU! YOU'RE SONJA BITTNER!
DO YOU... DO YOU WANT TO **SPAR?**
I ONLY EVER GET TO SPAR WITH MARISOL.
WHICH IS OKAY, I GUESS, BUT I KNOW **ALL** HER MOVES.
MY NAME'S **FOREVER,** BY THE WAY.
IT'S NICE TO FINALLY **MEET** YOU...

CARLYLE

ODERINT DUM METUANT

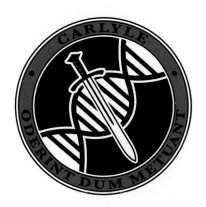

RIGHT: Cover artist **Owen Freeman's** original cover for **LAZARUS #20**.

Covers need to be designed several months in advance of an issue hitting stands, and in some cases, before an issue is even written.

Owen's pulpy, noir-ish image of Johanna was well-loved by the team, but the image was based on a scene that ultimately wasn't used, and so a new cover was created.

FOLLOWING PAGE SPREAD:
During the creation of **LAZARUS #16**, Owen Freeman and **Eric Trautmann** created "artifact" pages, treated as in-world objects, to help immerse the reader in Sister Bernard's story.

One such element, a video feed showing Morray Lazarus Joacquim in action, was cropped and rotated to fit on a single page, instead of the two pages originally scripted (in order to allow two prior scenes to get more space).

Presented on the two-page spread that follows is Owen's original version of that artwork, restored to its full size.

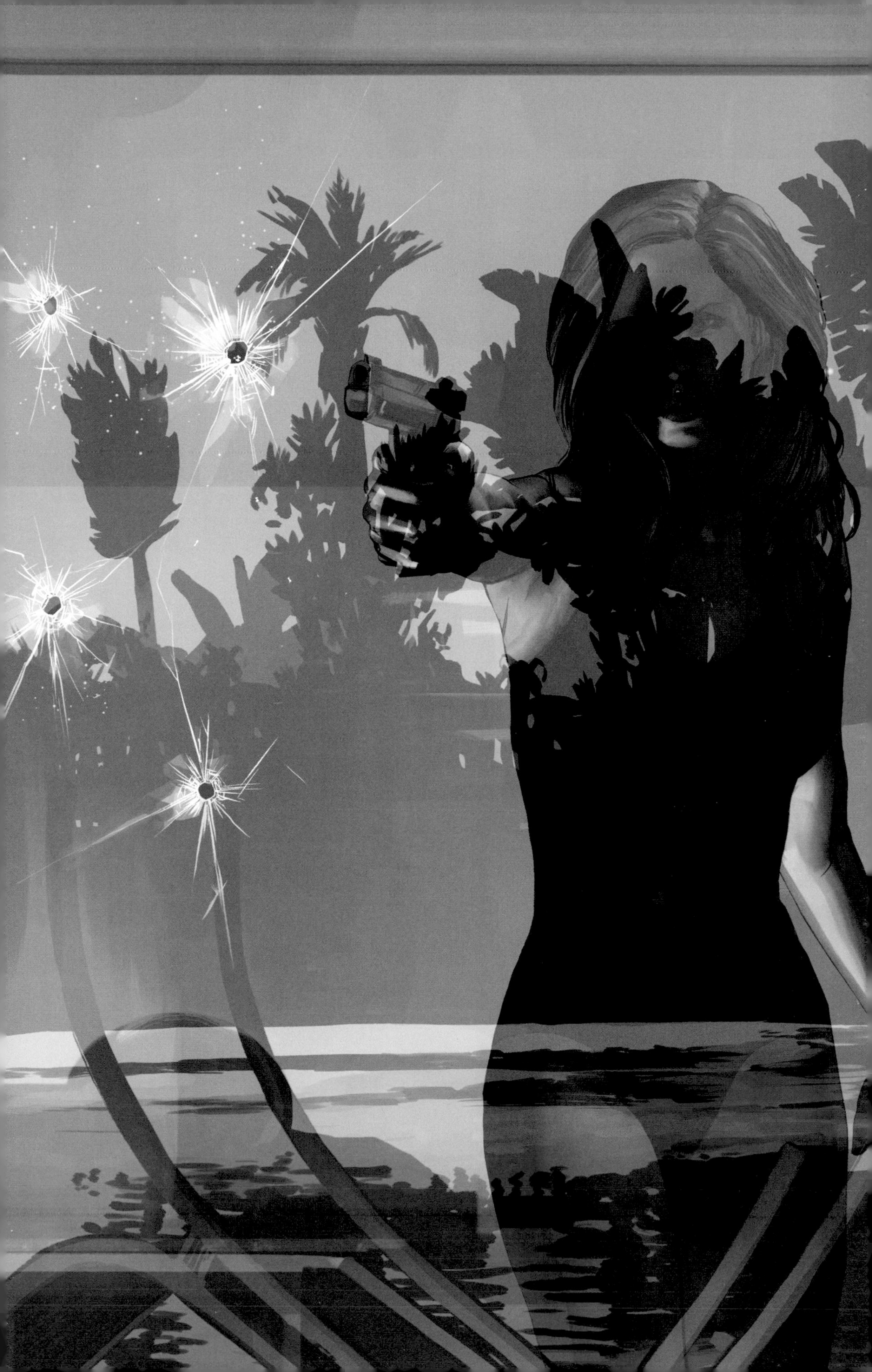

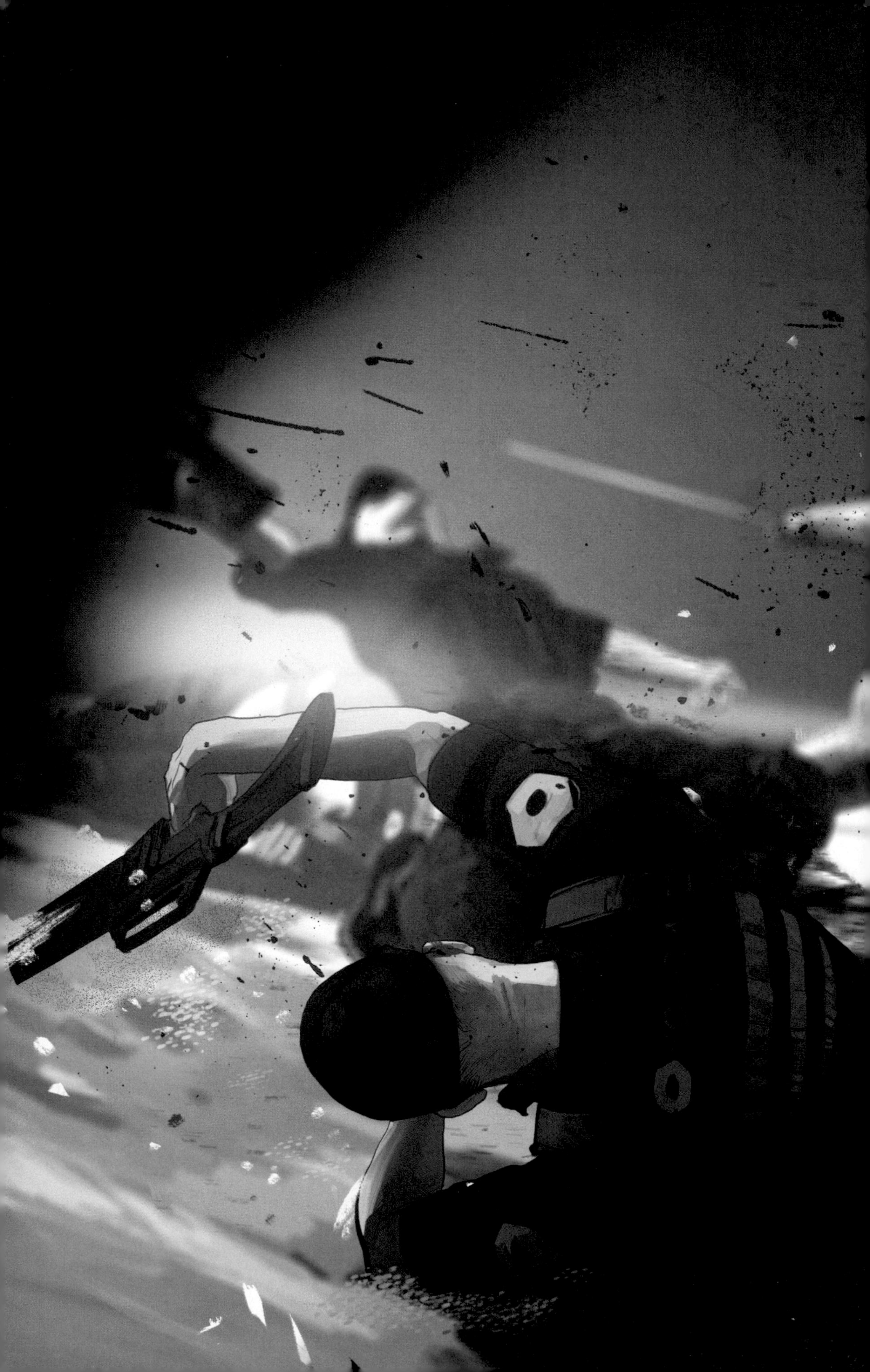

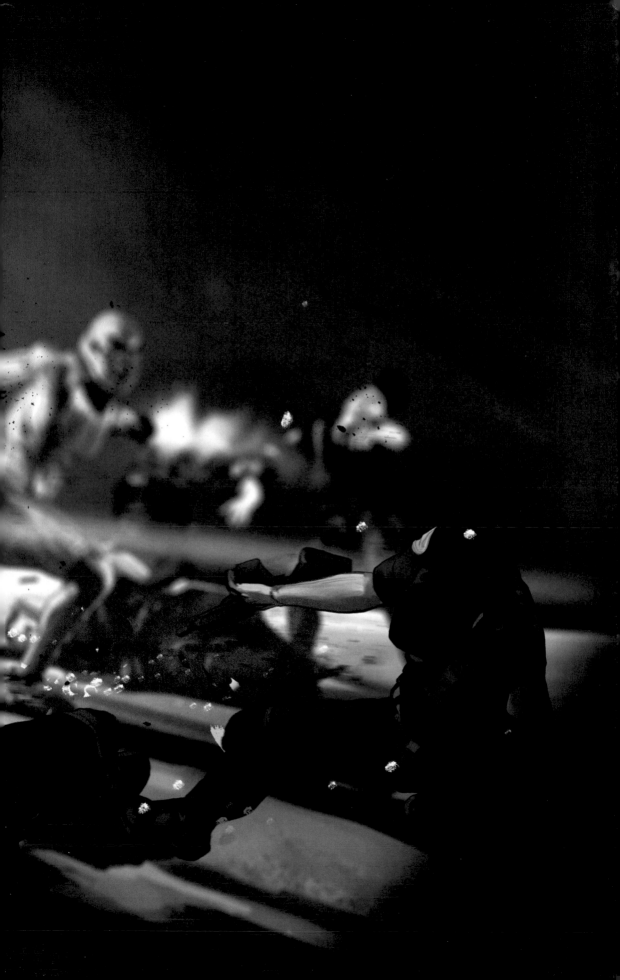

FOR FOREVER CARLYLE, THERE IS ONLY ONE LAW:

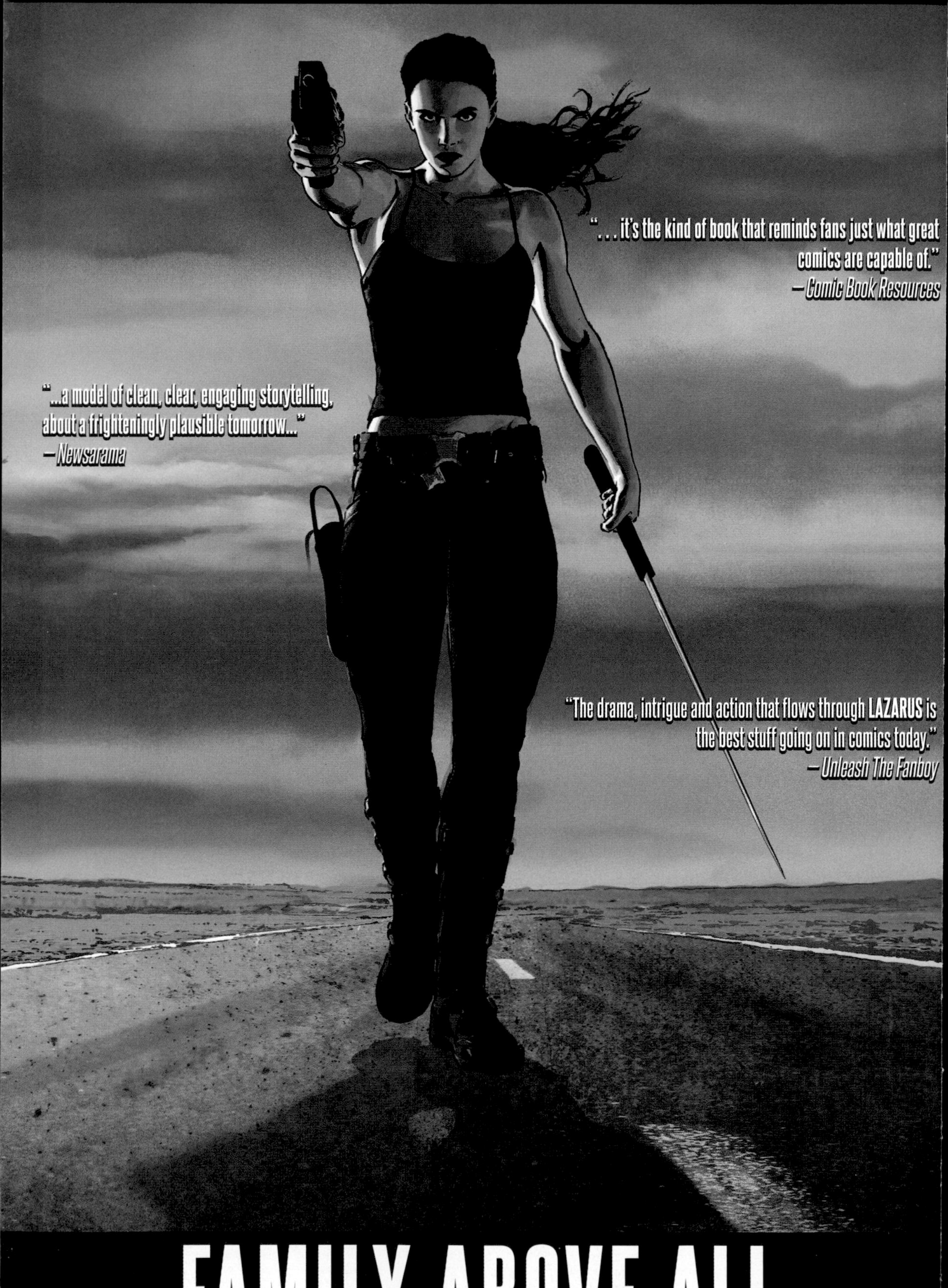
". . . it's the kind of book that reminds fans just what great comics are capable of."
—Comic Book Resources
"...a model of clean, clear, engaging storytelling, about a frighteningly plausible tomorrow..."
—Newsarama
"The drama, intrigue and action that flows through LAZARUS is the best stuff going on in comics today."
—Unleash The Fanboy

FAMILY ABOVE ALL.

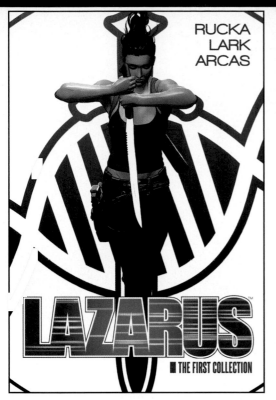

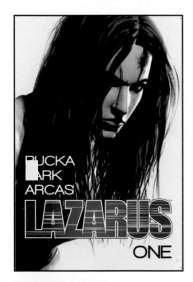
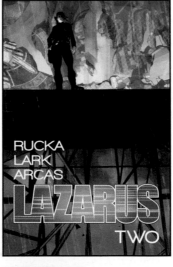
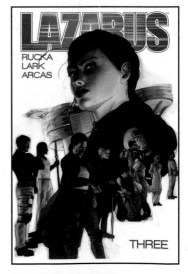

CARLYLE

ODERINT DUM METUANT

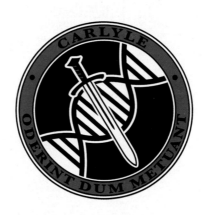